The Second Biggest Nothing

The
Second
Biggest
Nothing

COLIN COTTERILL

Published by
Soho Press, Inc.
853 Broadway
New York, NY 10003

Library of Congress Cataloging-in-Publication Data

Cotterill, Colin, author.
The second biggest nothing / Colin Cotterill.
Series: A Dr. Siri Paiboun mystery; 14

ISBN 978-1-64129-061-6
eISBN 978-1-64129-062-3

1. Paiboun, Siri, Doctor (Fictitious character)—Fiction.
2. Coroners–Fiction. 3. Laos—Fiction. I. Title
PR6053.O778 S43 2019 823'.914—dc23 2018057751

Printed in the United States of America

10 9 8 7 6 5 4 3 2 1

With my endless thanks to Tim, Martin, Bertil, Ernest CB, Howard, Mac, Dr. Leila, David, Kate, Bob, Shelly, Lizzie, Rachel, Ulli, Geoffrey, Magnus, Dad, Dr. Margot, Juliet, Cara, Shona, Scott, Pary and my wife and best friend, Kyoko.

In loving memory of Saigna.

TABLE OF CONTENTS

CHAPTER ONE
A City of Two Tails

Dr. Siri was standing in front of Daeng's noodle shop when she pulled up on the bicycle. It was a clammy day, but his wife rarely raised a sweat even under a midday sun. She leaned the bike against the last sandalwood tree on that stretch of the road and patted Ugly the dog. Siri shrugged.

"So?" he said.

"So what?"

"What did she say?"

Daeng pecked him on the cheek and walked past him into the dark shop house. He trotted behind.

"She said I have the body and constitution of a sixty-nine-year-old."

"You are sixty-nine."

"Then I have nothing to be disappointed or smug about, do I? I'm fit and healthy. I'm a nice, average Lao lady with supposed arthritis. She did, however, mention that most people my age in this country are dead. I think that's a positive, don't you?"

"But what about . . . ? You know?"

"She didn't say anything," said Daeng.

"She what?"

"Didn't mention it at all. She obviously didn't notice it."

"What kind of a doctor doesn't notice that one of her patients has a tail?"

"I've told you, Siri. You and I are the only people who see it."

"What about the shamans in Udon?"

"They didn't see it, Siri. They visualized it. Not the same thing."

"It's a physical thing, Daeng. You know it is. I can feel it."

"I know. And I like it when you do."

"But now Dr. Porn would have us believe that it doesn't exist, which means I must be senile," said Siri.

"It means we're both senile."

"Then, by the same account, if you don't have a tail, then obviously my disappearances are a figment of my imagination."

"Not at all," said his wife dusting the stools to prepare for the evening noodle rush. "All it tells us is that nobody else notices you're gone."

"I've disappeared in public before," said Siri with more than a touch of indignation. "Haven't I disappeared in the market? At a musical recital? In a crowded—"

"Look, my love," she said, taking his hand, "there is no doubt that you disappear. There is no doubt you cross over to the other side and learn things there and return and tell me of your adventures. There is no doubt you are possessed by a thousand-year-old Hmong shaman and communicate through an ornery transvestite spirit medium. There is no doubt that you see the souls of the dead just as there is no doubt that I have a tail that I received from a witch in return for a cure for my arthritis. But, for whatever reason, nobody else bears witness to our little peculiarities. And perhaps it's just as well. The politburo would probably have us burned at the stake for occult practices if anyone reported us. Even Buddhism makes them queasy. Imagine what they'd do if Dr. Porn wrote in her official report, '. . . and, by the way, Madam Daeng appears to have grown a tail since her last checkup.'"

"You're right," said Siri.

"I'm always right," said Daeng. She squeezed his hand and smiled and returned to the chore of readying her restaurant. She was startled by the sound of hammering from the back room.

"What's that?" she asked.

"Nyot, the doorman," said Siri.

"He's still here?" asked Daeng. "How long does it take to put in a door?"

Mr. Nyot, the carpenter, was busy hanging. Following the previous monsoons, the door had changed shape and would no longer close. Daeng was not afraid of intruders. Ever since it was installed when the shop house was rebuilt, that door had never been locked. Nobody could remember where the key was. There were no security issues in Vientiane. The Party wouldn't allow such a thing. All the burglars were safely behind bars on the detention islands. The ill-fitting door banged in the wind and Mr. Nyot had promised them a nice new door at a special price. But it was also a special door. Daeng went to inspect the work.

"What's that?" she asked, pointing at the missing rectangle of wood at the base.

"It's a dog entrance," said Nyot.

"It's a hole," said Daeng.

"Right now it may look like a hole," said Nyot, "but over there I have a flap with hinges that I will attach shortly."

"That's not what I ordered," said Daeng.

"Maybe not. But this door is five-thousand *kip* cheaper than the next in the range. And I did notice that you have a dog outside that seems unable to enter the building."

"That dog has never entered a building," said Daeng. "Not because it's unable to but because it has some canine dread of being inside."

"Well, when it gets over its fear this will be the perfect door for it."

She couldn't be bothered to argue and the saved five-thousand *kip* would come in handy even though it was a tiny sum. But she was sure that when the wind blew from then on, the dog flap would bang through the night and the hinges would creak and they would miss their old one. She was very pessimistic when it came to doors.

Siri laughed at their exchange as he wiped the tabletops with a dishcloth and thought back to his last contact with Auntie Bpoo, his unhelpful, unpleasant spirit guide. It had been a while. She had him on some kind of training program. He'd passed "taking control of his own destiny" and "awareness," and he was ready for the next test but for some reason she'd gone mute. He attempted to evoke her often, but the channel was off air. Often, he wished his life could have been, not normal exactly, but more under his own control. Daeng was saying something behind him.

"What was that?" Siri asked.

"I said the ribbon was a nice touch," said Daeng.

"What ribbon's that?"

"You didn't decorate the dog?"

"Not sure I know what you're talking about."

"The ribbon, Siri. You didn't see him out there? Ugly has a rather sweet pink bow on his tail."

"Nothing to do with me," he said walking to the street.

Ugly was under the tree guarding the bicycle. Sure enough, he was wearing a ribbon with a silk flower, and from the rear he looked like a mangy birthday present.

Siri laughed. "This looks like the work of a certain Down syndrome comedian I know," he said.

"Can't blame Geung and his bride this time," said Daeng. "In case you haven't noticed, we're doing all the noodle work here. He and Tukta won't be back from their honeymoon for another week. And Ugly was not so beautifully kitted out when I left this morning. Don't take it off. He looks adorable."

Siri was bent double inspecting the dog's rear end. There was more of a sausage than an actual tail so it was surprising the decorator had found enough length to tie on the bow and that Ugly would allow it.

"It appears to have a message attached," Siri said. "There's a small capsule hanging from it. Lucky he didn't need to go to the bathroom before you noticed it."

"A message?" She smiled. "How thrilling."

Never one to pass up a mystery, Daeng joined her husband on the uneven pavement. Ugly seemed reluctant to give up his treasure. He growled deep in his throat.

"Come on, you ungrateful mongrel," said Siri. "Who do you think pays for your meals and applies ointment to all your sores and apologizes to the neighbors for your indiscriminate peeing?"

It was a compelling argument and one that Ugly obviously had no counter for. He held up his haunches for his master to remove the capsule. It was a silver cylinder about the size of a cigarette. Its two halves could be pulled apart. Siri had seen its kind before but he couldn't remember where. Inside was a tight roll of paper, which he unfurled.

"Unquestionably a treasure map," said Daeng.

"Only words, I'm afraid," said Siri. "And handwritten."

Still pretending that his eyesight was as good as it had always been, he held out the slip at arm's length and squinted at the tiny writing. He would blame that arm for its shortness rather than admit to any deficiency in his eyesight. The note was just within range.

"It's in English," he said.

"What a shame," said Daeng.

He read it aloud with what he considered to be an English accent.

> *"My dear Dr. Siri Paiboun, it has been a while. By now I'm sure you have either forgotten my promise of revenge or have dismissed it as an idle threat. But if you had known me at all, you would have realized that my desire to destroy you and your loved ones is a fire that has burned in my heart without end. After such a long search I have found you and I am near you. I have already deleted one of your darlings. Before I leave I will have ruined the life you have established just as you did mine. I have two more weeks. That should be more than sufficient."*

It would be several hours before Siri and Daeng could fully appreciate the seriousness of their note because neither of them understood English. They knew French and could read the characters and they could guess here and there at meanings. But the languages were too far apart to cause either of them to panic. That would come later.

CHAPTER TWO
The Glory of Totalitarianism

At the end of 1980, Vientiane was a city still waiting for something to happen. It had waited through the droughts and floods, through the flawed policies, the failed cooperatives, the mass exodus of the Hmong and lowland Lao and, more recently, ethnic Chinese business holders across the Mekong. It had waited for inspiration, for good news, for a break. It had been waiting for five years but still nothing of any note had happened. So, what better way to celebrate five years of Communist rule than by inviting a large number of foreign journalists to observe the results of all those things that hadn't happened? There were those who argued that *nothing* was a good thing. For thirty years the Lao had been waging a war against their brothers and against the foreign powers that put them in uniforms. Wasn't *nothing* better than that?

It was what they called "a cocktail reception" even though none of the glasses being carried around on silver trays contained anything more exotic than weak whisky sodas and room temperature white wine. The hostesses who carried the trays wore thick makeup, military uniforms and uncomfortable boots. They smiled in a way that suggested they were under orders to do so. They did not enter into conversation with the already soused foreign journalists because they could not. They were from villages in distant provinces and even fluency in the Lao language was beyond their linguistic ability. And they had been warned by their superiors about these men from the decadent West and the shady East who bit the heads off babies and had sexual organs the size of ripe papayas. The girls trembled at every flirtatious glance, each beckoning whistle.

In its day, the nightclub of the Anou Hotel had been a gloomy cavern of nefarious goings on. When first the French, and then the American soldier boys played there, it was a mysterious grotto, so dark you couldn't see the age of your dance partner, so heavy with marijuana smoke you couldn't smell the fluids that had soaked into the carpets the night before. But on this evening, this glorious evening that marked the fifth anniversary of the founding of the People's Democratic Republic of Laos, the lights were all on, and there were no secrets. The gaps in the parquet tiles on the dance floor had been filled with cement and painted brown. The table vinyl curled up at the edges, and the light-blue paint peeled from the beams.

But, as Comrade Civilai said, perhaps this was the symbolism the Party wanted to pass along to the world. The decadent past had fallen into ruination. The last altars to the gods of depravity were crumbling and turning to dust.

"Or," Civilai added, "perhaps there was no other venue with a functioning sound system and a full bar."

Since he left the politburo he'd not been sure of the motives behind Party policy. Perhaps he never had.

Intimacy was obviously another government plot to

endear itself to the outside world. There really wasn't a great deal of space in the Anou. Sixty-four foreign journalists—all male—were shoulder to shoulder with Russian interpreters, most of the resident diplomatic community, selected aid workers and donors and the UN, even though nobody was ever really sure what the latter did to earn their living in Laos. All of the ministries were represented, each minister and vice minister with his own aide to help carry him back to the Zil limo at the end of the night.

Comrade Civilai—wearing cool, *avant garde* sunglasses—was there because of his distinguished service to the cause of communism in Laos and his apparent undying loyalty to the politburo. Chief Inspector Phosy was there because, despite several attempts to oust him by those who had become accustomed to graft and corruption, he was still the head of the police force. His wife, Nurse Dtui was there because it was a perfect opportunity to practice the foreign languages she'd taught herself with little or no benefit thus far. And Dr. Siri and Daeng were there because it was walking distance from their restaurant and a nice evening. They hadn't been invited, but no scruffy sentry with an unloaded AK-47 was going to turn away such a distinguished white-haired couple.

This small group of friends and allies sat at a table near the exit. They'd tired of attempting to snare any of the reluctant hostesses and instead had relieved the open bar of a half bottle of Hundred Pipers. With it they toasted anything that came to mind: to the miracle that they were all still alive, to Geung and Tukta on their honeymoon at a small vegetable cooperative outside Vang Vieng, to the peaceful, almost ghostly quiet streets of Vientiane, to the dizzying figure of 15 percent Lao literacy announced that afternoon, and, finally, to friendship. The bottle was approaching empty. Civilai had made more than his usual number of bladder runs to the bathroom because he'd hit a bad patch of stomach troubles following experiments with Lao snails in fermented morning glory sauce. The comrade was a pioneer in the kitchen and pioneers stepped on their own rabbit traps from time to time.

"What I don't understand . . ." said Siri.

"There must be such a lot," said Civilai, returning from the crowded toilet.

"I'm serious about treating this condition of yours," said Siri.

"I'm not letting you and your rubber glove anywhere near my condition, thank you, Doctor," said Civilai.

"Then, what I don't understand," Siri tried again, "is the significance of five years. Nine I can appreciate. Always been a lucky number. And ten has some decimal roundness to it. But five?"

"Well, young brother, it's quite simple," said Civilai. "The government is celebrating five years because, despite all its mismanagement and false hopes and poor judgment, it's still here. They never expected to make it this far."

"Who's going to kick them out?" said Daeng.

"Exactly," said Civilai. "That's the glory of totalitarianism. You can screw up for five years and admit you have no idea what you're doing and you wake up the next morning and you're still in power. You can experiment all over again."

"If you weren't suffering from dementia I'd arrest you for treasonous rhetoric," said Phosy.

"Look around, young chief inspector," said the old

politburo man. "Point me out one minister or vice minister here who isn't demented. All those grenades exploding too close to their brains."

"Uncle Civilai, you seem particularly nasty tonight," said Nurse Dtui. "Is it the snails?"

They charged their glasses and toasted to the snails.

"In a way, yes," said Civilai. "I'll tell you, sweet Dtui. Today, with no warning, no request, no discussion, I received a copy of the speech they expect me to give to all these pliable journalists at the end of the week."

"You could always say 'no,'" said Siri.

"And then what? They'd give the same script to some other doddery old fool to read the lies."

"So what are you planning to do?" Daeng asked.

"Harness the power of redaction," said Civilai.

"You'd get two minutes into the speech and they'd drag you from the podium," said Phosy.

"But what a glorious two minutes they would be," said Civilai.

"Except the simultaneous interpreters will be reading the original script," said Daeng. "The old king tried to change his abdication speech, and the radio station brought in an actor to read the Party version."

"An actor we could sorely use right now," said Siri, anxious to change the subject.

"I still have the floor," said Civilai.

"Oh, right," said Nurse Dtui, ignoring him, "your movie. I was going to ask about that. Don't you have a cast yet?"

"I feel nobody takes me seriously anymore," Civilai grumbled.

"The Women's Union has brought together a vast gaggle of would-be performers," said Siri.

"All we're missing is a functioning camera," said Daeng.

"The camera is functioning," said Siri, "and we are on the verge of acquiring a world-class cinematographer to operate it."

"Here I am about to re-educate the planet," said Civilai, "and you dismiss my plan out of hand."

"Perhaps we aren't yet drunk enough to take you seriously," said Daeng. "Another bottle might persuade us."

Civilai huffed and the hairs in his nostrils flapped. He walked off to the bar with a heavy smattering of umbrage and a noticeable stagger.

"He's not really going to sabotage the speech, is he?" Nurse Dtui asked.

"He's a politician," said Siri.

He'd planned to say more but realized that short phrase said it all.

"And the camera story?" asked Phosy.

The camera in question was a very expensive Panavision Panaflex Gold which had become 'lost' during the shooting of a film called *The Deer Hunter* in Thailand. Through the rice-growing underground it found its way to Laos and into the spare room on the upper floor of Madam Daeng's restaurant. Until then, all it lacked was someone with the ability to turn it on. But that small setback to the filming of Dr. Siri's ambitious Lao spectacular was apparently resolved.

"Our cinematographer has arrived and will begin his duties this weekend," said Siri with a smile. "Daeng and I and various relatives went to the airport to greet him and make sure he didn't change his mind and get on the return flight."

"And by 'cinematographer,'" said Daeng, "what Siri

means is a young boy with a certificate in film production and no experience."

"Yet more experience than all of us in the operation of a camera," said Siri. "I was born into a generation of candles and beeswax lamps. Electricity entered my life late. It wasn't until I arrived in Paris that I discovered the magic of *volts* and *ampères*. But by then I had decided to dedicate my life to medicine. If I had not, who's to say by now I wouldn't have been the one to invent the cassette player and the Xerox machine?"

"Is he legal, this camera person of yours?" the chief inspector asked.

"He's Lao," said Siri, "the cousin of Seksak who runs the Fuji Photo Lab. He's harking the call of the Party for its lost sons to come home to the motherland to share their new skills and savings."

"He left in the '75 exodus?" Dtui asked.

"Before," said Siri. "He made an orderly exit about ten years before with his father. Dad had a scholarship from the Colombo Plan. His wife died in childbirth, so it was just the two of them. They moved to Sydney. Bruce went to—"

"His name's Bruce?" said Dtui.

"His father renamed him when they got there," said Siri, "perhaps in an attempt to hide him amidst all the other Bruces. The boy had studied with the Australians here and become proficient in English. He sailed through high school and entered college."

"Why would he ever want to come back?" Phosy asked.

"His cousin believes he was disillusioned with the decadent West. His father had been killed in a car accident in Australia and Bruce was homesick. Missed his distant family. When our government announced we'd welcome expatriate Lao with no hard feelings, he was only too keen. His cousin told him about our film. He read my script and was delighted to join us."

"Can you afford him?" asked Dtui.

"Said he was happy to do it for nothing."

"Must be mad," said Civilai, returning with another half bottle of whisky, which he plonked down on the table like a memento of war.

"You could talk the crutches off a legless man," said Daeng. "How do you do it?"

"Those young fellows just need to know who's boss," said Civilai. "Look important. Don't say anything. Walk behind the bar. Pick up the bottle. Simple."

He sat at the table, his revolutionary fire apparently doused.

"And speaking of who's boss," said Daeng, "where's Madam Nong this evening?"

"My wife does not enjoy watching me drink," said Civilai. "She seems to think I devalue myself when I allow alcohol to make decisions for me."

"Whereas Madam Daeng here knows only too well that I am at my brightest and most perceptive with the Hundred Pipers playing the background music," said Siri.

"Sadly, as the music grows louder and the perception reaches a crescendo, the passion is known to wane," said Daeng.

There was a long silence at the table.

"We all know this is Daeng making a joke, right?" said Siri.

"I'm not so sure," said Dtui.

"Daeng, tell them," said Siri.

Daeng looked around the room.

"Daeng?"

The embarrassment was blurred by the voice of some-body leaning too closely into a badly wired microphone. Like announcements at the national airport, nobody knew exactly what had been said. But it was the signal for Siri's crew to down their drinks and head to the exit. It was speech time and their finely tuned instincts naturally sent them in the opposite direction.

It was only a short walk to the noodle shop, but Siri must have told them a dozen times that his wife was joking about his waning ardor. Still she kept mum and they were all shedding tears of laughter by the time they reached the closed shutter. High in a tree opposite perched Crazy Rajhid, the Indian. They could only see his silhouette against the moon, but it was obvious he was as naked as on the day he was born. They waved. He ignored them. He still believed that if he kept perfectly still he was invisible.

It was the time of the evening when the dusty streets were usually deserted and no other sound could be heard: no television, no radio, no hum of air-conditioning. But on that evening their drunken voices were carried across the river to Thailand to show the enemy that socialist Laos could still have a good time once in a while. In an hour, when the curfew took hold, their voices would be silenced too, but right now was as good a time as any to stand on the riverbank and yell abuse. It was nothing personal, just a friendly diatribe against a nation with an ongoing ani-mosity toward their inferior northern neighbors. It was therapy.

Once in the restaurant, Madam Daeng made a batch

of noodles to soak up the whisky and put something in everyone's stomach for the ride home. Only Civilai, still blaming the snails, forwent the meal.

"I think we need to approach the girl," he said.

"What girl's that?" Phosy asked.

"The blonde," said Civilai. "Acting second secretary at the American embassy. Looks gorgeous. Speaks fluent Lao. She was standing at the bar. I've met her at a few functions recently."

"He has these hallucinations," said Siri.

"In a room with two hundred men you really didn't notice one attractive woman?" Civilai asked.

"Even in a room with two hundred women I'd only notice Daeng," said Siri.

Daeng smiled and squeezed his hand.

"I was making all that up about his ardor," she said.

"At last," said Siri. "Why do you feel the need to approach the blonde, Civilai?"

"She has acting experience," said Civilai. "We need her for the film."

"In what role?" Siri asked. "Ours is the story of the nation through the eyes of two young revolutionaries not unlike ourselves. How many pretty blonde Americans featured in the birth of the republic?"

"We could write in a part for her," said Civlilai.

"As what?"

"I don't know. She could be the CIA."

"All by herself?" asked Siri.

"Why not?"

"I think you'll find most women in the CIA back then were making coffee and typing," said Madam Daeng.

"Look, it doesn't matter what she does," said Civilai.

"How many commercially successful movies have you seen that didn't have a glamour interest?"

"I believe we have one or two beautiful Lao women in major roles," said Dtui.

"That is admirable," said Civilai. "But if we're aiming at the international market . . ."

"Lao women aren't attractive enough?" said Daeng.

"They . . . you are lovely in the domestic sense," said Civilai, "but we need sexy. We need . . . we need a Barbarella."

Only Siri and Civilai knew who Barbarella was, and Siri wasn't about to disagree with his friend's choice. There followed a testy five minutes as the old boys tried to define sexy and explain why even the most attractive Lao in her finest blouse and ankle-length *phasin* skirt would not qualify. They dug themselves deeper into the muck with every comment. The discomfort was only eased when Civilai felt the need for one more visit to the toilet.

"Time for us to go pick up Malee," said Dtui. She stood to leave. "She's with a neighbor and they'll want to get to bed."

Despite his lofty position, Chief Inspector Phosy and his wife were still billeted at the police dormitory until their modest government house was completed. To his wife's mixed disappointment and admiration, he'd refused to move into the palatial two-story abode of his predecessor.

"Come husband," she said.

"I'm fine to drive the Vespa," said Phosy.

Dtui twiddled her fingers and he handed her the key. She knew that if he felt the need to tell her he was fine there had to be some doubt. Even in the carless streets of the capital there were potholes and sleeping dogs, and her husband had worked thirteen hours that day. He'd be safer on the pillion seat. They'd started toward the street when Siri remembered his letter.

"Oh, wait," he said, and pulled the folded paper from his top pocket. "A quick translation and you can be on your way."

He explained how the note had been attached to Ugly's tail sometime that morning. Nurse Dtui, hoping for a study placement in America, had put in many hours to learn English. In '75, armed with a scholarship and high hopes, she'd watched the Americans flee, and, like their Hmong allies, Dtui was stranded. She looked up from the words with an expression of horror on her face. Her English was competent enough to read Siri's letter and good enough for her to realize the menace it contained. She called Phosy back from the street and had the team sit once more around the table beneath the buzzing fluorescent lamp while she translated. Siri and Daeng appeared to be unmoved by the content.

"You don't seem that concerned," Phosy told them.

"It wouldn't be the first threat we've received," said Siri.

"Almost a weekly event," said Civilai.

"Well, I'm your friendly local policeman," said the chief inspector, "and I'm not going to let you laugh this one off. It isn't just a threat to you, Siri. The writer is promising to hurt your loved ones and that includes everyone at this table."

"I don't love him," said Civilai. "I'm not even that fond of him. That should let me off the hook."

"Ignore him," said Daeng. "He's having one of his difficult years. Go ahead Phosy. What do you suggest?"

"First, I suggest we look at the letter for what it does, not just for what it says."

"What's that supposed to mean?" said Civilai.

"Well," said Phosy, "the fact that it's in English sends a message in itself. As Siri doesn't speak the language I doubt he's antagonized too many English speakers in his life. And, even if the writer knows more than one language, why would he choose English for this particular threat?"

"I'm assuming you'll just be asking a batch of questions and have us fill in the answers later," said Civilai.

"I think that's a splendid system," said Madam Daeng. "Continue, Phosy."

"Secondly," said Phosy, "why does he only have two weeks to complete his mission? If he lived here there'd be no restriction."

"So, he's a visitor," said Nurse Dtui.

"On a visa," said Siri. "We aren't that generous in the immigration field."

"And we just left a room full of foreign journalists who are in town for exactly two weeks with nice fresh correspondent visas in their passports," said Phosy. "Any one of them could be our writer. Even the Eastern bloc boys would have a grounding in English."

"We can't interrogate all sixty-four of them," said Daeng. "We need to eliminate some."

"Well, he's certainly not Vietnamese," said Dtui.

"How do you know?" Siri asked.

"He gave Ugly a break," she said. "They still eat dogs over there. No Vietnamese is going to balk at slicing up a flea bitten mongrel if it serves a purpose."

They heard a low howl from the street. It might have been a coincidence but Siri doubted that.

"Okay, there are four Vietnamese journalists," said Daeng. "That takes us to sixty."

"Not much of a help," said Civilai.

"We need to start with the threat itself," said Phosy. "Siri, the writer made a promise that he would have his revenge. That his lust for vengeance is still burning inside him. I'm guessing that when he made that threat initially you would have sensed that it was more than just words. You would have seen him as capable of following through with it. It would have frightened you. For some time you would have been looking over your shoulder. On how many occasions have you experienced that type of fear in your life?"

All eyes turned to Siri. He looked up at the lamp and seemed to be fast-rewinding through his seventy-six years. He sniffed when he reached the end.

"Twice," he said.

"Then, that's—" Phosy began.

"Better make it three times," said Siri. "Just to be sure. Three times when I truly believed the nasty bastard meant what he said and had the resources to keep his promise. I'm not given to panic, but I confess to missing a few heartbeats on those occasions."

"Then that's where we start," said Phosy. "Who's first?"

CHAPTER THREE
Paris, 1932

I was sitting at an outdoor table in front of the Café de la Paix. I was alone, but I told the waiter in his long white apron that I was expecting someone. He was surprised to hear French from my lips. They usually were. He was unnecessarily polite. All the other tables were occupied by French sophisticates. White people as far as the eye could see. Dapper men with pencil mustaches and straw boaters. *Vogue* magazine women with bangs that restricted their vision to lap level. White silk dresses billowed in the wind. Champagne bubbled. You'd never have guessed France was in the middle of the Great Depression.

There was a sort of upside down racism in Paris those days. The French military had recruited thousands of Chinese for the war effort, and most of them had been killed in battle: ravaged by Spanish flu or just left to die slowly from neglect and hunger. They were expendable and soon forgotten. Their story would never have been released by the government but the bolshie French press got wind of it and exposed the disgrace in its national newspapers. The government had no choice but to apologize and thank the Chinese for their contribution to the Allies' victory over the Germans.

As I had an Asian face I got a lot of looks of remorse during that period. Those "we're sorry for what we did to you" looks. The looks never became words or actions, but I did get the odd smiles from pretty ladies in white. It was May and *la mode* of spring was the tennis look. The temperature was taking its time to catch up to the season. Hundreds of inappropriately dressed people sat shivering at their tables or walking briskly along the boulevard. Three ladies at the table beside me were cradling their coffee cups to keep their fingers warm. I smiled at them. They looked at one another before smiling back. As I was no slave to fashion, I wore mittens and a muffler.

I'd arrived in Paris on a steamer in 1924 at the age of twenty. Unlike the other Asians on board, I didn't have to shovel coal or stagger from the galley to the state rooms with trays of canapés and champagne buckets. I had a ticket. My cabin was small but comfortable. I was in the enviable position of having a sponsor who had taken it upon herself to turn me from a shoeless waif into a young man of letters. Madam Le Saux, more commonly known as Loulou, had first met me at a temple in Savanaketh. I had been dumped there at the age of ten by an uncaring relative who instructed me to learn all I could, then disappeared from my life. I learned everything the monks had to teach and read the French books in the small library over and over again. By the age of twelve I was bored.

Madam Loulou arrived one day in a yellow Peugot with a driver in a cap. She was tall and slim but for her midriff, where fat had gathered unkindly. She reminded me of a python I'd once seen digesting a pig. Hers was the first

French I'd heard spoken by a native speaker. My initial reaction was amazement at how clever she was to have mastered such a difficult language. Her face was so heavily cased in makeup it took some time for her expressions to match her words.

"Does anybody here speak French?" she called out. Her voice was manly, crumbly at the edges.

Nobody answered, not even the abbot whose French was by far the best at our temple. He slunk back into the prayer hall, took up a broom and started sweeping.

"My word," she said. "They sent me here because your temple has such a fine reputation. Yet I cannot find one person who understands me."

I don't know what possessed my skinny legs to walk me forward, nor how I dared look her in the eye.

"We all speak French, Madam," I said, "but we are embarrassed to attempt it in front of you."

She walked toward me, her heels sinking into the dirt with each step.

"And why would you be embarrassed?" she asked.

"Because we are not perfect," I said.

Despite the tightness of her dress, she crouched and wiggled her index finger in my direction.

"Come here, Little Prince," she said.

I shuffled forward close enough to see the wrinkles under her makeup.

"Only in nature can we find perfection," she said. "Man must settle for 'good enough.' And you are good enough for me. I choose you."

And, just like that, I became her project. She made donations to the temple for extra tuition. She produced excellent counterfeit documents proving my links to the

Lao royal family that gained me entry into the *lycée* in Saigon where she paid my fees. She attended my graduation and presented me with a second-class ticket on the *Victor Hugo* to France. In my pack, I had a letter of introduction from the governor general in Saigon to the director of Ancienne University and enough funds to cover my first-year expenses in Paris. Madam Loulou guaranteed me funds for every year that I achieved excellent grades until the day I became a doctor.

What she didn't guarantee was that she would stay alive long enough to honor that promise. Even as I was journeying across the Atlantic my sponsor succumbed to consumption and was dead by the time I docked in Marseilles. It wasn't until several years later that I learned of the background of my dear Madam Loulou. For many years, my sponsor had been the proprietor of one of the most popular whore houses in Saigon. She had amassed a small fortune mainly from the patronage of French army officers, one of whom was the aforementioned governor general. She had arrived in Vietnam early in the French campaign and in a city with more brothels than drain holes, she quickly made a name for herself. This was achieved, not from the beauty of her girls but from their unique skills. Madam Loulou had trained each one in the ancient art of fellatio. You might say she'd become a celebrity by word of mouth.

Loulou had never married nor produced offspring. She had nobody to share her wealth with. Somewhere along the line she got it into her head that she was on her way to hell: a belief loudly supported by the wives of the officers she serviced. A Catholic priest in Saigon—also a customer—suggested she might readjust her trajectory by saving poor orphans. And, in the shell of a nut, that's what led her to me and twenty other young boys. I still look for her in the back alleyways of the Other World, but I never see my darling Madam Loulou. And that, omitting several years of struggles and humiliations, of poverty, of retaking high school courses and accepting disgusting jobs to keep myself alive in France, explains why I was sitting in front of the Café de la Paix that chilly May morning. I was in my third year of medicine at Ancienne and doing moderately well, "for an Asian." But I'd run into a bad patch of my own doing and I needed counsel.

"Anybody sitting here?" came a voice.

The young fellow leaning over me was dark-skinned with a fine head of black hair greased back. He was dressed like half the men there at the café, and he grasped a tennis racket in his left hand. His right hand he held out to me. I grabbed it, laughed, and shook the hell out of it.

"Sit down, you fool," I said, "before someone challenges you to a game."

Civilai pulled out the chair and apologized in charming French to the three ladies behind him who needed to shuffle slightly to allow him to sit. They smiled. He gestured to the waiter, pointed to my cognac and held up three fingers.

"What makes you think I couldn't beat them?" he said.

"I doubt that racket's ever kissed a ball," I said.

"You're right. But see how impressed everyone looks. A Chinaman trained in the fine art of tennis. They'll go home and tell all their friends we can count to forty."

Civilai was, in many respects, my cultural savior in those tough years. We'd met at the Louxor, a small cinema in La Chapelle, where I worked as an usher and confectionary seller. I'd been there so long most of the patrons knew me by name. Civilai was from a wealthy family and never really had to work for a living. Our backgrounds were so different we really had no right to have become friends, but our love for the cinema drew us together. He told me that he was a Communist. At the time, I really didn't know what that meant. It seemed everyone in Paris had to have a cause. You had to be something other than your-self: a fascist, an anarchist, a poet. So I paid little heed to Civilai's constant references to Karl Marx and Lenin. He told me about his pal, Quoc, a Vietnamese who had great plans to go back to Indochina and rescue the slaves in the French colonies. Together they would establish a Communist state, just as soon as Quoc got out of jail in Hong Kong. He seemed, to my mind, to be spending a lot of time in jail.

As a child at the temple in Savanaketh, I hadn't had many dealings with the French administrators. In fact, I probably viewed them as great white gods educating us natives—through armed force—how to be civilized. I liked their uniforms. It didn't occur to me they were raping our land. We didn't have anything when they arrived and sev-eral decades later we had even less and were paying taxes on it. But, to a ten-year-old boy, that seemed to be the way of the world. If you had a big gun you had the right to do what you wanted.

But then, in France *entre deux guerres,* Civilai had become my grapevine to a country I had no other means to com-municate with. I had no friends or family back in Laos. Like all the bemused tribesmen and women, who had been corralled together under a Lao flag, I'd been born in a country that I still knew very little about. I'd written

'Buddhist' on the application to Ancienne, but the religion of my birth made no more sense to me than the Catholicism drummed into me at school. At 23 I'd already seen more of France than I had of Laos. Without Civilai I would probably have swallowed the colonial line that the country was working in the tropics to improve the lot of ignorant savages. Were it not for a generous fellationist, I would have been one of them.

"Do you ever order just one drink?" I asked my young friend.

He placed the newly arrived drinks like chess pieces on the checkered tablecloth and pushed one toward me: cognac to queen's pawn two.

"Monsieur L'Usher," he said, "one never knows when one's waiter might be struck down with a heart attack, leaving all those at the tables around his prone body deprived of their rightful *digestifs*. Always order as if these drinks might be your last."

"At these prices they undoubtedly will be," I said.

"Then consider yourself lucky that this very morning a handsome filly at Longchamp caught my eye. She almost begged me to put a hundred francs on her to win. And she did not disappoint me. Consider this afternoon my treat."

I knew there were no races at Longchamp in the morning. With Civilai, there was always a horse, a greyhound or a roulette table keen to cover the costs of our outings. He never once belittled me over my poverty nor offered to pay for my courses or keep up with the rent. My pride remained intact, but I was certain that if a disaster befell me, my friend would be there to help me out. I just had to ask. I never did.

"*Salut,*" he said and clinked my glass with his. We drank

to nothing in particular. "Shouldn't you be in school?" he asked.

"I don't go to as many classes as I used to," I said. "I work better from books. I tend to pick out the best lectures to attend. I went to one this morning on diacetylmorphine."

"Sounds fascinating."

"It was," I said. "It was one of those moments when you can be sure the world has just made another one of its serious mistakes."

"Like assassinating Archduke Ferdinand?"

"Potentially much worse than that," I said.

"Then tell me all about dicey mental morphine," he said.

"Diacetylmorphine is a pain reliever ten times more powerful than morphine. Morphine was first extracted from opium in 1805. It served us well medically, but it tended to be addictive. Scientists, searching for an alternative, synthesized diacetylmorphine, and it was an immediate success. The Bayer Company began mass production. Countries around the world hastily approved this new 'non-addictive' painkiller, and soon it was more popular than sex. And for good reason. A year after its launch in North America, 200,000 people had become addicted to this super drug that Bayer had named heroin. It was immediately banned worldwide for anything but medical or scientific use.

"But, of course, as soon as the drug became illegal, all the criminal networks went up a gear. The Chinese gangs already have refineries. The Corsicans are building labs right here in France under the noses of the *gendarmerie*. The lecturer believes that in the next decade heroin will outperform opium as the addiction of choice worldwide. It's less bulky and easier to hide."

"And this is what they're teaching you at medical school?" Civilai asked.

"You can pass on the information to your boss."

"Quoc? Why would he be interested?"

"Some of the most successful revolutions and coups in history have been funded by the drug trade. It's how the French maintain their presence in Indochina. You and your Communist buddies could get in on the ground floor."

"Siri, communism is all about empowering the workers, not debilitating them. When we take over from the French, the first thing we'll do is burn their opium crops."

"I admire your faith," I said, even though I didn't give it much of a chance.

"So anyway, what brings me here?" he asked.

"My postcard, I presume."

"It gave up so little information."

"I didn't want the French postal service to be the first to know."

"Excellent. I have an exclusive, and you want my advice."

"More, your blessing," I said.

"Oh, no."

"Oh, no, what?"

"I sense a liaison."

"More than a fling," I said. "I've asked her to marry me."

Civilai whooped and held up four fingers to the waiter.

"Does she know you have fifty centimes to your name?"

"She does. But she also has fifty centimes to hers. So between us we have one franc, which is the beginning of a fortune."

"Have I met her?" he asked.

"Yes, on your last trip to Paris. You and your Mademoiselle Nong joined us for the matinee of Mata Hari at the Louxor."

"Not the Lao beauty with the tight sweater?"

"The very same: Bouasawan."

"Why would a girl whose figure outperforms every erotic postcard on sale along the banks of the Seine agree to marry you?"

"I'm a catch," I said.

"You do know she's a Communist?"

"So are you."

"No, I mean she's a *Communist* said very loudly. I recall she discussed her motivation with Nong that day. She came to Paris for the sole purpose of joining the Party. She'd already memorized the manifesto before she arrived. She signed up with the CPF even before she registered at Ancienne. Nong believed she was a fanatic."

"Passion is a wonderful thing."

"I hope she can find time for you amid her obsession."

"This from a man who's leaving in a week to muster a proletariat and turn Indochina red?"

"I'm enthusiastic," he said, "not fanatical. I like to call myself a middle-path socialist. I appreciate the concept and the potential of communism. I think it could work to unite our people against the French. But I don't decorate my apartment with hammer and sickle wallpaper. I don't send photos of myself in a swimsuit to Lenin."

"You know she doesn't do any of that."

He was starting to irritate me.

"Don't get defensive, little brother," he said. "I'm just offering my opinions."

While the waiter was putting the new glasses on the table, Civilai knocked back the drinks he already had.

"How can I not be defensive when you disparage my choice of bride?" I said.

"Look, Siri, she's gorgeous. She'd make any man's heart turn somersaults. And there is no doubt she's intelligent or that she loves her country. I see no problem with her whatsoever. The only problem I see is you."

"I'm not good enough for her?"

"Like me, she obviously recognizes just how good you are. You are unique and supremely talented. But you don't believe in what she believes."

"I believe."

"You don't."

"I do."

"Convince me."

"What?"

"Convince me that you share her passion."

The cognac had warmed my blood and was making me disagreeable. I took off my muffler. I hadn't been planning to tell him but he'd left me no choice.

"I've joined," I said.

"Joined what?"

"The Party."

"Nonsense."

"It's true. I went to a few meetings with Boua and thought, well, this isn't so bad, is it? And I decided that, with a bit of work, this communism thing has a chance. So I paid my dues and got my card. I can show it to you if you like."

"I don't want to doubt your motives . . ." he said.

"I love her, Civilai. I've loved her since the first day I saw her in class. She's the most . . . the most substantial Lao woman I've ever met. She has dreams. She has unselfish ambitions. She smells nice. She can change the world, and I want to be beside her while she's doing it."

"Then all I can say is congratulations," said Civilai, and, as a fitting subject break, a coal cart was pulled over by a fat policeman right in front of us because the horse wasn't wearing blinkers. In protest, the horse shat all over the boots of the policeman who arrested the driver. He in turn protested that it was the horse that did the damage, not he. Some of the more intoxicated onlookers applauded the horse.

To my mind, our conversation became a little less amicable after that. We didn't part on the best of terms. If we'd known how long it would be before we'd meet again, we'd probably have drunk one more glass for the road, said *au revoir* with a handshake and wished each other luck. In retrospect, I wish we had because then I would have been late for my appointment and not become embroiled in one of the most unpleasant events in French history. Instead, still miffed about his comments, I told Civilai I had to leave in a hurry to pay a visit to the Hotel de Rothschild, where there was a sale of secondhand medical textbooks. But I made the mistake of mentioning that the main event of the book exhibition was its opening by the president, Paul Doumer, himself. I knew that would irritate him.

It was as if I'd pushed down on the detonation plunger of Civilai's personal TNT. He launched off on a tirade against the fuzzy-bearded gentleman that, were it not in Lao, would have shocked and offended all those around us. Drinkers tutted their disapproval at the volume, but Civilai ranted on. Doumer had been the Governor General of the colonies in Indochina. His were the taxes that drained the lifeblood out of the villages. His were the laws that favored the French over the natives; favored the lowlanders over the tribes people. His were the policies that made a success of their investments for the first time, all on the back of local suffering. More investors came to take the gamble that led to more pillaging and looting. When the Lao proved too backward and lazy to absorb this development, Doumer carted in Vietnamese administrators and laborers by the thousands. There were probably more Vietnamese in the country than Lao at that time.

And what funded all these grandiose projects? *La grande comtesse d'O.* Doumer took over the opium monopoly and used the profits to supplement the modest funds he received from France. It was not a new policy. He was merely continuing a historical precedent in the third world. But he was good at the game. His chemists processed raw Indian resin using a technique that made the opium burn faster, thus increasing the demand. He imported impure opium from China for the poor addicted coolies. While the world was seeking bans on the opium trade, Doumer was embracing it. So successful was his policy in the Far East that he returned to France a hero, and his rise through the political ranks was inevitable.

And in Civilai's mind, I was on my way to stand meekly in a chilly street alongside the type of people who adored celebrity. We would applaud as he arrived and applaud as he left, and we would go home and tell our loved ones how close we'd been to the great statesman. That could not have been further from the truth.

"I hope you two have a very good time together," said Civilai, throwing down his last cognac and leaving me with three untouched glasses of my own. His chair bumped our neighbors' table as he stood and he bowed in apology. He picked his way through the diners and stood at the border of the sidewalk. He looked back at me, winked and smiled before joining the passersby. On the table he'd left some bank notes and an unused tennis racket.

Of course, I'd heard a lot about Doumer from the news-papers and the orange box speakers in the parks of Paris. I needed textbooks, but that wasn't my only reason for attending the event at the Hotel de Rothschild. Even before I learned that it was true, I'd always believed that you could look into a man's eyes and see his soul. I wanted to see the face of a man who'd been so adept at shifting and shuffling human cargo that he'd been able to change the destiny of a people. The French had killed thousands of us in the name of advancement. Yet, there in Paris, the colonial overlords were saints, sacrificing their valu-able time to bring peace and hope to the poor nations. I needed to learn from Doumer—the great magician—how he'd pulled off this trick.

The previous year I'd gone to see the colonial exhibi-tion. I was one of the nine million people who queued to see an interpretation of life in the French controlled territories. Grinning Africans in ostrich feathers danced comically. The scent of homemade coconut sweets wafted through the crowds. On the Lao stage a handful of bored non-Lao actors were threshing rice and pounding in an endless loop. A black-and-white film showed scenes of jolly villagers welcoming men in uniform, working beside them in the fields, drinking together. Of native girls learning from a white woman in crinoline how to use a steam iron. Every country had its film and none of them made men-tion of the schools poor local children weren't allowed to attend or the slave porters carrying a new officer's house-hold goods, or natives being whipped for insulting an administrator. In fact, the actors at the colonial exhibition were all having such fun you'd want to hop on a steamer and join them. The French Communist Party ran an alternative exhibition showing the depressing truth of colonial occupation, but, naturally, very few people attended. Reality was such poor entertainment.

Getting from Café de la Paix to l'Hotel de Rothschild would have only taken me ten minutes on the Metro. It was cheap and reliable, but I always felt the tentacles of claustrophobia squeezing my chest when I was under the ground. Whenever possible, I would walk. Paris was a beautiful, vibrant city, and it felt disrespectful to be slinking around beneath her. The cool wind was at my back as I started off along rue Auber past the Grand Hotel. The edifices always felt like the faces of ornamental canyons around me. Ladies wrestled with their parasols. A man chased his boater. Remembering the horse at La Paix, I kept one eye to the ground when I crossed to Boulevard Haussmann. The trees there had been trained to lean away from the buildings, which made it appear that the apartments were lounging back against the grey sky. I passed the depressing, windowless Chapelle Expiatoire and—cognac and wind assisted—I reached rue Berryer in twenty-five minutes.

Any hopes I may have had of strolling up to the president as we perused the book display, looking into his soul and inviting him for a chat and an absinthe were thwarted when I turned the final corner to see that a large crowd had gathered opposite the hotel. Two *gendarmes* stood in the road in front of the onlookers motionless but for their black capes flapping like bat wings. There was no rope barrier, but the crowd comprised mainly elderly ladies and families with children holding small tricolors. An enter-prising shoe-shine boy was taking advantage of the boots on display. The policemen had apparently assessed the danger level and decided there was no threat, so they had their backs to the crowd.

It was very orderly and I could have probably slotted in amongst the old ladies, but I actually wanted to look at the exhibition and pick up a few bargains before they let in the public. Fortunately, we "Chinese" were at our most popular, so I ignored the police, who ignored me in turn, and entered an alleyway beside the hotel. I emerged at a rear door whose sign read TRADESMEN AND HOTEL EMPLOYEES ONLY. This was no fluke. Three months ear-lier, Boua and I had entered the hotel through this door whilst gate crashing a wine-tasting event. We had become quite competent at enjoying free French hospitality. On occasions, we'd even been able to convince people that we were the Japanese ambassador and his wife. Why not?

For a presidential visit I'd expected security to be tighter on this occasion, but the commissionaire's table inside the door was unattended. I was able to walk through the busy kitchen and the chambermaid's quarters unchallenged. Nobody knew what to say to me. And suddenly, there I was in the grand ballroom, which that day looked more like a book emporium. Men in monocles and tailcoat suites fussed over last-minute preparations, and hotel staff stood at attention in a line receiving their final in-house briefing. I was able to browse at leisure and even paid for and put aside my book selection at one of the secondhand booths.

A bell chimed from the direction of the reception area, and the staff hurried to the front of the hotel. I fol-lowed them because I admit I had become infected by the atmosphere. I wasn't even an employee, but I'd been there long enough to want the hotel to do its very best—even for a bastard like Doumer. I needn't have worried. The welcome committee was regimental. Everyone knew of his or her function and where they should stand. Except me. I retreated behind one of the stone pillars and from there I could see through the two enormous glass doors and beyond them I witnessed the arrival of two motorized police vans. The rear doors were thrown open and a dozen *gendarmes* stumbled out of each. Some took up positions on the hotel steps. The others wrestled open the doors, secured them in the open position, and spread themselves around the foyer. If they were armed, their weapons were well concealed. But I suspected there were more qualified plain-clothed officers strategically dotted around. One, quite obviously a military man with a crew cut and the nervous twitch of a security guard on alert, was in place behind the next pillar. I smiled at him and he ignored me. I'd expect nothing less from my bodyguard.

It was a very long, tense ten minutes before the President's Citroën arrived. An aide hurried to open the rear door but the president was already halfway out before he got there. I'd seen Doumer on newsreels at my cinema. He was a portly man with a fancy white beard, and I had a theory that this was what Father Christmas did for the other eleven months of the year. I couldn't help smiling at that thought as he stopped on the top step, turned and waved at the grannies and the bemused children. He entered the hotel and the male staff members leaned forward into a respectful bow. The women curtsied. There was silence apart from the manager welcoming the President on behalf of the hotel and the Fund for Wounded Soldiers.

A table had been set up in the foyer with the types of political books a president would have been expected to read. But I saw him as more of a detective fiction type. I was already an aficionado of Simenon and I decided that would be my opening gambit:

"I'm sure you'd prefer the exploits of Inspector Maigret," I would say.

I was practicing my pronunciation of that line and Doumer was alone at the table waiting for the photographer to adjust his lens. Doumer would laugh at my impudence and confess that he was indeed a crime novel fan. Leap forward five months and we'd be at his gentleman's club sorting out troubles in the Far East fairly and sensibly with not a shot fired.

I took a step forward but it seemed that by doing so, I broke some invisible thread and threw the ordered world into chaos. A shout came from the kitchen. It was a foreign language, but I wasn't alert enough to say which. A plate smashed. The kitchen doors flew open and a ruddy-faced man ran into the reception area. He had the build of a pasta chef and wore a suit so tight that it could only have been a relic from his slimmer past. A large serviette covered his right hand and forearm. It made him look like a waiter and perhaps it was that image: the head waiter emerging angrily from the kitchen after some unforgivable culinary incident that prevented the security detail from moving. We were a still photograph with only the man in the tight suit animated. He looked around the room, caught sight of Doumer, and staggered toward him.

He shouted again. This time I recognized his language as Russian. Then in French he said, "I do this in the name of the miserable ones who wait in Russia."

Then, like a birthday party magician, he pulled back the serviette to reveal an FN1910 pistol. I recall that he fired five shots, but I still don't know how many hit Doumer. Enough to make him dead, I could see that. He fell backward onto the book display and his blood ruined a number of first editions. By the time everyone realized what had happened, it was too late. I looked back at the security man behind the pillar. He had his gun drawn and aimed at the assassin, but he hadn't fired. In fact, I saw him look left and right, then return his pistol to his inside pocket. He watched the *gendarmes* tackle the gunman to the ground. He observed as the President's waistcoat changed from grey to crimson. And I couldn't be sure amid the chaos, but I fancied I saw the young man smile. I remember he had almost perfect teeth, which was quite unusual in those days.

He walked calmly to the hotel entrance and into the street. It was odd. Perhaps I was one of the few people there who didn't really care that the President had been shot. That's why I noticed him. Why had he not intervened? If he was a bodyguard, why was he leaving?

I wasn't yet doctor enough to offer to tend Doumer's wounds. He had a team of surgeons to care for him but none of them would make him any more alive. So, in pursuit of my own curiosity, I followed the short-haired man. He casually crossed the street and melted into the crowd even though the road had been cleared of traffic, and it would have been easier to walk there. I stayed with him. When he got to the first corner he turned, knelt, and pretended to be tying a shoelace. Even if he'd seen me I doubted he would have considered that I might be following him. You tend to notice only what you expect to be there.

He cut into a narrow lane with art and craft stalls on either side and picked up his speed. He stopped briefly at a stand with a display of ornamental mirrors, and there he made his second check for prospective followers. I'd put on a woolen hat I kept in my pocket and was almost beside him as he scanned the crowd through the mirror. If he'd looked to his right we would have met eye-to-eye. But he did not. Once he was through the maze of vendors he turned on to the boulevard at Faubourg Saint-Honoré, and I could see his shoulders relax. Now that we had distance between us I felt more comfortable. He sauntered along the northern pavement and I kept to the south side. We passed the saddlers and trunk stores, and he paused calmly to admire the fashions displayed in the windows of the high-class stores. Everything was going fine until he passed the foolish stone balloon monument and descended into the Metro at Ternes.

This was a problem, not just because of my claustrophobia, but because I had paid my last franc for the books at the hotel. I had nothing left for the Metro. But I was determined to stay with my man until I could work out what the hell had happened at the hotel.

The underground walkway to the station was long and tiled. Every sound echoed. My man wore shoes with metal tips. A blind person could have followed him. But the workday was not yet finished, and there were few people traveling. He was heading for a labyrinth of tunnels on the way to the platforms, and I had to stay close to see which he took. At each level and with each turn he could be there waiting for me. I was close enough to see him hand his 70 centimes to the kiosk cashier and receive his ticket. He showed it to the guard when he passed the gate.

I had neither ticket nor coins, but I had an ethnic brotherhood. The cashier was dark as cocoa, possibly Moroccan. I hoped he might have attended the colonial exhibition. I stood in front of him with the hangdog expression I used to get extensions on my essays.

"I have no money, brother," I said.

He could have told me to go jump in the Seine, but he cocked his head to one side, smiled a splendid set of teeth minus one at the front, and tore me off a ticket from the roll.

"Your lucky day," he said, "but don't try this shit again when I'm on duty. I got to cover shortcomings."

I could hear the metallic rattle of an East-West line train in the distance, but I couldn't tell in which direction it was headed. I ran past the guard and stood considering the options. There were two staircases. I chose west because my own instinct would have been to double back across the city. The stairwell seemed to go all the way down to Hades. I hit the empty platform after the passengers had boarded. The station assistant normally closed the metal gate when a train arrived, but it was open. Someone had failed to shut a door correctly, and the assistant was running along the platform blowing his whistle. It gave me time to look at the faces through the smoky glass of the windows. I reached the third carriage, and there I saw my man. He looked at me directly but with no sign of recognition or interest.

I walked to the fourth carriage, where the assistant was having trouble with the door. One of the hinges had dropped, and it took two people to lift it back onto its frame: the man outside, the train guard inside. We left the station seven minutes late.

At Courcelles I stepped off the train but my man did not. I climbed back on. The same happened at Monceau, and, by then, I had a sort of working hypothesis of what I'd witnessed at the Rothschild. My man was clearly not a part of Doumer's security detail, but he was armed and in a position to see all that happened. Even after the assassin had removed the serviette from his forearm, a good five seconds passed before he pumped his bullets into the president. My man's weapon was unholstered and aimed at the shooter, so why had he not fired? And why did he smile?

I was left with only one conclusion. The slurring Russian had been recruited by someone to shoot Doumer. Perhaps he had some grievance against the president about his treatment of Russians. He was clearly unstable but passionate. Someone had brought him into the hotel, perhaps as a guest. They'd provided him with a weapon and plied him with booze for Dutch courage. Only one thing was missing. The plan had to have a contingency. There had to be a second shooter in case the Russian folded or missed. Once the assassin had discharged his weapon, my man behind the pillar, a marksman, sober, would ensure that at least one bullet hit the target.

But the Russian did not fail. The president was dead, and the second shooter could return to his cabal and make his report.

At Villiers, my man stepped off the train and I was behind him. He was so confident that he no longer checked his back. I still had no idea what purpose my following him would serve. I wasn't yet clear-headed enough to assess what the benefits for France or Europe or the world would be with Doumer dead. I didn't really care. It just annoyed me that any idiot could undemocratically solve his problems with a gun or a sword or a stick of dynamite. Surely we'd progressed far enough from the ape to settle our differences without violence.

By the time I reached street level, I'd lost him. There were no large buildings nearby for him to have disappeared into so fast. It was as if the station had been built in the center of a large field in anticipation of development closing in on it. I could see all around but there was no sign of my man. I was embarrassed. Maigret would have been ashamed of me. I sat on a bench that had the view of just one tree, and I considered my next step. Who should I tell? What exactly would I say? Would anyone believe me? And, at that moment, my man walked out of the Metro exit. Somehow I'd passed him without noticing. The telephone. That was it. He'd stopped in the telephone booth. They were a new item in Paris, so it hadn't occurred to me. I imagined he'd reported that everything had gone according to plan.

He walked past my bench. I squeezed the cap in my hand and concentrated on the tree. I'd been a boxer and wrestler at university. Good in my weight class. But my man had a gun in his inside pocket. A lot of use the old one-two would have been against that. But, as before, he looked straight through me and crossed the park heading east. Perhaps it was there that I learned how to be invisible. I let him get fifty meters ahead then climbed back on his tail. He didn't go far. On Constantinople, he joined the queue at a tram stop. I didn't want to pass him, so I studied the headlines at the news kiosk. The newsagent eyed me with suspicion. The longer I stood there the deeper into me she glared. I had to make a decision. The tram was on its way. If I left it to the last moment and ran for it, I'd draw attention to myself.

Then there'd be another scene when the conductor asked me for money and found out I had none. But, if I didn't catch the tram I'd lose the second shooter.

The tram passed the kiosk. The driver clanged the bell and applied the brake. What if this was my man's final check? What if he left it to the last second before boarding the tram? That way he'd be certain he wasn't being followed. And then again, what if he had no intention of getting on board? And that, as Civilai would say, was the filly I put my savings on. I stood at the kiosk and waited for the passengers to board the tram. My man looked around, put his foot on the running board, then took it off and stepped backward. The conductor asked if he intended to get on, and my man waved him away.

"Hey, China," said the newsagent. "This what you're looking for?"

She reached inside a leather pouch and produced a very racy magazine. Some might have called it downright filthy. But I was a trainee surgeon and I'd seen all those parts before. The tram had pulled away, leaving my man alone on the sidewalk. He crossed the boulevard and walked directly to an expensive-looking apartment building opposite. He opened the main door and before it shut behind him, I noticed the uniformed concierge at the reception desk salute him. He lived there. Damn. I had to admire his audacity. Who would oversee an assassination three Metro stops from his home?

"Bravo," I said, but I wasn't going to let him get away with it. Neither was I likely to walk into a *gendarmerie* and file a report. And I wasn't about to seek help from my new comrades at the PCF. They'd have hoisted the assassin on their shoulders and treated him to a slap-up meal.

There was only one person I thought I could talk to. The following morning, I was due to attend the second lecture of three from an army general called Richard from the French medical corps. It was he who had described the rapidly approaching blight of heroin that morning. I'd been impressed by his distress and concerns about the drug business and his preparedness to accept the blame on behalf of the French government for its involvement in the opium trade.

After his lecture the following morning, I invited him for coffee in the university refectory. I told him what had happened after the assassination of Doumer. He asked why I hadn't filed a report immediately, but I could see he understood. He asked for my address but made no comment as to my actions or suspicions. I thought he might have considered me to be some sort of crackpot. I heard nothing for the rest of the day. I met Boua for lunch and told her I'd been at the book exhibition and witnessed the killing of Doumer. I'm not sure why, but I decided against telling her my theory of the second shooter and about my pursuit of him. It was the first time I'd withheld information from her but would not be the last, and we weren't even married yet. Perhaps I felt she'd consider it her duty to tell her Communist friends and things would have become . . . messy. I wanted to marry her without issues pulling us apart. Even then I was cautious of Boua's hypersensitive buttons and which ones launched missiles.

That evening, two young plainclothes army officers found me at my local café. Boua was at a policy meeting. The soldiers came directly to me even though we'd never met. They sat down at my table, introduced themselves and produced a manila envelope. From it they took two large photographs. Both were close-ups of my man.

"Is this him?" one asked.

"Yes," I said.

"Would you be prepared to act as an eye witness in the arrest of this person?" asked the other.

I said "yes" immediately but after they'd thanked me and left I started to think of all the reasons why I should have said "no." My life hadn't seen a great deal of excitement up until then. I'd studied, I'd traveled, I'd worked in a cinema. But I hadn't lived the adventures I saw on the screen. Then, suddenly, there I was front seat at an assassination and on the trail of a man with a loaded gun. I was playing the sheriff role but I honestly didn't know who the good guys were. What if the military had planned the kill? What if the shooter was a patriot? I knew Doumer was no angel. How dare I condemn his killers? But I'd pushed that wagon up to the top of the hill and those wheels had a habit of building up speed on the way down.

Late that night, I was awoken by the hammering on the door of our tiny apartment.

"Siri," someone shouted, "come and drink with us. We're celebrating."

I could only open the door a few centimeters when the bed was down and through the gap I saw my young military friends. They nodded and gestured for me to come. I told Boua a classmate had just . . . no, I can't remember what lie I told her. But she believed me because I'd been an honest man until then. If I felt any guilt, it was diluted in fear for my own life.

I was driven back to my man's apartment building opposite the tram stop. As we entered, the concierge was being led away. I was told to wait in the foyer. An older military man in a tracksuit silently waited with me. There were no sounds of doors being broken down, no gunshots, no shouted threats. But, ten minutes after our arrival, half-a-dozen soldiers in plain clothes came down the staircase escorting a man in pajamas with a sisal bag over his head. He wasn't cuffed or shackled, which made the situation more tense than was necessary. They stood their prisoner in front of me and pulled off his hood.

He still wore the crust of sleep around his eyes.

"Monsieur Paiboun," said one of the young officers, "is this the man you saw at the Hotel Rothschild pointing a gun in the direction of the President yesterday afternoon?"

I was distraught that he should have used my name. I put my trembling hands in my pockets.

"It's him," I said.

"And did you follow him from the hotel to this apartment at 235 Constantinople immediately after the assassination?"

"I did," I said.

"Should we not ask him why?" said my man.

There were six guards around him. Surely one of them could have told him to stop talking. But, no.

"Because, whoever little Monsieur Paiboun is," he said, "whoever he works for, we will learn of it. When I am released, I shall find him. If they foolishly decide to execute me, my brothers will find him. We will find him and we will take his life apart piece by piece, friend by friend. And when there remains only him, we will take him apart even more slowly and painfully, organ by organ, until there is nothing left. But long before the end he will have regretted this day."

At last the guards took his arms and half-carried him to the street and the waiting van. Before climbing aboard, he looked back at me and gestured a knife across his throat. And then he smiled. And the smile was more frightening than anything he'd said.

CHAPTER FOUR
The Widow Ghost

Siri and Daeng were sitting on their bamboo recliners on the bank of the Mekong looking out to the pinpricks of light on the far bank. Siri had crossed the river in both directions and could have been killed doing so a number of times in any number of ways. But Mother Khong always looked so innocent, as if you could just wade your way through it, pick up supplies on the Thai side and float back over. This time of year it was at its most sly. Escapees often waited for the end of the monsoon floods only to find themselves carried south on the current.

"I can't believe you haven't told me this story before," said Daeng.

"Have you told me all yours?" Siri asked.

"Not yet."

"Exactly," said Siri. "We have a combined age of . . . several hundred years. We need untold stories to entertain each other in our dotage."

"You don't think your involvement in the assassination of a president is a priority A-plus story?"

"I was just a witness. I have many more exciting stories than that. If I'd killed him myself it would have been the first story out of my mouth. I just happened to follow a coconspirator."

"One who promised to take you apart organ by organ. Did you ever find out who he was?"

"There was nothing in the press. No public trial. The only version of events on record is that of the drunken Russian *émigré*. Before his execution at the guillotine he claimed that he was driven in a trance to kill heads of state. Officially, the man I followed wasn't involved."

"And unofficially?"

"I met the army surgeon again a few years later. I was a qualified doctor by then. We were at a reception. He was drunk. He told me more than he was probably supposed to. He said the second shooter was a Corsican. He'd been in North America establishing a foothold for his family in various illegal activities. Some years earlier his two brothers had been in Annam setting up a network to send Chinese opium to Marseille. It was around the time Doumer was in Vietnam trying to find money to fund his projects. For two years he'd bought up the entire opium harvest and it still wasn't enough, so he started to eat away at some of the private contractors who had established networks. The Corsicans had set up such an organization. Doumer made an offer to take over their trade, but the brothers were answerable to the family. They refused him."

"And I bet they had an accident," said Daeng.

"A truck they were traveling in exploded. The authorities said it was a petrol tank leak, but some of the workers said they'd seen men with military haircuts creeping around the night before. Doumer denied any involvement but the Corsicans knew better. The younger brother, my man, was on the boil for a long time. That's why the family sent him to the States. But the Corsicans have short fuses and long memories. He watched the news of Doumer's return to France and fumed when the old man assumed the senate seat for Corsica. There were those who suggested Doumer was merely carrying his opium business home. The family suffered again at his hand and the elders finally gave the green light for the younger brother to return to France. By then, Doumer had become president and the rest we know."

"And you think the Godfathers still have a black list with your name on it, Siri?"

"It's not impossible, Daeng. There are still Corsicans in Laos left over from the opium heydays of the forties and fifties. They're married to Lao women and waiting for opportunities. Any one of them could be related to my man. There could be a contract out on me for old times' sake."

"You see, Ugly?" said Daeng to the dog. "This is what happens when you allow strangers to attach notes to your nether regions."

"And that's odd too," said Siri. "Ugly doesn't let anyone near him. A head pat's the most he can handle. He's not going to stand still for five minutes while an assassin ties a ribbon to his tail, is he now?"

"Yet, he obviously did."

"Curious."

Daeng poured them both a glass of homemade rice whisky, and they let it flow over their palates before allowing it to drop and burn holes in their livers. Around then, someone on the Thai side was apparently blown up by an illegal propane gas tank. They recognized the sound. It happened often.

"What I suggest . . ." said Daeng.

"Yes?"

". . . is that we do absolutely nothing."

"I thought that's what we were doing."

"We don't want paranoia to set in."

"Why does everyone on the planet think I'm paranoid?"

"Exactly. I suggest we just work on the small and solvable problems."

"Such as?"

"I'm glad you asked," said Daeng. "You remember Granny Far from the skirt bank?"

"How could I forget her?" said Siri. "We're keeping her alive, aren't we?"

The skirt bank was one of Madam Daeng's many community projects. More and more women she knew were running into financial strife and were selling what items of value they had to keep their families fed. Many had already sold their silk *phasin* skirts for far less than they were worth. Their family heirlooms were lost forever. Siri and Daeng had come into some good luck as a result of a drug deal that went wrong. They happened to have been in the right place at the right time. It was no fortune. Enough, Siri thought, for a nice little car and sufficient petrol to run it for a while. But Daeng had convinced Siri that they should use that money to set up a loan service. The women could deposit their *phasin*s at Daeng's shop. She would give them a fair price for the skirt and, one day, when the spirits were in a more convivial mood, they could pay back the loan and reclaim their goods.

The spirits were obviously in no hurry to heap blessings on the hapless women because Daeng's spare room was starting to look like a fabric warehouse. Mr. Geung, currently doing whatever it was that grooms did on their honeymoons at vegetable farms, was the curator of what he called the *sin* bin. He had no written records but he had a remarkable nose. If anyone returned and claimed their treasure he could sniff it out in no time.

Granny Far had long since lost her valuable *phasin* collection to unscrupulous dealers on the Thai side. But she still had an assortment of chain-link silver belts. Her children and grandchildren, and all but one nephew, had fled to the camps across the river. The anticipated arrival of money from her relatives in third countries had yet to materialize. So, from time to time, the old lady would ride her bicycle over to Daeng's noodle shop, have a bowl of her favorite spicy number two and call Daeng to one side to discuss a little business.

That evening, the business had been entirely different.

"Her nephew," said Daeng.

"What about him?" said Siri. "He's a nasty little shrew if I remember rightly. Did he run off with the old lady's belt collection? Wouldn't put it past him."

"No, he's dead."

"Ah, well. Then I apologize to his spirit for being so negative. Someone shoot him?"

"He died in his sleep."

"Really? How old was he?"

"Seventeen."

"Hmm."

"He'd worked the night shift in the kitchen at the Russian Club," said Daeng. "The curfew's flexible at the moment with all the journalists in town. He came home at two-ish and went to bed. Granny Far tried to raise him at nine but he was dead. No wounds."

"Any vomit—saliva?"

"No."

"Well, I hope our donations to the family were generous enough to cover a nice budget cremation."

"Siri, he's still there."

"Still where?"

"On his bed roll on the floor."

"Why?"

"Because I promised her I'd take you there to have a look at him."

"Oh, did you?"

"Yup."

"You do know I'm not a coroner anymore?"

"It's like riding a bicycle, Siri. You never forget."

"What about my replacement, the good Doctor Mot?"

"About whom you were quoted as saying, 'If they weren't stuck on, he wouldn't know a breast from a buttock'?"

"I did say that, didn't I? What about Dtui?"

"She and Phosy are taking care of their journalist group. And Granny Far specifically asked for you."

"Why?"

"There are . . . unusual circumstances."

The thing Siri liked most about his Pigeon bicycle was its padded passenger seat and the fact that Madam Daeng had to wrap one arm around his waist and push one breast against his back while they were riding together. Whenever he hit a pothole, a spontaneous samba ground them together. There were few potholes that escaped his attention. But Granny Far's house was only ten blocks away along the river. She was on the doorstep when they arrived. Ugly was with them of course. He hadn't expected to be on duty that evening, so he trotted drowsily to the spot where they parked the bicycle and collapsed beside it.

"Lucky it's not been a hot day," said Siri. "Or we should start to get a whiff of the boy by now."

He and Daeng followed Far to a room at the rear of the house, where the nephew lay beneath a grey mosquito net. The youth's face was contorted into a horrible death mask. His hands were poised in front of him as if warding off an attack. And he was wearing a nightdress; a woman's pink, sleeveless nightdress with Disney dalmatians printed all over it.

"I take it he wasn't given to homosexual tendencies?" said Siri.

"No, Doctor," said Granny Far, "he had a lot of young lady friends."

"And he didn't dress in girls' clothes at any other time of the day?"

"No, Doctor," said Far. "Would you like to cut him open now? I have an old plastic table cloth we could put down."

"No need," said Siri.

"Was he poisoned?" she asked.

"No, Granny Far," said Siri. "He wasn't poisoned. He was haunted to death."

"Oh, I say," said the old woman, and she held her palm to her chest. Siri was certain she had some good luck talisman hanging there. He had one too. It could often mean the difference between life and death. He instinctively reached for his own stone amulet beneath his shirt.

"Is there anything we can do?" Daeng asked.

"On the way in I couldn't help noticing the pile of furniture in the yard," said Siri.

"It's all the old stuff," said Far, "and wood from the old trees out back. I loaded it there this afternoon."

"So I take it your temple no longer provides a service?"

"All the monks have gone, bar one," said Far. "And his only functions seem to be grumbling and insulting anyone who wastes his time with dead loved ones."

"So you'd sooner do it here?" said Daeng.

"It's been the family home since the last century," said Far.

They wrapped the corpse in the old plastic tablecloth and carried it to the familial pyre, where they sat the nephew on a chunky Chinese chair. They knew they were supposed to inform the authorities and stand back and watch the cogs turn slowly, but there wouldn't have been much of the nephew left by the time they'd got his file up to date. There'd be the issue of lighting a fire without village headman permission, but Far said she could handle that.

"Doctor, could you say a few words?" said Granny Far, still attempting to ignite her candle with a cigarette lighter.

"What kind of words?" said Siri.

"I don't know. Something fitting."

"I don't know anything religious."

"That's fine."

"How's your French?" he asked.

"Non-existent, Doctor."

"Then here goes," said Siri.

"J'avais auparavant,
Vaincu de la jeunesse,
* Autres dames aimé,*
* Ma faute je confesse. "*

"That's lovely," said Granny Far. "What does it mean?"

"It is my desire that your nephew finds a comfortable place in nirvana," said Siri.

She offered him a silver belt for his trouble but he refused.

Back at the restaurant they locked up and retired for the night. They lay on the mattress in the familiar spoon position. Daeng caressed her husband's neck as they watched the moon rise through the open window.

"You've heard of that type of thing before?" Daeng asked.

"A lot," said Siri. "But since the beginning of the exodus—thousands of young men fleeing to the West—it seems to happen unsettlingly often. It's almost an epidemic. We hear about it in letters to relatives all the time. But I've never witnessed it first hand before."

"But what causes it?"

"Belief," said Siri. "Or should I say, misbelief. In many ways the young men feel they've failed in their duties as protectors of the family. They find themselves away from their support network. They don't have access to the shaman or to their village spirits or their ancestors. All those paths you could take in stressful times are closed. It makes them more susceptible to the malevolent spirits that have hitched a ride with them."

"But Far's nephew didn't go anywhere."

"But his family did and they took their beliefs with them. He felt he'd failed them by not going with them. He was left alone with the widow ghost who sucks out men's souls when they're sleeping. The Hmong call her *tsog tsuam*. In the beginning, she might make appearances like a movie extra in his dream. She'll have the role of a waitress or a passerby. But then he'll notice her . . . expect to see her.

And with every dream she becomes more prominent. He tries not to sleep but can't fight it. He's heard about her from his friends. He knows she's only interested in young men, so he goes to bed dressed as a woman to trick her. But, by then, it's often too late."

"How does . . . how could she kill them?" Daeng asked.

"The boys believe that she crushes their chests while they sleep. In the dream they're dead, and it's so convincing there is no point in breathing anymore. The spirit then takes the soul as a memento. She exists in many cultures with many names. But when you peel away her disguises and wipe off her makeup it always comes down to that one, same antagonist: *phibob*, the evil spirit that's responsible for most of the damage done to man's mind."

Siri tugged at the cord around his neck and pulled out the talisman from under his T-shirt.

"Feel this," he said.

"It's hot," she said.

"They feel threatened by this kind of talk," said Siri. "We have ours housetrained for the moment. But they continue to live on in the minds of thousands of lonely men around the world."

"How can you fight anything like that?" Daeng asked.

"I think I have an idea," said Siri. "I could—"

Daeng screamed and let go of the amulet.

"Hot?" Siri asked.

"I have an imaginary blister," said Daeng.

"Good, then it seems they know what I'm thinking. I've touched a nerve."

CHAPTER FIVE
Darts and Balloons

"I have so much gas in me Madam Nong has to tie a rope round my ankle and hold on to it so I don't float away," said Civilai.

"Yes, I'm sure we're all fascinated by your flatulence stories," said Siri.

"I didn't say anything about flatulence," said Civilai. "Gas is a different beast altogether. Gas is containable and controllable. Flatulence sneaks out at inopportune moments. You won't be hearing any wind instruments from me this evening. No, Sir. I'll know when it's time for me to empty my gas and I shall . . ."

"Civilai, spare us," said Madam Daeng.

". . . head off in an orderly fashion, open the valve, release the pressure and return with you all none the wiser."

"Except now we'll all guess where you're going and what you're doing," said Daeng. "Even if you're not."

"I'm feeling quite off my food already," said Bruce.

"Ah, Son, you'll have to put up with a lot worse than this before our film is complete," said Siri. "This is just a sort of test."

Bruce, alias Deesabun, had arrived back in Laos the previous week. He was twenty-two with dyed-blond hair, had an earring in his left lobe and carried eight kilograms more than he really needed. He'd been a quick learner in Australia and was already assured a lucrative career in TV production. But in the cutting room at SBS in Sydney he'd seen the conditions in the refugee camps and heard the struggling Lao government's pleas for qualified personnel to come home. His conscience got the better of him. It was a romantic notion to return to the country of his birth with something of value to offer. His cousin at the Fuji film lab had written to him about a group of visionaries who had written a film script. They had a Panavision camera they couldn't operate. They needed Bruce.

Upon his return, he'd met Siri and Civilai who had begun their romance with cinema half a century before in France. He was astounded by the depth and breadth of their knowledge of film. Their script, on the other hand—rewritten by the Ministry of Culture to incorporate Comrades Lenin and Marx, altered again by the Women's Union to raise the profile of women and returned to its original state by its writer, Siri Paiboun—would have been impossible to film in its present state. They had just the one camera, no permission to travel to locations and a budget that wouldn't have paid for sandwiches and lemonade on a B-movie set in Australia.

What they lacked in resources and ability, they more than made up for in alcohol. The first official executive directorial meeting was convened immediately after the evening noodle rush. The tables were clean, the utensils were spotless and a crate of Bordeaux sat at the feet of Madam Daeng, who wielded the corkscrew. The wine was the last from the cellar of the French Embassy, closed for the past two years due to a misunderstanding: the French thought Laos was still a colony.

Bruce was welcomed formally with a toast although Siri noticed Civilai sipped sparingly from his glass. They'd all warmed to Bruce's character—a sort of Lao/Aussie blend that made them smile. Siri particularly liked the fact that their cameraman was not afraid to speak his mind.

"Do you have good news for us?" Daeng asked.

"I certainly do," said Bruce. "I spent the afternoon with your camera, and I'm pleased to say it is now fully functional."

The directors cheered and drank to the victory. Bruce started to explain such things as fuses and batteries but he could see these details were fluttering hopelessly in the air some distance from the old folks' ears. So, he entertained them with other good news.

"I told you I had a surprise for you," he said. "Well, under the auspices of international aid for the third world, I was able to get a donation of a hundred and eighty hours of film and some video equipment. It's all in a crate sitting at the Customs shed at Tar Deua."

They stood with their drinks and saluted their cameraman.

"Excellent," said Siri.

"Our young hero," said Daeng.

Even sickly Civilai drank to the news.

"I just don't know how to get it out of Customs," said Bruce.

"Fear not," said Civilai. "It used to take a week of paperwork, but the process has been streamlined remarkably this past year. The current policy is for them to hold on to everything until someone shows up with an envelope full of money to thank the official for looking after their goods."

"Thank heavens for the return of corruption," said Daeng.

"Simplifies everything," said Siri.

"Ladies and gentlemen," said Civilai, "time is against us. I suggest we read through the opening scenes and put our collective minds together on how to win over the audience from the outset."

"You might have to take off your sunglasses so you can see the script," said Daeng.

"These aren't sunglasses, Madam," he said. "These are ultraviolet, light-sensitive lenses imported from Eastern Europe. Johnny Halliday wears them."

"They're from the morning market," said Siri. "And they have no more UV protection than beer bottles. And I'm sure even Halliday takes his off at night."

"All right, it's an image thing," said Civilai. "I'm looking for a hat to go with it."

Given his bad health, nobody had the heart to talk him out of it.

The script began by switching back and forth between the lives of two teenagers—one poor, one rich, but both causing havoc to the French colonial administration in Laos: a jeep disabled here, a phone line cut there. The military give chase but are always one step behind until they learn of the identity of the two boys. They torture the relatives who refuse to give them up. At last the boys meet for the first time at the port in Da Nang, about to stow away on a steamer to France. Both already heroes.

"Just out of interest," said Bruce, "and it really doesn't matter to me one way or the other, how much of this script is biographical?"

Siri and Civilai looked at each other and smiled.

"I'd say about . . ." Civilai began.

"At least . . ." said Siri.

They looked at Daeng, whose eyebrows were somewhere up by her hairline.

"A substantial amount," said Civilai.

"Wow," said Bruce. "So, the assassination of the French president in the thirties. . . ?"

The old boys laughed.

"Come on, Son," said Siri. "Who'd be foolish enough to admit to something like that?"

"It would be madness," said Civilai.

"Ridiculous," Siri agreed.

"But that reminds me," said Civilai, "I should take a look in the attic."

"For the . . . ?" said Siri.

"We'll need it for the assassination scene."

"You still have it?"

"The gun?" said Bruce. "Wow!"

Daeng smiled and refilled the glasses. Nobody had an attic.

The group sat together for another seven hours: Siri and Civilai attempted to expand the scope and grandeur of their film, while Bruce attempted to bring them all down to earth. But talking about something they loved was one of the happiest nights Siri and Civilai had spent together for a long time. When the tragedies began, Siri wondered how different everything might have been if he'd taken the threat more seriously. But, as it was, that night, with the warm buzz of expensive Bordeaux in their veins, they stood at the end of the meeting and, inspired by their Aussie cinematographer, they hugged. It was un-Lao but surprisingly therapeutic. Siri could feel all the bones in Civilai's chest and commented that it was like embracing a xylophone, but he didn't let go and Civilai was in no hurry to get away. They all felt that they were about to embark on a long hike through beautiful scenery with Civilai stepping into the bushes to throw up from time to time. But that didn't take away the magic. The completed film was in their heads. They'd started writing their Oscar acceptance speeches. This was a great moment and they all knew it.

Bruce was still negotiating with the government for the return of his father's property. In the meantime, he was staying at a guesthouse a few blocks walk away. They pointed him in the right direction and pushed. Civilai staggered to his lemon-colored Citroën. They were more concerned about his walking than his driving so nobody attempted to take the keys from him. He'd be alone on the road and the car barely hit forty kilometers an hour. Civilai, probably legally blind behind his Soviet shades, spent some time searching for the slot for the key, but, once engaged, the engine purred like that of a more impressive vehicle. He wound down the window.

"Little brother," he called to Siri.

Siri walked to the car and Civilai handed him a wad of papers he'd retrieved from the glove box.

"I forgot," he said. "I got the list. Here! Sixty-four journalists, one of whom is probably here for the sole purpose of killing you slowly and painfully and massacring the rest of us in the process. Their CVs, their blood types, their ages and all the way down to their favorite sandwiches. I've called in what few favors I have left to do background checks on them. I have hope we'll find him before he starts slicing slivers of skin off—"

"We can all imagine how he'll go about it," said Siri. "But don't you worry yourself. I have freedom-fighter Daeng and Ugly the Wonder Dog to protect me."

Civilai grabbed Siri's wrist.

"Siri," he said.

"Yes?"

"My little brother."

He didn't let go.

"What?" said Siri.

"I love you."

Even after three bottles of Bordeaux, there were some things men didn't say to each other. Siri could see his own embarrassment reflected in the dark of the glasses. Still Civilai didn't let go. It was as if he was waiting for Siri to say something meaningful back.

"Civilai," said Siri.

The doctor could feel his heart throb.

"Yeah?"

"Let go of my wrist."

"All right," said Civilai, and with two coughs of exhaust from a rusty tailpipe, he was off.

Nurse Dtui, the wife of Chief Inspector Phosy, had what they call an eye for language. She'd studied and absorbed Russian without the benefit of hearing it spoken. She'd learned how to pronounce the words from the six pages at the front of the textbook that laid it all out linguistically like a mathematical table. But that suited her style. She'd done the same with English even though that language was a bugger for inconsistency and exceptions to rules. As a member of the Lao administration team at the Moscow Olympics, she had proven her value as a translator, so it was only natural they'd find a role for her at the fifth anniversary celebration. Interpreters the Pathet Lao could trust were thin on the ground. Those who had learned English from the Americans were either having a dour time up north in reeducation camps or were on their way to the West. German and Russian speakers were starting to return from the eastern bloc with dubious technical skills, but their ability in those languages was a far cry from simultaneous translation. The majority of the press corps in town to cover the celebrations was from socialist countries. The Soviets, like the French before them, were keen to spark an interest in investment in this little landlocked country overflowing with natural resources and potential.

In fact, "potential" rather than "actual" was the adjective *du jour* in Vientiane that week. The organized visits were mostly to demonstration sites: samples of what a successful project might look like with a bit of luck and better handling. The groups were led by Soviet Embassy officials fluent in the languages of the socialist brotherhood and accompanied by Lao minders. The government officials understood little of the live commentaries that endorsed Laos the way Madam Loulou advertised new girls to her regulars: "She may not look like much, but she has hidden promise and a surprise or two."

And all this left Nurse Dtui's little pack of decidedly non-Communist English speakers wondering why they'd been invited at all. She and Phosy had met them that second night at the bar of the Vieng Vilai: the Constellation

Hotel of old. It was there that Air America pilots and CIA spies and USAID workers would gather in the days when the landlords of Sodom and Gomorrah still collected their taxes in Vientiane. The boys would down their cocktails at the Constellation before heading off to the late-night sin spots of the after-hours capital. Those were the days when the options were vast in number and bottomless.

No such choice in 1980. The bar of the Vieng Vilai was something of a graveyard. To order drinks one had to drag the manager from the reception desk. He had the only key to the drinks cupboard. Once Dtui had ordered on behalf of her group, it was obvious the manager wouldn't know an Old-Fashioned from a Vieux Carré. In '75, the hotels had been left in the hands of men who had never stayed in one. Since then, tourism had been nonexistent, and a number of hotels had been converted to dormitories for cadres and their families. The sudden and random government decision to open the city to tourists had thrown the hotel industry into a panic. The managers had no guest relation skills and no foreign languages. They most certainly could not recommend wines or explain the contents of a cocktail.

So, at the insistence of the chief of police, the manager of the Vieng Vilai handed over his keys, returned to his office and left the group to take care of itself. The journalists looked on in admiration as the policeman climbed over the bar and began to hand out drinks. They'd been there dry for three days. Under Phosy's management, there was no tab and no limit. The Australians would have ordered beer had the fridge been plugged in but they settled for tall Cuba Librés without ice. This was a third-world country after all.

They pushed two tables together, raised their glasses to Laos, and Dtui began to recite the welcoming address she'd memorized. Given her limited contact with English speakers, she did a fine job but didn't get very far. They applauded after her third sentence. The other ten would never be heard. During the free-for-all that followed, she realized the limitations of her medical textbooks. She was sadly lacking in vulgarities, recognition of accents, idioms, abbreviations and the words to rugby songs. This shortfall was soon addressed by the journalists as they set about her reeducation.

At one point in the ongoing translation for Phosy, who knew no English at all, she confessed that she had no idea what anyone was saying. And it was at that point that Marvin, a tall, blond Australian leaned forward, and, in fluent Lao, said:

"Perhaps we can help you in that matter?"

There were nine journalists at the table that evening: two Britons, two Australians, three Swedes, a Filipino and a Thai from the *Bangkok Post*, and all of them were competent in Lao. One or two might have been mistaken for Lao on the telephone. Even one of the Swedes, on his first trip to Indochina, had learned enough in the previous month to earn a trip to Laos.

"You see?" said Jim, a worldly Anglo-Australian photojournalist with a younger man's face, "Western newspapers aren't going to waste their budget on sending idiots to copy down whatever the Party tells them."

"It's been over two years since the last foreign journalist was here," said Sixten, one of the Swedes. "The world wants to know what's really going on."

With the bar open and no other guests in the room, the

evening progressed in a more traditional Lao fashion with bonds made and secrets shared. At one point, Dtui and Phosy were behind the bar fixing a round.

"I don't think they know you're the chief of police," said Dtui.

"I didn't tell them," said Phosy.

"They're very . . . open," said Dtui.

"What do you mean?"

"I mean, all that about the world knowing what's really going on," said Dtui. "Shouldn't they be a little bit more careful about what they say?"

"I think they're hoping for a reaction," said Phosy. "Our secret service people can't do anything when the world knows its journalists are here. If anything happens to them it would be a public relations nightmare. It would defeat the whole point of inviting them. They can say anything they like."

The evening turned to night and the guests decided it was time to go to eat. Three restaurants had been set aside for the visitors and they opted for the nearest. Despite a lingering paranoia honed over five years of not knowing whom to trust, Dtui liked the foreigners for their openness. Her favorites were Marvin, the gangly Australian, and Jim, the dirty-mouthed but funny Englishman who had given up his British passport and was currently based in Sydney. She and Phosy knew that the pair were already stoned when they'd first arrived. Perhaps they'd been expecting the worst and put up that marijuana force field to withstand another night of sober cultural pleasantries. Neither of them seemed the worse for wear from their smoking. They held their own in the noisy discussions. Marvin had signed on as a journalist for the *Sydney Morning Herald* but he was, in fact, a Lao scholar: an expert in Southeast Asian history and culture. He had come, as he said, "To see what a mess they'd made of his beloved Laos."

Jim had made a name for himself as a photographer at the height of the aggression in Vietnam. He still carried an interior tiara of shrapnel as a memento. The editor at the *Times* in England had passed on the Lao invitation to him in anticipation that he might get a picture or two that belied the Soviet claims of peaceful community development under its leadership. He'd suggested Jim write a vignette of socialist Laos with himself as a central character: *Sunday Times* magazine fodder.

Jim and Marvin went back a way. They'd shared a house in Vientiane in the sixties. They'd seen the country at its most corrupt and now they were seeing it at its most repressed. Both men were confident that it wouldn't be long before the repression subsided and the corruption made a triumphant comeback. Dtui had immediately recalled Civilai's description of the Customs department at Tar Deua.

"So, my boy, you're a plumber?" said Jim with his arm around Phosy's shoulder as they walked into the street.

It wasn't an outright lie. Phosy was very handy with a wrench and undertook most of the repairs at the police dormitory bathroom. He'd decided nothing would be gained by announcing who he was to the group. But he was with a canny crew of journalistic vagabonds. Jim sniggered.

"Something funny?" Phosy asked.

"Nothing at all," said Jim.

Phosy knew his cover was blown.

"What gave me away?" he asked.

"Oh, I don't know. Perhaps the manager calling you chief inspector?"

"I didn't think anyone heard."

"We're daft. Not deaf."

Phosy raised his voice for the crowd on the grassy pavement.

"Then I want you all to know I'm only here to chaperone my wife, for obvious reasons. I'm not spying. I'm off duty."

"Relax, Constable," said Marvin. "We've been riding around on bicycles all day. Nobody followed us. No guard post stopped us. I got the feeling nobody was interested in us at all."

"I imagine that's what the Soviets want us to write," said Bjorn, the oldest and most opinionated of the Swedes. "How free this place is. No shadowy characters taking notes. No hidden cameras. No bugs in the rooms."

"I got bugs," said Jim. "Big bastards in the bathroom."

"All we get is a jolly drunk policeman and his pretty wife," Bjorn continued. "How can we not write lovingly about this lie?"

"Here he goes again," said Marvin.

"Somebody has to," said Bjorn. "Because this isn't real, is it? The chief of police gives us free drinks. It must be such a liberal place. But it isn't. It's Vietnamese-style repression where you're paper-worked to death. And you Lao have your own style of zero truth. They don't say we can't interview inmates in the reeducation camps, but it will be too difficult to get a flight north at this time of year. We're welcome to speak with the minister who publically criticized the cooperatives, but he's out of town right now. Everything's possible, but nothing's doable. You're all cool about your history as colonized monkeys, but I don't see any French or American newspaper people invited here. You were kind enough to let the Americans keep their consulate open after you took over, but they're down to a diplomatic staff of six, and they aren't allowed to do anything. You nullify your critics with your smiles and your fake indolence."

There was a chilly Vientiane silence in the air for a second until Dtui laughed.

"Well I think I know who's going to mysteriously disappear overnight," she said.

A few more seconds for the chill to melt and the group fell into a swirl of laughter.

"At last, you've met your match, you grumpy old bastard," said Jim to the drunken Swede.

They applauded the nurse, blew her kisses and congratulated Phosy for marrying her. In five minutes most of them were on their way to dinner and Phosy and Dtui were left with Marvin and Jim in front of the dark hotel façade.

"Nice to see you've all got it worked out," said Phosy.

"Ah, don't listen to that flaky old hack," said Jim. "Nobody takes any notice of him. He's been in the region so long he can't see anything beyond his own bias."

"So, you don't agree with him?" Dtui asked.

"Some of it," said Marvin. "I mean, don't get me wrong. We're very fond of this place. We aren't going to belittle you in the press. But really, Dtui, what's this junket all about? The government's got nothing to show us apart from the fact you're still here, still surviving in spite of all those years of war and strife. You're a lesson to the world in tolerance, but I'm not buying the 'land of the free' angle."

"You do know I'm not a plumber," said Phosy.

"No, you're a public servant," said Jim. "And all the scary policies and cloak-and-dagger shit is put together at the Kremlins and the Stasi headquarters of the world, and I'd bet you're no more aware of the dark side of your country than the average farmer. No offence."

Phosy resented hearing it from a foreigner but he couldn't refute it. There were more secret police being trained by the Vietnamese in Laos than there were regular police officers. Even as chief of police, he wasn't granted access to the study venue or its graduates. Half of his investigations of missing persons were stymied with an official "Confidential. Do not proceed."

But he was proud of his country for what it had achieved, and he wasn't about to agree with a foreigner on its shortcomings. They walked the journalists as far as their Vespa and Dtui took the key.

"So, what do you two do when you're riding around on your bicycles?" Phosy asked.

"Observe," said Marvin. "Talk to the ladies in the market. Meet the unexpected character acquaintance from days gone by."

Phosy noticed a brief look from Jim that silenced his friend.

"What type of acquaintance?" asked Dtui.

"Probably one of the old girls from the White Rose," said Jim. "That's where he learned all about balloons and darts, if you know what I mean."

"Not to mention how to smoke ten cigarettes at a time," said Marvin. "And I consider this to be the perfect moment to change the subject. You two wouldn't happen to know of a doctor here in Vientiane called Siri, by any chance?"

"He's our—" said Dtui.

"It's a common enough name," said Phosy. "Why are you interested?"

"Just one of the Swedes was looking for him, is all," said Marvin.

"Do you know why?"

"No idea."

"I'll keep my eyes open for him," said Phosy.

They parted company with handshakes and the confession that the journalists probably wouldn't be catching the following day's 7 A.M. bus to visit the model collective. Dtui drove slowly back along the river road toward the dorm. They passed the Russian Club where the Soviet journalists failed in their attempts at Cossack dancing. They passed Daeng's noodle shop with Ugly on duty outside. They passed the grey padlocked shop fronts and the peeling white colonial buildings. They passed Crazy Rajhid being invisible in front of the Lan Xang Hotel, and they stopped for a while to admire the stars reflected in the water.

"Do they really know more about us than we know about ourselves?" Dtui asked.

"Dtui, when the only information you have about a place comes from the mouths of people who fled that place, you aren't going to hear many positive comments. You'll only get bitterness and anger and misinformation. That's why they were all invited here. To remind them we aren't evil. That we have the same dreams as them."

"What was all that about the darts and the balloons?" Dtui asked.

He looked at her with his eyebrows raised. "Yeah, I didn't get that either," he said.

"We should invite them to Daeng's shop," said Dtui. "I'd

love to see them lock horns with Siri and Civilai. They'd really have something to write about then."

"We'll see," said Phosy.

She kick-started the Vespa. The engine spoke up like the only voice in the whole of Laos. She wondered whether any of the English speakers would make it up in time for the early bus. She knew she wouldn't be meeting Jim and Marvin there. What she didn't know was that she'd never see them again.

CHAPTER SIX
Civilai's Own Brigitte Bardot

Siri's second threat arrived in the pouch of a postal worker early the next morning. The envelope was foolishly small like one of those wedding invitations impoverished couples sent out to save money. There were two stamps, both Lao: one with a picture of Lenin and one with the words *Royaume du Laos* with *Royaume* struck through. The old postman didn't leave. He was dressed in civilian clothes, with an armband and a battered hat as his only uniform.

"What are you waiting for?" Siri asked, "A tip?"

The old man's eyes and nostrils were already feasting on Daeng's breakfast noodles. Like the teachers, he hadn't been paid for several months. The modest Soviet funding hadn't stretched to the end of the year. Moscow and Hanoi were talking about reactivating some of the old opium plantations in order to cover government salaries in Laos. Siri stuffed the envelope into his shirt pocket and showed the postman to an empty stool. One more en-suite bathroom for Siri's charity penthouse apartment in heaven.

It wasn't till after eight, the office workers sated and at their desks, that Siri and Daeng could finally take a break.

"Tell me again," said Siri.

"They'll be back in seven days," said Daeng.

"What could they possibly do for two weeks on a honeymoon?"

"Well, during the day, they're learning vegetable cultivation," said Daeng. "The rest you'll have to use your imagination."

"Can't we . . . you know . . . hire someone till they come back?"

"Why, Siri? Don't you enjoy watching me work?"

"I do my share. And you know I love watching you work. You are the prima ballerina of noodles. But I would love it even more if I could sit at a back table with a strong coffee and a good book. I'm retired."

"You're sounding more like a Mandarin than a forty-something-year paid-up member of the Communist Party. Lording over the staff indeed. Shame on you. It's good for you to labor from time to time. Learn new skills."

"What's wrong, Daeng? Did my table-wiping ability not please you today?"

"What do you mean?"

"You're being grumpy."

"I'm not being grumpy. I am being both angry and anxious."

"Why?" he asked.

"You know why. I saw the postman, I saw the look on your face and I saw you stuff a letter into your pocket."

"Oh."

"Let's see it."

"It's probably just an ad for colostomy bags. They have a mailing list for everyone over—"

"Siri! I have a noodle strainer in my hand. In the

underground, they taught us thirty ways to disfigure a man using a noodle strainer, so don't push me."

Siri fished out the crumpled envelope and tore it open. They sat at the nearest table while Siri scoured the letter. He looked up.

"Well?" she said.

"Colostomy bags," he said.

Daeng reached across and thrust the strainer, missing his already-disfigured ear by a fraction.

"I can't read it," he said.

"English?"

"Same handwriting."

She took the letter from him, nodded, and slid it into her apron pocket.

Dtui was off at some cooperative with her group, so they had to wait until ten to get a translation. Bruce had an appointment to get a Lao driving license at nine. That involved taking his Australian license to the motor registry department, translating it for the clerk, and waiting an hour while she typed up a new one and attached a photograph to it. They insisted on taking the photograph themselves so Bruce arrived at the noodle shop with a license that looked like it belonged to a Solomon Islander.

"Makes your teeth look nice and white though," said Daeng.

"In fact they're all you can see," said Bruce. "They'll have to turn the lights out to ID me."

He was carrying a heavy cloth bag and a clip file. He put the file on the table in front of Siri and Daeng. They looked at it.

"Go ahead, open it," said Bruce with that big Solomon Islands smile.

Daeng flipped open the cover and there at the top was their title page held down with silver clips. They'd given their film the working title *Death to the Oppressors*. Both the Ministry of Culture and the Lao Women's Union had expressed their concerns, but Siri had assured them it was just a temporary filler until they had feedback from their marketing department. But it was *Death to the Oppressors* that stared back at them from the front page of the script. It was the most professional looking thing they'd ever seen: no typing errors, no cross throughs, no smudged or fading ink, no wine stains.

Daeng continued to thumb through the pile: the list of characters, the timeline. By the time the first page of the screenplay showed itself, Siri had already decided to adopt Bruce as his only son and leave him the Triumph in his will.

"How did you achieve all this?" Siri asked.

Bruce, as pleased as a papaya slice, unzipped the cloth bag and produced a clunky mechanical gadget that opened up to look like some science-fiction typewriter. It had a screen like a small television and a keyboard and other knobs and levers that gave the impression it could take off and fly.

"It's called a word processor," said Bruce. "Wordstar—just came out a couple of years ago, but it was already hot in the stores as I was leaving Sydney. The tech boys at UTS put together a Lao script version. You make all your mistakes in the screen here, correct them and print it out at the back. I took the liberty of retyping your script using a screenplay format. I can change it as we go along."

"Siri, you're dribbling," said Daeng.

"It's marvelous," said Siri. "Right, Daeng?"

Daeng wasn't nearly as excited. She was too focused on the letter in her apron pocket. Her instincts were tingling. Her tail was twitching. The two notes might have been the work of a crank—some dark practical joker—but she hadn't stayed alive this long by being complacent. If someone had gone to the trouble of contacting and threatening them, he was a troubled soul and anything was possible. Leaving Siri to drool over his new toy, she took Bruce to a table near the road and made him a coffee.

"Bruce," she said, "I was hoping you might take a look at something for me."

She handed him the letter and leaned back on her chair. He read it, looked up, then read it again.

"What is this, Auntie?" he said.

"One of the journalists was asking if he could help with the script. This is a sort of screen test. We want to know if we can use his idea in our film. Of course, we'd have to translate it, but . . . just see what you think."

The boy read through it again silently to be met by a smile from Daeng.

"I don't believe you," he said.

"Which part?" she asked.

"Any of it. This looks like the real thing to me. Am I wrong?"

"Perhaps you can translate it for me?" she asked.

He huffed and nodded his head.

"*Hello, Dr. Siri,*" he read. "*Let's face it; you wouldn't be afraid of me if I didn't give you a demonstration of my power. Threats without bodies to back them up are meaningless. Don't forget the theme of this maniacal obsession is 'loved ones' although there may be one or two collateral victims who fall outside those parameters. Since I arrived, I've been watching you. Clearly, the love of your life is Daeng. Then there's Civilai. We all know how close you are to him. So I've decided the order of departure of those remaining will be your best friend first and then your wife. I doubt you'll consider life to have any meaning once you've lost those two, but don't worry. Your own death will be so slow you'll have plenty of time to contemplate your loneliness.*

"*The cogs in the clock have started to turn and they are unstoppable. I look forward to watching your futile attempts to undo that which cannot be undone.*"

Bruce stared at her but her expression gave nothing away.

"Thank you," she said. "I think that was quite convincing, don't you?"

"Madam Daeng, we have to talk ab—" said Bruce.

"Oh look, Comrade Civilai," she said.

Civilai's lemon Citroën pulled up half on, half off the pavement in front of the restaurant. Siri broke away from his word processor trance and came to the doorway to see what was happening. He stood beside Bruce and Daeng. Civilai fought his way out of the driver's door and walked slowly around to the passenger side, using the car to prop him up. He opened the door and out stepped a classical blonde beauty in a sensible blouse and an ankle-length skirt.

"Ladies and gentlemen," said Civilai, "allow me to present Cindy, the new star of our movie."

Things were uncomfortable for a while. Cindy said "hello, how are you?" to everyone in impressive Lao and they all replied politely. Daeng invited their guest in for a cup of coffee. Cindy thanked her and said water would be fine. Coffee gave her migraines. Civilai leaned back against his car looking admiringly at his Brigitte Bardot. He had obviously not heeded the decision of the production committee that finding even a minor role for pretty Cindy would be a push. A starring role would be a feat of superhuman effort. Daeng decided it would be better to break the news to her sooner rather than later. It would probably shatter the girl's dreams but sometimes you had to shoot the pony rather than watch it hobble its way to a slow death. She took Cindy up to the *phasin* skirt room and got straight to the point.

"You're very pretty," she said.

"Thank you," said Cindy. "It has its drawbacks."

Daeng didn't bother to ask what they were.

"I'm afraid you can't star in our movie," she said.

"I can't?"

"No. In fact I can't even imagine a small part for you."

Cindy looked through the window. A flock of terns chose that moment to fly south. The sun reflected silver off their feathers.

"Thank God," she said.

"What?" said Daeng.

"Your Civilai was so insistent," said the woman. "I met him at one of our diplomatic social events. Several of them, in fact. He brought up the movie idea. I was totally against it but our head of mission suggested I cooperate. We can't afford to upset your government given our shaky status here. I've only just arrived so I didn't have much choice."

"You've only just arrived?" said Daeng. "But your Lao is . . ."

"I was an IVS here in '69. I was building latrines and

laying pipes for a year up country. Not everyone bothered to learn the language. Most said it wouldn't serve any purpose once we left. But I loved the sound of Lao and I have an ear for it, I guess."

Daeng looked at the young woman: simple clothes, unfussy hairstyle, straight-talking, obviously older than she looked. She must have known what an effect her looks had on men, men like Civilai.

"Did he flirt with you?" Daeng asked.

"Civilai? Yes, he flirted. He flirted like old men flirt, happy enough with a smile and a blush and a peck on the cheek. Just enough to let him imagine being back there when he was twenty and still available."

"He's been married to the same woman for forty-four years," said Daeng.

"Madam Nong. Yes, I know. He talked about her the first time we met. I got the feeling he was telling me he was happily married just in case I fell head over heels in love with him. He didn't want to disappoint me."

Daeng laughed.

"My Siri leaves it to the last minute to mention he's already taken just to be sure the young ones fall for him, and they do. But he isn't dangerous."

They clinked their water glasses.

"I've read the script," said Cindy. "I got a copy from the Women's Union. My reading's not that clever, but I got through it. A week with my head in a dictionary. But we don't have a lot else to do at the consulate these days."

"What did you think?" Daeng asked.

"Part historical, part political, part magical, part absolutely ridiculous. But what a ride. It would make a great movie."

"You think so? We've only got the one camera."

"I can help with budget."

"You can?"

"Sure. At the consulate we don't have an agenda anymore. But we have discretionary funds. We have a green light to help with education and the arts. No offence, but there aren't that many cultural activities going on right now. Your movie would qualify. What do you think?"

Cindy was invited to participate in the second production meeting that afternoon, and they came up with a budget that wouldn't break the State Department. They had a late lunch together except for Civilai, whose weight seemed to be dripping off him like wax from a temple candle. He settled for water. Bruce offered to take Cindy back to the consulate in the Willys jeep he'd picked up for next to nothing. They could see his pilot light burning just by being around her. He wasn't the best-looking young man to have fallen for her but he had ambition and a sense of humor. She seemed to like him. She screamed as the jeep left the ground and hit the empty road.

Which left Siri, Daeng and Civilai to go over the contents of the letter.

"Bruce didn't believe for a second it was fiction," said Daeng. "We might have to include him in on this."

"I doubt he imagined his return to Laos would be as full of excitement as it's turning out to be," said Siri. "Beautiful blondes and death threats."

"The question is," said Civilai, "when do we start to take it all seriously?"

"As you'll be the first to go," said Siri, "I suggest we stake you out over there beside the road like a house bantam and wait to see what bites you."

"Right," said Daeng, "we lie in wait and catch him in the act of whatever horror he has planned for you."

"I don't feel much peer support in this venture," said Civilai. "Have you alerted Phosy?"

"His people are going through the journalist files you left with me," said Siri. "We don't exactly have anyone at Interpol, so we can't verify that they've all told the truth in their CVs. But he sent copies to all the embassies and asked them to do background checks. They have no obligation to comply."

"I'm not sure I understand the letter," said Civilai. "What is all that about cogs and clocks?"

"My interpretation is that he's already set in motion whatever plans he has," said Daeng. "Either he's already hired someone to do the nasty . . . or there's a bomb in the basement on a timer," said Siri. "Luckily, we haven't got a basement."

"What if it's a riddle," said Civilai. "What if there are clues in his notes that will allow us to stop the ticking clock?"

"I don't get the feeling he's that accommodating," said Daeng, fishing the first note from her apron and turning it over to Dtui's translation. "The only thing that isn't immediately obvious is the line, '*I have already deleted one of your darlings.*' Does that mean he's already murdered one of your loved ones, Siri?"

"A few years back my dog was killed violently," said Siri. "I was very fond of her."

They heard a brief growl from the street outside.

"Siri, you know what I'm getting at," said Daeng. "Your first true love."

"Boua?" said Siri. "I'd prefer not to talk about her."

"Why?" Daeng asked.

"Because whenever I do, you sink into a foul mood for two or three days."

"That's just a woman thing," said Civilai. "Always comparing themselves to their predecessors, even when the ex is dead."

"Shut up, Civilai," said Siri and Daeng in tandem.

"It's true," mumbled Civilai. "Now look what you've made me do."

He headed off to the bathroom for the umpteenth time.

Once he'd gone, Daeng said, "I think we need to talk about her. Even at the expense of my flimsy female attitude. If this note refers to her, it means the killer was around when you were in Vietnam."

"It was suicide," said Siri.

He'd read Boua's suicide note so many times the paper had crumbled to dust. He read the final sentences now in his mind. *Can you ever forgive me for what I've done to you, and for what I have to do this evening? This is the only escape for us two.* Her one true love: communism, had been a disappointment. It had failed her. And once her vision was clear, she could see how she'd ignored and belittled the man who'd stood beside her for better and, decidedly, for worse. Thus, two hearts had been broken and she could not live with herself.

"Or it was made to look like suicide," said Daeng. "There are those who doubted the official report."

Daeng had never seen the suicide note and Siri had never mentioned it. That was the only real secret between them. He felt uncomfortable to be a part of the conversation now.

"By the time you got back to the camp they'd already

cremated her," Daeng went on. "So there was no evidence. Nobody really knows what happened. Around that time was there somebody you upset? Someone who might kill your wife but be prepared to wait twenty-five years to find you?"

CHAPTER SEVEN
Saigon, 1956

I arranged to meet Civilai in a coffee shop for old times' sake. We chose the Hotel Continental in District One because it attracted journalists and writers, and, as cinema people we fitted right in. Civilai intended to travel down on the train from Hue having crossed the seventeenth parallel on foot. I'd sneaked into the south from a field hospital in Ban Tangon on the Ho Chi Minh trail, although then it was still known as the north-south passage. I was a major general in the North Vietnamese army medical corps at that stage. The title was far more glamorous than the position. It seemed that no matter how many stars you had on your epaulette, the blood was always just as red, the mosquitoes just as thirsty and the chances of survival just as random.

Boua and I seemed to be stationed apart more and more often. She was a lieutenant colonel at the nurses' training facility in Dong Hoi. We saw little of each other. We'd returned to Laos from Paris in '39, still in love, I supposed. Altogether, I'd been in Paris for seventeen years. I loved the place. I'd imagined us with a cottage in Montreuil, three kids, a garden with an apple tree, and a Pomeranian called Loulou. There'd be a back terrace where Loulou and I would sit on Sundays. I'd drink coffee and cognac while Boua baked tarts in the kitchen.

Boua saw something slightly different. She saw hundreds of young Lao and Vietnamese being mowed down by French machine guns, their bodies rotting on battlefields. And over time, Loulou and the kids got fuzzier, and I could think of nothing more noble than returning to our homeland to overthrow the French—the same French who'd taught me and trained me and who'd brought me homemade *petits fours* to thank me for lancing their boils.

By the time we left France, Boua had made me feel so ashamed of my selfish ideas that I'd deleted them. For many years, I swore I'd merely tolerated the bastard French and their capitalist values. The mysterious *petits fours* haunted me in nightmares. When I arrived in Laos, I was every bit as passionate. Boua was passionate for Laos, and I was passionate for Laos . . . through her. Same destination, different route.

I admit I felt the adrenaline pumping as the steamer docked in Singapore, and we travelled north. We were warriors almost immediately. We spent our early years with the ragtag Free Lao militia fighting—or at least frustrating—the Japanese. In Vietnam, the OSS had identified groups of what they preferred to call "nationalists" led by a multilingual patriot called Ho Chi Minh: Civilai's old buddy Quoc after a number of name changes. The Americans provided weaponry and training. With the French off in Europe rescuing their motherland from Hitler, the Viet Minh assumed the mantle of protectors of Vietnam. By the war's end, the Vietnamese and Lao nationalists had accredited ourselves nicely, and we were certain we no longer needed the French. With trumpets blowing and new flags waving, we declared our independence. There was dancing in the streets, but they were slow dances to short tunes.

Pumped up from their victory in Europe, the French returned to Indochina in numbers to resume their usurper role. But the management had changed in their absence. The French set out to nullify all that foolish talk of independence and endeavored to put down the local rebellion, but it was a rebellion that would not lay still. With help from the Chinese, the North Vietnamese grew stronger and their influence spread. The French had a fight on their hands.

The Pathet Lao grew out of the Viet Minh momentum. Boua and I moved to the north of Laos where we trained medics and stitched up young boys who were fighting for the great cause of communism. But I noticed soon enough that not one of them knew, or cared, what communism was; they saw a banner of some sort that stood for equality and self-rule. But I'd lean over my patients by candlelight and listen to their whispered stories. And, without exception, they'd joined the Pathet Lao because they were tired of being shat on. They'd been shat on by the racist French, shat on by the corrupt Royal Lao army, shat on by fate, by the spirits, by Buddha. They just wanted a break from all that shit. And that was when my true passion for my country—a passion a longtime coming—took root. At last, I saw a point. The country boys put on a uniform and picked up a gun not because they stood for something, but because they wanted a fair roll of the dice. They didn't want victory as much as they wanted peace.

In '54 the rebellion of hope spilled over onto the

battlefield, and, in a fight that shocked the world, the French received a drubbing at the hands of a bunch of locals at a place called Dien Bien Phu. Boua and I were in Vietnam by then. We watched the final curtain from a ridge looking down at the despondent French army. I was saddened by the carnage, but I'd never seen my wife so joyful.

The international agreements were signed and the French dragged their feet until '56, when the last of the actors were to leave the theatre. And there I was in the coffee shop at the Continental watching it all happen. They had a parade that passed right in front of me. The drums of the Moroccan Sharpshooters' Band made ripples in my *café au lait*. In their big hats and their snowy-white uniforms and their confident stride, you'd never have guessed the French were the losers. Some of the crowd even cheered them as they passed. With nothing really to show for a hundred years of occupation, it struck me as particularly arrogant that they should hold their heads so high; that they should still be taller and heavier than us.

I'd been there at the café for forty minutes still nursing my cup with no sign of Civilai. I wondered whether he'd been stopped at the border or shot trying to cross it. Those were oddly unpredictable days. It crossed my mind a few times that I was the enemy. The '54 Geneva Agreement had sliced the country in half and we victors had been ordered to keep behind the line that divided a country we'd won. It was like the winner of the Tour de France being allowed to keep only the handles of the trophy.

I'm not sure we really wanted the south anyway. It had been flooded by Catholics escaping some imaginary genocide in the north. The suburban slums of Saigon continued to spread out like an ink blot. It was impossible to know who was from where or to police the mayhem. The South Vietnamese security forces had been trained hurriedly and indifferently by the fleeing French, and the task of supervising a city in transition was beyond them. For a while, anyway, anything was available and possible.

So, there I was, a Lao with no passport, undeniably an enemy agent, drinking coffee in the center of a city in denial. I could feel its incurable tumor. It still wore its foundation and its blush. Its pretty girls still cycled past in their beautiful silk *ao dai*, but you could see the bruises beneath the makeup. The men still strutted, but their heads turned often to look behind them. Saigon was keeping a brave face, but there was nothing holding the skin and bone together. A voice roused me from my thoughts.

"Anyone sitting there?"

I looked up and wasn't at all surprised by what confronted me.

"Did you really travel all the way from Hue with that tennis racquet?" I asked.

"Of course not," said Civilai. "Look around, little brother. French all over the city are trying to sell off their household items before they jump on the boat home. And imagine all those wealthy Catholic refugees who were forced to leave their china collections in the north. They would love nothing more than to pick up a new set here in the south. But, goodness me, they don't even have enough money to feed their fat children. They don't even have a real roof over their heads."

He waved his tennis racquet in the air.

"I picked up this beauty for almost nothing at a yard sale," he said.

Only Civilai would scour the suburbs to set up a joke.

"Sit down before somebody challenges you to a game," I said.

It was good to see him. We shook hands, and the nerves in our palms exchanged a familiar intimacy. We had kept in touch as much as an endless guerilla war allowed. He'd gone his way after Paris, organizing, activating, agitating. He was the only Lao on the central committee of the Workers Party of Vietnam. I'd seen him on the stage in Tuyen Quang when our Free Lao movement was hijacked by the Vietnamese-designed Pathet Lao movement. He was already a celebrity then, a visionary, a revolutionary, a genius but still an idiot. We'd reunited by chance at seminars and in bunkers. Whenever there was a lull in the fighting we'd go out of our ways to meet up and see a film or two. That war would never have been the same without Civilai. I was always glad he wasn't dead and he assured me that the feeling was mutual.

The note that had brought me to Saigon had been written in Lao and was, wisely, cryptic. He knew I'd come. He ordered a pitcher of beer from the one nervous waiter. Cafés in Saigon were bombed from time to time just to keep the enemy on their toes. It would have been an ironic end to our relationship to be blasted by a North Vietnamese hand grenade. The waiter knew that thanks to the influx of refugees he could be replaced. We, on the other hand, could not.

We drank our long-dreamed-of cold beer and caught up on the previous four months. I told him about the delta. He told me about Hanoi. We followed the progress of the drug trade. The Golden Triangle was producing half the world's opium, and the French, who had distributed the drug to fund their occupation, were now trafficking the product to pay for their withdrawal. As was our tradition, I asked him about his wife, Nong, who was teaching at Ai Quoc College, and he asked me about Boua. His marriage always seemed happier than mine, and I found myself inventing a perfect relationship to tell him about. I'm sure he knew I was lying.

"So, why are you here?" he asked, which surprised me considering he'd invited me.

"Because you need me?" I said.

He'd lost some weight and some hair since last we'd met. Jungle life took its toll on all of us one way or another. I'd long since forgotten the joy of hearing a solid stool thundering down to earth at our outdoor latrine.

"You are quite correct," said Civilai. "There was sympathy within my group when I told them of my findings. But when I asked for a team of commandos to accompany me here, they pointed out quite rightly that they were more likely to throw themselves under a tank than to accede to my request."

"Given the title of our assignment," I said, "you don't see it as a little ironic that two Lao would take it upon themselves to carry out a mission on behalf of the Vietnamese?"

"Let's just say that if we're successful—and I really hope we are—our little country will be owed a great debt of gratitude. One that I shall claim back over and over until the favor bucket is dry."

"How dangerous do you consider this to be?"

"At the very least we could be tortured and shot."

"In that case I doubt one jug of beer will be enough," I said.

Half an hour later we walked, perhaps a little unsteadily, the four steamy blocks to the National Museum of Saigon. We stood admiring its grand pagoda-like façade. There was a thick layer of gravel on the driveway, and we each selected the best specimens and put them in our trouser pockets. We paid our *piasters* to the indifferent young guard at the desk and put our names in the visitor's book. It hadn't been signed for four days. Oddly, considering what we were about to do, we gave our actual names. Civilai took time to write a comment.

We looked at the little map on the central beam and made our way to the north gallery. The guard didn't follow us, and there were no attendants in any of the rooms. So, there we stood in the middle of the Ly Dynasty: the golden age of Vietnamese art. Its ceramics were praised and sought after throughout the world and rightly so. The pots in front of us were elegantly slender with their emerald and light-green glazes and their distinct motifs. Every one of them was a work of art and literally priceless.

"They're beautiful," I said.

"Hard to believe they're over nine hundred years old," said Civilai.

"Hard indeed," I agreed.

"I'm guessing that the big grey-green one up there on the shelf will be the loudest," said Civilai.

"You think they'd mention volume in the tourist guide book."

"Perhaps nobody's ever tried to get a sound out of them before," said Civilai.

"Then let us be the first," I said.

I pulled a medium-sized hunk of gravel from my pocket, took aim and chucked it with all my might. Somehow, I

managed to miss the largest pot, but I did smash its neighbor to smithereens.

"That's the one I was aiming at," I said.

"Liar," said Civilai.

"Can you do any better?" I asked.

"I believe so."

He walked forward, stepped over the red rope, grabbed
two particularly elegant pieces of pottery and smashed
them together like cymbals. The sound was far more
pleasing.

"I didn't know that was allowed," I said, and I joined
him on the illegal side of the rope. We did a good deal
of smashing. I was just about to drop kick a potbellied
antique when the gallery attendant arrived, still wiping
baguette crumbs from his lips. He stood in the entry
way, eyes huge, mouth agape. My kick took out a whole
line of finely tapered pots, the shards of which landed
at his feet.

"What are . . . what do you think . . . ?" said the attendant.

"Destroying priceless artifacts," said Civilai, anticipating
the question. He went to the wall and elbowed the glass
on the fire alarm. The building rattled from the sound.
But the curator and his secretary had already arrived in
the gallery from the other direction. The curator staggered backward. The secretary, a plump young man in
steamy glasses, screamed and ran back along the corridor,
probably in search of a telephone to call the police. The
guard arrived. Nobody dared approach us maniacs. I sat
cross-legged on the ground, attempting to make a paper
airplane from a quite lovely sixteenth-century watercolor,
while Civilai attempted to lob his gravel into the last pot

standing. We had destroyed no fewer than eighteen price-less artifacts.

It was clearly the first crime scene the new South Vietnam-ese police force had had to deal with. The officers who arrived had no idea what to do. Officially, the commis-sioner general was the go-to person for matters of national importance. But he was due to leave in three days, and all he dreamed of was a trouble-free period in which to pack, to drink his way through as much of the wine cellar as pos-sible, and to disconnect tactfully from his mistress. All of his duties were handed over to the commander-in-chief, General Jacquot, who, in turn, passed these last-minute annoyances on to the prefect of the Saigon-Cholon region, Monsieur Blazer. He too had planned to escape peace-fully yet there in his anteroom stood two anarchists who had dared to ruin his orderly exit by destroying national treasures.

Blazer was still the prefect, and he could have ordered us executed there and then. It would have been a pro-found statement to make before launching a career in domestic politics. Exactly the kind of gesture he needed. But he seemed confused by our nonchalance.

"What do you have to say for yourselves?" he asked.

"They destroyed millions of francs' worth of antiques before our very eyes," said Marchant, the curator. He'd followed the police van to the prefect's house on his motor scooter. He was a sweaty, shifty-looking man with oily hair and an unimaginative body.

"I rather thought I was addressing these two villains," said Blazer.

"But I . . ." Marchant began.

"Your negligence at letting this happen I can deal with later," said the prefect. "Right now, I'm interested to hear the motivation behind this hooliganism."

He walked up close to us and I wouldn't have been surprised if he considered himself to be a threatening force. He came near enough for me to smell the wine on his breath, and I'm sure he could smell the beer on mine. He was tall and wide at the shoulders like a coffin standing on end. It was midday but he was in a dressing gown with a cravat. On his feet were the most outlandish carpet slippers. Were this a movie, the costumes department would have been chastised for its unlikely choices. It was hard for us to keep straight faces at such a sight.

"Do either of you speak French?" he asked, slowly.

"I did pick up a little at the Sorbonne," said Civilai.

"Are you mocking me, Monsieur?" he asked.

Civilai went on to list the years of his studies, the distinctions, and finally, the honors degree in Law. I had no doubt he was more qualified than the balding fellow standing in front of us. He turned his gaze to me.

"And you?" he said.

"Siri Paiboun," I said. "Merely a surgeon with a degree in medicine from Ancienne."

"I can check all this," he said. But we doubted he'd wait for the boat to come back with the answer to his inquiries.

"They should be executed immediately," said the curator, who appeared to be in an advanced state of agitation. Blazer ignored him.

"If you are truly academics," he said, "the act that you perpetrated today is even more inexcusable. You should be ashamed."

"And yet we aren't," I said.

"Then are you both mad?" he asked.

"Well, yes," said Civilai. "I would have to say we are mad in many ways. Only madmen would enter enemy territory and advertise their presence here in such an outlandish way. But we stand here before you with spines unbent and sanity unquestioned."

The weight of it all seemed too much for the prefect, and he sank into an overstuffed velvet armchair. All the rest of us, including half a dozen police, two French military types, three men in ties and a token woman, were left standing.

"Then I shall give you three minutes to explain yourselves before these gentlemen take you into the yard and shoot you," said the prefect. "I can think of no good reason for what you did at the museum."

"There is none," said the curator.

"Siri?" said Civilai, very generously considering this was his project.

"Very well," I said. "It's all very simple really. If we asked for an appointment to see the prefect on the week he was about to leave the country, the appointments secretary would have laughed at us. So, we had to find some subterfuge that would guarantee us instant access."

"What?" said Blazer. "You destroyed a museum exhibition in order to get an audience with me? That is indeed insanity."

"I don't know," said Civilai. "It worked, didn't it?"

"If I were armed I would shoot them both here and now," said the curator.

"Blood is a terrible stain to get out of a carpet," said Civilai.

"See?" said the curator. "They're making fun of you, Sir."

"In fact, we're only ridiculing you, Monsieur le Conservateur," I said. "We have the utmost respect for the prefect."

"Monsieur Blazer, surely you can't—" the curator began.

"Monsieur, could you stop talking?" said the prefect. "You're making my headache worse. All I need to know is what our maniacs here considered so important to say that they would cause mindless vandalism in order to say it."

"Perhaps we could sit with you over a glass?" said Civilai.

"Don't push your luck," said Blazer.

"After we've told you our story, you'll wish you'd made us comfortable," I said.

"Perhaps a spot of lunch," said Civilai.

The prefect laughed. "Of all the audacity," he said. "You'll stand, you'll remain in irons, and you'll have less than a minute to come up with a story."

"A firing squad is all they deserve," said the curator.

The prefect called to the sergeant at arms. "Escort Monsieur Marchant out of the room, Sergeant."

Two guards approached the sweaty man.

"In fact, it might be circumspect for the curator to stay," I said.

"Is this some sort of ruse?" said Blazer. "Is this the commander-in-chief playing a practical joke on me? A jolly deception as a farewell souvenir of Indochina?"

"I hear the commander-in-chief has no sense of humor," said Civilai.

"That's true," said the prefect. "Well then, for heaven's sake tell me what it is you have to say. Be brief. My lunch is waiting for me."

"Then, simply, the method we used to attract your

attention and the reason for wanting to do so, are one and the same," I said.

"I don't understand," said Blazer.

"On the black market in Europe, the Ly Dynasty ceramic and watercolor collection would be worth well over a hundred million francs to a collector," I said.

I reached under my shirt and every gun in the room was raised in my direction. I put up my hands.

"With your permission, Sir," I said.

The prefect nodded and I reached beneath my belt and pulled out a shard of pottery that had not been discovered when we were frisked.

"This," I said, "is a memento from our rampage this morning. The Ly collection is nine-hundred-and-sixty years old. This shard is two months old. From a distance, the pottery looks exactly the same. You only really notice the difference when you handle it."

"As we did," said Civilai.

"Nonsense," said the curator.

"Fakes are heavier than the originals, they're fired higher, and they have a sort of soapy feel to them. Antique ceramics are made of clay, and clay always has some impurities, often iron, but the collection in the gallery this morning had no rust spots at all. The exhibits on display at the museum comprised very clever fakes."

"Now I've heard everything," said the curator. "You think I wouldn't know the difference between genuine and fake earthenware?"

"You certainly would," said Civilai. "There's no doubt you knew that the ceramics in the museum . . ."

The curator walked swiftly toward the door. "I won't stay here to be insulted," he said.

"Stop him," said Blazer.

Two of the guards took Marchant by the arms and marched him back into the center of the room.

"How dare you treat me like this," he said. "I have some very influential friends in parliament, I'll have you know. You will certainly regret this."

"I've found from experience," said the prefect, "that people who actually have influential friends have no need to remind anyone of the fact. Go ahead, Doctor."

"You should find the originals in warehouse eleven at the airport," I said. "The crates are marked 'REPATRIATION32B.' According to the bill of lading the trunks contain household goods belonging to some of your senior people. You'll be looking specifically for crates eighteen, nineteen and twenty on the manifest."

"Have your people open them carefully," said Civilai. "We don't want any accidents. The names of the three army officers who colluded with the curator here and the names and addresses of the potters and painters recruited into the scheme are in a large envelope tucked into the back of the visitor's book at the museum. I was afraid it might have been confiscated and lost during my arrest."

"Or ripped apart in a hail of bullets," I added for effect.

The curator said nothing.

"How could you know all this?" asked Blazer.

"The Vietnamese who work under the curator and at the airport are no fools," said Civilai, "although their superiors treated them as such. The Vietnamese staff discovered the plot to replace the collection with fakes, but, given the influence of those involved, they didn't know who to tell. That's why they contacted us."

"And who are you exactly?" asked the prefect.

"A group of patriots who merely wish to protect Vietnamese culture," I said. "When all this colonial malarkey is out of the way, this will be a single nation again with a common history. It's probably best if you don't know any more than that."

We'd decided nothing would be gained by telling him we were Lao Communists.

"Naturally we'll have to verify these claims," said the prefect. "And while we are doing so, I shall keep you all here under guard. These are serious accusations and I cannot proceed without recommendations from my superiors. I shall return when we know more. In the meantime—I don't know—make yourselves comfortable."

There followed a peculiar hour during which Civilai and I sat on a divan and Marchant took the velvet chair. Each of us had an armed guard at our back. We had a front-row view of the curator passing through various shades of anger and into the vivid hues of fear. We had not been banned from speaking, so Civilai and I caught up on the films we'd seen on our respective 8mm show nights and the duties of our wives. We weren't careful about what we said. It was rare for foreign experts to come to the colonies and bother to study our languages. We were all supposed to speak French, so it didn't occur to us that the curator might be a linguist.

Much later, we went back over our conversation from that hour and began to question how much information we'd given away—if we'd mentioned places or names or whether we'd said anything in our own language that could have led to us being traced. Because, just before Blazer returned, we witnessed the look of Satan in the eyes of the curator. He leaned forward, and in fluent Lao, he said:

"Monsieur Civilai, Dr. Siri, you may be feeling smug about this victory. But it is only temporary. What you did today promises to ruin me financially and professionally. The prefect will not find the local artisans on your list because obviously I could not allow them to live given what they knew. I found I am something of an architect when it comes to murder. There will be nothing to tie me to the deaths of a few old potters. I will not be executed—our government cannot afford such a scandal—but when I return to France, my life will not be worth living. The only thing that will keep me sane from now on is the thought of finding you both and your charming wives and your children and doing to you all what you did to the pots. I shall crush you and destroy you, and I shall enjoy every second of your pain. It will be the fulfillment of my life's ambition to see you suffer."

We ate a late lunch at the prefect's table as we celebrated the rescue of Vietnamese national treasures. We drank probably the most expensive wine I'd ever tasted, toasted again and again by a late visitor, General Jacquot. It was true he did not have a sense of humor, but he had a remarkable capacity for wine. With such a victory under their belts thanks to us, the future of both men in national politics was assured. Whenever we met after that we drank to our success, but I never did forget the threat or the cold look of hatred on the face of the man who made it:

"I shall crush you and destroy you, and I shall enjoy every second of your pain. It will be the fulfillment of my life's ambition to see you suffer."

CHAPTER EIGHT
The Succubus Conductor

"So, if I'm reading this addendum to the screenplay right," said Bruce, "at a crucial moment in the battle, you and Civilai rip . . ."

"The two characters who may or may not be me and Civilai," said Siri.

"Right, anyway, these two characters rip off their shirts, grab the nearest machetes and charge down into the valley to confront the French forces at Dien Bien Phu."

"That's correct," said Siri.

"Why would you . . . they do that?"

"Good question," said Daeng.

"I mean, why machetes?" said Bruce. "There were guns everywhere."

"And why rip off their shirts?" said Daeng.

"It's cinema," said Siri. "It's symbolic."

"It's symbolic of insanity," said Daeng.

"I'm afraid I have to agree," said Bruce. "The movie's already two hours too long. Can't we just stick to the original script?"

"Things were getting dull," said Siri. "I wanted to inject a John Wayne moment."

Bruce seemed to be finding it harder to keep his team in order and focused. Civilai was taking more and more time off, and Daeng seemed preoccupied with other matters. Only Siri showed an unwavering commitment to the project. But then even he disappeared. Bruce turned toward the street for a second when a rare car went by, and when he looked back, Siri was gone.

The doctor found himself on a film set he recognized but couldn't immediately name. He was standing before a throbbing pink spaceship in a landscape of dry ice. He resented the fact that he was still not in control of these spiritual summonses. He knew who had called him to the other side and that he'd have to put up with more of Auntie Bpoo's mood swings. The old transvestite was his spirit guide. It was she who should have been at Siri's beck and call, not the other way around. Aladdin didn't have to go spelunking into the lamp to get things done.

"All right, I know you're here," said Siri. "Let's get this over with. I have a film to make."

"Huh," came a familiar voice. "That's one little chicken that won't ever make it out of the egg."

Bpoo appeared from behind the spaceship. She was finding it hard to walk in her skin-tight silver spacesuit. She'd gained a lot of bulk since their last meeting. She reminded Siri of a big balloon baby wrapped in tinfoil. Despite her weight, she left the ground and floated in her personal zero-gravity zone. She removed one of her gloves and lowered the zipper at her chest. Siri recognized the scene. It was Jane Fonda's erotic striptease from the beginning of *Barbarella*. The Fonda version had been one of his most memorable soft-porn moments in cinema, but he really did not want to watch the Auntie Bpoo interpretation through to its climax.

"What's all this supposed to mean?" said Siri.

"You should know. You're the host."

"*Barbarella*," said Siri. "1968. Is this a new test?"

"No, I just took a fancy to the costume. You know I'm naked underneath?"

"That's what I'm afraid of. But I'm going to have to stop you there. Our relationship is about to change. I don't have to put up with your idiosyncrasies anymore. I realized something the other day that explains everything about you. I understand why you're such a grump."

The spirit guide dropped to the ground like a suet pudding.

"You really know how to hurt a girl," said Bpoo.

"All these exotic locations, all the symbolism, all the drama and acting and cross-dressing, I get it now."

"I doubt you're that clever."

"No, you're right. It should have occurred to me a long time ago, back when you were still alive and making do with three dimensions. I should have seen it then."

"Are you telling me the offspring of a celebrated shaman has finally had an insight? The wait has been excruciating. Oh, Great Seer, what can you tell me?"

Sarcasm was rampant in the otherworld.

"The dress-ups," said Siri. "The tutus and stilettos and halter tops, the entire wardrobe that doesn't fit you. Clothes that you hate wearing. You have no choice, do you?"

"I have no idea what you're talking about."

"Don't you? I think most of your life, even into death, you've been stalked."

"Gibberish."

"The *phibob* found your weakness a long time ago. Somewhere back in your history when you were still a normal, polite young man with a real life, maybe even a career. The malevolent spirits decided to turn you upside down by visiting you in your dreams as a succubus. She became your lifelong nemesis."

"You should stop now, little doctor," she said.

Her spacesuit was liquefying and dripping off her like leaks in a gargantuan thermometer.

Siri continued, "You were so desperate to get her out of your life you started to sleep in a nightdress to persuade her you weren't male. You'd heard the rumors that she only took the lives of men. And it probably worked for a while, but she followed you, even into the daylight hours and haunted you. So you began dressing as a woman all day, all night, afraid to let down your guard even for the briefest time."

"This is a bad talk," said Bpoo.

"Of course your friends and neighbors ostracized you. They thought you'd gone mad. And you got to the point where you had no friends. You weren't homosexual or actually interested in cross-dressing, so those communities didn't want you. And you'd never attract a wife looking the way you did. So you became a bitter loner: miserable and obnoxious."

"No."

"And there you are now in the otherworld, still petrified to let down your guard. Still unpleasant. Still looking over your shoulder all the time. Because you're in their realm now, so there's no sleep for you. No rest. And you know the funniest thing about all this?"

"Make me laugh."

There was no scenery now. The spaceship was gone. They were facing each other in a green-screen room both dressed exactly the same in Siri's unfashionable attire. They were sitting on plastic bathroom stools.

"The *phibob* have only one weapon," said Siri. "All they can do is put their fear into you: the fear of death, of helplessness, of worthlessness. None of it is real. They plant an idea into you and sit back and watch you self-destruct. Ghosts don't kill people. People are eaten from the inside by their own terror. You've been living this lie all your life. Still, in the afterlife, you continue to be afraid even though they have no physical control over you. You are drowning in your own imagination. You still shroud yourself in all this symbolism because you think it puts them off your trail, but they aren't there, Bpoo."

"Is this you attempting to take control over me?" said the transvestite.

"Ah, so that's why you're being so defensive about it all. I have never and will never have control over you," said Siri. "But at least now I understand you. I'm sorry that you've spent so much of your life hiding and depressed. I'm sorry for all the times I've been rude to you. I've decided to go out of my way to like you. In fact, you've inspired me to put together a plan."

"To save me?"

"No, you're on your own. But I think I can save the boys your succubus has on her list. I might need a little help with that."

CHAPTER NINE
Collateral Deaths

"Oh, Siri, you made me jump," said Nurse Dtui.

"He sneaks up on you, doesn't he?" said Daeng.

Siri was back in the restaurant, but the sun was on its way down, and Dtui and Phosy had arrived in his absence. Bruce was still leaning over his processor.

"But where did you come from?" said Dtui. "I'm sure you weren't there when I came in."

"They used to call it 'out of thin air," said Siri. "But the air got thicker, and you have to fight your way through the pollution. Actually, I was in the bathroom. How's the screenplay coming along?"

"Well, when you ran off to wherever you went, and I gave up waiting for Civilai," said Bruce, "I decided to go ahead and cut all the extra scenes you've both been forcing on me. It's a lot shorter now."

"I wish to see the changes," said Siri.

"Right now, the movie is on hold," said Phosy. "We're putting our effort into your latest threatening letter. Bruce has read the note already, so we've drafted him into the team. We've got more important things to worry about than film scripts. This is getting serious. I've recruited my people to look into the case. I've made it a priority for the department."

"Any insights?" Siri asked.

"Well, it was obviously sent from inside the country," said Daeng.

"And the sender knows us and watches us," said Dtui.

"We talked to the people at the post office," said Phosy. "Nobody remembers seeing a foreigner buying stamps for a local delivery. Only airmail letters overseas. But of course he could have had someone local buy the stamps for him or procured them some other way."

"What about the writing?" Dtui asked.

Bruce put the two notes side-by-side on the table.

"I'm not a native speaker myself," he said, "but they both seem grammatically correct to me. Neat. Relaxed. He or she wasn't in a hurry."

"You think there's a chance it might have been written by a woman?" asked Daeng.

"Just saying it's not impossible," said Bruce.

"How are we doing with the list of journalists?" asked Daeng.

"The embassies just gave us copies of the standard application forms, the passports and their CVs," said Phosy. "A lot of them are on their first overseas assignments. If we're looking for someone bent on revenge for something that happened in the doctor's past, our choices are limited. There's only one old enough to have been around in Paris in '32. Dimitri Popov, Russian, sixty-eight years old. He was on the Pravda desk in Germany until the second war. Ring a bell, Siri?"

"No. I didn't go anywhere near Germany," said Siri.

"But no saying Popov didn't go to Paris," said Daeng.

"Why are the Soviets sending some feeble old journalist?" Dtui asked.

"They aren't going to spare someone with his own teeth for a dead-end mission like this, are they now?" said Bruce.

Siri cleared his throat loudly.

"If Civilai was here he'd beat the pair of you with his walking stick for disrespecting your elders," he said. "Compared to us lot, the Russian's barely out of diapers. But I don't think he's our man. His name doesn't ring any bells. Who else do we have?"

"Two Poles that covered our war with the French," said Phosy. "They fit the age bracket. Their names are Zielinski and Wisniewski. They would have been in Hanoi or on field assignments when you were in Vietnam."

"Don't forget this information came from their own CVs," said Daeng. "There were war correspondents who spent all their time overseas in bars and in various beds. They made up stories and the only excitement they had was what they wrote on their CVs afterward. We have to consider a lot of this data could be bogus."

"Anyone else?" Bruce asked.

"Just the one East German," said Phosy. "Ackerman. He was based in Hanoi during the war with America. Made a name for himself there. The embassy seemed quite proud of him. Made him sound like some sort of hero. It was a coup that they persuaded him to come to Laos of all places. They said he turned down more interesting offers."

"He's my favorite so far," said Daeng.

"Mine too," said Dtui.

"I don't know," said Siri. "I don't recall offending any Germans. I need to run all these names past my Dr. Watson."

"Who?" Phosy asked.

"Civilai," said Siri. "He's my facts and figures man. He could tell us if we met any of the journalists on the list. He has a remarkable memory for names."

"Madam Nong says he still has the runs," said Nurse Dtui.

"Well, that's very inconsiderate of him," said Siri. "If he didn't refuse point blank to accept my boundless medical experience, I'd ride over there to Kilometer Six and fill him full of aloe. Snails, indeed."

"Is somebody treating him?" asked Bruce.

"He swears by Dr. Porn," said Daeng. "He was on his way to see her when I had my medical appointment. He said she didn't find anything potentially fatal. Said he'd be right as rain soon."

"He wouldn't find a better doctor in this country than Porn," said Dtui. "Present company excepted."

Daeng laughed. Siri bowed.

"He says he prefers to visit a general practitioner because they make their decisions based on symptoms," said Daeng. "They're less likely to cut you open and take a look under the bonnet."

"After all these years he still sees me as a mechanic," said Siri.

"So until he's feeling better," said Dtui, "what do we do about the men on our shortlist?"

"I'll arrange translators for those that need them and have a talk with them," said Phosy.

"But, you know, we're really limiting ourselves," said Bruce. "We might not be dealing directly with the man who made the threat. He could have hired someone."

"I'm not so sure," said Daeng. "The notes seem personal."

"Then a relative?" said Bruce.

"That's the most likely," said Siri. "A vengeful son . . . grandson."

"Then it could really be any one of the sixty-four journalists here," said Daeng.

"I can't interview all of them," said Phosy. "And don't forget, we only have threats so far. No dead bodies."

Daeng said it was superstition, but Siri believed that talking about the dead increased the odds of encountering them. Fate had a wicked sense of humor. He immediately reached for the amulet beneath his shirt, but it was too late. Standing beyond the half-closed shutter was Phosy's deputy, Captain Sihot.

"Evening, all," he said.

"What is it?" Phosy asked.

"There's been a . . . an accident," said the captain.

"Anybody . . . ?"

"Two," said Sihot.

"I knew it," said Siri.

"I'm working sixteen hour days already," said Phosy. "Can't you just take care of it?"

The captain thought about it.

"No," he said.

The morgue at Mahosot Hospital had been opened for the night. It had the smell of a plastic bag that had once contained stale pork sausages. The two bodies were laid out side-by-side on aluminum dollies. A half circle of non-matching people stood staring down at them. Siri recognized the new Minister of Justice, a short army general by the name of Sing; Comrade Sikum who had taken over as head of the Public Prosecution department following the execution of his predecessor; Bjorn, the disagreeable Swede from the previous evening; the Australian ambassador and his translator; and a man in short trousers with a fishing net over his shoulder. Finally, there was Comrade Intara, the head of protocol assigned to the Ministry of Foreign Affairs and the coordinator of the journalists' visit. It was he who spoke first.

"Phosy, you have to do something about this," he said.

"I don't yet know what this is," said Phosy.

"I think I can tell you," said the Swede. His fluent textbook Lao felt overly fussy but it was understandable to all but the Australian. Phosy stepped up to the tables. He recognized the two men: the journalist scholar Marvin and the photographer Jim.

"I met you with these two last night," he said. "What happened between then and now?"

"Like these two here, I passed up the opportunity to visit the model cooperative this morning," said Bjorn. "No offence to the minister or the Lao government. I had a migraine and one of my Swedish colleagues agreed to take notes for me. I woke up late but in time to catch these two at breakfast. They were excited because they had, what they called, an adventure planned. They said they'd met an old friend who could get them access to the old Silver City, the nickname of the American OSB storage facility out past That Luang. It's where the Americans left behind the things they didn't have time to smuggle over the border when they were thrown out in '75.

"Jim had heard a rumor that one of the CIA boys had a 1952 red Ferrari that was locked away in a warehouse in Silver City. That car has developed something of a cult reputation among the Western press. Did it or did it not exist? Their contact confirmed that it was still there. When I met them at breakfast they were on their way to see it."

"I have to point out," said the protocol officer, "that Silver City is out of bounds. Access to the area is forbidden. I cannot think how this mysterious contact was able to obtain keys for the sheds."

"It wasn't guarded?" Phosy asked.

"There was no need. As I say, it was locked."

"Right."

"Then how did they drown?" asked Siri. He was leaning against a cabinet behind the group. They all turned around.

"How do you know they drowned?" asked the minister.

"It's not raining and they're wet and they're dead," said Siri. "Didn't need a medical degree for that one. Of course, I suppose one of you might have hosed them down before putting them on display, but there are other little telltale signs like froth around the nose."

The minister coughed. "I don't think Mr. Bjorn needs to be here for the further discussion," he said. "Thank you for your evidence."

The Swede huffed, obviously angry to have been dismissed so curtly. He glared at Siri before leaving the room.

"Then my question is, at what stage of their adventure did they happen to drown?" said Phosy.

"It appears that not only was the Ferrari still there," said the prosecutor, "but there were several cans of fuel— enough to fill the tank."

"And despite all the limitations we placed on the visiting journalists," said the protocol man, "these two gung-ho cowboys decided to take their stolen car for a drive. This, I must say, is exactly why we were against inviting anyone from countries with overly free presses. They think they can say and do anything they please. They adhere to no discipline whatsoever."

The Australian ambassador continued to smile and nod even though his interpreter said nothing.

"I'm assuming they lost control and drove into a river," said Phosy.

"A fish pond," said the man with the net. "I was lucky I wasn't standing four meters to my left. I'd just cast my net, pulled the draw string and felt the tug of a carp when this red monster leaves the road, takes off from the bank and flies into the water."

"And . . . ?" said Phosy.

"That was it," said the fisherman.

"You didn't go and help?"

"Can't swim."

"How deep exactly is that fish pond of yours?" Siri asked.

"Three or four meters at its deepest, I'd say."

"Then why didn't they open the door and swim to the surface?" asked Siri.

"Don't know," said the fisherman. "I was expecting something like that, but all I see is bubbles. I go to the local cadre's house and tell him, and, well, here I am and here they are. All a bit of a funny day really."

"How did you get the bodies out?" asked Phosy.

"The cadre sent his boys down," said the fisherman. "They smashed the windshield and dragged them out. They couldn't get the doors open."

"Hmm," said Siri.

Phosy turned to Captain Sihot. "Is anyone raising the car?" he asked.

"No," said Sihot.

"Where did this happen?" asked Phosy.

"Kilometer forty just past Ban Donhai."

"Okay, I want you to go out there and organize that. Make sure the cadre doesn't claim it as a souvenir. Bring it back here."

"We should get Dtui to start on these two," said Siri.

"Start on what, exactly?" said the minister.

"Determining the cause of death," said Siri.

"Obviously they drowned," said the prosecutor.

"I agree," said Siri, "but unless they were on some crazed suicide pact, two healthy, mentally astute men do not drive at speed into a pond and sit there waiting to drown."

"Well, you and your people are certainly not performing an autopsy," said the minister.

"We're not?"

"They're foreign citizens," said the prosecutor. "They were driving an old, poorly maintained vehicle. They had a terrible accident caused by their recklessness and they died. The Australian government would like their citizens returned as soon as possible."

The ambassador's interpreter awoke from his mute slumber and hurriedly summarized the prior conversation. The ambassador affirmed that he would take responsibility for the repatriation of both bodies. All was settled. The minister ordered the bodies to be locked in the morgue freezer before collection the following day. The officials filed out of the room, leaving Siri and Phosy.

"Anything you can do without cutting them open?" Phosy asked.

"I could take some samples. Do some tests. But I don't actually know what I'm looking for. If they were poisoned or stoned out of their minds, I'd need to get to the stomach. I think the car will tell us more than the bodies at this point."

Phosy stared at the doctor. "The second letter," he said.

"I know."

"It said there may be one or two collateral victims who fall outside the parameters of his mission. Do you think this could be his demonstration? The mysterious killer showing us what he's capable of?"

"In that case he'd be someone with access to Silver City or friends in high enough places to get him into the warehouse," said Siri.

He looked down at the photojournalist. The poor man had survived wars, yet here he was defeated in peacetime.

"Last night he said something about meeting up with an old acquaintance," said Phosy. "Marvin didn't want him to talk about it. I wonder if it was the friend who got them access to the warehouse. And I wonder if it's the person we're looking for. Perhaps he wasn't expecting anyone to recognize him, and he had to silence the two of them before his cover was blown."

"That's an awful lot of wondering," said Siri.

"He asked about you."

"Who did?"

"Jim. He said one of the Swedes was looking for you."

"That couldn't have been our man," said Siri. "He'd already found us."

"Perhaps someone was trying to warn you."

"This is too much conjecture for one old fellow to take on. Why didn't you mention this when we met today?"

"I don't know. You kept disappearing. I didn't have a chance."

Siri walked around the dollies and went over the chain of events in his mind.

"What do you suppose the Swede was doing here this evening?" asked Siri.

"Witness? Apart from the mysterious contact person, I suppose he was the last to see these two alive. He was the only one who knew what their plan was."

"But how would any of this crowd know that unless he volunteered the information himself?"

"I'll find out who it was that invited him," said Phosy.

"All right. But first things first. I'll start work on these two and see what I can find without leaving wounds. You follow up with the Ferrari and get someone to interview the other journalists. It won't be easy but see if you can find someone who hates me."

CHAPTER TEN
Hanoi, 1972

I remember the night of Hanoi Jane very clearly because it followed the first afternoon of Hanoi Hilton Henry. Both of these events, in their own way, made me think about misperception. I'd been without Boua for seven years already, but being without her was very much the same as being with her during those final years. She'd taken on the burden of hammering communism into the heads of the peasantry. She'd begun to show the signs of addiction. She'd never taken drugs, but she was so high on righteousness she could no longer listen to those of us who were witnessing her mental decline. She was untreatable. She was a total fool for a hopeless cause. Her suicide was not the most tragic event in her life.

The war we thought we'd already won raged on. But now the enemy no longer shouted insults in French from the trenches. Overnight the Tricolor had rearranged its colors, and we awoke to the sounds of Janice Joplin and The Doors. And the weapons were grander and more efficient, the budget ballooned and the motive for killing us was no longer merely to pillage. They were here to stop us reds from taking over the world. We all knew, of course, that if our new American minders hadn't stepped up to the plate, we would have flooded the planet with failed cooperatives and incompetent officials. But we had a weapon more effective than the B-52s, which could level a village in tenths of a second, and more slick than Agent Orange, which could strip a hillside and anyone standing on it, and more cunning than the bombies that burrowed into the soil and would blow the legs off buffalo and inquisitive children for decades to come.

We had heroin.

Boua wasn't the only one in Vietnam who'd lost all sense of right and wrong. My surgeon friend in Paris had been right. By late '71 there were already 560,000 heroin addicts in the US. Most of the product came via the Golden Triangle of Burma, Laos and Thailand. Seventy-five percent of urban crime was fueled by this addiction, and Nixon had called for a war on drugs. The CIA Indochinese opium policy had found its way back home.

A quarter of American troops in Vietnam were using heroin. Thousands were addicted, and the bad news for the gentlemen in Congress and the generals in their Saigon offices was that heroin made more sense to the reluctant soldiers than they did. It was a universally available brain tranquilizer. Any soldier could buy it on the roadside near the bases where young boys sold it along with snacks and soft drinks and cigarettes. The Vietnamese army was shipping and distributing it so nobody was afraid of getting caught. We in the north were being bombed to hell and back, but we were defeating the enemy one brain cell at a time.

That didn't make much of a difference to us on the ground in those days. I don't know how many young men and women I'd put back together as best I could. I'd cried with each failure. I'd drunk with officers who would be dead the next morning. Ours wasn't an army of guerilla soldiers. These were shopkeepers and farmers and teachers in uniform, and they were no less terrified of being in the jungle than the young American boys from the Midwest. But whoever it was there in the rain and the muck, they asked the same question. Down through the elephant mahouts of Hannibal, the foot soldiers of Kublai Khan, the Germans and English in the mud of the Somme—they all wanted to know the same thing: "What in God's name are we doing here?" But no matter what god you asked, you'd not get your answer because no god has ever seen any sense in war.

Which is all a long detour on the way to telling my story. You've probably worked out how it started. I was sitting at a table in front of the Metropole Hotel, which had recently rechristened the Reunification. There weren't many roadside bars in Hanoi back then. North Vietnamese had better things to do than lounge and booze. But there were some. There was a tourist trade of sorts. Curious foreigners came to see what it was like to party in a war zone. There was the Vietnam-American Friendship Association for one, shipping in anyone willing to pay their exorbitant prices. So there were cafés and restaurants and the odd bar, and there was me at the only occupied table at the Metropole that morning.

"Anyone sitting there?" came a voice I'd been expecting to hear.

I turned to see Civilai in full North Vietnamese Army dress uniform. His hair had retreated even further from his brow and he looked, I don't know, hardened. In his left hand, he held a rattan mango-plucker, which, from a very long distance, might have looked like a tennis racquet. I stood, kissed his cheeks and shook his right hand.

"That's the best you can do?" I asked.

"Do you know how hard it is to find a tennis racquet in war-torn Hanoi?" he asked.

"Sit down before someone asks you to harvest mangoes," I said.

He laughed and sat and looked around for a waiter. There was a greater chance of seeing a penguin stroll along Ly Thai To.

"How long are you in town?" he asked.

"Just long enough to pick up supplies. I head back to Vieng Xai on Thursday."

"Then I'm lucky I got to see you," he said.

"Always a pleasure. Why are you dressed like a postman?"

"It's . . ."

A waitress, obviously attracted by the uniform, came running out of the hotel. She had a permanently troubled scowl but pretty eyes. Civilai ordered four glasses of Cognac. She only had rum. He ordered Bacardi. She only had Saint James. He asked about beer. It wasn't cold. We settled for Saint James but ordered cola to take the taste away. That was warm too. The lengths we went to for a little alcohol buzz.

"And?" I said.

"And what?"

"The uniform."

"Right. It's the latest from Peking. Our allies want us to look stylish at the handover ceremony."

"Who's handing over what?" I asked.

"They're convinced that, with all the anti-American war demonstrations in the States and the obscene amount of money they're spending on eradicating us, it'll be over by next year."

"Haven't they been saying that for fifteen years?"

"Yes, but now we have uniforms so it's serious."

"Marvelous. I look forward to it."

The troubled waitress returned without a tray for some reason. They'd probably been requisitioned for the war effort. Instead she nuzzled the four full rum glasses, one bottle of cola and an ice bucket against her modest breasts. The bucket contained actual ice, which surprised us given that nothing else was cold. But we didn't bother to ask why. Those were hardship days. In her mouth she had the bill, which she handed to me. Perhaps the man dressed as a civilian was expected to pay for the soldier out of gratitude. Civilai grabbed it from me.

"Had a bit of luck in a card game last night," he said.

I didn't put up a fight. Even with ice and cola, the drinks were as bad as we'd expected. People passing in front of the hotel looked at us as if we were actors in some production that didn't need a camera.

"So," I said.

"Yes?"

"Any luck?"

"Six months since our last meeting and you want to start our reunion with a favor?"

"Yes. Did you do it?"

"In a way," he said. "But there's a catch."

"Any catches are acceptable if she said yes."

"She said yes."

I was so happy. I'd never wanted more to throw myself

at Civilai and rain kisses down on him. Naturally, I didn't. I merely nodded and said, "That's nice."

"But the catch is a rather large one," he said.

"Do I have to perform erotic acts with a member of the central committee?"

"Not unless you want to."

"Then there's nothing I wouldn't agree to," I told him. "Name it."

"Four American prisoners are to be released before the end of the year as a gesture of peace."

"After years of torture?"

"We prefer to call it 'custody with discipline.' In most cases it was just confinement. But over the years there may have been the odd renegade camp director with sado-masochistic tendencies. And there were factions that kept their own downed pilots like pets. It was hard to monitor all the jails."

"How long were these four locked up?"

"The longest was seven years."

"Seven years in a bamboo cage?"

"After a brief probationary period, they were all moved to one- or two-star accommodation. Some were quite comfortable."

It was one of my many sore points about our Viet Minh neighbors.

"Civilai," I said, "imprisonment should be punishment enough. Anything else is just gratuitous. Cruelty makes us look ignorant."

Civilai finished his first glass. The rum tasted better the more we drank.

"I don't want to get tangled up in this discussion again," said Civilai.

"Your average downed pilot has nothing more to tell you than—"

"Siri!"

". . . than you already know," I said.

"They've been bombing us for fifteen years," said Civilai. "Them and their Hmong puppets in Laos. They fly in. They press their button. They kill. They go home, have a nice meal and get drunk. They wake up the next day with a hangover and do it all over again. With their technology, it's like spraying ants. They're up there in their airplanes, and they have a pleasant flight over unspoiled jungle scenery, and they locate the village they've been instructed to liquefy, and they do as they're told. There's no accountability. They switch off all human dignity. When we shoot one down and a man survives, he carries the responsibility of all those who came and went before him. He needs time to be aware of what he's done. We give him time to think until he understands that it's not about targets; it's about families."

"So you want me to meet these four and assess whether they feel enough remorse?"

"No, I want you to go into each cell with a small medical team and make sure they're healthy. Treat whatever needs treating. Fix whatever's broken. And put together a brief medical report for them to take home. But while you're examining them, I want you to be yourself and joke and laugh and listen to their stories."

"Isn't it a bit late for that?" I asked.

"For what?"

"Basic love and kindness."

"It's never too late," he said. "But if you think it's too demanding . . ."

"You'd really blackmail me?"

"You said there's nothing you wouldn't agree to."

He gave me one of his looks and I gave him one of mine.

"I'll do it," I said. "But only because I've been looking forward to this evening for weeks. If I have to play Tom Dooley to earn it, I'll play the part. When do I meet the pilots?"

"Whenever you're free. They're at Clinic Twelve."

"Really?" I said. "The clinic behind the fuel depot?"

"That's the one."

"Do you think the B-52 pilots know that's where we're keeping them?"

"They should. We've leaked enough information about their whereabouts and we weren't subtle. Even the CIA should have understood."

We worked our way down our second glasses of rum. I could feel my intestines smolder.

"You do remember I don't speak English?" I said.

"Don't worry. It's all taken care of," he said. "And one of the pilots speaks Lao."

"How did that happen?"

"He was held by a militia group in Bolikhamxai for over five years. He learned it from his captors. See how accommodating we can be to our guests? Free language classes."

We decided against ordering another drink as I had to stock up on medications and that involved getting things signed. Those Vietnamese loved to get things signed. We stood to leave.

"Have you got time for a movie or two before I go back?" I asked.

Hanoi had an impressive network of living-room film

nights back then. Nobody dared congregate in numbers in a cinema for obvious reasons. So some bright spark had set up a smuggling route to bring up movie reels from Saigon. And they all had Vietnamese subtitles courtesy of the CIA propagandists. They had a department just working on translations. Nice of them.

"I'll see what's playing," he said. "And tonight, I want you on your best behavior."

"I can't think of what you mean," I said.

"Good-looking unattached older man, together with a strange woman in a hotel room. I'm afraid the temptation might be too much for her."

He handed me the mango plucker. "Here, take this. You might have to fight her off."

I still have that mango plucker somewhere.

I decided to get the airmen out of my schedule as quickly as I could, so I arranged to be there that afternoon. I arrived at Clinic Twelve at 2 P.M. The medical team Civilai promised comprised an unsmiling but naturally beautiful nurse in military uniform, an armed guard for our protection and a boy. He couldn't have been more than fourteen years old.

"Comrade Doctor," he said, "I'm Hung Lan, your interpreter."

"Hello, Little Comrade," I said. "And how did you get stuck with this job?"

"I excelled in languages in elementary school," he said. "I was recruited by the National Institute of Interpreters."

"I'm impressed," I said. "But aren't you a little young to be fraternizing with the enemy?"

"I am qualified and competent," he said. "But I admit

I was surprised to be chosen for this important mission ahead of my seniors."

I wasn't. This had Civilai written all over it: smart kid, beautiful nurse, senior Lao surgeon with a great sense of humor. He was showcasing communism. When the fliers were back home in front of the cameras they'd fondly remember the last people they met in Hanoi and forget the seven years of misery.

"Perhaps they aren't all bad," they'd say.

The nurse gave me the results of the pilots' blood, urine and stool tests. As you'd expect after years in the jungle there was a parasite orgy going on inside them. According to their medical history, two had made it through malaria. Three had survived dengue. One was currently still enjoying its effects. There was diarrhea and skin disease but, as far as I could tell from the records, nothing terminal. Or, at least nothing that would kill them in the next three weeks. And that was evidently our goal, to get them safely into the hands of American doctors who we could later blame if the pilots all keeled over on US soil. I doubted they'd ever be free of nightmares even when the physical symptoms were taken care of.

I gave each of the young men a thorough physical, noted breaks and bruises and sprains and scars the way a car rental shop might note down scratches and dents. The first three pilots were respectful and displayed an unexpected sense of fun. They joked through young Hung Lan who seemed more than capable of finding the right linguistic tones and textures. I bantered in battle-hardened black humor, and they responded with anecdotes from years behind bars. They weren't yet confident enough to criticize or blame. They'd start a story then stop, shake their heads, smile and think of something nice to say about their captors. They were still in enemy territory.

I tried to imagine what years in a cell might do to me. Would I become some other Siri? One that I didn't like? And how would I stop my mind from crusting over? What would I have to do to hang on to my memories, my knowledge, my sanity? And I'm sure it was that doubt about my own self-control that led me to leave Henry till last. They'd warned me about him. He'd spent five-and-a-half years in a bamboo cage in a remote, inaccessible area in the north of Laos. He'd been flying air support for a bombing mission over Vietnam, and his aircraft had been hit by random small-arm fire that brought him down. He broke his arm when he parachuted into the jungle and hit his head. He walked for a week, disoriented, ill, fatigued and was finally captured by a rebel militia unit. These were no regular PL troops—more a band of hill tribe bandits who sold themselves to whichever army offered the best deal.

The standing order from central command with regard to captured prisoners of war was to send them on to Vietnam via established prison camps, eventually to end up in the Hanoi prison network—known by foreigners as the Hanoi Hilton. But Henry never left the rebel camp. The commander of the group, a battered warrior of many campaigns named Yiw, was proud of his pet airman. He invited friends over to see him and poke sticks at him through the bars of his cage. He humiliated the American and starved and punished him when he thought his prisoner was showing disrespect. He was clearly certifiable.

But when Commander Yiw was off in the mountains, Henry befriended his captors, mostly young boys charged with preventing his escape. He learned Lao from them.

They brought him herbal medicines and natural poultices and tended his wounds until the next assault. They were every bit as afraid of their leader as Henry was, but they felt sorry for the man in the cage. Perhaps the most remarkable thing about this story was that Henry wrote a book during his years in captivity. The guards found him paper and pencils and he documented his experiences. When Yiw was in the camp, the manuscript lived in a plastic bag buried in the dirt beneath Henry's cage.

Yiw was killed in battle, probably no less than he deserved, and his second-in-command adhered to the protocol of the Pathet Lao and sent Henry to Hanoi. His only possessions were his dog tags, a shirt and shorts, a bamboo flute and reading glasses, all in one cloth shoulder bag. And sewn into the lining of that bag was his completed manuscript. The only reason I knew all this was that Hung Lan, my interpreter, had read it.

During his four months at the Hanoi Hilton, Henry had visitors. Some were priests who had refused to join the Catholic exodus south. Some were fellow American servicemen who had repented for their sins and apologized for their actions against the Viet Minh. But some were tourists. Visiting incarcerated POWs was on the itinerary. Curious foreigners were escorted to the jails where they could ask questions and take photographs. And it was to one of these visitors that Henry entrusted his manuscript. The tourist, afraid she might be arrested, owned up to the collusion and handed the script to the tour guide. Hung Lan was asked to read and summarize the text. He told me the highlights. It would have made a splendid movie.

I'd expected Henry to be friendly like the others. But he was not. He refused to speak English through the interpreter. It felt odd to be conversing with him in Lao. He had a strong, confusing accent and wasn't nearly as fluent as he thought he was. It shouldn't have worried me. He was a foreigner who had gone to the trouble of learning my language, and he'd been through a horrific experience, but I felt uncomfortable with him. I didn't want to dislike him, but I found it impossible to engage. And there were other things that worried me.

Despite the conditions he'd lived in for so long, he'd somehow avoided most of the parasites currently gorging on his countrymen. He'd had a bout of dengue some time back, and there was some liver damage that may have been a result of hepatitis, but apart from that he was in pretty good shape. He even had a belly.

"So what are you saying?" he asked.

"Just observations from the point of view of a doctor," I said. "I've always been fascinated by how different people react to hostile environments. As a foreigner, you wouldn't have any natural defenses against conditions in the jungle. Yet you've somehow been able to counter all the usual enemies of the human body. How did you fight off insects and treat their bites? How did you make sure the water you drank was decontaminated? How did you survive?"

My medical team sat around us in the cell obviously frustrated that they had no idea what was being said. I was already fond of Hung Lan—he's probably a rich property tycoon by now—but I liked being free of my interpreter.

"You do know I don't have to answer any of these questions?" said Henry.

"I know."

"But I tell you, Older Brother, I earned the respect of those savages."

I wasn't that fond of being his older brother, and I wondered whether I'd be able to respect anyone who called me a savage. He launched off into a narrative I felt he'd practiced beforehand.

"Despite my horrible injuries, when they found me I put up a fight," he said. "I took them on, hand-to-hand, fought to what I thought would be my death. Once they had me in the cage I constantly tried to escape. Bravery was what jungle fighters expected and respected. They saw me as a real man. They wanted to be like me. I could tell they had no respect for that bastard Yiw. He was cruel to everyone. So when he was away, they treated my wounds using natural remedies that had been passed down through generations. They gave me medicine and balm to prevent illnesses and keep the mosquitoes at bay. I learned their language very quickly. I have a knack. They were in awe. Soon, I was like their brother. They loved me. But they were scared shitless by what the commander might do if he found out we were allies. So I put up with it, played along so my captors wouldn't get into trouble. It's all in the book."

"Right," I said. "The book. You don't seem very upset to have lost your manuscript."

He winked. I had a problem with winking too. I took it to mean he had a plan B. I wondered if he'd left a copy with his close friends at the border. Great foresight, that, to make two copies of a manuscript written in pencil in extreme conditions. I assumed the village didn't have a Xerox. Either way, he seemed very confident.

I conducted my standard physical tests while he described some of the torture he'd endured. He had a number of recent bruises that he put down to "misunderstandings" with the guards at the Hilton although nobody recalled having cause to beat him up. His broken arm had healed beautifully, and he had a messy scar on his head that would have benefited from sutures that were obviously not available. A torn ligament that he said was caused by being dragged behind a buffalo cart by the ankle had left him with a limp. I had no X-ray to check that. Suddenly, and unexpectedly, he switched to English.

Hung Lan jumped to his feet. "You're going to pay for this," he said.

"For what?" I asked through the interpreter.

"The traumas your people have caused me," he said.

"We're letting you go," I reminded him.

"So?"

"So, I suggest that until you're on the plane, you feign a little gratitude and save your complaints. It's not too late to give your ticket to someone else."

He gave me a dirty look and in him I saw the ugly Dr. Siri I'd probably have become after five years in captivity. I'd probably be intolerable after five months. When we left the room, I spoke of my concerns to my team and assigned them some tasks. I had time before my date that evening to pay visits to two old friends.

Bao Ninh was at his desk at the department of statistics at Hanoi University. He'd been collating data since the beginning of the war. The Vietnamese loved collating and recording. He had records on everything from pelicans being shot accidently by antiaircraft fire to tanks sinking without a trace beneath the mud of the monsoons.

From there I still had time to stop by the office of General Xuan of the People's Army of Vietnam. Being a field surgeon, I often had the good fortune of saving the lives of important people. Xuan was in his office and alive only due to the fact that I'd removed half a ton of shrapnel from his chest. He was a man who greatly appreciated being alive. We shared a jug of coffee and some reminiscences, and I left him with homework I knew would be completed thoroughly.

I returned to my dorm, changed into clothes that looked exactly the same as the ones I'd taken off but were cleaner and took a bicycle *samlor* back to the Reunification. I was an hour early. The interior bar had come alive since my earlier visit. If I'd taken a photograph I doubt anyone in the world would have guessed the setting was a bar in a city that was about to be bombed to oblivion. Attempting to describe the international crowd there that evening would have been like identifying extras in a Fellini movie. I wanted to ask where all the freaks had come from—how they'd got there—why they'd bothered. But I had to rehearse my speech. I had my notes on a napkin. I didn't know how long we'd be alone together. She spoke French, I heard, so we could communicate without an interpreter. But I wanted to hit the right tone. It went something like this:

"Boys in their twenties in America are calling themselves 'veterans.' I'm sixty-eight. I've spent thirty-odd years fighting for something that I have eventually come to believe in. That, is what a veteran is. Those boys returned with the medals they'd been awarded for being wounded and they called our war 'The biggest nothing in American history.' And that hurt and offended me. You made a one-act appearance in a fifty-act play, and you killed more of us than were murdered in the entire century before and you called it nothing. And when it's all over for you, when the white-water flow of money abates and your leaders find something sexier to support, we'll still be here fighting for our lives against the next tyrant, or poverty, or nature. And by then you will have forgotten us. That's what I want your Hollywood to tell everyone. Tell them it's only *nothing* for you. For us, it's survival and hope."

That was going to be my big finish. I could perhaps squeeze out a tear or two and make my voice crinkle a bit and do my bulldog long-jowled expression. She'd give me a glass of whisky to make me feel better and . . . well, as Civilai said, one thing would doubtless lead to another.

The wobbly bottomed secretary found me in reception and led me up the staircase to the fourth floor and what they jokingly referred to as the "royal suite." A queue of ten to twelve people stood at the end of the corridor, and the secretary placed me at its tail. But before I'd taken a step forward, the hotel siren sounded. Some in the queue panicked and ran. Others, like me, held their ground. There was a policy for air raids. We'd all been shown the nearest bunkers and been directed to areas like schools or hospitals that were supposedly only hit by accident. There were a lot of accidents those days.

And then the door to the suite was thrown open, and a small scrum of people directed by a hotel official passed us in the hall headed for safety. Jane Fonda was at the rear, propped up by a large man in a baseball cap. She seemed smaller than I remembered her from *Cat Ballou*. She was wearing jeans and a sweatshirt rather than her silver space suit, and her hair was mousy brown. In her natural state she was even more naked than Barbarella. I noticed she held a ballpoint pen in her hand. She spotted me at the end of the queue and pulled away from her minder. I was holding the serviette with my speech notes. She smiled, took it from me, turned it over and signed it. She smiled again, said something I didn't understand and followed the entourage to the hotel bomb shelter.

There were no bombs that night. They'd be raining down in force soon enough during Operation Linebacker II, which made a mess of the northern capital and killed a lot of people. We all remarked later how limited the imaginations were of the men who came up with the name. Surely they couldn't have run out of sports references. But Jane and her team left the next morning without my message to Hollywood. I had her autograph and I cherished it until one day when I had the flu and thought it was a tissue. It was the nearest I'd been to a movie star. She'd smiled at me.

So, as there'd been no romance in the royal suite and I still had a tank of adrenaline, I put all my energy into my next interview with Henry. I seem to recall there was me, Civilai, General Xuan, the child interpreter Hung Lan and a CIA liaison person who was supervising the orderly release of his pilots. I can't remember his name. Two guards escorted Henry to the canteen. Something in the way he walked told me he was confident this was to be his release day. We sat him down and he smiled only at the CIA guy, who didn't smile back. As I was technically the lead attorney, I spoke to the prisoner in Lao, and Xuan translated into Vietnamese, which Mr. CIA seemed to understand. It was messy but it worked.

"Henry," I said. "I've been learning a lot about you."

He looked confused.

"I was able to trace the records back to the day you crashed," I continued.

"June 1966 flying an F-100," said Henry, smiling.

"They never did find your plane," I said.

"Lot of jungle out there," he said. "It may never be found."

"Perhaps because we're looking in the wrong place," I said.

"Once my instruments short-circuited there was no way of being sure where I was," he said. "Like I say, there's a lot of unoccupied land out there."

"Lot of river too," I said.

He looked at me for the first time.

"What's that supposed to mean?" he said.

"It means that a North Vietnamese radar unit plotted your course that day and had you a hundred kilometers off your designated route on the west of Bolikhamxai. You were over the Mekong when the blip disappeared."

Henry looked at the men in front of him and realized for the first time that this was not a handover committee.

"What is this?" he said.

"Your plane wreckage was not found in the jungles of Bolikhamxai because you put it down in the river a hundred kilometers west."

"Bullshit," said Henry.

"It's undoubtedly still there," I said. "But we'll have to wait for the war to end before we go scavenging. You parachuted, not into hostile Laos, but, as you planned, into Thailand."

Henry spoke not one more word that day. He just glared angrily into my eyes as I untangled his lies.

"You'd had enough of this war and the mindless killing," I said. "And you wanted to get out of it. We can all understand that. And, what better place to escape a war than Thailand? Pretty women. Low prices. Nobody asking questions. I'm not sure where you'd put down the roots to this new life, but it's unlikely you'd go to Udon Thani with its secret American airbases we all know about. You'd avoid big cities. There was always a chance you'd be recognized in the bars. I'm guessing you buried your parachute near the river, changed into civvies and jumped on a local bus to somewhere like Ubon Ratchathani. You had money saved—probably already set up a Thai bank account. And it seemed back then you could probably live off your savings forever.

"Not a lot of difference between northeastern Thai language and Lao," I said. "You probably married a local girl who taught you the language in a feminine kind of way, and you got confident because everyone understood you. But you aren't that good. There are differences between Isan Thai and hill-tribe Lao. In fact, I doubt you'd find a band of hill-tribe rebels fluent enough in Lao to be able to teach you anything. Yours is the Lao of Thai bars and yours is the body of the soft life. Whatever maladies you picked up were treated at the local hospital. Those last bruises and scrapes were probably thanks to you running head first into a wall or punching yourself in the face."

The early evening mosquitoes were flocking around the onlookers planning a sundown assault, but the audience was rapt and I was the star. Nobody else spoke.

"In the beginning, I imagine you had no intention of returning to the West," I said. "You were safe and you were happy. You had your secret Nirvana, but you were young and illegal. And there was a world out there you hadn't seen. You became dissatisfied, and your money ran out. Your banana farm and your lychee plantation and your pig pens or whatever you thought might make your fortune, they all failed and you were left dissatisfied and frustrated. You needed to get back to America. But how do you do that when everyone believes you're dead? The Central Command listed you as MIA. There was only one way to come back with dignity. You'd read about other US fliers imprisoned for years. The ones that made it back home had options and probably received a pension. But you had a bigger idea. You wrote about your fictional incarceration in a full-length manuscript. You could see movie and TV rights at the end of the tunnel.

"Someone you met in the north of Thailand knew about a gang of thugs on the Lao side that rented themselves out as mercenaries for the PL. My friend the general here knows about them. Their commander had recently shot himself whilst as drunk as a cellar rat, and his gang was in need of guidance and money. So you headed up there with your manuscript and you made a deal. You handed over what little money you had left and promised them a share of the fortune you'd be making from your book. All they had to do was say they'd kept you a prisoner for almost six years under orders from their boss. Then they march you to the nearest legitimate PL camp and drop you off. It was a brilliant plan. You knew the Viet Minh were bringing all the MIA together in Hanoi for an eventual handover. What were a few months of discomfort in the Hanoi Hilton compared to the alternatives?

"The book was a clever idea too. You were aware it might have been discovered but if it was, it would make you stand out from the other prisoners. Perhaps the Vietnamese would feel remorse for your cruel treatment over the border. Perhaps they'd respect you for your many attempts to escape. If it was successfully smuggled out by the tourist it would have been an immediate hit Stateside. But if it wasn't, that was fine too because—and I'm guessing this last part—your wife had the original, probably resplendent with dirt and bloodstains. All she had to do was post it anonymously to the US embassy in Bangkok with a note that a deserter had brought it to Thailand. You couldn't fail either way."

We'd left Henry alone in a cell that morning. He'd been exposed as a fraud so all of his dreams of back pay and compensation and book and film royalties, of one day getting a visa for his Thai wife, of being repatriated as a hero, that was all gone, thanks to me. The Vietnamese and the CIA fellow patted me on the back as we walked away, and I might have gloated just a little and Henry probably noticed that.

Civilai and I sat on the front porch of a small house over in Ba Din that evening talking about Hanoi Hilton Henry. We were waiting for a showing of *The French Connection* with subtitles. It was R rated but we had IDs.

"Why did you first doubt him?" Civilai asked.

"I don't know," I said. "There's what you see and what you perceive. Jane's perception was that I was an elderly fan desperate for an autograph."

"Which wasn't so far off the mark."

"I was more perceptive. I sensed there was something wrong with Henry. Unlike you in your penthouse suite and endless rounds of cocktail receptions here in the capital, I've been living in the jungle on and off for the past twenty years. Nature leaves scars. Some medical conditions are unavoidable, especially if you're in the open air and unprotected. But he looked too . . . too hale and hearty. If he'd been tortured as he claimed, why were there so few historical wounds? And some lies are obviously lies. His arm had been broken as he said but not from parachuting from a plane six years ago and left untreated. There was little evidence of trauma. The bone had clearly healed when he was a child and had continued to grow. The break was at least twenty years old. It was arrogant of him to think we wouldn't have qualified people here who'd notice things like that. I thought if he could lie about that, what else was he lying about? The liver disease could have been a result of hepatitis, but I have a nose for alcoholism."

"It takes one to know one, little brother."

I didn't think a lot about Henry for the next few months because I was too busy getting bombed by Nixon. Christmas was celebrated in style with the heaviest bombing raids since World War Two. Hanoi took the brunt of it. For the first time, the hospitals had more civilians being put back together than military personnel. There was something desperate about the attacks, like a boxer down on points in the last round coming into the ring with a machete. And it did promise to be the beginning of the end. I was back in Hanoi for New Year's, and I found a Christmas card in my mail pouch. I have no idea how it got there. It began pleasantly enough with the words *Season's Greetings* in glitter on the front. But when I opened it, the message became a little less agreeable:

To you and your loved ones. With nothing but unnatural death to look forward to. I shall kill you all. I'll be seeing you, Siri Paiboun. I promise you that.

CHAPTER ELEVEN
Mindless Assassin of the Century

"So, there are our three top contenders for mindless assassin of the century," said Daeng. "If the line in the first note, *I have already deleted one of your darlings*, refers to your lovely Boua, that would rule out contestant number three. Boua died in '65. You destroyed Henry's life in '72. Have you had any other loved ones bumped off since then?"

"Not including dogs?" asked Siri.

They heard a mournful howl from the street.

"No," said Daeng.

"Then I can't think of any," he said.

"What about the bread woman?"

Siri stared at his wife. They were together at a table, straightening aluminum spoons and forks. The cheap rubbish from China tended to curl up after a few months of sweaty palms.

"The bread woman?"

"You should have known I'd find out."

"What's to find out? We had one date and that was a disaster."

"You liked her enough to ask her out. Tell me about her."

"Really? All right. The bread woman, a.k.a. Lah, is, as far as I know, alive and well and baking baguettes with her sons. When I was still at Mahosot, Civilai and I would get our lunch from her cart and sit and eat on a log beside the river. Damn, I should really go and see how Civilai's doing. He's been bedridden for two days. I'll go in the morning and force some doctoring on him. I know if it was serious, Dr. Porn would contact us; she's looking after him, but a second opinion can't hurt."

"We can take him a bottle of something to cheer him up," said Daeng.

"Did Phosy say anything else about the journalists?" Siri asked.

"He ruled out the two Poles because they didn't arrive in the country until two days after we found Ugly's letter. And the Russian died of old age six months ago. He was replaced at the last second by someone much younger."

"That only leaves the East German," said Siri.

"Phosy talked to him. He was certainly in Hanoi when you were there and you might have met up with him in the caves at Vieng Xai. He wrote some pieces from there, being careful not to give away the location."

"Anything about me?"

"He claims never to have heard of you."

"Then we have to learn as much as we can from our two dead ones," said Siri. "Apart from the fact that they unquestionably died of drowning, I didn't see any signs of violence. The tall one hit his head, probably on the dashboard. That might have been enough to knock him out. There were no seatbelts. The photographer's airways were clogged. I'm guessing he suffered from allergies. I doubt that was serious enough to kill him."

Daeng looked up and sniffed.

"What is that smell?" she asked.

"I'm boiling chicken bones in the back garden in a tin drum," he said.

"What on earth for?"

"I'm afraid I cannot disclose that information."

"If you are planning to serve them with my noodles, it's very much my business."

"Goodness me, no. You can't eat them. They're old."

"Where do you get old chicken bones?"

"At the dump," said Siri. "Ugly dug them up for me. He's a natural. We managed to recover some thirty kilograms of the things."

"Thirty . . . ? That's disgusting. How did you get them back here?"

"I hired a bicycle *samlor*. It stank the thing up completely. It'll have to be fumigated. I had to ride the bicycle along behind him with a peg on my nose. I gave him a nice tip."

"And you're really not going to tell me what it's all about?"

"A man has to have a hobby that's all his own, Daeng. Can you watch the drum for me? Keep the fire going for another couple of hours?"

"Why? Where are you going?"

"I told Phosy I'd take a look at the red Ferrari," said Siri. "It just got back."

The Ferrari had finally been dragged from the fish pond and towed to the city behind a tractor. It was parked looking a little sorry for itself in the police parking lot. Phosy and Bruce were standing in the shade of a maiden's breast sandalwood tree when Siri arrived on his bicycle, followed shortly by Ugly. Captain Sihot was standing guard.

"Sorry I'm late," said Siri. "Bending spoons. Boiling bones. You know how it is. Time got away from me."

Phosy and Bruce stepped up to the car.

"We've been over it once," said Phosy. "We just needed your coroner's insight to take another look."

"Has anyone interfered with it since it went in the water?" Siri asked.

"No," said Sihot. "I accompanied it all the way home. Nobody's been anywhere near it apart from our police mechanic, and I was with him the whole time."

"And what was his conclusion?" asked Siri.

"He said the brakes and the steering were in great shape for an old car. Somebody obviously loved it and took care of it. He said he doubted it left the road due to some mechanical malfunction. He did offer a sort of explanation as to why the two of them couldn't get out. The lock latches were rusty. You couldn't open the doors from the inside. You'd have to wind down the windows and open them from outside. But with the pressure on the glass from the water it would have been hard to open them."

"Were the latches tampered with?" Siri asked.

"Didn't look like it, Doctor. Just natural rusting over time."

"I doubt anyone could have planned to have the car leave the road exactly where it did," said Bruce.

"That's right," said Sihot. "It's got all the signs of an accident."

"But what made the driver leave the road at all?" said Phosy.

"Drugs?" said Siri. "Booze? Speeding? Asleep at the wheel? Without an autopsy, we'll never really know."

"Was there anything inside?" Bruce asked.

"There's a bag behind the driver's seat," said Sihot. "We didn't touch it. There were beer bottles on the floor, so it's pretty obvious they were drinking. I think the driver just lost control."

"They seemed to have a very impressive tolerance for alcohol from my memory," said Phosy.

While he fished out the bag, Siri walked around to the front of the Ferrari and looked through the broken windshield.

"That's odd," he said. "There must be a dozen mimosa leis hanging from the rearview mirror."

"What's odd about that?" said Bruce. "A couple of old Lao hands want to go for a drive in the countryside. They remember the old days when everyone hung flowers inside their vehicles to keep the road gods happy."

"But that's exactly it," said Siri. "The old days. There's nothing on the road but military and government vehicles these days. Nobody sells leis anymore. Where would they get them from?"

"Temples still make them for festivals," said Sihot.

"When there's a fair they prepare them but not before. They don't have spare leis laying around just on the off chance someone wants one."

"The journalist welcoming committee," said Bruce. "They handed out leis at the airport."

"That was over a week ago," said Siri. "These are still pretty fresh."

"Why are we so hung up about flowers?" asked Sihot.

"It's called brainstorming," said Siri. "You just say things for no apparent reason until you accidentally stumble upon a truth. It's like politics."

Phosy had recovered a black camera bag from behind the seat. He got into a coughing fit from the fumes.

"Sihot, don't let anyone smoke around here. The interior stinks of petrol. The tank must be cracked."

"I'll get the mechanic to empty it," said Sihot. "Can't afford to let petrol evaporate in this day and age. It's hard to come by."

Phosy laid the bag on the ground and unzipped it. It contained three very expensive looking lenses, several sodden packets of film and one plastic bag with a day's supply of marijuana with soggy papers.

"These boys were serious," said Bruce.

"It was a bit early in the day to get stoned," said Phosy. "There's no paraphernalia in the front seat. Just the beer bottles."

"And more important than what's in the bag," said Siri, "is what isn't in the bag."

"Right," said Phosy. "I doubt a photojournalist would go on a trip without his camera. He'd be prepared for unusual sights. He'd have it with him on his lap or over his shoulder."

"The cadre swore his boys didn't take anything from the car or go through the foreigners' stuff," said Sihot. "But I'll go see him again. Those professional cameras are expensive. A year's salary for some of them."

"Have them go back into the pond too," said Phosy. "See if anything got dropped when they dragged out the bodies."

With cloths over their mouths and noses they conducted one more thorough search of the car interior but found nothing of any relevance. They agreed that the most-likely cause was that they'd been drinking and lost control of the car. Phosy drove Sihot to the station and took Bruce home. The Aussie had moved out of the guesthouse and was living with a relative until he could find a place of his own. It was on the way. He asked to be dropped off at the end of the lane so he could get some snacks at the roadside stall. The chief inspector offered to put Siri's bicycle in the back of the jeep and give him a ride to the restaurant but was reminded that Ugly wouldn't be able to keep up with them. And, besides, it was a cool, overcast evening, and he could take a leisurely ride along the river.

As Siri negotiated the dirt track in front of the Women's Union, he noticed that there was plenty of activity inside. From the doorway he could see that Dr. Porn was still at her desk. He wondered if she ever went home. Very few doors were locked in Vientiane, and, like Siri, most householders couldn't remember where they'd put their keys for safety.

He pushed open the front door and called out, "It's only me."

Porn's office still had no door of its own. She looked up from the logjam of files on her desk and seemed relieved to have a distraction from her bureaucratic combat.

"Siri, you old goat," she said. "Come in."

Even before he reached the desk she had a cup of tea poured for him from her thermos. They exchanged a warm handshake that told of many years of friendship and cooperation.

"How are the eyebrows coming along?" he asked.

It was a standing joke that only he found funny. Porn had shaved her eyebrows for a brief period as a nun and they hadn't grown back.

"I always dream that your mentioning them again and

again will be motivation enough for them to make a come-back," she said. "How are you, good doctor?"

"I'm sparkling," he said. "And you?"

"Tired," she said.

"Work?"

"Family."

"You have a family?"

She laughed.

"Yes, it comes as a surprise to me too."

"You never talk about them."

"It's my policy to keep my private life private. I stay here as long as I can every evening, so I don't have to deal with domestic issues. But you aren't here to listen to my woes. How is your blockbuster film progressing?"

"I think we're on hold for a while until we can sort out a few other issues."

"Then that's not why you're here?"

"No. I have two other matters to discuss," he said. "Firstly, how good are your contacts in the camps?"

"The refugee camps?"

"Yes."

"How good do you need them to be?"

"Let's imagine that I have a commodity that I would like distributed amongst a certain faction of the camps' residents."

"What is it?"

"I can't tell you yet."

"Is it legal?"

"Absolutely."

"Religious connections?"

"You really think I'd be proselytizing at my age? No, it's a good thing. Call it a gift. Would you be able to distribute it?"

"Is it bigger than an elephant?"

"Smaller than a house lizard."

"Then I think I can. For you."

"Excellent. I'll have all the details for you beforehand, I promise."

"And the other matter?"

"Right. I have a friend."

"You do?" she looked surprised. "When did that happen?"

"*Touché.* This friend is exhibiting certain, what could be called symptoms. And as a doctor I am concerned because the symptoms suggest to me a condition—one that I have been expecting for some time."

"Siri, you aren't the type of doctor who needs a second opinion. Why are you telling me? Treat him!"

"I'm not his doctor."

"Who is?"

"You."

Porn blew on her tea even though it wasn't that hot.

"And you think I've misdiagnosed a patient of mine?" she said.

"I hope not."

"Then you'll have to tell me his name. I'm full-time here at the Union. I have very few patients these days, and they're only at my house some evenings and during the weekends. If I'm making bad decisions because of overwork I need to know about it. What's his name?"

"Civilai Songsawat."

She sat up straight then laughed again.

"Civilai?"

"Yes."

"Our Civilai?"

"The one and only."

"Siri, I haven't seen Civilai as a patient for three years."

"You didn't see him last week after Daeng's physical? He was arriving at your house as she left. He said you gave him a clean bill of health. Told him he was in great shape. Just had a touch of diarrhea."

"I did examine Daeng, and, yes, Civilai did arrive as she was leaving. But I didn't examine him. He brought me homemade scones and we chatted for twenty minutes until my next patient arrived."

"You're not his doctor?"

"No. He insists you've been his doctor for so long he would never dream of seeing anyone else. He said it would be a betrayal. I daren't interfere."

"The lying bastard," said Siri. "He's not once let me examine him."

"Why would he lie about something like this?"

"Because he's a stubborn old bastard. Because he knows he's sick and doesn't want to worry anyone. He's too proud to let anyone take care of him."

"What symptoms have you seen?"

"Loss of appetite, nausea, bruising, and he's been hiding his jaundiced eyes behind dark glasses hoping I wouldn't notice. He's been in bed for a couple of days with his supposed diarrhea. I believed he was getting treated by you. If you'd considered it serious I was sure you'd get in touch with me. I should have—"

"Do you have transportation?" she asked.

CHAPTER TWELVE
Let Me Get This Straight. You're Dead?

It was certainly the worst movie Jane had ever made. It was in competition for the worst movie made by anyone. But Siri believed that no man, having watched Barbarella groaning through her ten-minute orgasm in the excessive pleasure machine, could have avoided milking the goat when he got home. It was blatant soft-porn sci-fi and he and Civilai were disappointed that she'd agree to make it. But that didn't stop Siri from putting up a *Barbarella* poster in the mobile ward to cheer up the injured soldiers.

And here he was piloting the throbbing pink 41st-century spacecraft, looking through the windshield at a blackboard dotted with fairy lights that was supposed to be the universe. And supposedly floating in that two-dimensional space at the end of a rope was Civilai in a Chinese postman's uniform.

"What are you doing out there?" Siri shouted. "You're ruining the scene."

"The scene ruined itself," said Civilai without the benefit of a microphone. "Will you stop trying to rescue this movie and its low budget special effects? Here I am supposedly in space with no oxygen tank, and I'm dangling rather than floating. With Jane in the driver's seat, nobody noticed the scenery. But you . . . ?"

"What exactly are you doing in my dream?" Siri asked.

"Not a dream, Siri. This is the reality. You speeding out to Kilometer Six on the back of Dr. Porn's motor scooter, that's the dream. You with a heart thick as sticky rice, tears streaming down your face, that's the dream."

"This feels like one of Auntie Bpoo's mind tortures," said Siri.

"No. Sorry. Bpoo's off in her trailer sulking. I don't know what you said to her, but it really upset her. She's wearing a football kit, boots and all. So you can't blame her. She has nothing to do with this scene. This is just your imagination and me, old pal."

"And what's the moral?" Siri asked.

"There has to be a moral?"

"Usually."

"Oh, I don't know," said Civilai, attempting to cut the rope with a nail file. "How about, 'All good things come to an end.' I like that one. Or, there's always, 'Don't trust people who drink too much.' Which reminds me, I'm supposed to warn you and Daeng to cut down on the rice whisky intake. I know there's a canary's chance in a jet engine that you'll take any notice of that. I certainly wouldn't."

"So, let me get this straight. You're dead?"

"Brilliant."

"How does it feel?"

"Death?"

"Yes."

"It feels like . . . I don't know. It feels like I'm a part of the big it."

"A part of what?"

"Mass."

"I don't get it."

"Well, you know when they take the unexploded ordnance to the smelting works and melt it all down and it sort of blends together and you can't tell what was a bombie and what was a wok because it's all one? Well, that's what this is except there are no unexpected explosions. You can't tell a tree from a Boeing 747 from a toothbrush. It's all a big *blancmange.* I was going to do the tennis racket gag to give you a laugh, but there are none over here. Or, at least, they're no longer identifiable. Shame. It would have been a good exit line."

"We had some good times," said Siri.

"A million of 'em, but let's steer clear of clichés, shall we?"

"Are you scared?"

"A little bit."

"I'm sorry you had to go first."

"A bit sooner than the universe had in mind, but we'll be together soon enough."

"Thank you for making this easier for me."

"What are friends for?" said Civilai. (Although he vehemently denied having said it.) "All right. You get back there to your devastation and grieving, and I'll catch up with you on the set of a much better movie sometime soon."

The nail file severed the rope and the backdrop became a long, stretched-out lava lamp display and Civilai was sucked into it. He shouted, "Wheeeeh."

And he was gone.

Dr. Porn's fifteen-year-old motor scooter sounded like a Harley Davidson in the silent compound. The heavily armed guards at the gate had been undecided as to what to do, so they waved the bike through. Elderly Party members and their wives tended to look alike after seventy. You could never be too cautious. The lights were all on at Civilai's house. Porn stopped in front of the gate. Madam Nong was on the front steps hugging her knees. Sitting beside her, mirroring her actions, was Rajhid, the crazy Indian. He was dressed, which seemed appropriate, and his hair was greased up into a point like a pencil. How he knew . . . how he got there . . . what he was thinking, nobody would know. But he was there.

Madam Nong seemed not to notice the motor scooter until it was silent. She looked up to see Porn and Siri looking down at her.

"You'll want a drink," she said.

Her face was ashen but dry. Her skull seemed to have grabbed at her face and pulled it tight.

"Where is he?" Siri asked.

"In bed," she said. "I'll get him for you."

It was a line so common to her lips she didn't even realize she'd said it.

Dr. Porn sat on the other side of her and put an arm around her shoulder. Siri stepped over them and took off his leather sandals before going into the house. He walked through to the bedroom. Civilai's body in Muay Thai boxing shorts and an *Apocalypse Now* T-shirt lay comfortably on the mattress. There was no question that he had a smile on his face. There was a chair beside the bed.

"Anyone sitting there?" Siri asked.

There was no objection so he sat beside his friend. In the films you only had to pass your palm across the eyes to close the lids. In reality you had to poke and prod and wrestle the bastards shut. So, even though it was a little bit creepy, Siri left the eyes open. They were as yellow as mustard. There was nothing to say. On the bed was a body that had once belonged to a great man. It was empty of soul and mind now, so there was no point in engaging it in conversation. There'd be time for that later.

Siri looked around the tidy bedroom. A glass cabinet with crockery and an unused tennis racket. Framed photographs on the dresser: Civilai and Nong in their sixties and their forties and back and beyond. The colors fading into memory until there were only pastel ghosts in ghostly locations. One photo of Siri and Civilai each shaking a hand of the last governor general of Indochina, a bogus smile of gratitude on his bloated face. One photo of the two couples: Siri and Boua, Civilai and Nong, black and white, a professional picture from a man who made a living from his art—the Eiffel Tower looming over them, the date, 1931. And Siri realized his hands were wet and noticed the steady drip from his cheeks but could not stop it and did not want to. He heaved the tears up all the way from his chest like an old pump emptying a flooded basement. He groaned out each spurt. Nobody came to investigate.

And when he was dry and silent he continued his study of the tidy room. And his eyes rested upon the bedside cabinet and a single pill box and the handwritten label attached to it:

Dr. Porn Chaisak Clinic. December 1st, 1980.

CHAPTER THIRTEEN
Begone the Boulangere

Death to the Oppressors was postponed if not abandoned completely given the circumstances. There was a cremation to arrange, and the greatest challenge was to relieve the Politburo of the responsibility of organizing a state funeral for an ex-Politburo member. Nong and Siri and all who loved Civilai, and Civilai himself, wanted a quiet, intimate ceremony so they could say goodbye in their own way. No cavalcade. No trumpets. No insincerity. No long meaningless wait.

Daeng had kept close to her husband these past two days, watching his smiling eyes, hearing his witty banter with the customers. Even when Mr. Geung and Tukta returned from their vegetable honeymoon and resumed their duties at the restaurant, Siri stuck around, wiping tables, washing bowls, hanging thirty kilos of blanched chicken bones on the lines in the back garden. But he didn't leave the building through the front entrance in all that time. It was as if the road outside might drop into the river at any moment.

On the third day after the Ferrari deaths, Phosy and Sihot arrived at the shop. It was the eve of the grand ceremony of the fifth anniversary of the republic—what Siri had begun to refer to as "the second biggest nothing." The news of the two dead journalists had been met with sadness in the West, but, given the recklessness of their accident, not much respect. The obituaries mentioned their wild pasts as if it were inevitable they'd have sticky ends. "It's how they would have wanted to go." No mention that perhaps they didn't want to go at all. Articles leaned heavily toward apologies to the Lao for spoiling their celebration. The bodies were sent to Australia and the case was closed.

"Is he in?" Phosy asked.

Daeng was presiding over the usual madness of noodle primetime.

"He's upstairs," she said. "Try to get him out into some fresh air, will you?"

"Do you think he can handle any more bad news?" Phosy asked.

"I don't know what he's thinking or feeling," she said. "It's as if he's inside a big puzzle, and he's trying to think himself out of it. He's certain one of the stories from his past has sparked something here in Vientiane. He's sure the death of the journalists is connected to the two letters and the man who sent them. But now that Civilai's death is a part of it too, he can't seem to rest until he's worked out the how of it."

"Well, Daeng, what I have to tell him isn't going to make him feel any better," said Phosy. "I think you should come up and hear it too."

She delegated noodle duties to her returnees and followed the detectives upstairs. Siri had formed a sort of nest in the skirt room and had notes all around him as if he were trying to solve a gigantic riddle. They went with him to a room at the back that contained nothing other than themselves.

"The bread woman," said Phosy.

"Lah, I was afraid of that," said Siri.

"What about her?" Daeng asked.

"She died on the second," said Sihot. "Apparently of natural causes."

"That's it," said Siri. "She died on the second. The journalists—the collateral victims—died on the fifth. Civilai died on the eighth. This is it. This is the threat realized."

"We've already had the paranoia conversation," Daeng reminded him.

"Oh, Daeng," said Siri. "How can this be paranoia? He's following up on his threat but he's making it look like natural causes. Look at the victims. Look at the order. And you're next."

"I'm afraid it's become impossible to ignore," said Phosy. "Daeng, I need to put you somewhere."

She laughed. "We have some empty cupboards in the skirt bank room," she said.

"You know what I mean," said Phosy. "We have to send you somewhere safe so I can work this out."

"I think that's a splendid idea," said Siri.

"You do?" she said.

"Yes."

"Siri, for the benefit of our guests here, can you tell us what happens when we arm wrestle?" said Daeng.

Siri blushed. "I don't see that as . . ." he began.

"There's a point," said Daeng. "What happens when we arm wrestle?"

"You beat me."

"Once or twice?"

"I have an old war wound," he said. "A bullet . . ."

"Always, Siri," said Daeng. "I always beat you. So what chance do you think you and your policemen friends here have of dragging me to a safe house and having me squeeze pimples off my backside while you stumble around trying to find the man who wants to kill me?"

"Daeng, this is no laughing matter," said Phosy. "He's causing people to die."

"Then you'll just have to catch him before he causes me to be one of them, won't you?" said Daeng. "And if the cogs are indeed already in motion as he said, it would appear he's already infected me with his evil magic. So there's really no point in my going anywhere."

There followed the type of silence that comes from hitting a wall of obstinacy. Siri rebounded.

"Phosy," he said. "I have to do an autopsy on Civilai."

They looked at the doctor as if he were suffering from dementia.

"Isn't it obvious what he died from?" said Phosy.

"I need to be sure."

"He's your friend," said Phosy.

"He's not anything anymore," said Siri. "He's dead. All I have there in the morgue is his slowly decaying flesh. But that meat can speak to me. People are dying in the order predicted and I want to know how he's killing them and how to stop him."

He didn't mention the box of pills he'd recovered from the bedside cabinet, nor the words "sooner than the universe had in mind" that had stuck with him since his conversation with Civilai's spirit.

CHAPTER FOURTEEN
Reunion at the Morgue

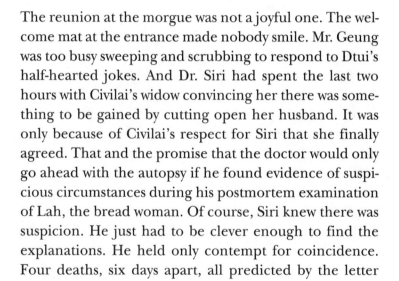

The reunion at the morgue was not a joyful one. The welcome mat at the entrance made nobody smile. Mr. Geung was too busy sweeping and scrubbing to respond to Dtui's half-hearted jokes. And Dr. Siri had spent the last two hours with Civilai's widow convincing her there was something to be gained by cutting open her husband. It was only because of Civilai's respect for Siri that she finally agreed. That and the promise that the doctor would only go ahead with the autopsy if he found evidence of suspicious circumstances during his postmortem examination of Lah, the bread woman. Of course, Siri knew there was suspicion. He just had to be clever enough to find the explanations. He held only contempt for coincidence. Four deaths, six days apart, all predicted by the letter writer.

He pulled up three chairs beside the corpse of the bread woman and he, Dtui and Mr. Geung sat there like hospital visitors.

"Before we start," said Siri. "Let's plan our tactics. Let's begin with the hypothesis that our nemesis was responsible for the deaths of the two journalists. In his letter he made it sound random, that he'd just kill someone as a show of his intentions. But what if it wasn't random?"

"You mean he had a reason to kill them?" said Dtui.

"One of them had met someone he knew," said Siri. "Perhaps our friend hadn't planned to kill them, but they recognized him from the old days. His cover, whatever that was, was blown. He had no choice but to do away with them."

"You don't think it was an accident?" said Dtui.

"Before I went to see Madam Nong, I stopped off at the police car lot," said Siri. "I took my boy wonder, Geung here, with me."

Mr. Geung snorted through his nose and laughed.

"As you know, Mr. Geung's senses are more active than my archaic system," said Siri. "We took a look at the Ferrari. Geung's nose led him straight to the mat under the driver's seat. He pulled it out and there were three puncture holes in the floor. The petrol had been drained but he could still smell that the holes went right through to the tank. Someone had deliberately made those holes so the fumes would fill the car."

"Why?" asked Dtui. "To make an explosion?"

"No," said Siri. "That was my first guess too. But there wasn't much chance they'd ignite the fumes unless they lit a bonfire in there."

"The killer wants them to-to-to breathe it," said Geung.

"Exactly right," said Siri. "As the temperature rose, the fumes would have filled the car. They wouldn't notice because there was a much stronger smell there."

"Flowers," said Geung.

"Someone had put together a whole bunch of leis and hung them from the rearview mirror. Jasmine in a confined space tends to overpower other scents. If they'd smoked their weed they might have noticed the subsidiary smell of petrol fumes because grass tends to heighten the sense of smell, but they didn't. They drank beer. One of the bottles had been re-capped. I had Geung take a sniff."

"I could s-s-smell rotten egg," said Geung. "Like, like antibiotic."

"And why would anyone put antibiotic in a bottle of beer?" Siri asked.

"Beats me," said Dtui.

"Some antibiotics deaden the sense of smell temporarily," said Siri. "So, what if the killer gave them the leis and the beer to see them off on their journey. But also to make sure they didn't notice the petrol fumes?"

"But why?" Dtui asked.

"I couldn't do an autopsy on Jim, the photojournalist, but I did notice he had sinus problems. I guessed he'd had allergies. If his condition was chronic and he didn't have access to medication, the fumes could have been enough to kill or at least incapacitate him. He's drinking, driving too fast on bad roads in a car without seatbelts. He has an attack. It either kills him outright, or he drives into a tree or a house."

"Or a pond," said Geung.

"The killer couldn't have planned for both of them to die," said Dtui.

"It didn't matter if only Jim had recognized him," said Siri. "Perhaps they'd met in the war, stationed at the same press corps. I don't know. But he got lucky. The two of them ended up in a lake and both drowned. And anything Jim had told Marvin about the reunion drowned with them. Our killer had cleaned up."

"And he could use the deaths to show he was serious," said Dtui.

"And capable," said Siri.

"How did the k-k-killer man know about the ah, ah . . . ?"

"The allergy?" said Siri. "That's a good question. If they'd worked together it wouldn't have been much of a secret. If Jim used an inhaler it would have been noticed."

"Any of the journalists here for the festival could have seen him use it," said Dtui. "And they didn't recover an inhaler from the car wreckage."

"It could have floated away," said Siri. "We'll get Phosy to ask around when we're done here."

"And what are we looking for with your girlfriend Madam Lah," Dtui asked.

"Any evidence that the death wasn't natural."

"It wasn't," said Geung.

Mr. Geung, either under the influence of Siri and his spirits or through some innate Down syndrome sub-ability, had certain senses that reached into the realm of the dead. His intuition was rarely wrong.

They'd talked to Lah's sons. The only existing condition they knew of was her insomnia and, for that, she'd been taking herbal magnolia bark for years. But they recalled that recently their mother had heard reports on Thai radio and had switched to pharmaceuticals. They didn't know where she acquired them or how much she used. They gave Dtui all the drugs from their mother's medicine cabinet in a plastic bag. There was nothing to be learned from the containers. Only one had a label and that was for heartburn powder. Another two or three pill boxes were unmarked and a large bottle with only a centimeter of liquid inside had a handwritten sticker that said: *Two glasses before bed.*

Siri recognized the pills in one of the boxes. China was flooding the market with its cheap versions of European drugs, and they made their products look as much like the originals as they could. The drug was a variety of benzodiazepine commonly prescribed for insomnia, and, in certain cases, for depression. By itself it presented no danger. With alcohol it could be fatal. But, according to the sons, their mother drank alcohol rarely and in moderation.

There were no obvious signs of drug abuse. In fact, as they foraged inside the bread lady, Dtui commented that the woman was in great shape internally. They took samples and Dtui and Geung retreated to the lab. The days of guesswork and comparative color-chart tests were behind them. The Soviets had funded a room with equipment and chemicals to test the fluids and flesh. Only Dtui could read the directions and instructions, and, without her, the room remained locked.

Siri sat under a tree with the chemistry lab goats and drank sweet coffee and ate sticky buns—the specialty of the Mahosot canteen—and waited for news.

"You were right about the benzodiazepine," said Dtui. She sat beside the doctor on a pile of tractor tires. "High concentration but not enough to kill her."

Mr. Geung joined them on the grass, greeting the goats by name.

"Anything else?" Siri asked.

"We don't have results from blood and urine," she said, "but we did an analysis on the contents of the bottle the boys gave us. Some sort of liquid morphine. Again, a high concentration and mixed with something sweet. I guess it was to take the taste away. Geung sampled it. He said it was like a milkshake."

"Yummy," said Geung.

"Lucky it wasn't poison," said Siri.

He thought back to his days there at the hospital. To their lunches on the river bank. To Lah, and her hand-made baguettes and pretty smile. And he recalled one week when she was away at the Soviet hospital, a small operation on a rather aggressive mole. She said it had been particularly painful because she had a low tolerance for opiates and had refused pain killers.

"That's how he got her," said Siri. "The combination of the opiate and the psychoactive drugs on an elderly woman. It would have shut down her central nervous system. And if he got the doses right he could have timed it to within a day of his schedule."

"So, someone knew about her intolerance," said Dtui.

"Must have," said Siri.

"Somebody's playing God," said Geung.

His stutter had become less pronounced since his marriage.

"Exactly," said Dtui. "He's blurring the line between natural and unnatural death. But how can he have access to everyone's medical history? A colleague talking about his allergies is one thing, but Lah was a Lao bread maker with no foreign contacts and a life that was limited to a few city blocks. How does he find out . . . ? Siri, she must have been seeing a doctor."

Siri knew Dtui would arrive at that conclusion soon enough. He still had Civilai's medicine bottle with Dr. Porn's label in his pocket. He'd known the doctor since he arrived in Vientiane and he respected her. He'd trusted her with his secrets. He didn't want to believe she'd have a role in this macabre drama but nothing in those odd days of Lao noir was out of the question. Only one thing could vindicate her.

Siri jumped to his feet and the goats scattered to the ends of their tethers.

"All right, team," he said. "Let's get back inside."

"Are you sure you're up for this?" Dtui asked.

"He'd have expected it of me," said Siri. "When I next see him, he'll be complaining about the rust on the scalpels and the coldness of the dolly under his arse. No pleasing some people."

Dtui probably took that as a comment designed to lighten the mood, but Siri knew it was true.

Mr. Geung had placed a hand towel over Civilai's face and it helped. The comrade's eyes, despite hours of manhandling, had refused to close. It was as if the old fellow was keen to see what had finally defeated him. They were surprised to see the scars of at least two bullets and one long, poorly stitched wound from a knife or machete. And that was only the front. Siri knew a politician would invariably have more knife wounds in his back.

He left the Y incision to Dtui and even before she was down to the navel all three of them stepped back in horror. The liver looked like someone was smuggling an over ripe durian inside him. His spleen was bloated and fatty deposits sat here and there like clouds on a break. Thick bands of fibrous tissue tried, to no avail, to hold everything together. But, most importantly, there was congealed blood. Lots of it.

"This happened too fast," said Siri.

"What do you mean, Doc?" Dtui asked.

"If he'd been bleeding like this he wouldn't have been

able to function for months. He certainly wouldn't have been sipping Hundred Pipers last week and annoying everyone and acting out scenes from our film. A week ago, Civilai was himself, albeit dying slowly from cirrhosis. Then, almost overnight we have the glasses to hide his jaundiced eyes and the loss of appetite and the bruises and the trips to the bathroom to throw up. It was as if he went from ignoring his condition to freefall and death."

"You think it was accelerated to fit into the killer's time-table?" Dtui asked.

"I think we need to see what's in his gut," said Siri.

At that point the temperamental air-conditioner let out a rare puff of cold air, and the hand towel on Civilai's face lifted and wafted away like a magic carpet. Siri found himself staring into those jaundiced eyes and returning that cheesy grin.

"You bastard," he said.

Siri sat at his desk and again left the analysis to Dtui and Geung. In his heart, he knew what they'd find. Someone had given Civilai anti-coagulants. If they tested the jar in Siri's shoulder bag they'd find Aspirin or Warfarin or some such. And again he'd return to the same three questions: How did the killer learn of Civilai's condition, why would Dr. Porn prescribe him something potentially lethal, and why did she lie when she said she hadn't been treating him at all? Was she doing him a kindness? Did he go to her office and ask for something to end the pain? She was surely too professional to agree to that and there was still a lot of pain to be had in bleeding to death. Siri had no choice now but to tell Phosy of his findings and have the lady doctor brought in for questioning.

"Are those tears, boss?" said Dtui from the office doorway.

"My face leaks from time to time," said Siri. "It's the old pipes."

"Time to switch over to PVC," she said.

"What have you got for me?" he asked.

"It's conclusive. What's your guess?"

"Aspirin?"

"Ibuprofen."

That afternoon, while Siri was at the morgue, the third letter arrived. Bruce was upstairs tinkering with the Panavision. He was the only one who still believed their film would be made. It seemed to give him a purpose for returning to his homeland. What else would he do? Daeng held out the envelope to him. It had the same odd combination of stamps attached to it. He didn't take it from her.

"It's to Dr. Siri," he said.

"He's not here."

"We should wait."

"Open it," she said, then threw in a half-hearted "please."

Reluctantly, the young man took the letter and tore open the envelope. He read it through silently first and sighed. He looked into her eyes and she nodded. He translated.

"My dear Dr. Siri," he began. *"I'm sure you can see that the countdown has begun. Loved ones A and B have kicked the proverbial bucket. Loved one C is already under my spell and there's nothing you can do about it. Grief would kill you eventually, I suppose, but I don't have time to wait for that. You'll be following*

close behind, doctor. And my promise to you will be consummated
and I will be able to breathe again. Fare thee well, you shit."

It wasn't until later that night that Daeng showed Siri the
letter and told him what it said. They were on a grass mat
on the bank of the river drinking Daeng's own homemade
rice whisky with wild apricot juice. That minor fruity addi-
tion made it feel more medicinal. Less likely to kill them.
The mosquitoes had apparently tired of Lao blood and
were off in search of foreign journalists. The moon was
hopping from cloud to cloud. It reminded Daeng of the
bouncing ball in song lyrics but the only music was from
the cicadas and the frogs.

"So, if I'm next," said Daeng, "what existing condition
is he going to exploit?"

"I've been racking my brain," said Siri. "You're so annoy-
ingly healthy. Your tail's not even long enough to strangle
you."

She knocked the top of his head with her fist.

"Why doesn't he just shoot me?" asked Daeng.

"What?"

"If the objective is to wipe out your loved ones because
you directly or indirectly ruined his life, why not get it over
with as quickly as possible? He has a limited time. Guns
and various explosives are readily available for a small fee.
He could have just wiped us all out in a couple of days and
honored his threat. Why the show?"

"What are you saying?"

"I'm saying he's gone to all this trouble to make a point.
He's doing to you what he thinks you've done to him."

"Used natural causes to kill someone?"

"Something to do with a physical condition that was

aggravated because of something you did or didn't do? I don't know. He's playing God because he thinks that's what you did. You made him lose face or made him poor or put him in jail, where he picked up a disease. I don't know. You need to go back over those three threats and find out what happened to the men you incensed."

"How do I do that?"

"Has bereavement really left you so empty of ideas? The French have released their records on their involvement in the colonies. Their reports are on public record. It shouldn't be that hard to locate a major incident that occurred during the last few days of French control in Saigon. And our good friend, Seksan, acting caretaker-cum-ambassador at the politically clogged French embassy, has a lot of time on his hands. I'll send him over some noodles and see what he can do."

Siri smiled. Daeng was at her most desirable when she was organizing. Nobody did it better.

"Now, as for the Americans," she said, "I'm sure they can tell you what became of long-nose Henry once they found out he was a fraud."

"We still don't speak English," he reminded her.

"Which would have been a problem before the gorgeous, speaks-fluent-Lao, movie star Cindy came on the scene. They don't have a single thing to do at the US embassy. I'm sure she'd be delighted to thumb through a few files, especially if you were leaning over her, breathing onto her neck."

"You'd trust me alone with her?"

"I know your fancy: mature, slightly overweight and armed."

"That's true. She could never compete. What about Paris?"

"As you are one of the few residents of 1932 Paris still alive, I think we need help from someone with a good memory. And I reckon we'd have a chance with the oral history traditions of the Corsicans."

"And where do we find a Corsican at this time of night?"

"How about this for a suggestion," said Daeng. "We stroll ten minutes down the road to the Nam Poo fountain, where we will find the open-air bar of Dani and his Lao wife."

"Dani's a Corsican? I thought he was Serbian."

"Dani's father was a pilot with Air Opium in the glory days of trafficking. I'm sure he could help us with some history, and, if we're good, with a cold pitcher of beer."

"Dr. Siri," she said. "What a nice surprise to see you here."

"They told me this was a famous hangout for foreign diplomats," said Siri.

The bar at the Nam Poo fountain was popular with foreigners even though the fountain never spurted and the beer was never cold enough to please everyone. When Siri arrived they saw Cindy drinking with a handsome young Asian man built like an athlete. It was dark, but he had sunglasses perched on top of his head. She let go of his hand when Siri arrived and didn't introduce him.

"How's the film going?" she asked.

"On hold," said Siri.

"Yes," she said. "We heard about Civilai. You and he were very close."

"We were brothers."

"I'm so sorry."

"Thank you."

He didn't feel a lot of sincerity coming from her direction. She was clearly drunk and impatient to get back to her liaison.

"I was hoping you could find me some information about a pilot who was shot down over Vietnam in '66."

"Much of our records are still classified," she said.

"This one should be open enough," he said, and told her about Henry. He kept it brief because he felt he was intruding. She threw back a tall rum and Coke and signaled to the waitress for another while he spoke. He got a feeling her Grace Kelly looks wouldn't be accompanying her into her forties.

"We all have to go to the parade tomorrow," she said. "But I'll see what I can find after."

"I appreciate that."

He nodded at the young man who merely glared back, and he went in search of Daeng on the other side of the fountain. They were in the middle of the city but there were no street or shop lamps around, so he used the table candles to light his way. He almost missed his wife, who was sitting at a shadowy table with Dani and Chanta, the owners of the bar.

"Siri," said Daeng. "We may have some good news at last."

"I don't know," said Siri. "There was something uneasy about her."

He was sitting in front of Phosy's desk at police headquarters telling them about his brief encounter with Cindy the night before.

"And perhaps she had something to be uneasy about,"

said Sihot who was leaning against the wall behind his boss.

"Why's that?" Siri asked.

"I was talking to the Swedes last night," he said. "One of them said he saw your friend Cindy talking to Jim the photographer the night before he died."

"That would have been after Dtui and I talked to them," said Phosy.

"You think Cindy was the mysterious contact?" Siri asked.

"They're sure to have spare keys for Silver City at the embassy," said Phosy.

"You'd think we'd have been smart enough to change the locks," said Sihot.

"There were no keys on the bodies," said Phosy. "So, whoever tampered with the car had to be there to wave them off and lock up."

"The embassy has its own guests turning up for the parade today," said Sihot. "They were given leis at the airport when they arrived. They have a supply."

"So, she gets there early," said Phosy, "fills the tank, punches the holes in the floor, puts up the flowers and leaves the doors open until the Australians get there. They're already on cloud eleven from whatever they'd been ingesting the night before, so they're not completely tuned in. She joins them in a few sips of beer and off they go."

"It's not impossible," said Siri. "And Jim, wanting to document everything, insists on taking her photo. So, somehow, in the confusion of the departure, she makes sure the camera doesn't travel with them."

"I don't know," said Phosy. "I don't think a photojournalist would be separated from his camera that easily."

"The Swede said everyone was aware of Jim's allergies," said Sihot. "He's been using an inhaler for years. He bought a fresh one the day he arrived in Vientiane. Always liked to have a spare in case of emergency."

"So, where were the inhalers?" Siri asked.

"They didn't see any at the pond," said Sihot, "but they were looking under the water. Inhalers would have floated. I sent someone to talk to the fisherman, see if he caught anything plastic."

"Did you find out why the Swede was asking about Siri?" Phosy asked.

"Something about writing an article for a French magazine," said Sihot. "The life of an Ancienne graduate fighting against the French. We have no way of checking whether that was true or not."

"Oh, so close to stardom," said Siri.

"Look," said Phosy. "I'll be leaving all this with you two. I have to attend this damned stupid parade at That Luang and listen to a National Day speech moderately altered from every other National Day speech I've ever sat through. At least I can take some files and sign stuff. Siri, how are the arrangements for the funeral going?"

"The Party's having its state funeral on Friday," said Siri. "It's symbolic so they don't need a body. Or, at least they won't be getting one. They're not having Civilai lying in state, although he'd really get a kick out of it. Not that it would matter if he were there. The average villager couldn't identify a politburo member even if he had his name tattooed across his forehead. I doubt there'll be a cheer squad or women throwing themselves in front of the hearse. The actual funeral will be this evening."

"I'll be sending my people to both," said Phosy. "I want

photographs of the mourners and the gawkers. There's a good chance our killer will attend one or both of them. If he . . . or she, has put as much effort into all this as it seems, he or she will be there to admire his or her work. Siri, I don't want you or Daeng anywhere near the parade today."

"Oh, what a disappointment," said Siri. "Daeng will be devastated."

Despite the threat to his life, Siri rode his bicycle back to the restaurant with Ugly trotting alongside, without giving a thought to snipers or tossed grenades.

"You do know you started this whole mess?" Siri shouted. "What are you doing allowing a complete stranger to tie notes to your tail?"

Ugly's ears and tail drooped and he assumed a repentant expression all the way home. They arrived in time to find Daeng at a table with two Europeans. One was Dani, the owner of the Nam Poo bar. The other looked a lifetime older than Siri. The doctor pictured the old fellow lashed to the mast of a sailing ship for his entire life braving the storms and the baking sun.

"This is Dani's Uncle Joe," said Daeng. "He's visiting Dani and his family."

Siri shook the old man's hand. He had one hell of a grip. The experience was like putting your hand on a railway track and having a train run over it.

"Dani says he never forgets anything," Daeng added.

Joe sipped his coffee.

"Tell him," said Joe in gutter French. "Tell him I was there in Paris in '32 when the president got shot."

They'd obviously discussed Siri's request already.

"Tell him yourself," said Dani. "He speaks better French than any of us."

"What?"

"You tell him," said Dani.

"He's a Chinaman," said Joe.

"Try him," said Dani.

"You speak some?" shouted Joe.

"Only what I picked up from the whores on the old rue Bouterie," said Siri.

He'd never actually been to the old rue Bouterie and had never learned anything of value from a whore, but his comment had its desired effect. Joe looked at the doctor and laughed so hard he couldn't keep the coffee in his cup.

"Good luck to you," said Joe.

"I was in Paris in '32," said Siri.

"So Dani here tells me," said Joe. "You anywhere near the shooting?"

"I witnessed it," said Siri.

"You don't say," said Joe. "You don't say. Fancy that."

Daeng refilled his cup.

"They told me the Russian they arrested for the killing was just a patsy," said Siri.

"A madman," said Joe. "A drunken fool so high he had no idea why he was pumping bullets into the guy. It was all set up by the family. Doumer had two of the boys killed over there in Annam."

"Do you know why?" Daeng asked.

"All drugs," said Joe. "Those were nutty days. Drugs bring out the worst in people. The third brother, Marcel, he was sworn to avenge the death of his kin. He was there at the . . . I don't remember the name of the hotel."

"Rothschild," said Siri.

"That's it. That's it. He *was* there," said Joe pointing at Siri. "Marcel was there to make sure the Russian wasn't so out of it he'd miss the president and shoot himself. It all went great but Marcel got himself arrested somehow. I don't know how that could of happened."

"What became of him?" Siri asked.

"Not a lot, as far as I can remember. He was in jail for a week or so then the *gendarmerie* gave him some money for the inconvenience and sent him home."

"What?" asked Siri.

"As far as I remember," said Joe.

"Why?"

"Now, that's another story," said Joe. "He didn't shoot no one, did he? And there was a little matter of repercussions."

"About what?"

"Doumer had been the state representative for Corsica before stepping on a few heads and hitting the big time. There's those that say it was drug money that got him up there. They say he'd feathered his nest over there in Annam and brought the trade home with him. If Marcel had been formally arrested and charged, there would of been a lot of evidence leaked to the newspapers to that effect. The government was struggling to keep everyone happy during the Depression. They didn't want the presidency besmirched. And they had their assassin. They didn't need Marcel, did they?"

When the guests had left, Siri and Daeng went outside to sit on the two barbershop chairs that had arrived on the current one day and snagged in the weeds. Once they'd dried out they were surprisingly comfortable. Ugly lay between them.

"So, you didn't actually ruin Marcel's life," said Daeng. "A week in jail is hardly purgatory."

"I doubt he even remembered me when they let him out," said Siri.

They drank in the river air and considered Joe's story.

"It looks like we're just about to learn whether our crazed killer is behind door number two," said Siri.

Daeng looked up to see a short plump man riding a bicycle. In white chinos and a pink brushed-silk shirt, he was dressed more for cocktails than exercise. On the otherwise empty road he stood out like an Easter egg on wheels. Monsieur Seksan was French with Lao parents. But France wasn't ready for an ambassador to Laos of Lao ancestry. The compromise was that he could look after the embassy after diplomatic relations had broken down as a sort of high-level janitor. He showed his resentment of this slight by drinking all the wine in the cellar and damaging things.

He kicked down the bicycle stand and hurried toward the couple.

"I thought you were anti-exercise," said Daeng.

But the man sidestepped her question, barged into Siri, threw his arms around him and wept on his shoulder.

"I just heard," he said through his sniffling. "I'm sorry. I'm so sorry. So, so sorry."

He then repeated it all in French. It took them a while to calm him down. They sat him on one of the barbershop chairs and Daeng patted his hand.

"Give him the talk, Siri," she said.

"All right," said Siri. "Here we go. Siri and Daeng and Civilai were elderly people who had lived for many years in an area rife with weapon fire, tropical diseases and falling coconuts. There were any number of ways our three heroes could have been snuffed out. They may have leaned a little too heavily on alcohol from time to time to get through it all, but get through it they did. And by some miracle they stayed alive until ripe old ages. They knew the grim reaper of infinite patience was sitting on a stool at the end of the tunnel ready to claim their penitence. And so the first pin fell. It was unfortunate that Civilai left them. They'd miss him. Given the amount of booze he'd thrown down his throat over the years, they could hardly have been surprised. It would have been a bigger surprise if none of them died. No, Monsieur Seksan, a lifetime is more than enough."

And, with that, Siri pushed the Frenchman away from his damp shoulder and asked him what he was doing there. After a few seconds of self-gathering, Seksan took a deep breath and said, "Yes, let's all be brave about this."

Siri smiled at Daeng.

"Let's," said Siri.

"I found the records you requested," said Seksan. "Before our little diplomatic standoff, Paris sent the no-longer secret files referring to the last few days of our occupation of Indochina. The staff here locked the files in the strong room and didn't even get a chance to open the dispatch folders before they left. I took a look. Page after page of bureaucratic dross. But, as I'm blessed with having no distractions, I was able to dig down to the inci-dent you mentioned."

"You found it?" said Siri. "Excellent. Did you see men-tion of Civilai and myself?"

The name Civilai sparked another emotional response from the ambassador janitor. It took a while for the dry sobs to clear.

"No," he said at last. "But they did mention the incident.

They wrote that French agents had uncovered a plot to steal valuable artifacts from the national museum in Saigon."

"Bastards!" said Siri.

"That army officers were involved and that they were court-marshalled and executed by firing squad whilst still on Vietnamese soil," Seksan continued.

"And the museum curator?" Siri asked.

"He was to return to France for a civilian trial. He was escorted by a French agent. On the ship home, according to the report, he pushed the agent to whom he was handcuffed overboard. The agent was a large man who couldn't swim and the bodies were never found."

"And then there was one," said Siri.

CHAPTER FIFTEEN
The Lightning Bug Angel

They'd chosen Hay Sok temple for a number of reasons. It was small and intimate and it had a history. Siri's first Vientiane house, before it was blown to bits by a mortar, had overlooked the temple grounds. He and Civilai had often sat at the kitchen window there and drank too much and finished one another's sentences. One night, Civilai had alerted Siri to a surprisingly large swarm of lightning bugs gathered around the main stupa.

"They're trying to tell us something," Civilai had said. "I feel this is a crucial moment in our lives."

Siri had been head down at the time, engaged in conflict with a wine bottle. He was holding it between his knees and gouging at the foil top with a corkscrew. He completely missed the significance of Civilai's sighting.

"I must be losing my touch," he said.

"It's incredibly beautiful," said Civilai.

"There was a time I could just rip these things off with two fingers."

"No, I see it," said Civilai. "I see the shape clearly now. It's an angel."

"I'm bleeding here."

"She's beckoning to me."

"They must be using some new alloy."

"I'm coming, my darling."

"I need a hacksaw."

"This is where I shall be laid when it's all over," said Civilai, looking down at his young brother spouting blood.

"What?" asked Siri.

"My cremation. It will be here."

"Then this will be the death of both of us."

"Siri, what are you doing?"

"I'm trying to get to the cork."

"There is no cork."

"Eh?"

"It's a screw cap, Siri. You're hacking through metal."

"Sacrilege," said Siri. "Since when did wine come in screw tops?"

"A present from Australia. You don't have to drink it if it offends you."

"Don't be ridiculous."

Siri hadn't seen the lightning bugs and he had to take Civilai's word for the angel, but he referred to it often. So it was decided that Hay Sok temple was where they'd barbecue old Civilai. And they'd do it at night because fire in the daytime always seemed like a wasted opportunity to watch the spirit take off. There was only one monk minding the temple, and it wasn't the same ghost monk Siri had once talked to. This was an ex-mathematics teacher whose wife had swum the Mekong to get away from him. He'd decided that becoming a monk in a city that had little respect for monks was preferable to giving chase. And it seemed fitting. They didn't want some religious fanatic telling them how their sins could be forgiven. Siri and Daeng were fond of their sins and they wanted credit for them.

It was just as well the math teacher didn't have a lot to say because the guests wanted Civilai on the bonfire and on his way so they could get to the wake. Despite the overwhelming sense of irreverence, there was a healthy crowd there to pay respect. In Bruce's bag of magic tricks there was a Super 8 home movie camera. He was entrusted with the task of filming everyone in attendance. If Phosy was correct, the killer was somewhere in the crowd. Siri didn't know everyone there but there were a number of old friends. He was hoping to see Dr. Porn and have her explain the tablets beside Civilai's bed, but there was no sign of her. Sitting around on the grass with lit candles dancing in the breeze were Madam Nong and Daeng; Crazy Rajhid in a white nightshirt; Phosy and Dtui with Malee on her lap; Mr. Geung and his bride, Tukta; non-Ambassador Seksan; the Swedes (although nobody remembered inviting them; Cindy and two others from the US embassy; the entire household of Siri's government residence still given over to the homeless; and an assorted collection of people who had felt Civilai's warmth and kindness over the years. There was nobody from the politburo.

To the math teacher's dismay, Civilai had written very simple instructions for his trip to the pyre: tell a couple of jokes, pour some accelerant on the body so it doesn't take all night to burn, and go get drunk.

"How can you celebrate his death with alcohol when it was alcohol that took him from us?" asked the annoying latest girlfriend of Mr. Inthanet, the puppet master.

"If he was run over by a bus, would you force the guests to find their own way to the temple on foot?" asked Daeng.

"If he drowned in the river would you tell everyone they couldn't bathe for a week?" asked Siri.

The bemused girlfriend scurried back into the crowd and Siri and Daeng performed their own version of a high five. Of course, Civilai would haunt them all for eternity if there was no booze at the wake.

Across town the fireworks had begun, marking the last leg of the journalist's visit and the end of the second biggest nothing. After an arduous ceremony at the stadium, seemingly endless speeches and an embarrassing display of military might, the guests would have been enjoying the last of the freebees. Those that could be bothered would have read the Xerox of Civilai's posthumous speech Siri had delivered to their hotels that afternoon. At least there would be one small belt of honesty for them to consider on their journeys home.

The firework show was limp compared to what they had seen at the Olympics, but the timing was perfect. Civilai's journey to Nirvana or heaven, whichever he best qualified for, was accompanied by whooshes and bangs and one or two "ooh" moments. As predicted, the whole thing was over in thirty minutes. Siri had brought a pack of sparklers and they caught the last flames of the pyre and waved them as Siri and Daeng sang Civilai's bawdy Lao version of "La Marseillaise." Siri had marshmallows and wooden skewers in his shoulder bag but decided at the last minute that only he and Civilai would see the funny side of that.

Daeng announced that everyone was invited back to the restaurant to drink a toast to their old friend. That afternoon, Madam Nong had driven to Daeng's in Civilai's yellow Citroën jam-packed with her husband's leftover bottles, so there was plenty to drink that night. The temple was only four blocks from the restaurant so very few of the guests refused the invitation. One of those apologizing was Cindy. She approached Siri with a large brown envelope under her arm. Ugly sniffed at her leg. She was clearly one of the police department's favorite suspects for the killings but Siri felt no fear. It was as if Civilai's death had made him not invincible but indifferent to attempts on his life.

"Dr. Siri," she said. Already she was slurring. "You asked me if I could find you information on the downed pilot. I was able to pull this file after the parade. It seems to me there are a lot of inquiries going on about the . . . I don't know, about the accidents? The journalists and now Civilai. You know? Perhaps if you could confide in me what you're looking for exactly, I could help. I have resources."

"So it seems," said Siri, holding up the envelope. "Perhaps after I've looked through this I'll have requests. Are you not going to join us for the wake?"

"I'm obliged to attend the closing ceremony, however briefly," she said. "Then I have to pack."

"Where are you going?"

"I'm on my way to Phnom Penh," she said. "This was just a temporary posting."

"You're fluent in Lao and they send you to Cambodia?"

"I speak a fair bit of Cambodian too."

"Multitalented."

"My offer of help still stands."

"You've only been here, what? Nine days?"

"Fourteen," she said, "but my work here is done."

"Two weeks? That's most efficient of you," said Siri.

CHAPTER SIXTEEN
The Wake

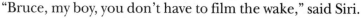

"Bruce, my boy, you don't have to film the wake," said Siri.

"It's like they say back home in Sydney," said Bruce. "You can make a bit of money filming a wedding, but you make a hell of a lot more filming the honeymoon."

Siri laughed and slapped him on the back. The restaurant was packed to the point where they'd had to move the tables out to the roadside so the guests could fit inside. Daeng had felt obliged to make noodles for everyone, but Siri had put his foot down. Instead they chewed on baguettes with assorted dips and salads.

"You think this gathering might degenerate into an orgy?" Siri asked.

"You never know, Doctor," said Bruce. "Sometimes you just have to point the camera and it makes things happen."

Daeng arrived, put her arm around her husband and asked to borrow him.

"Phosy and Dtui and Sihot are upstairs," she said. "We're looking at the US documents. You want to join us?"

"It's Civilai's wake," said Siri.

"He'll understand."

◙ ◙ ◙

They sat cross-legged on the floor in the skirt-bank room. With Malee asleep on a pile of *sins*, Dtui did her best to translate the relevant documents. There were a lot of them.

"All right," said Phosy. "Originally, I thought we were down to the last threat. We can pretty much discount the first—the Corsican in Paris. I'll get back to the second suspect later."

"What do you mean?" said Siri.

"One at a time," said Phosy. "We'll start with Henry in Hanoi in '72. The last contact you had with him was Christmas that year. He sent a Christmas card to you, Doctor. You picked it up on your next visit to Hanoi. What do you remember about that card?"

"Reindeer. Glitter," said Siri.

"Not helpful," said Daeng.

"Let me remind you," said Phosy. "The message read *'To you and your loved ones. With nothing but unnatural death to look forward to. I shall kill you all. I'll be seeing you, Siri Paiboun. I promise you that.'* Once the pilot had been exposed as a fraud, the North Vietnamese plan was to fly him to Saigon with the other three pilots and let the US military sort out the punishment."

"That's the last I knew," said Siri.

"The records we got from the US embassy start on December twenty-eighth," said Dtui. "Apart from a break for Christmas Day so the pilots could have some nice roasted chicken and a cold beer, Hanoi was spattered with ordnance for eleven days straight. As they couldn't leave, Henry was still in a cell at the clinic where you met him. The US bombed the fuel plant and missed. They leveled a suburb for four blocks in either direction. The clinic was reduced to rubble. One of the pilots was killed but not Henry."

"What happened to him?" Daeng asked.

"In the chaos of the bombing, thousands were killed, communication networks were destroyed and the surviving MIA pilots were forgotten and left to fend for themselves. Despite the fact that their country was raining bombs from B-52s on the Vietnamese, they gave themselves up to the authorities. I'm guessing they had no other choice. Henry wasn't amongst them. He'd fled."

"How could an American remain unnoticed in Hanoi?" asked Daeng.

"There were foreigners in Hanoi, even through the bombing," said Siri. "There were Eastern European advisors, press, tourists. All he needed to do was get a change of clothes."

"Even so, he wasn't about to walk out of Vietnam during the heaviest bombing of the war," said Phosy.

"But he could fly," said Dtui, flipping over the page. "The last entry in Henry's file is this mention of a group of American folk singers staying at the Reunification. While they were down in the bunker hiding from the air raids, someone broke into the room of a guitar player and stole his passport and air ticket as well as a large sum of money. When they noticed the robbery the next day it took forever to find someone to report it to. The Committee for Solidarity with the American People in Hanoi was obviously not quite as enamored of their American guests as they had been before the bombings. It would have taken some time to arrange replacement travel documents for the guitarist. But, that morning, a commercial flight left for southern China. On board, having successfully changed the date of his flight was someone claiming to be the guitarist. That same person made an ongoing flight to Bangkok. There's no firm evidence that it was Henry who stole the passport, but there was no trace of him in Hanoi."

"When I interviewed him he had a two-month old beard," said Siri. "He could have easily passed for a folk singer. I'm sure Immigration didn't look too closely."

"And that brings us back to his Thai family," said Daeng. "His plan had failed. He was still poor. But by now the Thai authorities would have been alerted to look out for him. The Americans were on his trail."

"If he was thirty-three in '72 he'd be forty-one now," said Phosy. "Even married to a Thai he'd need a passport to stay there all this time. He'd have to apply for residence every year."

"Or pay a local cop to keep his mouth shut," said Sihot.

"He couldn't take on the guitarist's ID because the passport had been reported stolen," said Phosy. "But it's Thailand. You can buy a whole new identity there."

"He'd need money for that," said Siri. "He stole some in Hanoi but not enough to start up a new life."

"I don't know," said Phosy. "He's a conman. He almost convinced two governments he was a POW. He's cunning. His type is never short of a money-making scam. He could get away with anything. He might be in Vientiane as a diplomat or a journalist or an aid worker. You never know."

"He'd still need documents to get into the country," said Daeng.

"Or a boat," said Sihot.

"All right, so what's the other news?" asked Daeng.

"What other news?" asked Phosy.

"You said there was information about the second suspect."

"The Frenchman, right."

"He drowned," said Siri.

"Presumably," said Phosy. "Again, no evidence. But following your suspicions I sent some men to your friend Dr. Porn's house. She's bolted. It looked like she'd packed in a hurry."

"Front door was open. Lights were still on," said Sihot. "Something had spooked her."

"Perhaps the fact that we were on to her," said Phosy.

"I don't believe Dr. Porn's involved in all this," said Daeng.

"Well, she's certainly hiding something," said Sihot. "Her motor scooter was gone. I couldn't find a passport. But I did talk to a neighbor. What do you know about your Dr. Porn?"

"Not a lot," said Siri. "I first met her here in '75. The Women's Union trusted her enough to give her a top position. I know she was with the resistance for a while."

"Did you know that she was in Saigon?"

"I don't recall her mentioning that," said Daeng.

"She was there for quite a while during the French occupation, evidently. Long enough to take a French lover."

It was then that Siri remembered where he'd seen the tube that had contained the original note. The one tied to Ugly's tail or one very similar to it had sat in a glass souvenir cabinet in Dr. Porn's office.

"This information is from the neighbor?" said Daeng. "Hardly a secret then."

"She was a bit sketchy on details," said Phosy. "I've called for the records from the Union. Evidently, the lover was multilingual. Spoke Lao."

"You don't think . . . ?" said Siri.

"Brokenhearted," said Sihot. "Her lover arrested and shipped to France. The thought of revenge the only thing keeping her going. I don't—"

Bruce and his camera appeared in the doorway. He was drunk and giggly.

"Afraid you have to either look soused for the camera or come down and poin the . . . join the party," he said. "People are leaving. No hosts. Bloody poor show."

"He's right," said Daeng. "There's nothing we can do tonight. Come, young Bruce. Follow me from guest to guest and I'll disclose their most intimate secrets for the camera."

"Bravo," said Bruce. "I'll have enough footage to produce my own documentary. In fact, that's a bloody good idea."

"Stay with Daeng," Phosy told Sihot.

"Not so close her husband will get jealous but near enough to take a bullet for her," said Siri.

The party was over and nobody had died. Siri and Daeng lay on a patch of grass at the river's edge, close enough to feel the spray from the water dashing against the rocks and getting whisked up on the breeze. They were holding hands and had been since they staggered down the bank. They heard a splash. Crazy Rahjid had abandoned his white nightshirt and was backstroking naked against the current. He should have been carried away by the force of the water but he remained, neither ebbing nor flowing, as if he were anchored.

"Will you have a wake for me?" Daeng asked her husband.

"No."

"Why not?"

"Because you're not dead."

"When I am."

"I'll be dead ten years before you, and I'll be in far too advanced a state of decay to think about all that organizing."

"He said I'm next, Siri."

"I know. You're not the type to worry about dying."

She sighed. "I just don't want to go without knowing who he was and how he did it. How sad will it be if our final mystery together remains unsolved."

"I'm afraid to say Dr. Porn isn't looking that innocent," he said. "Maybe it is solved."

"But so many questions are still unanswered."

Rajhid vanished below the surface of the water. He was something of an aquatic animal, but, instinctively, Siri and Daeng began to mentally count the seconds. Siri must have lost count because when the Indian reappeared near the far bank, the doctor had him under for an hour.

"Have you seen him?" Daeng asked.

"He's over there," said Siri.

"No, I mean, Civilai. Since . . ."

"Yes."

"You didn't tell me."

"Sorry. We had a bit of a chat the night he died. I disappeared in Dr. Porn's office when she went to get her motor scooter."

"Was he . . . natural?"

"He was suspended at the end of a rope with lava lamp effects all around him."

"No, I mean, did he seem different? Is the other world like an afterlife?"

Siri gave it some thought. "I don't think so," he said. "I mean we won't be lying there hand in hand in our halos sipping cocktails."

"But we can communicate?"

"Until eternity."

"Then that's good enough."

With the help of Rajhid, Siri and Daeng climbed the riverbank, crossed the dusty road and negotiated the challenge of the staircase to bed. Rajhid turned off the downstairs lights and closed the shutters. Daeng collapsed fully dressed— for now—on the mattress. Siri, always orally aware, went to the bathroom to brush his teeth. He smiled at himself in the mirror as the toothpaste dribbled down his chin. His teeth always seemed more desperate for a good clean when he was drunk, and he had time on his hands. He opened the medicine cabinet, which usually contained nothing but old razor blades and various balms and ointments for the elderly. But that night he saw four bottles he didn't recognize. Still brushing, he focused on the label of one of them. He was confused. He read it again and the brush dropped from his hand and into the toilet. He grabbed the bottle, ran into the bedroom and shook Daeng awake. She came to reluctantly and in poor humor.

"Look at this," Siri shouted, holding the bottle in front of her face. "Look."

She tried to focus.

"How many of these have you taken?" he asked.

"What?"

"How many?"

CHAPTER SEVENTEEN
Porn

By midday on Wednesday they had all the evidence they needed to convict Dr. Porn. All they were missing was the doctor herself. Phosy and his team had worked since sun up to put together all the pieces. The fisherman at Ban Donhai had caught two inhalers. The refills in both were empty. But the label on the newer one was clearly from the office of Dr. Porn.

The sons of Lah, the bread woman, recalled that their mother had obtained her benzodiazepine from Dr. Porn's surgery as well. The locked cabinet in Porn's office contained a bunch of keys that were labeled "Silver City/ USAID." And the final clue had been in Siri's bathroom all along. Since Daeng first started seeing Dr. Porn, she'd been prescribed methotrexate: 7.5mg to be taken once a week to treat her arthritis. It would have been far too difficult to explain how she had been cured of an incurable condition so she'd said nothing. She'd stopped off at the doctor's surgery and picked up her prescription from the housekeeper. Daeng didn't notice at the time, but the doctor had upped the dosage to 10mg a day. At least that was the amount handwritten on the label. That concentration would be fatal in a woman of Daeng's age. Daeng accepted and paid for the medication—but she had no reason to take it. So it sat there, unopened in the cabinet until Siri brushed his teeth the night before. The only element missing now was motive, and they agreed the French lover angle was now worth pursuing more than ever.

The morning noodle rush had not helped remove the pain that frog marched back and forth across the brains of Dr. Siri and Madam Daeng. They had the headaches they deserved.

"It's this," said Siri, as he dipped the tips of his old chicken bones in a pot of yellow paint. Daeng had sent Mr. Geung and Tukta on some unnecessary errand to stop their overly loud laughter. They regretted having promised Bruce access to their heads to complete his documentary, but at least he and his camera were silent.

"What?" she said.

"This is the reason we shouldn't drink," he said. "Not liver failure and death. Death is by far the better option. The hangover. That should be our incentive to give it up. Why do we persist on having mornings after, given how horrible they are?"

"No, I can't use any of this," said Bruce, switching off his camera and loading a new three-minute cartridge. "We're reaching the climax here. You have to focus. The world wants to know—"

"The world's watching your film?" asked Siri.

"Are you kidding?" said Bruce. "This could be compelling. You're about to tell the audience how you unmasked a killer. We need your thoughts. We need to know why a woman you trusted and liked should want you and your loved ones dead."

"But we don't know why," said Daeng. "I thought we were all friends."

"That's fine," said Bruce turning the camera back on. "That's the relationship we need to establish. But first, we need atmosphere. Something undeniably Lao. I know. Follow me."

Bruce settled on the skirt-bank room for background. He draped the *sin*s elegantly and had Siri and Daeng sit cross-legged on the floor in front of them. They were concerned that his decision to have them drinking coconut water from actual coconuts was a little hokey. But Bruce convinced them Aussie audiences lapped up all that sentimental ethnic content. And they couldn't deny the cool sweet water was exactly what they needed to douse the cinders in their brains.

"I'll edit this all in the right order after," he said. "We'll get to the 'why' later. Let's start with what you think happened."

Their cameraman was far more energized than the old couple in front of him. He could obviously picture commercial success and personal fame. The more excited he became, the more pronounced his Aussie-tainted accent was.

"Start with the dead Australians," he said.

"One of the first things Jim did when he arrived here was buy a new inhaler refill," said Siri. "We're guessing he knew Porn from the time he lived here. I don't know if he contacted her, or if he bumped into her at the surgery. But it obviously screwed up her plans that she was recognized. Maybe he knew something about her background in Saigon. Hard to say until we find her."

"There's still a lot that doesn't make sense," said Daeng.

"Like what?" asked Bruce.

"Like why she'd be so stupid as to put her labels on all of her bottles and refills," said Daeng. "Either she wanted to get caught or she was sure nobody would notice. She knew, given the seriousness of his condition that Jim wouldn't survive an attack without his inhaler."

"What about Silver City?" Bruce asked.

"The Women's Union had keys for all the USAID buildings—I guess because there was a lot in the warehouses that could be used or sold. Although as yet, nobody has done so," said Siri. "Porn was here in the old CIA days, so she'd remember the famous Ferrari and know what a coup it would be for a journalist to get a ride in it. She had time and opportunity to puncture the tank and set up the leis. She couldn't have anticipated the pond. She'd have been hoping the car hit a tree or went over a cliff and caught fire, destroying all the evidence."

"And given what she did to Madam Lah and your dear friend Civilai, you still like her?" asked Bruce.

"It takes time to hate someone you love," said Daeng.

"If she did this—" said Siri.

"If?" said Bruce.

"All the evidence points to her, I agree," said Daeng. "But after a lifetime of experience, it seems like you should be able to judge a person. If you're totally wrong, it's as much a reflection on you as on her. Look, you know, Bruce, this has been a real drain on both of us. Why don't we give it a break now and come at it again when we're fresh."

"We're both buggered," said Siri.

"I completely understand," said Bruce. "Look, I've got two minutes left on this tape. How about I ask just two more questions and we'll call it a day?"

"Fair enough," said Siri.

"How was Dr. Porn planning to do away with you, Daeng?"

"She'd been treating me for rheumatoid arthritis for a couple of years," said Daeng. "She prescribed methotrexate. Originally, I was supposed to take it once a week. After our last appointment she changed the dosage to once a day."

Daeng yawned and leaned against her husband.

"And what's the problem with that?" asked Bruce.

"It's very toxic in high doses," said Siri. "Daeng has been known to have a drink every once and a while. That and methotrexate combined would have been enough to kill her."

"So, why isn't she dead?" asked Bruce.

Siri could barely keep his eyes open.

"All right, Son," he said. "Time for a nap."

He tried to stand but the room twisted.

"I said why isn't she dead?" asked Bruce.

He had raised his voice as if talking to the deaf. The camera was down at his waist. He was clearly angry that nobody was answering his question. Daeng's usual flashing light warning system was dull. Siri tried to lunge forward but his reflexes were shot. He looked at Daeng and—with the few facial features that still worked—they shared an expression of apology. The window shutter was open but they couldn't shout for help. The clouds outside grew cumbersome and heavy and dropped to the ground, followed by the sky.

CHAPTER EIGHTEEN
The Thai that Binds

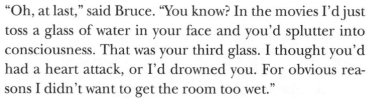

"Oh, at last," said Bruce. "You know? In the movies I'd just toss a glass of water in your face and you'd splutter into consciousness. That was your third glass. I thought you'd had a heart attack, or I'd drowned you. For obvious reasons I didn't want to get the room too wet."

Siri was the first to come around. He could see the young man in a blur and hear his words, but it was as if he were in the audience watching a scene from a play. He blinked a few times to clear his sight. He and Daeng were lying on the floor back to back, tied together at the wrists with their ankles bound. He tried to speak but whatever the boy had put in the coconut water was powerful stuff. The Lao skirts had been piled around them a meter high and Bruce sat on the top of one pile like a mischievous elf. There was a scent of lighter fluid in the room.

"Yes, it was perhaps a bit stronger than it needed to be," said Bruce. "But I really didn't expect you to drink that much."

Daeng groaned.

"I'm not sure I'll have the time for both of you to regain your speech. I have a plane to catch this evening. At least your ears are working. Two weeks, just like I promised. Not as smooth as I'd hoped. It all started off so well too. Good fortune with the journalists, eh? Right on time. Civilai desperate for sleep popping the Ibuprofen I prescribed for him. And you, Lady Daeng, my only failure. So proud of yourself. But, Daeng, you should have gone with the drug option. Burning to death is so . . . icky. With all this antique cotton you'll go up a lot faster than Comrade Civilai, but it'll still be a wicked way to go. And it'll be a shame for you to leave this earth without knowing what the point was, right? So I'll chat for a little while, if you don't mind."

He was flicking the top of an engraved Zippo lighter open and closed and rolling the flint wheel with his thumb. Daeng stirred.

"I'll begin at the end. Or, a bit before the end because the end hasn't happened yet. Seksak who runs the Fuji Photo Lab did have a cousin named Keophoxai who went to study in Australia when he was ten or thereabouts and eventually became Bruce. That much is true. But it wasn't me. Theirs was a big extended family with more cousins and nephews and nieces than you could spray with insecticide. Your dear old friend Dr. Porn was his unpopular aunt. She'd gone off to fight the royalists, so she wasn't the most loved family member. But I'll get back to her later.

"The Australian embassy had language classes back then and Bruce was their brightest student. They arranged a scholarship for him, and he breezed through high school in Sydney, got into university and studied film production. Again, all true.

"And then, there's me. I'm Thai from the northeast so, technically and historically, I'm Lao too. I was a keen student but I came from a poor family and I didn't have any opportunities to study. My mother was a widow from a young age. My father got shot by the border patrol. Smuggling. I was the only son so I stayed home and worked the fields. We struggled. My mother went away to the town for a few weeks from time to time. She said she'd found work in a shop but I wasn't stupid. I could smell booze on her clothes and I knew what she'd been doing. But, good luck to her, was my philosophy. Better than starving to death. She was pretty then and we needed the money. When it ran out she'd get back on the bus. I got used to the system.

"Then, one day, and I'll never forget it, she came home with a *farang*—a white guy. She introduced him to me as Uncle Henry. He was tall. He had a blond buzz cut and phenomenal teeth—even and white like the man in the Darkie toothpaste ads. He said something I didn't understand and held out his hand to me. I didn't know what to do with it.

"Shake his hand, Dom," my mum said.

"Dom, that's me. So I grabbed his fingers and shook that hand the way you'd shake dust out of a mat. And they laughed. I didn't know why. But I laughed too. And that was the start of the happiest two years of my life. As he taught me English, I learned that Henry was a pilot and that he had a disease that stopped him being able to fly anymore. The US Air Force had given him money so he could retire. And he chose our house for his retirement. Nobody worked. The rice paddies dried up and cracked in the drought. The vegetables got overrun with weeds. We ate all the pigs so there were none to mate in the fall. But if we needed something we'd drive to the market in the old truck Henry bought and buy whatever we needed. It was as if the money would never run out.

"Henry bought a generator and fixed up our cabin nicely. There was nothing fancy. He didn't want to draw attention to us. There was no TV. Nothing that you'd call a luxury. But we were a happy family. Every afternoon Henry tutored me in whatever subject we could find books for. He always said I was the brightest kid he'd ever met. I ate up everything he said. I wanted to please him. He told me stories about his parents who were both university teachers who were short-listed for Nobel Prizes, and his sister who won the Miss California beauty title in 1967, and his brother who was working his way up to being the President of America. And my mum said that nothing would make her more happy and more proud than if her son could study in a real university and become a doctor.

"And I guess they decided that I'd go away to study. I hated the idea of being away from the house, but Henry convinced me that school wasn't a lifetime. That I'd . . ."

Siri coughed. "I don't . . ." he said in a breathy voice.

"Ah, good," said Dom. "Communication. It can never be overrated. But, right now, you can't interrupt me. I'm on a roll. I have a lot to say and the clock's ticking. You'll have your moment. Where was I? Right, he told me that in no time I'd be back with skills and a degree, and I could support my family and be someone important in the community. I told him I wanted to be a pilot like him. But he said that pilots just kill people and that I should be a doctor and help people instead. He said it would make my mother happy. And she was. After a life of abuse and struggle I could see that finally the spirits were on her side. I couldn't disappoint her.

"I travelled to Bangkok with Henry. We went to the Australian embassy. At the time I wondered why he'd want me to go to Australia rather than America. It was several years before I really understood."

Siri's senses were returning. First came his sense of smell. The lighter fluid wasn't on the skirts. It was on him. He felt Daeng's index finger tapping against his hand. Dom, the boy who was not Bruce, droned on.

"I took tests in Bangkok that were obviously designed for idiots. I was embarrassed at how easy they were. And the next thing you know I'm on a Qantas flight to Sydney. Then the blur. The classes. The bullying. The cultural explosion. The A grades, the distinctions and, wham, I'm accepted at Sydney University to study medicine. And the only thing that kept me centered through it all were the monthly letters from Henry. My mother couldn't write so I learned of their life through him. They were such happy letters in the beginning. Every semester, money arrived in my account to cover my study fees. I didn't socialize so my income was more than enough. My only two objectives were to graduate and go home.

"It was 1972 when I received the letter that changed everything. Henry's condition had deteriorated to the point that he had to go to Vietnam to see a specialist."

Siri tried to say something but the words crumpled together before he could organize them.

"Yes, Good Doctor Siri," said Dom. "I can feel your excitement. Because now is when you appear in this story. Daeng, my darling, this is the bit I want you to hear. The specialist was you, Siri, remember? Educated in Paris. Trained in tropical medicine. How could he fail to find you? As I was into my second year of study, Henry decided that I was ready to learn about his condition, echinococcosis. He described it in detail. It was a horrible, debilitating disease but it was curable. If Henry had come to Sydney he would have recovered. But he didn't. He found you instead. He was in your clinic for four months being treated for something erroneous. You withheld his letters to me during that time. He sent me no money because you were draining his account for medicine unrelated to his illness. He sent that same medicine to my mother who had the same disease. By then he was too sick to go to America so he returned to Ubon. And there he found that my mother had died in his absence. A disease that would have been cured if you had prescribed the correct medicine."

"All . . . bull," Siri managed at last. It was barely audible but the Thai was too engrossed in his own story to notice the interruption.

"Out of his love for my mother he stayed on at our house. Any time he wrote for the next year, he mentioned you in his letters. Your cruelty. Your incompetence. And every letter concluded with the same line: *'Siri Paiboun the fake Lao surgeon has done this to us. He has destroyed our family. He must atone. This is my final wish.'* I couldn't stand it anymore. The payments into my account stopped. I didn't have any money to return to Thailand or to continue my studies. I took a menial job and saved as fast as I could. In 1976 I received a letter from the village headman telling me Henry was dead. I had loved him even more than I loved my mother. Suddenly, I had nobody."

Siri coughed again and forced out the words, "Henry was a . . . a compulsive liar."

"Of course, Fake Doctor. What else could you say to protect your reputation? But me? I had been told I had to discontinue my studies. I had passed every course. I specialized in pharmacology. I was offered a post at a research laboratory. But by then I had a bigger ambition: to avenge the deaths of Henry and my mother. I befriended the Lao community in Sydney. It wasn't too hard to convince them I was one of them. They were quick to adapt to life in Australia. We spoke English together. Then, in '75 when the floodgates of refugees opened, I was already a respected member of the Lao welcoming committee. And through them I heard of your whereabouts, Fake Doctor. I learned where you worked and where you lived and who you loved.

"I learned about Dr. Porn in Vientiane who had a nephew studying in Sydney. His father had died and the boy was alone. I contacted him and became his friend—in a way. I hadn't yet formed my plan to—"

"You should just stop and listen to the stupidity you're talking," growled Siri. "None of it makes sense. I was in Hanoi. Why would a US pilot go to Hanoi for medical treatment in the middle of a war? And there is no echinococcosis in Thailand. He just selected the name from a medical dictionary. You—"

Siri fell into a coughing fit. The boy reached behind him and found his can of lighter fluid. He removed the cap and sprinkled the remainder of the liquid, not on Siri, but on Daeng. Her finger percussion became frenzied.

"Nearly done," said Dom. "A little bit more and we can all go on our respective ways. It turned out that Dr. Porn's nephew wasn't a great communicator. He rarely wrote home. Never sent photos. Even less often after his sad demise."

"You killed him too?" Siri asked.

"Not really," said the Thai. "It turned out he had a weak heart. I introduced him to cocaine: the heart-attack drug of choice. It was my first experiment with death by existing conditions. It was nothing like murder, you see. If I'd given him the cocaine and he didn't have cardiovascular disease, I'd have been doing him a favor. It's not at all like being a poisoner. I haven't directly killed anyone. If you feed your friend peanut butter sandwiches every day he'd thank you and scoff the lot and suffer no more than weekly stomachaches. But, what if he was allergic to peanuts? Oops. It led me to look more closely at the sometimes lethal combinations of conditions and medicines. I got away with young Bruce's deliverance and nobody found the body. I adopted his ID. I started to communicate with the family in Laos pretending to be him. I'd learned the Lao alphabet when I was a kid. My Lao writing wasn't fluent but appropriate for a boy who'd spent fifteen years in Australia. Spoken Lao was easier. My village dialect was easy enough to adapt. I apologized for my slackness at not writing. Telling them how close I was to graduating. Saying I wanted to return to my homeland. I wrote to my dear Aunt Porn who was the family's black sheep: anti-royalist, registered Communist. Nobody else spoke to her. She wrote back to me. She was surprised I knew about her. It was like Pandora's box opened up in front of me. She told me all the gossip: about relationships, about the resources she had at her weekend surgery. I stole pharmaceuticals and sent them to her for her stock. We became close.

"I had Bruce's passport. We looked similar. I put on some weight and dyed my hair like him—he had this peroxide fixation—and we could have been twins. The family met me at the airport. They hadn't seen Bruce since he was ten so it wasn't hard to fool them. They wanted me to stay with them but I insisted on going to a hotel. I was waiting for Dr. Porn to invite me to stay with her. She lived alone so she was reluctant at first, but we soon became comfortable with one another, and I moved into her spare room behind the weekend surgery. I pretended to like her but she was sloppy. She wasn't one for security. Her filing cabinets weren't locked and the medicine cabinet was always open. I'd alter the labels, change the contents and she'd hand over the drugs that would kill her patients."

"Why the journalists?" Siri asked.

"See? I knew you'd be interested. I was planning to start my attack with the bread woman but there I am at the market and this guy comes up to me—this *farang*—and he says, "Bugger me, if it isn't little Dom." I recognized him from Ubon. It was Jim. He was one of Henry's drinking and toking buddies. He'd come to stay with us a few times when he was doing stories up country. I tried to convince him he was mistaken, but he'd watched me grow up. We'd played soccer together. I guess he had that photographer's eye that never forgot. The hair and the added weight didn't fool him. I guess my face hadn't changed that much. It really screwed up my plans.

"Porn had told me about the red Ferrari and Silver City. The keys were sitting there in her office cabinet. So I got the two Aussies all fired up about taking the car for a drive. I'd emptied the inhaler he asked me for, opened a couple of beers to see them off and dropped some antibiotics in the open bottles to deaden their senses to the smell of the gasoline. I'd arrived a couple of hours early to—"

"Boy," said Siri. "Henry had reason to hate me, but it had nothing to do with disease or misdiagnosis. Your mother's boyfriend was AWOL. He was a deserter and a coward and a liar."

The Thai threw the empty fluid can at Siri, and it caught him on the side of the head. The cut bled. Daeng's tapping grew frantic.

"I'd like to consider myself something of an expert now," said the Thai. "Take you for example, old man. You're the antidepressant type. If things hadn't gone wrong here I would have had dear Aunt Porn give you antidepressants from her stock. I'd already substituted her low dose with much higher potency pills. After losing those near to you, you'd be distraught. You'd pop paroxetine until they put you to sleep and made you care less. But you're also an alcoholic. You can't stop yourself. You'd mix booze and pills and whittle yourself down to nothing, and I wouldn't have had to do another thing. You'd have been on self-destruct. I'd just check for your obituary from time to time knowing you were spiraling down a toilet."

"How did you kill your aunt?" Siri asked.

Dom smiled. "What makes you think I killed her?" he asked.

"It's only logical," said Siri. "She wouldn't have just up and left. She wasn't the type. I'm guessing she found out what you were doing."

"The nosey cow went through my things. Found my real passport. With the Mekong pumping away at the rate it is she should be somewhere near Cambodia by now."

"So you aren't as clever as you thought you were," said Siri. "You're just a common or garden murderer. There's nothing smart about throwing an elderly lady in a river or setting fire to an old couple."

"That is your fault, Fake Surgeon," said the Thai. "And I'm in a hurry to get it over with. So if you'd just be kind enough to tell me why your charming wife here isn't dead in spite of a heavy overdose of methotrexate . . ."

"Yeah, you know, that wasn't clever either," said Siri. "That had nothing to do with existing conditions. Rheumatoid arthritis was never going to kill Daeng naturally."

"Whatever! Why didn't the medicine kill her?"

"Because she didn't have rheumatoid arthritis."

"Of course she did. I've been through her file."

"She got over it."

"People don't get over arthritis," said Dom.

"My wife did. She's remarkable. You should have considered that in your flawed plan. She has skills too. Did you know she can whistle?"

"What?"

"Whistle. She could whistle the eyeballs off a buffalo."

"What are you talking about?"

"Go on, darling," said Siri. "Show the foolish boy how loud you can whistle."

Daeng whistled. It was impressive but no world record.

Dom laughed and he flicked a flame from the Zippo.

"I've got better things to do," he said.

He reached behind him for the rolled-up newspaper and lit the end. It took a while to catch. Siri cocked his ear toward the door but there was no sound. He needed a few more seconds.

"How did you get the Ibuprofen to Civilai?" he asked.

"Didn't need to," said the Thai. A healthy flame had engulfed one end of the newspaper. "His wife came to the clinic regularly. She'd mentioned that her husband couldn't sleep. I put together a little pill box and delivered it myself when Civilai was away."

Siri heard a scamper of footsteps on the landing and

suddenly the confused face of Ugly appeared in the doorway.

"Hello, my friend," said Dom. "I hope this wasn't your backup plan. This dog's loved me from first sight. Sorry, boy. I didn't bring any cheese today. Amazing how many dogs are cheese junkies. They can't—"

Having looked at Siri and Daeng, who were suddenly screaming for help, tears pouring down their faces, Ugly ran full speed at Dom and buried his fangs in the back of his neck. It was the perfect attack spot. The victim couldn't punch or kick him away. Dom dropped the newspaper, which continued to burn, on top of the skirts which had yet to catch fire, and dragged the dog across the hill of fabric. Despite his prey swinging from side to side, the dog didn't let go. Dom screamed and cursed.

"This is stupid!" he yelled. "He'll get tired. There's nothing to be gained from this."

Siri and Daeng had pushed together into a standing position. Dom continued to scramble around on top of the *sins*, eventually edging closer to the old couple. Siri leaned forward, and, using their bound wrists as a pivot, Daeng left the ground and swung her legs through the air. Both feet connected to the Thai's head. The force of the blow shook off Ugly, but it also stunned the killer. Siri and Daeng stood breathing heavily in the cleared space in the center of the room. The newspaper continued to smolder, but the material in the heap was packed together too tightly to burst into flame. The Thai was out cold on the skirts.

"Nice one," said Siri.

He looked around.

"What do we do now?" he asked.

"I haven't thought that far ahead," said Daeng.

"How did you know Ugly would come inside?"

"Instinct," said Daeng. "Mine and his."

In the distance they could hear the squeak of the hinges on the dog door. Dom began to stir.

"*Merde,*" said Siri.

The boy took a while to get himself oriented, but just as he reached for the Zippo, a dark figure appeared in the doorway—a dark, completely naked figure. Crazy Rajhid was much faster at assessing the situation than Ugly had been. He dived across the skirts, grabbed Dom's Zippo hand and wrestled him down. Ugly went for the ankle. But the attack seemed to unleash the beast in the intruder. He snarled and flailed and seemed to draw on a pool of strength from deep inside him. Rajhid weighed no more than a Wednesday. Dom threw him off, bouncing him against a wall. The dog got a kick for his troubles and fell into the central clearing where Daeng and Siri stood helpless, back to back. Someone downstairs was banging on the restaurant shutter. It was past noodle time.

Dom made for the rear window. It was narrow but open, and he was about to dive through, when Rajhid with his second wind made a flying rugby tackle at Dom's legs. The boy's chest fell heavily against the window frame. He tried to kick free of the tackle but what Rajhid lacked in bulk he more than made up for in adhesion. He now had an unbreakable grip. But the Thai still had the Zippo. He flipped it open, produced a tall flame and tossed the lighter in the direction of Siri. It landed at the doctor's feet and immediately ignited the slowly evaporating fluid. The flames engulfed one leg of his trousers.

Rajhid made the call. He let go of Dom, grabbed the nearest skirt, and threw himself at the fire. He wrapped the cloth around Siri's leg and smothered the flames. When Siri looked up, he saw that Dom was gone. Rajhid crawled to the window, looked down and shook his head. They'd lost him.

CHAPTER NINETEEN
Works Like a Charm

Almost a week had passed. The journalists had departed and the city went back into social hibernation. The border was still closed. At the market, for the equivalent of a dollar you could get a potato or a lifetime supply of marijuana. The appearance of cooking oil caused a stampede. In the end-of-year review, someone calculated that the country had fourteen thousand kilometers of road, most of which was impassable in the wet season. Another thousand cooperatives had folded and industry still comprised one percent of the economy. There were three unexploded ordnance incidents a day, many of them fatal. The schools still had no textbooks, and the teachers were being paid in rice because the budget didn't stretch to education.

Civilai would have had some sarcastic comment to make about it all. Nobody of any personal importance to him attended his state funeral. Even Madam Nong had to pull out at the last moment due to a touch of migraine. She was replaced on the bleacher by somebody who looked a little like her. A lot of photographs were taken and there was an article about Comrade Civilai in the *Pasason Lao* newsletter and a forty-minute special on Lao radio. But the live turnout was sparse and the sincerity shallow. Civilai had always spoken his mind and socialism wasn't cut out for such foolishness. That final speech had raised hackles throughout the Party.

Probably the most pertinent news of the week was that there had been no sign of the murderous Thai. The chicken ropes that crisscrossed Siri's backyard had broken his fall from the upstairs window. Where he went from there was anyone's guess. Once Phosy was alerted, every available policeman was on the streets looking for a plump young man, probably hiding his blond hair beneath a cap. He hadn't turned up for his booked flight on the day he attempted to cremate Siri and Daeng. He wasn't seen at any guard posts along the roads leading from the city. There were no sightings of him crossing the river. He'd just vanished. Neither had Dr. Porn's body been recovered. But the Mekong was a huge winding stretch of water with no end of crevices and gnarled roots to trap a body.

Siri and Daeng fell back into a routine. It wasn't the first escape from near death for either of them, but they weren't getting any younger. Survival was hard work and even a week after the incident they were drained. They couldn't get the scent of lighter fluid out of their nostrils. Both were philosophical about death and had no ambition to claim more life than they were owed. Daeng was probably as pleased to have preserved the antique skirt collection as she was to have preserved herself. They still had their lives thanks to a dog and a naked Indian and for that they would be forever grateful. But, until Dom was caught there could be no rest.

Siri had packed all of his chicken bones, each one exactly three centimeters long with a yellow stain at one end. He'd had no template for his design but decided it didn't matter. It was most certainly the thought that counted. Before her sad demise, Dr. Porn had arranged transport for his cargo to three refugee camps on the Thai side. Madam Khunthong, who had taken on the responsibility for this shipment, had called Siri into her office to have him explain once more what it was all about. She hadn't quite grasped the concept. Khunthong was a jolly, football-shaped woman with no chin and a high forehead.

"Tell me again what they are," she said.

"They are small lengths of chicken bone with dobs of yellow paint at one end of each," he said.

"And how many, in total, do we have here?"

"Twelve-hundred in each box."

"And we give them to . . . ?"

"One to every single man in the camps under the age of twenty-five," said Siri. "And a handful for families to hand out to single Lao men they meet in the countries they're accepted by."

"I'm assuming we don't tell them these are chicken bones."

"Absolutely not," said Siri. "These are ancient amulets blessed by generations of shamans. They should find a strong length of string and wear them around their necks. They're infused with magic. They are more powerful than even the most evil of night seductresses."

"Night seductresses?"

"That's what you tell them."

"But it isn't true."

"It doesn't matter."

"You want our people to lie to them?"

"Yes."

"I don't think I can tell them to do that."

"Madam Khunthong," he said. "These boys already believe lies, and those lies are killing them. A silly story becomes a rumor, which becomes a legend, which becomes a reality. Our boys are dying in their sleep, killed by malevolent spirits that take advantage of their naivety and susceptibility. Once you believe enough in something, it becomes real. Believe me. I have inherited a whole dimension through belief. These young men are afraid to go to sleep because, in their dreams, there lurks a woman who can suck out their souls. And in their sleeping hours she becomes real. And in their dreams she kills them. And they believe they are really dead. So they have no option other than to die. Here!"

He held out one of his bones.

"This is magic," he said. "It looks simple but it is blessed. It contains enough karma to ward off any evil spirit woman who walks the night. It's a false belief sent into battle a false belief."

She looked into his eerie green eyes.

"Are you sure this will work?" she said.

"I know it will," said Siri. "There's only one thing."

"What's that?"

"You'll have to charge for them."

She laughed.

"I knew it," she said. "Porn told me it wasn't a scam but I—"

"It's not," said Siri. "It only needs to be a hundred *kip* or a baby chick or some embroidery. It's a token. You can use whatever you earn for any projects you have running. But it can't be free, you see? Quite rightly, we Lao have learned not to trust anything free. For this to be credible it has to have a price."

◙ ◙ ◙

Daeng awoke with the sky as black as blindness outside the window. She turned around to see a familiar empty space on the mattress beside her.

"Siri, are you in the bathroom or in the other world?" she shouted.

There was no answer.

He was in the other world.

"You're a being of extremes," said Siri.

"I can't think what you mean," said Bpoo. He had finally shed the 'Auntie' skin. He was dressed in a man's three-piece-herringbone suit with a tie and flip-flops. He sat opposite Siri at a metal table in a conventional police interview room. One wall had a long mirror that would have been disappointing if it wasn't two-way.

"I suppose I'll have to take my own credit for getting you out of skintight lamé and unwalkable stilettos," said Siri. "But now you're overdoing the macho. I expect you to pull out your rubber hose and start beating a confession out of me. There's middle ground, you know? I'll probably miss your elaborate sets and rampant symbolism, but I'd be quite happy to meet you on the bank of the Mekong over a metaphorical baguette."

"Do you have a point?" said Bpoo. "I have a darts tournament in half an hour. What do you want?"

"What do I want?" said Siri. "I thought you summoned me."

"Doesn't work like that. I sense your desire to have a chat and I enable your crossing over."

"What? That's useful to know. I conjure up a desire and you appear? You couldn't have told me that a year ago? It feels more like the sort of relationship we're supposed to have."

"Do you have a question, Oh Master?"

"We still need to work on that sarcasm. Here's the deal . . ."

Siri told him about his chicken bone project and raised his eyebrows hopefully at the end.

"So?" said Bpoo.

"So, I was wondering whether you'd be able to . . . you know . . . bless the bones or something."

"Do I look like the pope?"

"Isn't there some mechanism over there to promote supernatural activity in inanimate objects? Sprinkle a little bit of fairy dust or something?"

"You really are bad at this," said Bpoo.

"You said this world exists in my subconscious," said Siri. "I want to explore the outer limits of our relationship. Like the homework I gave you during our last visit two days ago. I bet you haven't done it, have you?"

"You see?" said Bpoo. "You don't even understand what our relationship is. I am not your private detective. I lead you through the labyrinth of your mind; I do not find missing persons."

"So, you failed."

Bpoo made a furtive glance at the mirror.

"I'm not authorized to give such information," he said.

"Who's behind there?" Siri asked.

"It's just a mirror," said Bpoo. "I was just checking my hair."

"In that case, I desire to go home to bed," said Siri.

Bpoo hesitated.

"There is one thing I am at liberty to tell you," he said.

"Yes?"

He looked again at the mirror.

"The person you inquired about is not deceased."

CHAPTER TWENTY
Siri Down

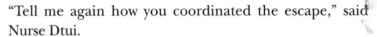

"Tell me again how you coordinated the escape," said Nurse Dtui.

The noodle shop tables had been pushed together, and the usual gang sat around the large square. From left to right there was Dtui and the ever-snoozing Malee, Chief Inspector Phosy, Mr. Geung and Tukta, Siri, Daeng and a large Donald Duck balloon standing in for the absent Civilai. A late evening shower had brought out the fire ants in such numbers Daeng had been forced to close the shutter, turn off the lights and illuminate the table with two temple candles. It gave the gathering the air of a séance.

"We didn't exactly escape," said Siri. "We were just as tied up and incapacitated at the end of it all, but we did organize the whistle for Ugly and we got in one good kick."

"It's called the tap code," said Daeng. "It's like Morse Code for beginners. The POWs in the camps developed it when they were banned from speaking. It's alphabetical. You have a letter grid in your head and you count the number of taps you hear until you've spelled out a word.

One quiet night Siri and I developed a French language version."

"Why?" asked Dtui.

"You never know when you're going to be incarcerated and have your tongue cut out," said Siri.

"He's right," said Daeng, "You don't."

"So Daeng's there tapping away, and I'm doing my best to keep a count and concentrate and talk to a maniac at the same time," said Siri. "And after a very long time I realize my wife was putting our lives in the hands . . . the paws of a neurotic mongrel."

There came a muted howl from the street.

"I put a lot of faith in our dog," said Daeng. "I hoped he might sense our fear. He'd stood looking at the dog door many times, but I'd never managed to coax him inside. I guess a building's a frightening proposition for a dog that spent most of his life in the jungle."

"I hoped we'd built up enough gratitude points from all the meals and affection for him to break his rule just that once," said Siri. "Then I get the second plan tap coming through explaining the two-man Bruce Lee kick. But tapping's a painfully slow process so we hadn't really outlined the whole thing. And then it was too late. Ugly was there and we just relied on the warrior spirit to make it work. And there's Daeng flying through the air."

"Not bad for a woman with chronic arthritis," said Phosy. He'd read Dr. Porn's files.

"It was the sedative," said Daeng. "I could feel nothing below my waist."

"It hadn't occurred to us that Crazy Rajhid would be skinny enough to get through the dog door," said Siri, keen to get off the topic of arthritis. "But given his girth

I shouldn't have been surprised. He'd seen the noodle crowd gathering and heard the whistle and the shouts from upstairs. He leaped three garden fences to get here. He should get a medal."

"Where would we pin it?" asked Tukta.

She didn't say much, but what she did say usually hit the spot. They drained a lot of laughs out of that, had one more drink and found other things to laugh about. Then they had one more drink. All but Civilai, who was on water. Served him right.

"And why," asked Phosy, "did your stash of antique *sins* not go up in flames at the mere scent of fire?"

"Now, for that we have to congratulate our resident genius, Mr. Geung here," said Daeng. "In his role as keeper of the *sin* bin he took it upon himself to cover every contingency. As you may recall, we have already been victims of vandals and nothing would tickle the fancy of your average arsonist more than a room full of dusty cotton and silk. So he fire retarded them."

"How on earth would you go about such a thing?" asked Phosy.

"Borax," said Geung. "It . . . it's quite easy."

"Evidently, it's a sort of laundry additive," said Daeng. "You soak your natural material in it and let it dry and it makes it hard to ignite."

"Not exactly f-f-fireproof," said Geung, "but good enough."

"How do you know all this stuff?" asked Dtui.

"The spirits of the *s-s-sins* told me," said Geung.

They all laughed, even those who were sure it wasn't a joke.

"How about Dom's movie camera?" Daeng asked.

"It's on its way," said Phosy. "I'd like to take it myself but sometimes you have to trust the Thais to do it right. And I suppose this is as much their case as ours. It's okay. There'll be someone watching over them."

"I think the brief, euphoric life of another generation of flying ants is over," said Siri.

"Right," said Mr. Geung.

He hopped to his feet and hurried to pull back the screen. They needed the river breeze. Tukta turned on the lights.

"Where do you think he is?" Daeng asked.

"Dom?" said Phosy. "No idea. But I'm guessing he's back in Thailand. It's not easy for an outsider to disappear in Vientiane. He doesn't have any relatives or friends here. He's not the type that could survive in the jungle. All I can guess is that he found a boat and floated home."

"But he's not finished," said Siri. "Perhaps he'll reorganize and try again some—"

"Dr. Siri!"

Geung had dragged open the shutter and was standing in the entrance.

"Come," he said. "Quick."

Everyone rushed to the street. Ugly, unconscious, lay in a pool of blood in front of the restaurant. Siri went down on one knee and felt for a pulse.

"He's—" he began.

The crack of the rifle carried along the river in a watery echo. Everyone froze. Siri looked briefly at his wife then dropped to the ground. Daeng screamed. Phosy and Geung ran for the trees and used them as cover as they headed in the direction of the shot. But there was no more gunfire. They saw nobody.

◙ ◙ ◙

Under the glare of the electric light, Daeng, Dtui and Tukta carried Siri inside and into an alcove not visible from the street. They lay him down and he sat up straight away.

"Bring in the dog," he said.

Tukta returned to the pavement with a towel and scooped Ugly from the roadside as if he weighed nothing. She lay him beside the doctor.

"You sure you weren't hit?" Dtui asked.

"I think I'd know if I was," said Siri. "I only went to ground under orders. Good thinking, Wife."

"We needed the shooter to believe he hit his target," said Daeng. "Otherwise he'd have kept shooting. How's the dog?"

Siri was looking for a wound.

"He's been drugged," he said. "This is where all the blood came from."

He pointed at the tail, or what was left of it. The last six centimeters had been hacked off.

"A lot of blood," said Dtui. "Nothing fatal."

"Looks like Dom's forgiven Ugly for turning on him," said Siri. "Still couldn't bring himself to kill the beast."

Dtui went to check on Malee, who'd slept through the drama. Phosy and Geung returned.

"No sign of anyone," said Phosy.

"Not even Rajhid?" said Dtui.

"He's not exactly on the clock," said Daeng. "He could have an appointment with some dolphin up river for all we know. We're just fortunate to get him when we can."

"Will Ug-Ugly make it?" Geung asked.

"His wagging days are over," said Siri. "And he's never going to trust cheese again. But he'll be fine. Just a bit light-headed for a day or so."

CHAPTER TWENTY-ONE
You're on Candid Camera

The next two days flew by in a blur. The police checked every deserted building, every guesthouse. They rechecked the houses of anyone connected to the original Bruce, went through Dr. Porn's basement, even visited the few seedy opium dens that everyone denied existed. Once again, Dom had vanished. Still, Siri remained out of sight at his official government residence by the That Luang monument.

The missing camera belonging to Jim was retrieved from the house of Dr. Porn. Dom had obviously lifted it from the Ferrari before the journalists set off. Once developed, the film showed four very clear photos of Dom and the car and the journalists, taken on the morning of the day they died.

The handheld movie camera and twelve developed films arrived at Phosy's office from Thailand and with Dtui's help, the chief inspector went through every second, constantly pausing and replaying. But after no more than ten minutes it was obvious to both of them what had motivated Dom to act the way he did. That evening, Siri broke cover and cycled to police headquarters.

"Siri, what are you . . . ?" said Phosy.

"Is that what I think it is?" said Siri, nodding at the film projector.

"Why are you here?" asked the policeman.

"I know where he is," said Siri.

Dom was awoken by the rattle of a key in a metal lock. The echo bounced around the building like a disoriented bat. He took out a pistol and an M16 and climbed to the top shelf level of the storage facility. In the shadows of the hampers and heavy equipment he couldn't be seen from the ground. In nine days, this was his first visitor.

Apart from one red Ferrari, Silver City remained virtually untouched since the Marines locked it up in '75. They deposited the keys with the embassy, and, under duress, the embassy handed one of those bunches to the PL. But it was an administration without balls. Nobody dared make decisions. Nobody would commit a signature to an order. So, apart from a visit by the Russian circus performers who were forced to camp in the grounds outside, Silver City had been frozen in time. Officials made brief visits, an inventory was taken, but nobody removed anything. The doors were relocked and the keys deposited with the Women's Union. It was perhaps because those keys still hung in Dr. Porn's office that nobody thought to look there for Dom.

The main warehouse was a treasure trove of household goods, various electrical equipment and enough weaponry to launch a third world war. Dom had wondered why an aid agency would need so much military hardware. He'd made copies of the keys as soon as he realized their significance, and after his escape from the fake surgeon's restaurant he set up his secret command post slap in the middle of the city. From there, his plan had been to follow through on his threats and assassinate the widow first. But he'd let himself down again. He was no marksman even though that modern equipment came with manuals. All he had to do was get the target in his sights and squeeze the trigger. Or so he thought. He could see her in the crosshairs. He wasn't that far away. Yet somehow he'd missed the wife and hit the doctor. Better than nothing, he decided. He saw him go down. He saw them carry the lifeless body into the restaurant. He needed first to be sure Siri was dead, then he'd return and do away with the widow.

But now he had to lose this unwanted visitor at the storage facility. He crawled to a spot where he could see the entrance. Someone was there locking the door from the inside. He was dressed like a farmer. He wore a broad straw hat so he wasn't recognizable from above. He had a two-wheeled market trolley that held a cardboard box. Dom crawled to the edge of the stack where there was an uninterrupted view of the ground. The visitor had moved a small table into the space and placed it beside a large white industrial refrigerator. He opened the box and took out a compact movie projector. As there was only one of its kind in the country, Dom recognized it as the one he'd brought from Australia. The newcomer unreeled a long extension cord and plugged it into a socket on one concrete post. Dom remained silent, unseen but fascinated as the man turned on the projector and pressed a switch that produced a neat rectangle of light on the side of the fridge.

"Dom, I have some good news for you," shouted the man. The voice was familiar but a little distorted in the windowless chamber. Dom was shocked to hear his actual name.

"I should have realized earlier where you'd be," the man continued. "You could probably live here for the rest of your life. Plenty of survival rations to eat. Lots to entertain you. You won't be able to see the picture from up there but the volume's probably loud enough," he said. "Of course you'd know, seeing as it's your equipment, right? Hope you don't mind us borrowing this and the camera. If you do want to watch, feel free to come down. I'm not armed. All you'll see on the screen is a couple of drunks in a bar alcove talking. You should recognize both of them. One of them I think you took a shine to when you met her here. Our pretty blonde. The other's changed a lot since you last saw him but it should be quite obvious who he is."

The intruder pressed play, walked to the wall by the door and sat down on the concrete floor. He took off his hat.

Dom couldn't believe his eyes. The audacity. Dr. Siri— uninjured, unarmed and alone—was no more than thirty meters from him. It was as if the old man was giving him a second shot.

"You're either brave or stupid," said Dom.

"Bit of both really," said Siri. "I didn't tell anyone I was coming. I doubt they'd have let me be here alone if I did. All I ask is that you watch the film before you shoot me. You've got plenty of time. And it'll make things easier the closer to me you are, right? You're not much of a marksman. No offence."

Voices emanated from the projector.

"Better hurry," said Siri. "The show's started."

"What's to stop me from shooting you dead first and watching the tape after?" said Dom.

"Nothing, except then you wouldn't get the punch line, would you? And that's the best part."

Dom came down the ladder on the far side of the stacks and walked cautiously to the table. His gun was trained on Siri the entire time. He squinted at the screen. There were two people: a middle-aged overweight man with thinning hair and a beautiful blonde woman who looked quite drunk. He was holding her hand. The Thai recognized her as Cindy from the US consulate but couldn't place the man.

>"No, Darling, you're a legend round the bars of Ubon," said Cindy. "Everyone knows you. I've heard a lot about how amazing you are. I bet you've got some great stories."
>
>"You sure you aren't with the CIA?" asked the man. "'Cause if you are I'd have to shoot you."
>
>"Do I look like the CIA?" she said.
>
>He laughed and looked into her cleavage.
>
>"You sure don't," he said.

"Recognize the man yet?" Siri asked.

"No."

"Imagine him fifteen years younger and ten kilos lighter."

"I don't . . ."

The truth hit Dom with the force of a stack of crates landing on top of him. He looked up at Siri, who raised his hands to the heavens and shrugged.

"It can't . . ." said Dom. "When was this video taken?"

"Three days ago," said Siri.

"That's not possible," said Dom. "It's just someone who looks like him."

"Stay tuned, viewers," said Siri.

"What have you heard?" said the man on the screen.

"Just some things that can't be true," said the blonde.

"Try me."

They were drinking Thai rum with ice and soda. The man was constantly topping up their glasses.

"They said something about you convincing the US government you were a POW for six years. It would be awesome if it was true."

He smiled and raised his eyebrows.

"No?" she said.

"Almost got away with it too," said the man. "I even wrote a book about my six years in captivity."

"You're kidding me."

"True as I'm sitting here," he said. "I was this close to a hero's welcome and a million-dollar movie deal."

"What happened?"

"Some shitty little Lao doctor is what happened. But I can't tell you any of that. It's kind of classified."

"Oh, come on."

"No, I shouldn't."

She topped up his drink and stirred in a cube of ice.

"Well, you sure know a way to a man's heart," he said. "Okay, I'll tell you. But it can't go any further than this bar, you hear?"

"Cross my heart," she said, making a finger X on one breast.

"All right," he said. "You see, I was quite a well-known anti-war activist in the States. I'd written a book and other stuff. I was invited to run for Congress on a peace ticket, but we had a plan. I was already a decorated pilot."

"You were a pilot? Wow!"

She squeezed his arm. He flexed his muscle.

"I enlisted so I could operate from inside the insidious war machine," he said.

"From minute five to minute eight you'll notice there was a lot of bull dung getting tossed around," said Siri. "It's not easy to separate the fact from the fiction. We only edited out his trips to the bathroom and our girl changing the cartridges. The rest is verbatim. But just bear with it. We make our appearances toward the end."

Dom was stooped over the screen, the gun limp at his side. He didn't react to Siri's comment.

"To cut a long story short, I stole an airplane," said the man. "An F-100. I flew it away from the war zone and landed it in a Communist controlled area. Of course, I disabled it so the enemy wouldn't use it against my brothers. I hiked a week to the border. I'd broken a leg landing it, but I had jungle training. I knew how to lash it and tolerate the pain."

"So where were you for those six years if you weren't in a POW camp?"

"Here," he said. "I shacked up with a Thai whore and her mental son—as a front, mind you. And I continued to fight for our pacifist cause incognito from a village in Ubon. I had to come in to the bars and spend time here, earning the trust of servicemen and journalists and learning their confidential information. I'd pass on this intelligence to the anti-war movement in the States. I knew them all. Jane Fonda was a close friend. She came to visit me here several times. We had

a sort of . . . fling. She was serious but I didn't need all that baggage."

"I'm jealous," said the blonde.

"No need, Honey. I've got plenty of loving to share."

"So you were like a real spy," said the girl.

"I was a master of disguise," he said. "I could change identities overnight. I have a knack for convincing people I'm somebody else."

"Give me an example," she said.

"Well, languages and accents. I can do accents. Australian's one of my best. I remember I took the whore's son to Bangkok and got him on a scholarship to Australia by convincing the embassy he was the top student in my school in Ubon. I didn't have a school but I had all the fake paperwork to say I did. And I had an Australian passport I'd stolen from some drunk here. Even the Aussies thought I was one of them."

"And they accepted the boy to study there?"

"They were desperate for kids from the third world who could speak English to meet their quota and they had a lot of funding for education."

"Did the boy know he was there under false pretenses?"

"He had no idea. I told him the money was from me, but I didn't have to pay a penny. It was all Colombo Plan funding."

"Why send him to Australia and not the US?" said the blonde.

"Why not what? Send him Stateside? You seem like a clever girl. You've probably worked out I'm persona non grata *in America these days after all my agitation. They'd never let me back in without throwing me in jail. But the Aussies have a family reunion visa. The boy goes*

to school, gets residence and I can apply to join him there as his legal guardian. I faked that document too. I can go anytime I like. Just got a little bit tied down here with, you know, business."

"You're a real conman, aren't you?" she said. She was leaning against him. Another shirt button had popped open.

"What went wrong with the POW scam?" she asked.

"It was my last chance to get back into the US legally," he said. "As a hero I could convince them they were wrong about me stealing the plane and operating undercover. I was a week away from getting on that flight. I was having a final medical. I'd spent four months in a sort of up-market prison camp in Hanoi. I figured it was worth the inconvenience. I grew a beard and let my hair sprout wild. I got the shit bitten out of me by insects. I ran into a few walls, collected some grazes and bruises. And I picked at the food they gave us so I'd lose weight. After those four months I looked the part. Could have convinced anyone, I thought. But then this smart-assed little bastard Pathet Lao doctor comes and examines me. He decides I'm not sick enough. Haven't been ravaged enough by diseases.

I mean, shit. All he had to do was sign a release, god damn it. They should have been happy to be rid of me. But, no. This guy wants to do the full Edgar J. Hoover investigation to make himself look good to his Vietnamese bosses. He lied about a bunch of stuff, but they believed him and bumped me from the flight. Tried to get me into CIA hands. But I escaped."

"You remember his name?" she asked.

"I'll never forget it," he said. "Fake Doctor Siri

Paiboun. His name still comes to me in nightmares. But I've fixed him."

"How?"

"I set the mental son on him. I have to tell you there was always something scary about the boy. He was crazy about me to the point that he'd have done anything I told him to. In fact, he was clingy. Deranged, I'd say. I told him me and his whore mother had a disease. Got it into his head that Paiboun was responsible for us dying. She's not dead either, the mother. She's still putting it out there for old geezers. I see her slumming around the bars some nights. The boy was easy enough to stir up. I arranged for his scholarship to be cancelled, blamed Fake Dr. Siri for that too. So I knew he'd be pissed, knew he'd find a way to get revenge on behalf of his dead mother and dear old Uncle Henry. He promised me in the last letter I got from him. That's when I 'died' and left him in vengeance limbo. The guilt would have been too much for him not to go through with it."

"Ah, I hear my name," said Siri. "You must have got to the meat in the sandwich. We're not far from the end."

Dom's weapon was on the ground beside him. He was leaning with both fists on the refrigerator, blocking half the picture. The bar conversation continued.

"So, what have you been living on all these years?" the woman asked.

"I'm surprised you haven't heard," he said. "I run a very profitable import-export company here in Ubon. Made quite a fortune off of it. Of course, I'm still very active in the international peace movement."

"There really is no end to you, is there?" said the blonde.

"Look, this is a bit embarrassing," he said. "I've left my wallet in the Benz. Could you get this and we'll go somewhere quieter."

"Sure," she said.

"You're staying at the hotel, right?" he asked.

"Yeah."

"What say we get another bottle and burn off some calories over there?"

"Sounds peachy," she said. "But, hey. Do you mind if we take those two guys sitting at the end of the bar?"

She nodded in that direction. The man followed her gaze.

"What?" he asked.

"Yeah, we kind of came together," she said.

Two Western men in casual clothes appeared in the picture, grabbed Henry by the arms and stood him up. Their heads were all out of the frame now.

"What are you doing?" said the man.

"First I'll retrieve my camera from my overnight bag and make sure it's working."

The woman approached the camera. The picture went dark briefly then returned. She was holding the camera now and pointing it to another table where two Thai men sat drinking beer. They made V signs.

"If they could speak English," she said, "those two plainclothes Thai police gentlemen would probably say, 'You're under arrest.'"

"On what charge?"

"Where should we start?" she smiled. "You've just confessed to a dozen illegal things you really did, and

another dozen that you probably didn't do. We've traced
several postal scams back to you already. But we can start
off with immigration violations and work our way up to
inciting murder. That should keep us busy."

Siri got to his feet and stretched his stiff old back.

"Good show, eh?" he said. "I'll leave it up to you to sort
the mushrooms from the toadstools in that salad, but I
think you've got the gist of it. He had no connections to
the peace movement. That was a story he perfected
to explain why he'd been there for so long. But even if
every word he spoke was a lie, you can surely see how you
and your mother fit into his world of fantasy. And perhaps
he really believed all the garbage he said. Dementia works
in odd ways. He was never a successful businessman. He
taught English—made just enough for his next drink. It
seems his world pretty much existed in the postal service.
In his apartment they found begging letters and applica-
tions and scams. They found some letters to you he hadn't
sent. They all asked for help with money."

"This is all a setup," said Dom. "You put this all together
to mess with my mind."

He reached down for the gun.

"Don't do it," came a voice, and the building echoed
with the sounds of gun hammers cocking behind him.
While Siri had kept Dom engaged, Phosy and a few select
officers had entered through the rear door and taken up
positions.

Dom laughed.

"I had you in my sights, you know?" he said.

"I know," said Siri. "But secondhand revenge is rarely
effective. You were carrying someone else's vengeance.

Those few seconds it took to step into your stepfather's shoes were enough to throw off your timing."

"I don't believe that was Henry on the film," said Dom.

"Yes, we thought that would be the case," said Phosy. "That's why we've arranged for a family reunion."

"With Henry?" said Dom.

"You're under arrest in Laos which probably won't be a lot of fun for you," said Phosy. "Our prisons aren't the most hospitable. So we've arranged a happy moment for you to take to jail with you."

"Our American colleagues were delighted to hear of Henry's whereabouts. He's been on their wanted list for a long time. Our friend Cindy was only too pleased to join our sting operation. They've transported your daddy to the US consulate here before flying him down to his own oblivion via the embassy in Bangkok," said Siri. "His dream of being repatriated will come true, but I think he'll be admiring the land of the free through barred windows for a very long time."

EPILOGUE ONE

"Hey, Say," said Monh, "not putting on your stockings tonight?"

Say and Monh and two other Lao were in a corrugated tin hut in Bangkok. They'd worked on the site till it was dark. Then they ate instant noodles and went to bed, too exhausted to listen to the radio or look at pictures in magazines. That's the way it was seven days a week, and, for Say with his nightmares, it had been hell. He'd nearly died in an accident a few weeks before. He'd been so exhausted he almost fell from the thirty-fifth floor of the unfinished building. Monh had grabbed him at the last second. It was because of this that his relatives at the camp had sent him the charm. It was ancient, that much was obvious. It was yellowing with age. His mother told him it had belonged to a great shaman. It hung on a simple string and weighed no more than a bubble but it contained great magic.

He'd worn it the day it arrived, and for the first time in a year he didn't see her in his dream—the succubus. She didn't taunt him. Didn't attempt to seduce him. The next night he left off the nightdress but wore the stockings. He dreamed about fields and chickens and friends from the old days. She was afraid of the charm. He knew it. And tonight he'd be leaving off the stockings, and his room-mates wouldn't mock him again.

Because Say had the power.

EPILOGUE TWO

"It's quite mundane, isn't it?" asked Daeng.

"What is?" asked Siri.

"Life without an assassin breathing down your neck."

They were on the veranda at the French embassy enjoying one of Civilai's leftover bottles of Merlot. Seksan, the not-French ambassador, was in the kitchen frying up another batch of crêpes. The moon was just an unconvincing smile in a tar sky. Ugly had reverted to form and remained on the pavement beyond the barbed wire–garnished wall. Like Daeng, he continued to wag a tail that only he could see.

"How did they get along?" she asked. "Fraudulent father and homicidal son?"

"Phosy said they were together for five minutes before the boy attempted to garrote Henry with his belt."

"Families. What can you say?"

They looked at the inflatable Fred Flintstone punching bag that sat at the head of the table. He hadn't touched his drink.

"Still not talking to us, Civilai?" said Daeng.

"He'll get over it," said Siri. "I haven't spoken to him

about the whole murder thing yet, but I imagine he'll be more angry at being a victim of a lie than at being dead."

"It's another one of your biggest nothings, isn't it?" asked Daeng. "America believing their war was justified. Laos believing we have something to boast about. And this, a young man fooled by a pack of lies."

"People are basically stupid," said Siri. "We're easy to dupe. Nobody asks for proof anymore. A lie told with confidence is indistinguishable from the truth."

The scent of sweet crepes frying reached their nostrils.

"Any other news from police HQ?" Daeng asked.

"No sign of Dr. Porn's body," said Siri.

"I'm glad she wasn't involved in all this," said Daeng.

"She kept quiet about her past but now that the files have been released it appears she was in the same business as you."

"Noodles?"

"Subterfuge, deception, insurgency, revolution, counterintelligence, spying."

"It's good for a country girl to have interests other than sewing," said Daeng.

A strong breeze cut through the embassy garden and Fred Flintstone rocked back and forth.

"See?" said Siri. "Civilai always did appreciate a good joke."

And as the evening wore on and the warm air currents mingled in the embassy grounds, Civilai danced with his trademark lack of coordination, and Siri smiled in his direction, and they told stories about the old fellow that would have been farfetched . . . were they about anyone else

FIC   Tyler, Anne
TYL   The clock winder

DATE DUE

OCT 27 1987	JAN 1 8 1994	JAN 0 3 1997
JAN 1 1 1988	FEB 1 92	NOV 0 4 1998
JAN 2 7 1988	FEB 7 92	
FEB 2 1 1991	OCT 13 93	
FEB 2 7 1991	SEP 30	
MAR 2 1 1991	APR 19 '95	
	SEP 29 '95	
APR 1 1991	JAN 24	
MAY 2 9 1991	MAR 2 8 1996	
JUL 2 2 1991	JUN 2 1 1996	
AUG 2 6 1991	SEP 2 7 1996	

1050

HAS CATALOG CARDS

DEMCO

Also by Anne Tyler

A Slipping-Down Life (1970)
The Tin Can Tree (1965)
If Morning Ever Comes (1964)

These are Borzoi Books,
published in New York
by Alfred A. Knopf

The Clock Winder

THE CLOCK WINDER

by *Anne Tyler*

Alfred A. Knopf

NEW YORK   1972

THIS IS A BORZOI BOOK
PUBLISHED BY ALFRED A. KNOPF, INC.

Copyright © 1972 by Anne Tyler Modarressi.

All rights reserved under International and Pan-American Copyright Conventions. Published in the United States by Alfred A. Knopf, Inc., New York. Distributed by Random House, Inc., New York.

Library of Congress Cataloging in Publication Data
Tyler, Anne. The clock winder.
I. Title.
PZ4.T979Cl ₍PS3570.Y45₎ 813'.5'4 70-178966
ISBN *-394-47898-3

Manufactured in the United States of America

First Edition

The Clock Winder

◙ 1 ◙

1960

The house had outlived its usefulness. It sat hooded and silent, a brown shingleboard monstrosity close to the road but backed by woods, far enough from downtown Baltimore to escape the ashy smell of the factories. The uppermost windows were shuttered; the wrap-around veranda, with its shiny gray floorboards and sky-blue ceiling, remained empty even when neighbors' porches filled up with children and dogs and drop-in visitors. Yet clearly someone still lived there. A pile of raked leaves sat by the walk. A loaded bird-feeder hung in the dogwood tree. And in the side yard, Richard the handyman stood peeing against a rosebush with his profile to the house and his long black face dreamy and distant.

Now out popped Mrs. Emerson, skin and bones in a shimmery gray dress that matched the floorboards. Her face was carefully made up, although it was not yet ten in the morning. Whatever she planned to say was already stirring her pink, pursed lips. She crossed the veranda rapidly on click-

3

ing heels. She descended the steps gingerly, sideways, holding tight to the railing. "Richard?" she said. "What is that I see you doing?"

"Just cutting back the roses is all," Richard said. His back was turned to her. He waved a pair of pruning shears behind him, hip-high.

"I meant what you're doing at this *moment*, Richard."

"Oh, why, nothing," Richard said.

It was true. He was zipped up by now, free to turn and beam and click his shears on thin air. Mrs. Emerson stopped in front of him and folded her arms.

"Don't try to get around *me*, Richard. I looked out my window and saw you. I thought, *Richard?* Is that Richard?"

"I was preparing to cut back the roses," Richard said.

"Is that what you call it?"

Richard had a special set of gestures he made when embarrassed—pivoting on his heels with his head hanging down, working something over in his hands. He twisted the rubber grips on his shears and said, "It's getting time, now. Fall is coming on."

"That house you are standing by is Mrs. Walter Bell's," said Mrs. Emerson. "In full clear view of her dining room window. Don't think that I won't hear about this."

"*I* wasn't doing nothing, Mrs. Emerson."

"Oh, hush."

"I was only cutting back the roses."

"Just hush. I don't know, I really don't know," said Mrs. Emerson.

"You're just distraught nowadays, that's all."

"Distraught? Why would I be distraught?" said Mrs. Emerson. "Oh, give me those shears, hand them over. You're fired."

Richard stopped twisting the shears. He looked up at her

with his mouth open, his face jutting forward as if he had trouble seeing her. "Ah, now," he said.

"I'll cut back my own damn roses."

"Now Mrs. Emerson, you know you don't mean that. You'd never just *fire* me. Why, I been working here twenty-five years, not counting the war. Planted them roses myself, watered them daily. Do I have to tell you that?"

"I don't know what kind of watering you're talking about," said Mrs. Emerson, "but you're leaving anyway. Don't expect wages, either. It's only Monday, and you were paid Friday. You've been here not half an hour yet and most of that time ill-spent. Oh, I looked out that window and thought I was seeing things. I thought, What have we come to, after all? What's it going to be next? First Emmeline, letting my transistor radio run down, and then no sooner do I let *her* go than *you* start in. Well, you can send your new employers to me for a reference but don't expect me to cover up for you. 'Works well,' I'll say, 'but tinkles on the flowers.' Maybe *some* won't mind."

"Couldn't you just take a little longer over this?" Richard asked.

Mrs. Emerson raised her chin and looked past him, twiddling with the empty sleeves of her sweater. She said, "Longer? Why should I take longer? I've made up my mind."

"But if you gave it your thought, some. Who could you find that would work as good as me?"

"Whole multitudes," said Mrs. Emerson, "but I won't be looking. I'm too disappointed. Everywhere I turn there is someone failing me. Well, that's the end of that. From now on I'll do it all myself."

"Paint the shutters? Keep that creaky old plumbing fixed? Climb up to clean the gutters in them little spiky shoes?"

Mrs. Emerson had already turned to go. She paused, lifting one hand to test a curl. It was a sign of uncertainty and Richard knew it, but then he had to go and ruin it for himself. "You'll be calling me back, Mrs. E.," he said. "*You'll* call."

"Never," said Mrs. Emerson.

Then she went off on tiptoe, to keep from sinking into the lawn.

She kept a pack of playing cards on the dining room table. She sat down on the edge of a chair, smoothing her skirt beneath her, and reached for the cards and began laying out a game of solitaire with sharp little snaps. Her breathing was too rapid. She made a point of slowing it, sitting erect, aligning the cards carefully before she started playing. But unfinished questions kept running through her head. Should she have—? How could he—? Why had she—?

The sun from the bay window fuzzed the edges of the sweater draping her shoulders, lit the flecks of powder across· the bridge of her nose. She had once been very pretty. She still was, but now that her children were grown there was something brave about the prettiness. She had started having to work for it. She had to fight the urge to spend her days in comfortable shoes and forget her chin-strap and let herself go. Mornings, patting a pearly base coat over her cheekbones, she noticed how she seemed to be falling into separate pieces. Her face was a series of pouches tenuously joined by transparent skin, reminding her of the tissue-covered frames of model airplanes that her sons used to make. Her close-set blue eyes were divided by minute cracks. Her mouth had bunched in upon itself so that she permanently wore the sulky look she had once had as a child. All she had left was color—pink, white, blond, most of it false. Weekly she went to the hair-

dresser and returned newly gilded, with her scalp feeling tight as if it were drawing away from her face. She dressed up for everything, even breakfast. She owned no slacks. Her thin, sharp legs were always in ultra-sheer stockings, and her closet was full of those spike-heeled shoes that made her arches ache. But when her children visited and she stood at the door to meet them, wearing pastels, holding out smooth white hands with polished nails, she had seen how relieved they looked. Relieved and a little disappointed: she had survived their desertion, she had not become a broken old lady after all.

She put the red seven on the black eight. Now the six could go up. She looked across the table, out the bay window, and saw Richard standing exactly where she had left him. His shoulders were slumped. The pruning shears were dangling from one hand. Would still more be expected of her? But as she watched he dropped the shears and started off toward the toolshed behind the house. She would have to put the shears away herself, then. She had no idea where they went.

She turned an ace up. Then another. Along came Richard, carrying an old suit jacket, a brown paper bag, a thermos bottle. He was plodding, that was the only word for it. Thinking she was watching. Well, she wasn't. She snapped the last card down, checked for possibilities one more time, and then hitched her bracelets back and gathered the cards into a deck again. When she next looked out the window, Richard was gone.

This house was full of clocks, one to a room—eight-day pendulum clocks that struck the hour and half-hour. Their striking was beautifully synchronized, but the winding was not. Some were due to be wound one day, some another. Only her husband had understood the system. (If there *was* a

system.) When he died, three months ago, she considered letting all the clocks run down and then restarting them simul-
taneously, so that she could stop puzzling over which day to
wind which one. But the symbolism involved—the tick, pause,
tock, the pause and final tick of the grandfather clock in the
hall, the first to go—made her so nervous that she abandoned
the plan. Anyone else would have just wound them all tightly
on a given day, and carried on from there. Mrs. Emerson
didn't. (Wasn't there something about overtight mainsprings?
Wouldn't her husband have done that years ago, otherwise?
Oh, what was in his mind? What was the meaning of these
endless rooms of clocks, efficiently going about their business
while she twisted her hands in front of them?) Evenings she
wandered through the house bewildered, opening the little
glass or wooden doors and reaching for the keys and then
pausing, her fingertips to her lips, her eyes round and vague
as she counted back over the days of the week. She was not a
stupid woman, but she was used to being taken care of. She
had passed almost without a jolt from the hands of her father
to the hands of her husband, an unnoticeable sort of man who
since his death had begun to seem much wiser and more
mysterious. He knew answers to questions she had never
thought of asking, and had kept them to himself. He had
wound the clocks absentmindedly, on his way to other places;
he had synchronized their striking apparently without effort,
without even mentioning it to her—but how? The grandfather clock in the hall was now a quarter-minute ahead of
the others, and that was as close as she could get it after half
a morning spent irritably shoving the hands back and forth,
waiting for the whir of the little hammer as it prepared to
strike.

It struck now. Then after a pause the others began: ten
o'clock. And here she was with nothing to do, no one to talk to,

alone in a sealed house with the last of her supports sent away. She rose from the table, touching a hand to her hair, and went to the front hall. On the bureau was a vase of marigolds which she spent minutes rearranging, changing nothing. She smoothed the linen runner beneath the vase. Then she opened the front door, intending to stir the dim, dust-flecked air. She was about to close it again when she caught sight of the outdoor furniture, which spilled in an uneven line down the veranda and on around the corner of the house. It would stay there year-round; it always had. No wonder this house was so depressing. She remembered how dismal the wicker loveseats looked in winter, the seams of their soggy cushions harboring wisps of snow; how the aluminum chairs dripped icicles and the rattan ones darkened and split and overturned in the wind. The picture came to her like an answer: everything would change for the better, if she moved the furniture before fall set in.

She rushed out with her skirt swirling around her, picked up the round metal tea-table and clicked down the front steps with it. Then around to the back yard—more forest than yard, slanting downward as steeply as a mountainside all the way to the garage, which was out of view. She passed two empty trellises, a toolshed, a rotting gazebo, a stone bench, countless frayed, cut-off, cruel-looking ropes her children had once climbed and swung by. Spongy moss gave way beneath her heels, and brambles snagged her stockings. Birds started up from bushes as if she had no right to come this way. When she reached the garage she found that the side door was stuck. She gave it a kick with the pointed toe of her shoe. Then she heaved the table inside and started back up the hill. Already she was out of breath.

Next came a loveseat, bulky and awkward. She flung the sleeves of her sweater behind her and bent to tug at one

wicker arm, but the legs kept catching on the floorboards. When she had pulled it to the steps she stopped to rest. Then someone on the street said, "Need a hand?"

She turned. A tall girl in dungarees was watching her. "I could take the other end," she was saying.

"Oh, *would* you?" said Mrs. Emerson.

She stepped to the side, and the girl moved past her to scoop up one end of the loveseat. "It's not heavy but it's *clumsy*," Mrs. Emerson told her. The girl nodded, and followed her down around the house with the base of the loveseat resting easily in her hands. She certainly didn't believe in wasting words. Every time Mrs. Emerson looked back at her to smile apologetically (she really should have warned her about the distance they had to cover), all she saw was the top of a bent head—dark yellow hair hanging straight to her shoulders, a style Mrs. Emerson considered drab. The girl didn't comment on the steepness, or the brambles, or the fact that it seemed ludicrous to cart furniture through an apparently endless forest. When they reached the garage she disappeared inside, righted the tea-table, and reached out for the loveseat. "Any more going in?" she asked.

"Yes," Mrs. Emerson said.

"Well, then," said the girl, and she moved the two pieces of furniture down to the far end, opposite the car, making more space. Mrs. Emerson waited outside with her arms folded. She could use this breathing spell. Now, should she offer a tip? But that might be an insult. And there was always the question of how *much* to offer. Oh, where was her husband, with his desk-size checkbook and his bills on a spindle and his wallet that unfolded so smartly whenever she was sad, offering her money for a new outfit or a trip to Washington?

The girl emerged from the garage, wiping her hands on the seat of her dungarees. "I certainly do appreciate this,"

Mrs. Emerson told her. "I hope I haven't held you up too much."

"Didn't you say there was more?"

"Oh, yes, all that's left on the veranda."

"I'll stay and help you finish, then."

"Well, goodness," said Mrs. Emerson. She was glad of the help, but she wondered what kind of person would let herself get so sidetracked. Weren't there any fixed destinations in her life? As they climbed back up the slope she kept glancing sideways at the girl's face, which was pretty enough but Mrs. Emerson thought it would take a good eye like her own to notice. Not a trace of make-up. What a nice bright lipstick could have done! She wore brown moccasins, shapeless and soft-soled. Ruining her arches. Her white shirt was painstakingly ironed, the creases knife-sharp across the shoulders and down the sleeves. A mother's work, for certain —some poor mother wondering right this minute where her daughter had got to. But she hadn't the strength of character to send her on her way. The girl looked so capable, hoisting up two chairs at once when they reached the veranda and swinging through the side yard with them. "Any time you get tired, now," said Mrs. Emerson, compromising, "or have to be somewhere, or meet someone—" The girl was already too far down the path to hear her.

When they were climbing the slope again Mrs. Emerson said, "I *used* to have a handyman. Did until this morning. He would have made short work of this. Then I caught him mistaking the nearest rosebush for the men's room." The girl laughed—a single, low note that made Mrs. Emerson look up at her, startled. "Well, I fired him," she said. "I can't have *that*."

The girl said nothing. They rounded the house, climbed the front steps side by side. There seemed to be more furniture

now than before; they hadn't made a dent in it. "Where did they all *come* from?" Mrs. Emerson said, poking a chair with her foot. "I can't remember ever buying any of this."

"Outdoor furniture is capable of reproducing," said the girl. Which made Mrs. Emerson pause for a moment before she went on with her own train of thought.

"Our family was once so big, you know," she said. "Seven children, all grown now. One married. And a grandchild. When they were still home these chairs got filled soon enough, believe me. Children and friends and boyfriends and neighbors, all just having a grand time." She was staring vaguely at a wooden rocker, although the girl was already halfway down the steps with her own load. "Ask anyone in these parts, they all know my children," she said. " 'It's the Emersons,' they'd tell each other, when we'd go sailing past in the car with everybody sitting in everybody's lap. I am Pamela Emerson, by the way."

"I'm Elizabeth Abbott," said the girl.

She had stopped on the grass. She waited while Mrs. Emerson dragged the rocker down the steps. Mrs. Emerson said, "Abbott? It's funny, I can't remember seeing you here before."

"I haven't *been* here. I come from North Carolina."

"Oh, I have cousins in North Carolina," said Mrs. Emerson. "Not to know personally, of course. Are you just visiting?"

"I'm going to see these people about a job."

"A job. Goodness," Mrs. Emerson said, "and here you are moving furniture. Do you usually go at things in such a roundabout way?"

Elizabeth smiled. The whole of her face smiled. "Always," she said.

"I just hope you won't arrive late, that's why I asked. The last thing I'd do is interfere but *I* have daughters, work-

ing daughters, and I can't help telling you: first impressions are all-important. Promptness. Neatness."

She was looking at Elizabeth's shirt-tails, but Elizabeth didn't notice; she had moved off now with her chairs. "They don't know to expect me, anyway," she called back. "I saw their ad on a bulletin board in a thrift shop. I like getting jobs from bulletin boards. What they want is a mother's helper, and I need to find out if that means housework or babysitting. Babysitting wouldn't be good at all. I don't like children."

"Is that right?" Mrs. Emerson said. She was trying to remember if she had ever heard anyone else admit to such a thing. She puffed along with the rocker, taking short rapid steps to keep up. "Now, I would have thought you were still in school."

"I am. I'm earning money for my senior year at college."

"In September?"

"I'm taking a year off."

"Oh, that's terrible!" said Mrs. Emerson. They had reached the garage by now. She set down the rocker to stare at Elizabeth, who seemed undisturbed. "Interrupting like that! It's terrible. Why, one thing may lead to another and you may never get back. I've known that to happen."

"It's true," Elizabeth agreed.

"Couldn't you get a scholarship? Or a loan?"

"Oh, my grades were rotten," she said cheerfully.

"Still, though. It's no good to have to stop something in the middle. What does your father do, dear?"

"He's a minister."

"Nothing wrong with *that*. Although a lot depends on the denomination. What denomination is he?"

"Baptist."

"Oh."

"If this job is babysitting," Elizabeth said, "I'll just have

to find me another bulletin board. But the friend that dropped me here said Roland Park was the likeliest neighborhood."

She stacked her chairs inside the garage and reached for the rocker. Mrs. Emerson said, "Do you know the people's name? The ones you're going to see?"

"O'Donnell."

"O'Donnell. Well, I've never heard of *them* before. If it's people I don't know they're generally young. New young people buying up these old houses for a song and moving in with children. But *children* aren't so bad. What is it you have against them?"

"I don't like people you can have so much effect on," Elizabeth said.

"What? Goodness," said Mrs. Emerson.

They climbed back up the hill. It seemed to have grown steeper. Mrs. Emerson's palms were sore, and two fingernails had broken, and her stockings were in shreds. "If only my boys were home," she said. "If only I'd thought of this some-time when they were visiting. They'd have been glad to help. But I just never did, and then I asked myself, Why wait until they come? Why not do it myself, while the weather's still warm and the sun so nice?"

She paused to catch her breath, one hand clamped to the small of her back. Elizabeth stopped too. "Would you like me to finish up for you?" she asked.

"No, no, I wouldn't hear of it."

"It'll only take a minute."

"I'm all right."

They gathered up the next load and started back down. Mrs. Emerson's heels kept slipping on dead leaves. This was all Richard's fault. He couldn't even rake properly. Slick brown leaves were scattered here and there, with moss or smooth earth beneath them instead of the grass he should have

been growing. The chair she carried was knocking against her knees. Mean little tangled bramble bushes kept snatching her sweater off her shoulders. What would her husband say, if he could look down now and see how her life was turning out? She sighed raggedly, hitched the chair higher, wiped her forehead on her upper arm.

Then when they were just descending the steps to the garage, Mrs. Emerson caught her heel and fell. She landed on top of the overturned chair, scraping both knees and the palm of one hand. "Oops, there!" she said, and gave a little tinkling laugh. Tears were stinging her eyelids. She reached for Elizabeth's hand and struggled to her feet. "Oh, how ridiculous," she said.

"Are you all right?"

"Of course I am." She jerked her hand away and began brushing her skirt. "I just caught my heel," she said.

"Maybe you should rest a while."

"No, I'm fine. Really."

She lifted the chair again and one of its legs fell off—a white metal tube, rust specks seeping through a sloppy paint job. It clattered down the rest of the steps. She felt the tears pressing harder. "It's broken," she said. "Isn't that ridiculous? It's just not my day. And Richard gone, too." She fixed her eyes on the chair leg, which Elizabeth had picked up and was examining. "If I had fired him *tomorrow*, now. Stayed in bed where I should have and kept my head under the covers and fired him tomorrow instead. Some days just anything I do is certain to bring ruin."

"It can easily be mended," Elizabeth said.

"What? Oh."

"The screw must be somewhere around. I can fix it."

"Yes, but—*why* did I fire him? What got into me?"

"You said—" Elizabeth began.

"Oh, that. He's been tinkling on the roses for twenty-five years, not counting the war. Everybody knows that. It was just his flaw, something we avoided mentioning. Well, I *would* have, but I was uncertain how to bring it up, you see. What phraseology to use."

"Now, was there a washer to this, I wonder?" Elizabeth said. "Or just the screw."

"I certainly never meant to *fire* him for it!" said Mrs. Emerson. "I didn't even know I was going to."

She dropped to the steps, pulling a flowered handkerchief from her belt with shaky hands. By now the tears had spilled over, but she smiled steadily and kept a tight rein on her voice. "Well, I'm being very silly," she said.

"Could you move your feet a minute?" said Elizabeth. She was patting the ground in search of the screw. Her face was turned slightly away; possibly she had not even noticed the tears. Mrs. Emerson straightened her back and blew her nose, silently. "*All* help is difficult, I suppose," she said.

Elizabeth's hands were square and brown, badly cared for, the nails chopped-looking and the knuckles scraped. But their competence, as they located the screw and fitted it into the chair, was comforting to watch. Mrs. Emerson blinked to clear her blurred eyes. "Emmeline was another one," she said. "The maid. Now I'm having to make do with a girl from State Employment, a shiftless sort that chews tobacco. Half the time I can't even count on her to come. And the house! I'm ashamed to look at it too closely. Oh, it seems I've just been left all alone suddenly. No one stayed with me." She laughed. "I must be hard to get along with," she said.

Elizabeth had pulled a red pocketknife from her dungarees. She opened out a screwdriver blade and began tightening the screw. "My," said Mrs. Emerson, making an effort to

lighten her voice. "Is that the kind with all the different blades? Corkscrew? Can opener?"

Elizabeth nodded. "It's Swiss," she said.

"Oh, a Swiss Army knife!" Mrs. Emerson blew her nose once more and then folded the handkerchief and blotted her eyes. "Matthew wanted one of those for Christmas once," she said. "My oldest son. He asked for one."

"They come in handy," said Elizabeth.

"I'm sure they do."

But she had given him, instead, a violin and a record player and a complete set of Beethoven's symphonies. Remembering that made her start crying all over again. "I'm sorry about this," she said, although Elizabeth still had not looked up at her. "It must be bereavement. The aftermath of bereavement. I just lost my husband three months ago. At first, you know, things are very busy and there are always people calling. It's only later you notice what's happened. After the people have left again."

She watched the pocketknife being folded, the chair being set in the garage. "Goodness, *that* didn't take long," she said.

Elizabeth returned, dusting off her hands. "I'm sorry about your husband," she told Mrs. Emerson.

"Oh, well. Thank you."

Mrs. Emerson rose from the steps. All her joints ached, and her knees felt tight and stiff where they had been scraped. They started together up the hill. "My friends say it's often this way," she told Elizabeth. "The delayed reaction, I mean. But I never expected it *now*, three months after. I thought I had felt bad enough at the time. Sometimes this terrible idea comes to my mind. I think, if he was going to die, then couldn't he have done it earlier? Before I was all used up and

worn out? I could have started some sort of new life, back then. I would have had some hope. Well, *that's* a stupid thing to say."

"Oh, I don't know," Elizabeth said.

It was this girl's silence that made Mrs. Emerson rattle on so. Mrs. Emerson had a compulsion to fill all silences. In an hour she would be wincing over what she had spilled out to a stranger, but now, flushed with the feeling of finally having someone stay still and listen, she said, "And I *can't* go for comfort to my children. They're not that kind, not at all. Oh, I always try to look on the bright side, especially when I'm talking to people. That makes me tend to exaggerate a little. But I never fool *myself*: I know I'd have to attend my own funeral before I see them lined up on this veranda again talking the way they used to. They are always moving away from me; I feel like the center of an asterisk. They *work* at moving away. If I waited for my sons to come carry this furniture it would rot first, they never come. They find me difficult." She climbed the front steps and turned to flash a very bright smile at Elizabeth, who was looking at her blankly. "Those auto rides," she said, "with all of us crammed inside. 'There go the Emersons,' people would say, and never guess for an instant that behind the glass it was all bickering, arguing, scenes, constant crisis—"

"Oh, well," Elizabeth said comfortably, "I reckon *most* families work that way."

Mrs. Emerson paused; her thoughts snagged for a second. Then she said, "They *live* on crisis. It's the only time they're happy. No, they're never happy. They lead such complicated lives I can't keep up with them any more. All I've seen of my grandchild is one minute little black-and-white photo of a bunch of total strangers, one of them holding the baby. A lady I'd never seen before. Elderly. The last time we were all

together was by necessity, for the funeral—and they left the baby with his other grandmother. Two of my boys live right in this area, but do I see them? Well, Matthew, when he can get away. Timothy never. The only one just dying to come is Andrew, and him I'm supposed to discourage because he's a little bit unbalanced. He's not supposed to leave his psychiatrist. He's not supposed to come home and expose himself to upset. It's unhealthy of him to want to."

"It sounds," Elizabeth said unexpectedly, "as if he's in somebody's *clutches.*"

For a moment Mrs. Emerson, who had already opened her mouth to begin a new sentence, had trouble following her. She looked up, startled, at Elizabeth's earnest, scowling face. Then she laughed. "Oh, my," she said, and reached for her handkerchief. "Oh, my, well . . ."

Elizabeth straightened up from the railing she had been leaning against. "Anyway," she said, "I'll just take this last load of furniture down."

"Oh, will this be the last?" Mrs. Emerson said. She had suddenly stopped laughing.

"There's only these two."

"Wait, don't hurry. Wouldn't you like to rest a minute? Have some milk and cookies? You said you hadn't made an appointment. You could finish up any time."

"I just did have breakfast," Elizabeth said.

"Please. Just a glass of milk?"

"Well, all right."

Mrs. Emerson led her into the house, through the ticking hallway toward the kitchen at the rear. "My, it's so *dark* in here," she said, although she was used to the darkness herself. As she passed various pieces of furniture—the grandfather clock, a ladderback chair, the chintz-covered armchair in the kitchen, all of them scuffed and worn down around the edges

from a lifetime with children—she reached out to give them little pats, as if protecting them from a stranger's eyes. But Elizabeth didn't even glance at them. She seemed totally unobservant. She pulled an enameled stepstool toward the table and sat down on it, doubling her knees so as to set her feet on the top step. "I just don't want to hit the O'Donnells at lunch," she said.

"No, no, you have plenty of time," said Mrs. Emerson. She poured out a tall glass of milk. Elizabeth said, "Aren't you having any?"

"Oh. I suppose so."

Ordinarily she never touched milk. She only kept it for cooking. When she settled herself at the table and took the first sip she had the sudden sense of being back in her mother's house, where she used to have milk and cookies to ease all minor tragedies. The taste of milk after tears, washing away the gluey feeling in the back of her throat, was the same then as now; she stared dreamily at a kitchen cabinet, keeping the taste in her memory a long time before taking another sip. Then she set the glass down and said, "I hope you don't think I'm one of those people that gives notice all the time."

"Notice?"

"Firing people."

"Why should I think that?" Elizabeth said.

"Well, all this talk about Richard. And then Emmeline. But those two have been with me half a lifetime; it's only lately that all this unpleasantness came up. They took advantage, knowing the state I was in. Oh, I don't blame them entirely, I know I haven't been myself. But how could they expect me to be? Ordinarily I'm a marvelous employer, people can't do enough for me. You can tell by their name that family will have too many children."

"Um—"

"The O'Donnells. Babies and toddlers and little ones in diapers, I'm just sure of it. I believe I know them. Don't I?"

"I thought—"

"They'll run you off your feet over there."

Elizabeth finished her milk and set her empty glass down. She wiped the back of her hand across her mouth. "I think you must be offering me a job," she said.

"A job," said Mrs. Emerson. She sat straighter and placed her palms together. "That is something to consider."

"Are you asking if I'd like to work for you?"

"Well, would you?" Mrs. Emerson said.

"Sure. I'd make a better handyman than babysitter, any day."

"Handyman!" said Mrs. Emerson. "No, I meant housework. Taking over for Emmeline."

"Why not handyman? It's what you need most. You already have a maid, you said."

"But *gardening*. Painting. Climbing ladders."

"I can do that."

"Well, I never heard of such a thing."

"Why? What's so strange about it?" Elizabeth said. She had a habit of rarely bothering to look at people, Mrs. Emerson noticed. She concentrated on objects—pulling threads from a seam of her dungarees or untangling the toaster cord or examining the loose knob on the peppermill, so that when she did look up there was something startling, almost a flash, in the gray of her eyes. "You wouldn't have to pay me much," she said, looking straight at Mrs. Emerson. "If you let me live in I could get by on next to nothing."

"It's true, it scares me just to think of looking for another colored man," said Mrs. Emerson. "Nowadays you can't tell *what* to expect."

"Well, I don't know anything about that."

"But carrying firewood! Digging compost!"

Elizabeth waited, looking perfectly comfortable, picking leaves off the soles of her moccasins.

"I do get nervous at night," said Mrs. Emerson. "Not that I am *frightened* or anything. But having someone down the hall, just another human being in case of—"

She fell silent and raised a hand to her forehead. This world expected too many decisions of her. The girl's good points were obvious (calmness and silence, and the neat twist of her hands mending the chair) but there were bad points, too (no *vivacity*, that was it, and this tendency to drift into whatever offered itself). She sighed. "Oh well," she said. "It can't hurt to try you out, I suppose."

"Done," said Elizabeth, and reached a hand across the table. Mrs. Emerson was slow to realize that she was supposed to shake it.

"Now, I was paying Richard fifty a week," she said. "But he wasn't living in. Is forty all right?"

"Oh, sure," said Elizabeth, cheerfully. "Anything." How would she earn her way through college, talking like that? Then she stood and took her glass to the sink. She said, "I guess I'll get the last of those chairs taken care of."

"Fine," said Mrs. Emerson. She stayed where she was. That was her privilege, now that she was paying. She listened to the front door slamming, the chair legs scraping across the veranda. Then she heard Elizabeth crashing through the woods. She thought of living in the same house with her— such a lanky, awkward, flat-chested girl—and she raised her eyes to the ceiling and asked her husband what she had let herself in for.

2

"It's simple," said Elizabeth. "That stump is the chopping block. There's the axe. And there sits the turkey, wondering when you'll start. What else could you want?"

"If it's all that simple why ask *me* to do it?" the boy said. He was standing beside her in the toolshed doorway, looking at the turkey in its crate. The turkey paced three steps to one side, three steps to the other, stopping occasionally to peer at them through the slats.

"Look at him, he wants to get it over with," Elizabeth said.

"Couldn't we call in a butcher?"

The boy was a college senior named Benny Simms— pleasant-faced, beanpole-thin, with a crewcut. He lived two houses down, although his mother was beginning to question that. "He lives at *your* place," she told Mrs. Emerson on the phone. "Every weekend home he's out visiting your handyman. Handywoman. What kind of girl is she anyway? Who are her people? Do you know anything *about* her?" Elizabeth had heard of this call, and other mothers' calls just like it,

23

from Mrs. Emerson, who reported it in a voice that tried to sound amused but came out irritated. "This is one problem I never had with Richard," she said. "I find there are drawbacks that I hadn't foreseen when I hired you." She was still trying to switch Elizabeth over to housekeeping, which was probably why she sounded irritated. She tapped her fingernails on a tabletop. "I don't know, people surprise me more all the time. 'Above all else, be *feminine*,' I used to tell my daughters, and here you are in those eternal blue jeans, but every time I look out the window some new boy is helping you rake leaves."

"Oh, well, the leaves are nearly gone by now," Elizabeth said.

"What's that got to do with it?"

"I'll be indoors more. They won't be stopping by so much."

"It's more likely they'll just start invading my kitchen," Mrs. Emerson said.

Benny Simms picked up the axe that was leaning against the toolshed. He ran a finger down the blade and whistled. "I just did sharpen it," Elizabeth told him.

"I guess you *did*."

"Did you know the Emersons have a whetstone wheel? The old-fashioned kind, that works with a foot pedal. I found it in the basement."

"Nothing about the Emersons would surprise me at all," Benny said.

"I like things like that. Things without machinery to them. Machinery is something I don't understand too well."

"I would've thought you'd know all about it," Benny said.

"No. *Yard* work now, or carpentry, or plumbing—things that you can see reason to right on the surface . . ."

"Then why can't you kill the turkey?" asked Benny.

"Well."

He handed her the axe. Elizabeth turned it over several times, studying the glint of the blade very carefully but moving no closer to the turkey. She was wearing what Mrs. Emerson called her uniform—moccasins, dungarees, and a white shirt, and a bulky black jacket with a rib-knit waist now that the weather had turned cool. A wind from the east was whipping her hair around her face. She kept brushing it back impatiently without lifting her eyes from the axe. "I'm not too certain about that bevel," she said. "It looks a little bluish. I hope I didn't go and ruin the tempering."

"I don't know what you're talking about," said Benny. "What'd you take this job for, if you can't kill turkeys?"

"Well, how was I to know? Would you expect that to be a part of my job? First I heard of it, in she walked yesterday carrying the crate by the handle. Passed it over to me without even slowing down, walked on through the house peeling off her gloves. Said, 'Here you are, Elizabeth, take care of this, will you? Have it ready in time for Thanksgiving dinner.' Tomorrow! I didn't know what to say. I suspect," she said, setting down the axe, "that she planned it all on purpose, to turn me to housekeeping."

"Most people get their turkeys from the supermarket," Benny said.

"Not her."

"All plucked and wrapped in plastic."

"Not Mrs. Emerson. She won it at a church bazaar."

"Oh, is that what you win? I've heard of prize turkeys before but I thought they'd have their feathers off."

"Nope. You do it all yourself."

"Do you know how to pluck them?"

"Oh, sure," said Elizabeth. "The feathers and the innards, *that's* no problem."

Benny was brushing his crewcut on end, over and over. "Innards. Jeepers," he said, "I'd forgotten them. You'll have to fish out all those half-made eggs."

"I tend to doubt that," Elizabeth said. She smiled suddenly and shut the toolshed door, dropping the wooden cross-bar into place. "Oh, well, I don't know why I asked you anyway. If you can't, you can't."

"I'm awful sorry."

"That's all right."

They started up the hill toward the front yard—Elizabeth ahead, with her hands deep in her jacket pockets, Benny still brushing up his crewcut as he walked. "What I stopped by for," he said, "was to ask if you wanted to come with me this afternoon."

"I'd love to."

"I'm going—don't you want to know where you'd be coming with me *to?*"

"Where am I coming with you to?"

"I'm going out to the country for my mother. Picking up some pumpkins for pumpkin pie."

"Oh, good," said Elizabeth. "Maybe I'll get Mrs. Emerson a pumpkin too. Big as a footstool. Drop it in her lap and say, '*Here* you go, take care of this, will you? Have it ready in time for Thanksgiving.'" She laughed, but Benny didn't.

"I don't know why you stay with that woman," he said. "Couldn't you find someone else to work for?"

"Oh, I like her."

"What for? The whole family's crazy, everyone knows that."

Elizabeth had stopped to empty bits of leaves from one moccasin. She shook it out, standing one-legged in the grass. "Other people have said so too," she said, "but I don't know yet if they're right. So far I've only seen Mrs. Emerson and Matthew."

"Matthew. Well, he's okay but *Andrew* is stark raving mad. Wait till you see *him*."

Elizabeth bent to put her moccasin back on, and they continued toward the street. Squirrels were racing all around them, skimming over the grass and up the skeletons of the trees. "Lately we've got squirrels in the attic," Elizabeth said. "No telling how they got there, or what I do to get rid of them."

"When I was little Mrs. Emerson used to scare me to death," said Benny. "Also Andrew, and Timothy a little too but that might have been just because he was Andrew's twin. I wouldn't even come in for cookies, not even if Mrs. Emerson called me herself with her sweetie-sweet voice. I'd heard stories about them since I was old enough to listen. That Andrew is *violent*. And do you know that Mrs. E. went to pieces once because she thought her first baby got mixed up in the hospital?"

"I hear a lot of people have that thought," Elizabeth said.

"Maybe so, but they don't go to pieces. And they don't try and give the babies back to the hospital."

Elizabeth laughed.

"I wonder if my mother would care to hire you," Benny said.

"It's not too likely. Besides, I believe I'd like to stay and meet these people."

"When would you do that? Some don't come home from one year to the next."

"Well, one's coming today, as a matter of fact," Elizabeth said. "The one here in Baltimore. Timothy. That's what we're killing the turkey for."

"I could ask my mother if she needs any carpentry done."

"Never mind," said Elizabeth. She tapped him lightly on the shoulder. "Go on, now. I'll see you this afternoon."

"All right. I hope you manage that turkey somehow."

"I will."

She climbed the steps to the veranda, unzipping her jacket as she went. Inside, the house was almost dark, filled with ticking clocks, smelling of burned coffee. The furniture was scarred and badly cared for. "Mrs. Emerson," Elizabeth had once said, "would you like me to feed the furniture?" Mrs. Emerson had laughed her tinkling little laugh. "Feed it?" she had said. "Feed it what?" "Well, oil it, I mean. It's drying out, it's falling to pieces." But Mrs. Emerson had said not to bother. She had no feeling for wood, that was why—the material that Elizabeth loved best. The hardwood floors were worn dull, black in some places where water had settled in, the grain raised and rough. In a house so solid, built with such care (six fireplaces, slate in the sunporch, a butler's pantry as big as a dining room, and elegant open inserts like spool-bed headboards above every doorway), Mrs. Emerson's tumble of possessions lay like a film of tattered leaves over good topsoil, their decay proceeding as steadily as Mrs. Emerson's life. Strange improvements had been tacked on—a linoleum-topped counter, crumbling now at the edges, running the length of the oak-lined breakfast room, dingy metal cabinets next to the stone fireplace in the kitchen. In the basement there were five separate servants' rooms, furnished with peeling metal bedsteads and rolled-up, rust-stained mattresses;

on the second floor most of the doors were kept shut, darkening the hall; on the third floor there was an echo, the wallpaper was streaked brown beneath the shuttered windows, the floor outside the bathroom bore a black ring where someone had long ago left a glass of water to evaporate, unnoticed. The two attics off the third-floor rooms were crammed with playpens, cribs, and potty-chairs, bales of mouse-eaten letters, textbooks no school would think of using any more. There was a leak beside one chimney which only Elizabeth seemed concerned about. (Periodically she was to empty the dishpan beneath it; that was all.) Mrs. Emerson, meanwhile, set antique crystal vases over the scars on the dining room buffet and laid more and more Persian carpets over the worn spots on the floors. The carpets glowed richly, like jewels, calling forth little sparkles of admiration from the ladies who came to tea. Elizabeth hated Persian carpets. She wanted to banish all their complicated designs to the basement and sand the floors down to bare grain—something she knew better than to suggest to Mrs. Emerson.

She climbed the stairs, creaking each step in turn, trailing her hand along the banister. In the hall she stopped a moment to listen to Mrs. Emerson, who was in her bedroom talking to the maid. "Now, Alvareen, if Mr. Timothy gets here by lunchtime I don't want you serving any bread. He's gained fifteen pounds since he started medical school. Heart disease runs in the family. Give him Ry-Krisp, and if he asks for bread say we don't have any. Can you understand that? Meanwhile, I want to see a little cleaning done. I don't know how things have been allowed to slide so. The baseboards are just furry. Do you know what Emmeline used to do? She ran along the baseboard crevices with a Q-tip, down on her hands and knees. Now that's cleaning."

"Yes'm," said Alvareen.

"Are you out there, Elizabeth?"

Elizabeth crossed the hallway to the bedroom. Mrs. Emerson was sitting at her little spinet desk, wearing a dyed-to-match sweater and skirt and a string of pearls, holding a gold fountain pen poised over a sheet of cream stationery. She looked like an advertisement. So did everything else in the room—the twin beds canopied with ruffles, the lace lampshades, the two flowered armchairs that turned out to be shabby only if you came up close to them. It was hard to imagine that Mr. Emerson had lived here too. He had died of a heart attack, people said, in one of the twin beds— almost the only Emerson to do things without a fuss. Now the beds were neatly made and there were little satin cushions arranged at the heads. The only thing out of place was Alvareen, a black hulk of a woman in a gray uniform, standing beside Mrs. Emerson with her hands under her apron. "Mrs. Emerson, I'll be going now," she said.

"Yes, yes, go on. Elizabeth, have you taken care of that turkey?"

"Not yet," Elizabeth said.

"Why not? I can't imagine what's holding you up."

"I was just going to fetch an old shirt," said Elizabeth. "I don't want to get all bloody."

"Oh. Now, I'm not interested in the details, I just want him seen to. At one o'clock tomorrow I want to find him stuffed, trussed, and ready to carve. Is that clear?"

"Who's going to cook him?" Elizabeth asked. "Not me."

"Alvareen, but I'm having to pay her double for the holiday. No one *else* will do it."

She smoothed the lines between her eyebrows, looking tired and put-upon, but Elizabeth didn't offer to change her mind about cooking. One piece of housework, she figured, would turn her magically into a maid—and just when Mrs.

Emerson was getting used to her as a handyman. At teas, catching sight of Elizabeth as she climbed the stairs or passed a doorway, Mrs. Emerson would cry, "Wait! Girls, I want you to see Elizabeth. My handyman, can you imagine?" And the ladies would round their mouths and act surprised, although surely the news was all over Roland Park by now. "Oh, Pamela, I swear," one of them said, "you always find some different way of doing things." Mrs. Emerson beamed, setting her cup soundlessly in its little fluted saucer.

"I've brought you in some firewood," Elizabeth said, "and later I'll drive out for the stuffing mix. Would you like a big old pumpkin?"

"Excuse me?"

"A pumpkin. I'm going out to the country with Benny this afternoon."

"Now, what would Alvareen know to do with a pumpkin? She can barely warm up a brown-and-serve pie. I don't remember giving you the afternoon off."

"I did a full day's work in the morning," Elizabeth said. "Carried in the firewood, caulked three window frames, mended the back porch railing, and sharpened all your tools. Also I oiled the whetstone."

"What whetstone is that?"

"The one in the basement."

"Oh, I never knew we had one. Well, Richard worked five full days a week. Morning *and* afternoon."

"Richard wasn't on hand round the clock whenever you called for him," Elizabeth said.

"Oh, never mind that, can't you just stay? Timothy's coming home."

"I won't take long."

Mrs. Emerson rose and went to her dresser, where she began going through a little inlaid box full of bobby pins. She

dug out bobby pins and put them back in and dug out more, as if some were better than others. Then she began shifting hairbrushes and perfume bottles around. "I don't know what I depend on you for," she told Elizabeth. "You're never here when I need you."

Elizabeth said nothing.

"And the country, all these trips to the country and anywhere else that comes to mind. Washington. Annapolis. Lexington Market. The zoo. Any place you're asked. It's ridiculous, can't you just stay put a while? Timothy said he might be here by lunch. I was counting on your standing by to help me."

"Help you do what?" Elizabeth asked.

"Well, maybe we'll need more firewood."

"I just got through telling you, I brought some in. MacGregor delivered a truckload this morning."

"What if we burn more than you'd planned on? *Some* problem will turn up. What if we need a repair job all of a sudden?"

"If you do, I'll see to it later," Elizabeth said. "And Timothy will be here."

"To be truthful, Elizabeth, it's nice to have things thinned *out* a little when just one of my children is here. Somebody to lighten the conversation. Couldn't you stay?"

"I promised Benny," Elizabeth said.

"Oh, *go* then. Go. I don't care."

When Elizabeth left, Mrs. Emerson had started opening all her bureau drawers and slamming them shut again.

Elizabeth's room was across the hall from Mrs. Emerson's. The air in it smelled heavily of cigarettes—the Camels Elizabeth chain-smoked whenever she was idle—and there was a

clutter of paperback detective stories and orange peels and overflowing ashtrays on the dresser. In the lower drawers were odds and ends belonging to Margaret, who had lived in this room until she left home. Her Nancy Drew mysteries were still in the bookcase, and her storybook dolls lined one wall shelf. The other children's rooms were stripped clean; Margaret's was different because she had left in a hurry. Eloped, at sixteen. Now she was twenty-five, divorced or annulled or something and drawing ads for a clothing company in Chicago. "And moody, so terribly moody," Mrs. Emerson said. "The few times she's been back I've wondered if she'd go into a depression right before my eyes." Mrs. Emerson had a way of summing up each child in a single word, putting a finger squarely on his flaw. Margaret was moody, Andrew unbalanced, Melissa high-strung. But coming from her, the flaws sounded like virtues. In Mrs. Emerson's eyes anything to do with nerves was a sign of intelligence. Other people's children were steady and happy and ordinary; Mrs. Emerson's were not. They were special. On the bookshelf in the study Margaret's pale, pudgy face scowled out from a filigree frame, her lipstick a little blurred, her lank hair a little mussed, as if being special were some storm that had buffeted her. In this pink lacy room she must have seemed as out of place as Elizabeth, who sat on the satin bedspread in her dungarees and scattered wood chips across the flowered carpet whenever she was whittling.

Wood chips marked the doorway to the room, and trailed across the hall and down the top few stairsteps. "You must think you're Hansel and Gretel," Mrs. Emerson once said. "Everywhere you go you drop a few shavings." She had seen Elizabeth's carvings—angular, barely recognizable figures, sanded to a glow—and not known what to make of them, but apparently they had settled her mind. Before then she kept asking, "What are you going to do, in the end? What will you

make of your life?" She liked to see plans neatly made, routes clearly marked, beelines to success. It bothered her that Elizabeth had just bought a multi-purpose electric drill that would sand, saw, wirebrush, sink screws, stir paint—*anything*—which she kept in the basement for her woodworking. "How much did that thing cost? It must have taken every cent I've yet paid you," Mrs. Emerson said. "At this rate you'll never get to college, and I have the feeling you don't much care." "No, not all *that* much," Elizabeth said cheerfully. Mrs. Emerson kept nagging at her. That was when Elizabeth showed her the woodcarvings. She dragged them out of her knapsack, along with a set of Exacta knives and a sheaf of sandpaper. "Here you go, I'm planning to set up a shop and make carvings all my life," she said. "Are you just saying that?" Mrs. Emerson asked. "Or do you mean it. It's a mighty strange choice of occupations, and I never knew you to plan so far ahead. Are you just trying to quiet me?" But she had turned the carvings over in her hands, looking at least partly satisfied, and after that she didn't nag so much.

Elizabeth pulled the knapsack out of her closet and dug down to the bottom of it, coming up finally with a man's ragged shirt that was rolled into a cylinder. She shook it out and put it on over her jacket. Down the front of the shirt were streaks of paint in several different colors, but no blood. She had never even killed a chicken before. Not even a squirrel or a rabbit, and that at least would have been killing at long distance.

Across the hallway Mrs. Emerson was talking into her dictaphone. "This is going in Melissa's letter. Melissa, are you sure you don't need that brown coat with the belted back that's hanging in the cedar closet? Something else, now. What was it I wanted to say?" There was a click as the dictaphone was shut off, another click to turn it on again. "Yes. Mary.

Now, the last thing I want is to offend that husband of yours. I'm not any ordinary mother-in-law. But would you be able to use my old fur coat that I got four years ago? I never wear it, I was just going through my winter things this morning and stumbled across it. Young men can't generally afford fur coats so I thought—but if you feel he'd be offended, just say so. I'm not any ordinary . . ."

Elizabeth stood by her window, flattening the rolled sleeves of her paint-shirt and wondering what she would do if it took more than one chop to kill the turkey. Or could she just refuse to do it at all? Say that she had turned vegetarian? But that would give Mrs. Emerson an excuse to clap her into housework. Elizabeth had nothing against housework but she preferred doing things she hadn't done before. She liked surprising herself.

"Andrew, I understand about Thanksgiving but on Christmas I set my foot down," Mrs. Emerson said. "I'm not thinking of myself, you understand. I'm managing quite well. But Christmas is a *family* holiday, you need your family. Tell your doctor that. Or would you rather I did? It doesn't matter to *me* what he thinks of me."

She could go on like this all night, sometimes. To Elizabeth it seemed like so much busywork. If she couldn't write those messages right then, or bother remembering them, were they worth committing to tape? Maybe she just liked pressing all those buttons on her little beige machine. But Mrs. Emerson said, "I take pride in my correspondence, letter-writing is a dying art. I refuse to turn into one of those people who sit themselves at a desk to say, 'Well, nothing to report at *this* end, everything going as usual . . .'" At two or three in the morning, waking just enough to shut her window or reach for another blanket, Elizabeth would hear sudden, startling sentences floating across the dark hallway. "I resent what you

said in your last letter, Melissa. Everyone knows I am not the sort of mother who interferes." "Where is that necklace I lent you? I never said you could *keep* it." Her voice was clear and matter-of-fact, the ordinary daytime voice of a woman who had been awake for hours. "How could you just hang up on me like that? I've been thinking and thinking, the older you get the less I understand you." "Do you have Emily Barrett's address?" "Someday *you* will be alone." "Where is the photograph you promised?"

On the student desk in the corner sat Elizabeth's own mother's letter, weeks old, sheets and sheets of church stationery hoping for an answer.

. . . Honey if you were going to be gone so long you should have said so when you left. We would never have let you for one thing and for another we would have cooked you a finer last meal and made a bigger to-do. I could just cry thinking of that plain old meat loaf and succotash I gave you. But your sister's wedding was still on my mind and I never knew you were planning anything but hopping off for a short summer job. I thought sure you would be back for school. Well the college called and I didn't know what to say, I remembered you had talked about taking time off but we never thought you were serious. And we thought you meant to go by bus like ordinary people, not with just a wedding guest that none of our side knew. How could you be sure what he drove like? Nowadays they let just anyone on the road, all kinds of things can happen. But there you went and didn't say a word more about it. I don't know if you were planning to be gone so long or it just happened. You often do get carried away. Anyway here you are now in Baltimore you say. You should see all the times I've crossed addresses out and written new ones in for you since you sat here back in May eating that meat loaf and succotash.

Well there is not too much to report here. Everybody is fine although as usual your father is working too hard. He just lets these women walk all over him, taking up his time for missionary circles and all kinds of lectures and tea-parties and slide-showings and paltry illnesses and so forth, when I tell him he should rest more and behave like ordinary pastors, confine himself to sermons and funerals and maybe a few deathbeds. He eats it all up, I believe. He wouldn't know what to do with himself if they would stop pestering him. Now Mrs. Nancy Bledsoe has gone and given him a dog, a female collie that chews up everything including magazines and table legs, and you know how scared he is of dogs and never would have anything to do with them. She says it is a token of appreciation for all he did while her mother was dying. He said thank you kindly although I notice he has no notion what to do with the thing, doesn't know how to pet it, backs off when it jumps on him, asked me right out one day after a lot of hemming and hawing what was wrong with her that she squats to piddle when everyone else's dogs raise their legs. Now Christmas will be coming up which is the busy time for all those deaths and melancholies as well as church services and so on.

Polly is looking so sweet and pretty now that she is married and she is just real active in the Young Wives Fellowship. I don't know if she has told you yet about the event they are expecting in March. Me a grandmother, I'm just tickled pink. I always did want to have someone to spoil rotten but hand back when he got to fussing. Honey I just wish you would settle down yourself some, finish at Sandhill College or get married, one. I know you don't like to hear me say that but I just have to tell you what's on my mind. Mrs. Bennett talking the other day said there is always one in every family that causes twice as much worry as all the others, not that you would love them any the less for it, well, I knew what she meant although of course I didn't say so.

Dommie Whitehill still comes calling on us and asks all

*about you, where you are and what you are doing and who
you are going around with and so forth. I could just cry for
that boy. You will never find anyone sweeter than Dommie,
I don't care how far you look, and that is something that is
getting mighty hard to find these days and nobody waits forever.*

*Elizabeth I have oftentimes told your father he should
drop you a line. He says it is up to you to write first and take
back all you said so I wish you would. Honey he is just so hurt
but would never show it for the world, you know how proud
he is. Nobody is as strong as they look. I have thought of calling you on the long distance but not knowing how your employer might feel about it I didn't. You could, though. Just
one word is all it would take and it would make him so . . .*

Elizabeth changed into older dungarees, tattered and
spotted and faded white at the seams. She took a leather belt
from her dresser, but instead of putting it on she raised it over
her head and spun it by the buckle like a lariat, in a huge wide
beautiful circle. The tongue of the belt flicked a storybook
doll—Margaret's doll but Elizabeth's room, no one's but her
own. She awoke here every morning feeling amazed all over
again that she had finally become a grownup. Where to go
and when to sleep and what to do with the day were hers to
decide—or not to decide, which was even better. She could
leave here when she wanted or stay forever, fixing things. In
this house everything she touched seemed to work out fine.
Not like the old days.

When she descended the stairs, threading the belt
through her jeans, she found Alvareen in the front hallway
wiping the baseboards. "I'm going to take care of that turkey
now," Elizabeth told her.

"That right?"

"You wouldn't like to do it, I don't guess."

"Not me." Alvareen sat back on her heels and refolded the dustcloth. "Honest to truth, you think she could find the money somewhere to *buy* one. What you all have for supper last night?"

"Tuna fish on saltine crackers, open-face, topped with canned mushrooms."

Alvareen rubbed her nose with the back of her hand, a sign she was amused. She loved to hear what was served up on her sick-days.

"For vegetables she spread oleo on celery sticks, with a line of green olives straight down the middle."

"You making this up?"

"No."

"Can't be *anyone* to cook as bad as that by accident," said Alvareen. "Must be she wants to discourage your appetite. She's tight with a dime."

"Elizabeth?"

"Just going," Elizabeth called up the stairs.

"I thought you'd have left by now."

"Just on my way."

She waved a hand at Alvareen and walked out the front door, crossing the veranda briskly but slowing as she reached the yard. There wasn't a person in sight, no one to offer to help. She dragged her feet all the way to the toolshed. When she opened the door the turkey rushed to the back of his crate with a scrabbling sound. Elizabeth squatted and peered inside. "Chick, chick?" she said. He strutted back and forth within his three-step limit, his wattle bobbing up and down. Away from the light his wings lost their coppery sheen. He looked drab and shabby, his feathers a little ragged, like someone who had slept with his clothes on. "Well, anyway," Elizabeth said after a moment. She untwisted the wire that held the crate shut and reached in, carrying out a set of motions that she had

rehearsed in her mind. One arm circled his body and pinned his wings down, the other clutched his legs. He struggled at first and then relaxed, and she straightened up with the turkey tight against her chest. "You surely are a *big* buster," she told him. There by the chopping block lay the axe, right outside the toolshed door, but it would take her a minute longer to get herself prepared. She set the turkey down. He was too fat to run far. He ambled out the door and down the hill, jerking his neck self-righteously with each step, while Elizabeth followed a few feet behind. She could still grab him up if he started running, but neither of them seemed in any hurry. They walked single file through the trellis, past the blackberry bush, under the rotting roof of the gazebo that showed squares of sky between its warped shingles. Then back again, toward the toolshed. That turkey had no sense at all. He circled the chopping block twice, and still Elizabeth let the axe stay where it was. He headed back through the trellis. They walked like two people filling time, sauntering with exaggerated carelessness, trying to look interested in the scenery. Then the turkey started speeding up. He didn't run, just took longer and longer steps, never losing his dignity. Elizabeth walked faster. Trees and shrubs and the second trellis skated past them, perfectly level. Then they reached the end of the yard and Elizabeth suddenly darted beyond the turkey and skidded down the bank into the alley, heading him off. A car screeched to a stop not two feet from her. The turkey became interested in something on the ground and stayed there, just at the edge of the bank, pecking unconcernedly.

The car was a dirty white sportscar. The driver was a round-faced blond boy wearing an Alpine hat with a feather in it. When he climbed out he bumped his head against the doorframe. "I wish you would watch where you're going," he said.

"Sorry," said Elizabeth. She couldn't give him more than a glance because she had to keep her eyes on the turkey. Without looking around she reached toward a bush behind her, snapped off a switch, and started up the bank. "Shoo, now, shoo!" she said.

"Out walking your turkey, I see," said the boy.

"I'm getting up nerve to kill him."

"I see. Are you Elizabeth? My name's Timothy Emerson. I knew we were going to have a turkey dinner, but Mother never mentioned it was still on foot."

"It may be *forever* on foot," Elizabeth said. "This whole business is harder than it looks."

"Can I help?"

But he wore a plaid sports coat and wool slacks, much too good for killing turkeys in, and even the effort of climbing the bank after her had turned his face pink. "Just stay where you are, keep him off the road," Elizabeth told him. "That's all I need."

"I could run over him with my car if you like."

She smiled, but her attention was still on the turkey. She gave a flick of her switch and the turkey moved away, slowly now, still examining the ground. "What you need is a leash," Timothy said.

"I can get him to the chopping block easily enough, but then what? I just hate to tell your mother I'm not equal to this."

"Let him run off," Timothy said. "Buy one at the supermarket. Mother'll never know."

Elizabeth bent one ankle beneath her and sank down to the ground, still holding the switch. The turkey moved a few steps further off. "Is it you that the unicycle in the basement belongs to?" she said.

"Me? Oh, no, that's Peter's. I was never one for exercise.

I'm sure he wouldn't mind if you used it, though."

"I was just hoping to *see* it used," said Elizabeth. "I'm not one for exercise either."

"Really? I thought you would be."

"How come?"

"I expected to see you out playing football with the little neighborhood boys," Timothy said.

"What would I want to do that for?"

"Well, you are the handyman, aren't you?"

"Sure," said Elizabeth, "but that's got nothing to do with football. I wonder if other people have the same idea? I've been getting the strangest invitations lately. Tennis, bicycling, nature walks—if there's one thing I don't like it's nature, standing around admiring nature. I come home feeling empty-headed."

"Why go, then? Look, your turkey is heading toward the road again."

The turkey was a good twenty feet off, but Elizabeth merely glanced at it and then settled herself more comfortably on the ground. "I *always* go where I'm asked," she said. "It's a challenge: never turn down an invitation. Now, does Peter really know how to ride that unicycle? I mean, bump downstairs on it? Shoot basketballs from it, like they do in the circus?"

"Your *turkey!*"

Elizabeth looked around. The turkey was picking his way down the shallowest part of the bank, talking to himself deep in his throat. "What about him?" she asked.

"Aren't you afraid he'll get away?"

"Oh, I thought I was going to give up on him and go buy one from the supermarket."

Timothy stared at her. "Well, I only said—you didn't seem—I never heard you make up your *mind* about it," he

said. So that Elizabeth, for the first time giving him her full attention, wondered why he wore such a jaunty feathered hat set at such a careless angle. He sounded like his mother, who was forever tying herself into knots over plans and judgments and decisions. But his eyes must have been his father's—narrow blue slits whose downward slant gave him a puzzled look —and she liked his hair, which stuck out in licked-looking yellow spikes beneath the hat. She smiled at him, ignoring the turkey.

"Are you really going to let him just walk off?" he said.

"Sure," said Elizabeth, and did—rose and brushed off her dungarees, stood on the edge of the bank to watch the turkey cross the road at an angle and start up someone's back yard. Finally he was only a jerking coppery dot among the trees. "Now I have to go to the grocery store," she said. "Anything you need?"

"Maybe I could take you there."

"Oh no, I like to drive. You could get your car off the road, though."

"Or I might come with you. Is that all right? I'm always on the lookout for something to do while I'm home."

He hadn't been home at all yet, but Elizabeth didn't bother reminding him. "Fine," was all she said, and she reached under her paint-shirt to pull, from her jacket pocket, a set of keys dangling from Mrs. Emerson's lacy gold initials.

The car was a very old Mercedes with a standard shift that tended to stick and make grinding noises. Elizabeth was used to it. She drove absentmindedly, keeping the clutch halfway in and watching the scenery more than the road, but Timothy changed positions uneasily every time she shifted gears. He kept one hand tight on the dashboard, the other along the

back of the seat. "Have you been driving long?" he asked her. "Since I was eleven," Elizabeth said. "I haven't had time to get a license yet, though." She swerved neatly around an on-coming taxi. The roads here in the woods were so narrow that one car always had to draw aside when it met another, but Elizabeth made a game out of never actually coming to a full stop. She ducked in and out of parking spaces, raced other drivers to open sections of the road and then rolled easily toward their bumpers as they backed to let her by. "I can see that I'm making you nervous," she told Timothy, "but I'm a better driver than you realize. I'm trying to save the brakes."

"I'd rather you saved us," Timothy said, but he loosened his grip on the dashboard. Then they hit Roland Avenue, and he settled back in his seat. "I don't suppose you know if Andrew's coming," he said.

"He's not."

"I was afraid to ask Mother on the phone. She can go on and on about things like that. But Matthew will be there."

"Nope."

"What, no Matthew? He practically *lives* there."

"He used to," said Elizabeth. "Then your mother said he was wasting his life on a dead-end job. Running a dinky country newspaper and getting all of the work but none of the credit. *I* don't know why."

"The owner drinks," Timothy said.

"She said for him to come back when he got a decent job. He never did. It's been three weeks now."

"Matthew is the crazy one in the family," Timothy said.

"Oh, I thought that was Andrew."

"Well, him too. But Matthew is downright peculiar: I don't believe he hears a word Mother says to him. He visits her every week, no matter *what* she's up to. Brings tomatoes he's grown himself, stays an hour or two."

"Not any more he doesn't," Elizabeth said. "Will he get another job, do you think?"

"No."

"Well, what then? Won't he ever come home again?"

"Oh, sooner or later Mother will give up. Then he'll wander in again and that'll be the end of it."

"I doubt if he's crazy at all," Elizabeth said.

She parked haphazardly in a space barely longer than the car, and they climbed out. Standing on the curb she peeled her paint-shirt off, shut it in the car, and brought a curling vinyl wallet from her jacket pocket. "I wonder how much turkeys cost," she said.

"Let me pay. It was my idea."

"No, I have enough."

"Aren't you saving up for college or something?"

"Not really," Elizabeth said.

The grocery store was vast and gloomy, even under the fluorescent ice-cube trays that hung from the ceiling. There was a smell of damp wood, cardboard, cracker crumbs. They had barely stepped inside when someone said, "Timothy Emerson!"—a sharp-edged woman in a fur stole, one of Mrs. Emerson's tea guests. "Don't tell me you're honoring your mother with a visit," she said. "Did she recognize you?" She flung out a little peal of laughter. Elizabeth slid past her and went over to the meat counter. "I'd like a turkey," she told the butcher. "Kind of fat."

"Fifteen pounds? Twenty?"

"I wouldn't know. Could you let me hold one?"

He disappeared into a back room. Mrs. Emerson's friend could be heard all over the store. ". . . never known a braver woman, just so sweet and brave. Disappointments never faze her. I said, 'Pamela,' I said, 'why don't you sell that big old house and find yourself an apartment now that—' 'Oh no, my

dear,' she told me, 'I'll need all that space for my children, if ever they choose to come home.' "

The butcher reappeared, carrying three turkeys. "This one?" he said. "This one?" He held them up one by one, while Elizabeth frowned and twirled her car keys. "Let me try that last one," she said finally. She reached across the counter for it and weighed it in her hands. "Wait a minute. I'll be back."

"How is your twin brother, dear?" the friend was saying. "I understand he's in the care of a doctor again. Now, wouldn't you think he should be in his own home? New *York* is no place for a, for someone who's . . ."

"Try this," Elizabeth told Timothy. "Add intestines and such. Feathers. Feet. Do you think he's about the right size?"

Timothy, who had lit a pipe, stuck the pipe between his teeth and took hold of the turkey. "Feels okay to *me*," he said.

Mrs. Emerson's friend said, "It's Elizabeth, isn't it? How are *you* this fine day? Planning for a great many dinner guests?"

"Well, not exactly," Elizabeth said. "Forget you saw me buying this." She left the woman staring after her and went back to the butcher. "I like it," she told him, "but I could do without that piece of metal in his tail."

"That's to pin his legs down."

"I'd prefer it without, anyway," Elizabeth said.

While he was wrapping the turkey she went off in search of stuffing mix. Timothy by now was coasting down the aisle on the back of a shopping cart. He took several long strides and then hopped on the rear axle, leaning far forward to keep his balance. The pipe in his round face looked comical, like a snowman's corncob. "This is something I've always wanted to do," he told her when he had coasted to a stop. "Mother

never took us to grocery stores; she telephoned. Up until Margaret ran away with the delivery boy."

"Telephoned!" Elizabeth said. "Didn't it cost more that way?"

"Why not? We're rich."

He wheeled the cart over to the meat counter, where they collected the turkey. Then Elizabeth went off to find snacks for Alvareen's sick-days. Timothy followed, pretending the turkey was a baby in a carriage. "Who do you think he favors?" he asked, and he lovingly rearranged a patch of butcher's tape. Then he hopped on the cart and coasted off again. "I must find Mrs. Hewlett," he called back. "She has such a consuming interest in little Emersons." Periodically, in her trips down the aisles, Elizabeth caught sight of him. He whizzed past sober ladies and grim-faced clerks, a flash of yellow hair topped with a red feather. When she met him at the check-out counter he had parked the cart and was carrying a gigantic sack of dog food that hid his face and reached to his knees. All she saw were his hands clutching the sides of it. "I know we don't have a dog," he said, poking his head around the sack, "but I can never resist a bargain, can you?" And he turned to put it back again, his· knees buckling, staggering beneath its weight, all to make her smile.

But when they were back in the car his mood had changed completely. He sat hunched in his seat, staring out the side window and fiddling with his pipe but not smoking it. "I'd have liked to find a turkey with a couple of feathers left," Elizabeth told him. Timothy didn't answer. Then when they stopped for a light he said, "Maybe we could just drive around for a while."

"Where would you like to go?" said Elizabeth.

"I don't know. Nowhere. Home," he said, and he

slouched down in his seat and tapped his dead pipe on his knee all the rest of the ride.

Elizabeth parked in front of the house. The minute the car doors slammed Mrs. Emerson appeared on the veranda, stepping forward and then back on the welcome mat with both hands clasped in front of her. "Timothy!" she said. "What are you—why—?"

"My car is down back," Timothy said. He climbed the steps and bent to kiss her on one cheek. Mrs. Emerson's face was tilted up to him, her eyes half closed by the frown she wore, and she kept her hands pressed tightly together. "I still don't understand," she said.

"How are you, Mother?"

"Oh, just fine. I'm doing beautifully. I'm managing very well."

"You *look* well."

Elizabeth passed them and went into the house, carrying the groceries. As soon as she reached the kitchen she dumped the whole bag in one swoop, stripped the turkey of its wrappings and set it on the counter. Then she put the other items away more slowly and folded the paper bag. Alvareen came in with a scrub pail full of gray water. "Is that *him?*" she asked, looking at the turkey.

"Pretty neat job, wouldn't you say?"

"Then what's that other feller doing, running around out back?"

"Oh, Lord."

Elizabeth went out the kitchen door and found the turkey squatting by a basement window. "Shoo!" she said, and clapped her hands. The turkey moved a few feet off before he stopped again. "Shoo, boy! Shoo!"

Mrs. Emerson appeared on the back porch, followed by

Timothy. "Now, how on earth—" she said. "I thought I told you to kill that thing."

"I was just getting set to," Elizabeth said.

"Then what did I see in the kitchen? What is that creature on the counter?"

Timothy handed his pipe to his mother and came down the porch steps. "Drive him this way," he told Elizabeth. "I'll be here to grab him."

"I would rather drive him off again."

"Explain that, please," Mrs. Emerson said. "I gave you a perfectly simple chore to do, one that Richard would have seen to in five minutes. The only thing in my life I ever won and you shoo him off like a common housefly. Then try to fool me with one from the butcher. That *is* what you did, isn't it? That's where you and Timothy came in from together, looking so smug?"

Because neither Elizabeth nor Timothy felt like answering, they concentrated on the turkey. They closed in on him tighter and tighter, although the last thing they wanted to do was catch him. The turkey did a little mumbling dance with himself, stiff-legged.

"I can't trust anyone," Mrs. Emerson said.

"Oh, Mother. What'd you ask her to do it for, anyway? She's too tender-hearted."

"Too *what? Elizabeth?*" Mrs. Emerson set the pipe down, in the exact center of the top porch step, and folded her arms against the cold. "It isn't the turkey I mind, it's the deception," she said. "The two of you going off like that, laughing at me behind my back. Conspiring. That naked, storebought-looking bird lying on my kitchen counter."

Timothy had driven the turkey to a spot directly in front of Elizabeth, but Elizabeth made no move to catch him. She

was watching Timothy, who was growing pinker and stonier but not answering back. He stood so close to her that she heard the angry little puff of his breath when his mother spoke to him.

"This was *your* idea, wasn't it. Elizabeth never did such a thing before. I always felt I could rely on her. Now I don't know, I just don't know. It isn't enough that you leave me all alone yourself, you have to drive everyone else off too. Isn't that it? Isn't that what you're hoping for?"

"Good God," said Timothy, and then in one swift lunge he scooped up the turkey and carried it squawking and flapping to the toolshed. He took such long steps that Elizabeth had to run to keep up with him. It seemed that the whole upper half of his body had turned into beating, whirling, scattering feathers. When he reached the chopping block he jammed the turkey down on it and held it there. Then for a moment everything stopped. The turkey held still. His head lay limp on the block, his eyes seemed fixed on some inner thought.

"Timothy? Wait," Mrs. Emerson called.

Timothy reached for the axe without looking at it, hefted it in his hand to get a better grip and chopped the turkey's head off. It took one blow. The turkey's wings began flapping, but with doomed, slow beats that carried the body nowhere. The beady eyes stared at a disc of blood. Mrs. Emerson cried, "Oh!"—a single, splintering sound. Elizabeth said nothing. She stood at Timothy's side with her hands in her jacket pockets, staring out over the trees and pinning her mind on something far away from here.

◙ 3 ◙

Two weeks before Christmas there was a heavy snowfall. Timothy had a date with Elizabeth, and it took him nearly an hour to make the drive to his mother's house. Downtown was difficult enough, but once he reached Roland Park his was the only car on the road, laying new black tracks which wavered slightly if he traveled at more than a creeping pace. He hunched over the steering wheel and squinted through a fan of cleared glass while handfuls of soft snow floated soundlessly around him. His gloves were lost, his heater was broken, and he had forgotten to have his snow tires put on. The only comfort was his radio—a news announcer telling him, over and over, that Baltimore was experiencing a heavy snowstorm and traffic conditions were hazardous. "Exercise extreme caution," he said. His voice was friendly and concerned. Timothy carried out a token pumping of his brakes, relieved that someone else had noticed these dreamlike puffs of white.

He had begun to have spells lately of worrying that he had died, and that everyone knew it but him.

The lights of the houses along the way were circled with

bluish mist. Parked cars were being buried, quickly and stealthily. "If you don't have to drive, stay home," the announcer said. "Keep off the roads." Timothy had no need to drive at all, and should have been safe in his own apartment, but he felt like seeing Elizabeth. He had started taking her out two and three times a week. They went to dinner or the movies, or sometimes they stayed home and played whooping, dashing games of chess, with Elizabeth making bizarre moves and sacrificing quantities of pieces whenever she grew bored. Timothy was more scientific about it. He knew all the famous matches by heart, and could solve any chess problem the newspapers offered him. But Elizabeth had a psychological trick of swooping into his territory from some unexpected corner of the board, stunning him with the swift arc of her long arm, so that even when the invasion was harmless he was taken off guard and made some unlikely move to counter hers. Their games ended in giggles. Everything they did ended in giggles. He kept trying to get on some more serious footing with her, but every time they saw each other they went sailing off into some new piece of silliness. He caught it from her; laughter came shimmering off her like sparkles of water. His mother watched them with a puzzled, anxious smile.

The house was lit in every window, casting long yellow squares across the white lawn. He climbed out of the car and braced himself for a trip through the snow without boots, but before he took his first step Elizabeth rounded the house carrying a snow shovel. Sparks of white glinted on her cap, which seemed to be one of those fighter-pilot helmets with ear-flaps that little boys often wear. "Halt!" she said, and raised her shovel like a rifle. Then she placed herself squarely in front of the steps, set the shovel down at a slant, and started running. A narrow black line followed her magically, pausing each time she was stopped short by the creases be-

tween sidewalk squares. The rasping sound brought Timothy's
mother to an upstairs window—a silhouette against yellow
lamplight. He laughed and waved at her. Then the blade of
the shovel arrived at his shoe-tips and Elizabeth faced him,
laughing too and out of breath. "There," she said, and turned
to lead him up the black carpet she had laid for him.

They stamped their feet on the doormat. Elizabeth had
on huge rubber boots with red-rimmed soles and flapping
metal clasps; he had the feeling they were once his father's.
The cuffs of her jeans were stuffed into them, and her jacket
collar was turned up so that her hair, streaming from the
helmet, fell half inside and half out in honey-colored tangles.
Other girls could waft through his mind in chiffon, or silk,
or at least ruffled shirtwaists, but not Elizabeth. Elizabeth
forever wore that thick, shabby jacket, and wore it badly—
hands deep in her pockets, waist hiked up in back, shoulder
seams reaching halfway to her elbows and the zippered front
bellying out below her chest. He thought of the way she
dressed as another joke played on him by the universe. If he
was going to get so tied up with her, couldn't she have at
least one romantic quality? Couldn't she smell like flowers, or
be as light on her feet as a snowflake? But she smelled of wood
shavings. When she stamped her boots, gleaming drops shot
out to dampen his trousers all the way to the knees.

"We still going to the party?" she asked.

"If you want to. It's still on. But you didn't have to clear
the walk for me, it'll only get snowed under again."

"Oh, snow-shoveling's my favorite job," she said.

So she would probably have done it anyway; it wasn't for
him at all.

They stepped inside, into a blast of hot air. While Elizabeth bent to take her boots off Mrs. Emerson came down the
front stairs. She kept her head perfectly level, one hand

weightless on the banister. "Timothy darling, I can't imagine why you tried driving on a night like this," she said. She came up to him and took one of his hands between her own, which were so warm they stung him. "Mercy! Where are your gloves?" she said. "Where are your boots?"

"I must've lost them."

"You're surely not going out again. Are you? Stay here at home."

"Well, there's this party I want to hit."

"Fiddlesticks," said his mother.

She drew him into the living room, skirt swirling as she turned. If anyone looked dressed for a party tonight, it was she. Surely not Elizabeth, who had taken off her jacket to expose a shirt that seemed to have mechanic's grease down the front. "In a minute we'll have the fire built up," Mrs. Emerson said. "Matthew's out getting more wood."

"Oh, is Matthew here?"

"He got some time off."

"From what? Did he change out of the dead-end job?"

His mother looked uncomfortable, but only for a minute. She picked up a poker and rearranged a pile of embers. "No," she said, "but I had him come anyway. I hated to think of him out in that shack of his. He's going to be working over Christmas, did you ever hear of such a thing? Well, no one *else* there could get a paper out."

"Are any of the others spending Christmas here?"

"Andrew is, but not for long. Just two days." She put the poker in its stand and began pacing in front of the couch, where Elizabeth was sitting now to slide her moccasins back on. "Mary will be with her in-laws. Margaret I haven't heard from yet. Melissa," she said, and frowned briefly but then shook it off, "is traveling with someone to Bermuda. It worries me *who*, I think I have some right to know these things, but

in her last letter she ignored all my questions and she doesn't answer her telephone. Peter's going skiing with his roommate in Vermont." She had ticked off the names on her fingers, like a hostess planning a dinner party. Now she looked over at Timothy, one last finger waiting to be tapped. "*You* will be here," she said.

"I guess so."

She settled herself in a wing chair. At the back of the house a door slammed, a log crashed to the floor and rolled with a splintery sound. Matthew appeared in the living room doorway with an armload of firewood. "Hello, Timothy," he said, and crossed the room to shake hands. He was trailing clumps of wet snow, and had to reach awkwardly around a stack of logs that rose to his chin. Depend on Matthew to find the hardest way to do anything. When he dumped the wood beside the fireplace, bark and dead leaves flew across the rug. More bark clung to the front of his jacket, which was a plaid logger's shirt whose sleeves did not cover his wristbones. No sleeves covered his wristbones. He was the longest, lankiest, knobbiest man Timothy had ever known. His face was bony and sad-looking, with clear-rimmed glasses forever slipping down his narrow nose. His straight black hair had last been cut months ago, probably by himself. If any jeans could be more faded than Elizabeth's, his were, and when he hunkered down to build the fire Timothy saw that his ankles were bare, red and damp-looking above soggy gray sneakers. "Jeepers, Matthew," he said. "It makes me uncomfortable just *looking* at you."

Matthew only smiled and went on laying logs in the fireplace. He worked so deliberately that the others fell silent. They were willing sparks not to fly, logs not to slide, kindling not to sift through the grate. That was what Matthew's way of moving did to people. In a family full of noise and con-

fusion and minor accidents, he was the quiet one. He touched everything as gently and awkwardly as if he had broken some precious object years ago that he would never forget; yet he had always been that way. The only fuss he caused was the irritation his family felt when they watched him hold his fork too cautiously, smooth down too kindly a rug he had just stumbled over, stack each stick of wood so meticulously with his long, bony fingers when he was laying a fire.

"Why don't you let Elizabeth do that?" Timothy asked.

"I didn't want her out in the snow."

"How come? She was just now shoveling the walk."

Matthew lowered a stick of wood that he had almost set in place. He looked over at Elizabeth.

"It's nice out there," she told him.

He set the stick on top of the pile. It fell off again.

"In a few days," Mrs. Emerson said, "Elizabeth goes off to New York for her vacation. I tell her it's a mistake, especially if the snow sticks. I want her to spend Christmas with us."

"Bus or train?" Timothy asked Elizabeth.

"Car," she said.

"Car? You're driving?"

"A fellow named Miggs is. I got him off a bulletin board."

"Elizabeth is so devoted to bulletin boards," Mrs. Emerson said. "I never even knew they existed. She finds them everywhere—laundromats, thrift shops, university buildings. She always knows who is driving where and who has lost what and who is selling their old diamonds off."

"In this weather a train would be safer," Matthew said.

"I prefer cars," said Elizabeth. "They give you the feeling you can get off whenever you like."

"But why would you want to get off?" Timothy asked.

"Oh, I wouldn't. I just like to know I can."

Matthew said, "Did this man Miggs show you any references?"

Timothy stopped lighting his pipe and looked at him.

"He's only a student," said Elizabeth. "He goes to Hopkins. On the phone he sounded very nice."

The fire had caught. It blazed up, spitting as it reached the snowy logs, and Matthew squatted back to watch it with his hands dangling between his knees. "My, isn't that lovely," Mrs. Emerson said. "Isn't this pleasant. Why would anyone want to go out on such a terrible night?"

She was cuddled between the wings of her chair, with the firelight turning her face pink and soft. Timothy imagined that a struggle was going on within her: Should she be rejoicing that he was coming by so much lately, or should she be worrying over his choice of dates? (Such a shambling sort of girl, not at all like the ones he usually went out with.) "Aren't you going to stay longer?" Mrs. Emerson would ask, and instead of his usual evasive answer Timothy could say, "No, but I'll be back day after tomorrow. I'm taking your handyman to the movies"—choosing the word "handyman" on purpose, gleefully watching the two different reactions tangling her smooth face. (The *handyman?* But he did have to come home, after all, to get her.) Whenever she saw them off at the door she would fuss over Elizabeth, offering to retie her scarf or lend her a lipstick, "something to brighten your face just a little, a touch of color is always nice although of course you're looking very pretty as it is." Then Timothy, in the midst of enjoying himself, would shoot a glance at Elizabeth and suddenly wonder: did she have to wear that wristwatch *everywhere*, with its huge luminous dial and its paint-spattered leather band? Even on a date? Even dressed up? He was split between wanting to defeat his mother's expectations and wanting to live up to them. He would rock

on his heels, blank-faced, hoping for Elizabeth and his mother to settle things without him. "Maybe next time you could borrow my curlers," Mrs. Emerson would say. "A tidy hairdo is always nice for special occasions." Elizabeth never seemed bothered by her. *Nothing* bothered Elizabeth; that was part of her charm. It was also very irritating. He sighed and looked over at her, where she sat on the couch peacefully curling the red cellophane strip from a cigarette pack. Matthew had taken the seat beside her. The two of them looked something alike, both scruffy and ragged and lost in their separate trances. "We should be going," Timothy said.

"Oh, is it time?"

"But it wouldn't hurt to put a dress on."

Elizabeth shrugged and uncoiled from the couch. "All right, back in a minute," she said, and padded out of the room in her rundown moccasins. She left behind her a silence that spread and hardened, until Mrs. Emerson came to herself and sat straighter in her chair.

"I was just thinking," she said. "This is the first Christmas we'll be spending without your father."

"That's true," said Timothy.

"He always did love Christmas so. Just like a child."

"I remember he did."

Matthew said nothing at all, although he was the one who had been closest to their father. Sometimes Timothy had trouble even picturing what their father had looked like. He was a forgettable man. He had come up from nothing, from nowhere, married a Roland Park debutante and made a fortune in real estate—a line of work so beneath notice that no one had ever thought of suggesting it for his sons, least of all Mr. Emerson himself. Only strangers considered him important. "At the settlement on our house," Timothy had once heard someone say, "things got so tangled I thought they

never *would* straighten out. Fortunately I happen to know Billy Emerson personally. I just popped in his office and said, 'Billy—' "—as if Billy Emerson were a name worth dropping. That conversation had made Timothy stop and think. Was there something about his father that he had overlooked? Something he should reconsider? But his father's only talent, after all, was for making money. Money sprang up around whatever he touched, a fact that he seemed to take for granted. He never mentioned it, at least not to his family. "Money is essential," Mrs. Emerson said, "but not important." Her children had no trouble understanding her.

"When you were all little," Mrs. Emerson said now, "he used to take you to visit Santa Claus. Do you remember that? Urging you all to make lists beforehand, practically sitting in Santa's lap himself just to overhear what you asked for. And all of you so hard-headed you never believed in Santa for an instant, not a one of you. Remember, Matthew?"

But if Matthew remembered he didn't say so. He was slumped in one corner of the couch, examining the helmet Elizabeth had left behind. He straightened the chin-strap, tucked the ear-flaps in, pulled them out again and then held the helmet up on the tip of a finger to frown at it.

"He would have had that yard lit up like the Fourth of July, if I hadn't begged him not to," Mrs. Emerson said. "Always so fond of Randolph. Rudolph. The reindeer. *I* don't know why. And birthdays! How he loved birthdays!" She narrowed her eyes at Timothy, who shifted his weight uneasily. "I don't suppose you remember what day it is tomorrow," she said.

"It's my birthday," said Timothy.

"It's your birthday. Andrew's and your birthday. Will you be spending it with us?"

"I don't think so, Mother."

"*Andrew* likes birthdays." She pulled off a ruby ring and twisted it in the firelight. "He always sends me a dozen roses, thanking me for having him."

"How do you know? Maybe he's congratulating you."

"*You* would be." She shoved the ring back on. "I used to give you double birthday parties, remember that?"

"Yes," said Timothy, and remembered Andrew, thin and frantic and overexcited, aiming a sputtery breath at his side of the cake, suffering even then from some jerkiness of mind which Timothy had feared a twin could catch like a cold.

"I sent him his presents in plenty of time," said Mrs. Emerson. "How is school going, dear?"

For what *she* feared was that twins had to split a single share of intelligence between them—something she had read in a long-ago ladies' magazine and never forgotten, even after the twins had turned out to be the brightest of her children. Timothy had spent too long assuming she was right to be able to laugh it off. "You asked me that *yesterday*," he said.

"Oh, did I?"

"Do you imagine you should still be signing my report cards?"

"Timothy, dear, I was only interested."

"That's more than I am," Timothy said. "I think it's all a bore."

"Oh, how can you *say* that? *Medical* school?"

"It's a bore."

"Well, it was your decision, not mine. I was never the kind of mother to interfere in her children's lives."

"Oh, Lord."

"Now, let's just sit and enjoy the fire. Shall we? You've done a very good job with it, Matthew. I believe the last time you built a fire you left the flue shut."

The last time Matthew had built a fire was when their

father died, in June, and their mother kept insisting the house was cold. Oh, everything she said nowadays was attached to other things by long gluey strands, calling up other days, none of them good, touching off chords, opening doors. All he could do was tip his head back against his chair and sink into his own private tunnel while she pattered on.

"I'm ready," Elizabeth said.

She had changed into a bulky wool dress that fit haphazardly, and nearly all of her hair was caught up by one flaking gilt barrette. Her nylons were wrinkled at the ankles and her squashed-looking black pumps curled at the toes. She swung her vinyl handbag like a waitress just getting off work. Mrs. Emerson looked up at her and sighed, sharply. But Matthew gave Elizabeth a happy smile, and she stood in front of him smiling back until Timothy rose abruptly and took her hand. "Come on, come on," he said. "We're late already."

"Elizabeth, dear, your hair is falling down," Mrs. Emerson said.

They had a long drive ahead—past the city limits, out on a superhighway filmed with slippery snow. Elizabeth had to keep clearing the mist off the inside of the windshield. When she wasn't doing that she was switching radio stations—from one song to the other, in the middle of a note, which was something Timothy rarely did himself. He felt an obligation to hear songs through to the end, even if he didn't like them. He also finished books that bored him, and had never in his life walked out on a movie. The fact that he and Elizabeth were so different, even on this small point, deepened the sense of uneasiness that had been growing in him all evening. Here they were out on a snowy road, probably driving to their deaths, and he didn't know anything about this girl. Every-

thing he asked her was batted back at him, or turned into a joke. "Elizabeth," he said, "why is it we never have a serious conversation?"

"Why should we?" she asked.

"You never say anything you mean. Never talk about your family, or that place you're from—what's-its-name—"

"Ellington."

"Ellington. Have you got something against it?"

"Oh, no. I liked it," said Elizabeth, and she smiled at a lone house swaddled with blue Christmas lights. Then she began tracing spirals on her window, and just when he thought the conversation had reached a dead end she said, "I probably would be there still, if my father didn't get so het up about reincarnation."

"About what?"

"He doesn't believe in reincarnation."

"Well, who does?"

"I do," said Elizabeth. Then she giggled and said, "This week, anyhow."

"You couldn't possibly," Timothy said.

Elizabeth only sat back in her seat, tucking her hands in her sleeves for warmth.

"*Do* you?" he asked.

"Oh, well. It was one of those last-straw deals," she told him. "I was enough of a thorn in his side not being religious. Reincarnation was the end."

"What do you want to go and believe in a thing like *that* for?" Timothy said.

"I just think it's a nice idea. You can stop getting so wrought up about things once you know it's not your last chance. Besides. It gives me something to say when old ladies tell me I shall pass this way but once. 'Oh, well, or twice, or three times . . .' I tell them."

"How far do you carry this business?" Timothy asked. "Do you think you were once a high priestess in Egypt? Do you feel we knew each other in Atlantis?" He was hoping for her to give some crackpot answer, something that would disenchant him, but it wasn't that easy. "Who knows?" was all she said. "What would it matter, anyway?"

"You just thought this up to irk your father," Timothy told her.

"Well, maybe so," she said cheerfully.

"And he wouldn't have started a fight over a little thing like that."

"Of course he would. Besides, he didn't like this boy I was seeing."

"Oh," said Timothy. "What was wrong with him?"

"He just considers me a trial. Always has. You can't really blame him."

"No, I mean the boy."

"Oh. Well, nothing, to the naked eye. He was just a State College student. Then he got arrested for robbing laundromats."

Timothy swerved to avoid an abandoned car. "You certainly know some funny people," he said.

"Why do you say that?"

"Did he tell you what he was doing? Did you know?"

"Oh, no, just that he was working. I wondered what at."

"You could have guessed, if he wouldn't say. *I* could have guessed. You could have been a little more curious, and maybe stopped him."

"I would never change someone else's affairs around," Elizabeth said.

That kept him silent for a full five minutes; he couldn't think of a thing to say. He concentrated on driving, which was growing more difficult. The road felt like cotton beneath

his wheels. The few cars he met were barely creeping along, shapeless white igloos eerily glowing beneath a white sky. "How can you see? I can't," Elizabeth said, and Timothy said, "I don't understand you. Fighting with your father! And here I thought you were Miss Easy-Going. Miss Fix-It. I wondered how your family was managing without you to patch the plaster."

"At home I break things more than fix them," said Elizabeth.

Then she rolled the window down with a jerk, which was unnecessary. Their breaths seemed likely to freeze in front of their faces. A new wave of mist fogged Timothy's vision and he hunched forward, peering for the turnoff. "Can't see a thing," he said, but he found it, anyway—an overhead sign swinging and whipping in the wind—and turned blindly.

"I thought they had snowplows up north," Elizabeth said.

"Well, this burglar," said Timothy. "Are you supposed to be visiting him or anything? Waiting until he gets out?"

"Waiting for what?"

"Well, to get married, maybe."

"He wasn't going to be in *that* long, it was only laundromats."

"The reason I'm asking all this," Timothy said carefully, "is that you and I seem to be going out together a lot. I wanted to know if you were committed in any way."

"Committed?"

"Not tied to this burglar or someone."

"Why do you keep calling him a burglar?" Elizabeth said. "He was a chemistry major. We hardly even knew each other."

Timothy gave up. "Would you like to go out to dinner tomorrow?" he asked.

"I can't. I'm going to see Matthew's house."

"Matthew?" He turned to stare at her. "How did *he* get into this?"

"Why not? I like him."

So this was where all the uneasiness had been going: Matthew. "Break it, can't you?" he said.

"No," said Elizabeth. "I want to see his house. Besides, I never turn down an invitation."

"Do you *have* to keep *telling* me that?"

Then he slammed into the Schmidts' driveway and cut the engine and piled out. He didn't open the door for Elizabeth. She followed on her own, calmly swinging her handbag and shuffling up the narrow groove of cleared sidewalk. Timothy waited on the front porch with his back turned, ignoring her. She didn't seem to notice.

It was Ian Schmidt who opened the door—a classmate of Timothy's. He said, "Oho! We thought you weren't coming. This is Elizabeth, isn't it? We met one night at a play."

"That's right," Elizabeth said.

He showed them into a living room papered with travel posters. Guests sat around in clumps, not yet at ease, and a small, square baby was being passed from lap to lap. "That's Christopher Edward. Our son," Ian said. "Today's his six-month birthday." He was so proud of that that he kept them standing in the doorway, fully wrapped and shedding snow-flakes, while he scooped the baby up and brought him over. "Say hello, Christopher, say hello." The baby stared, poker-faced, at Elizabeth. She stared back. "Hmm," she said finally, and began tugging her boots off. Lisa Schmidt appeared to show her where to put her jacket. As they passed each group of guests she stopped for introductions, and Elizabeth nodded

gravely once the names were said. The profile view of her, with her chin-strap dangling and her stiff, cold hands clutching her purse, sent a sudden stab of love through Timothy that left him feeling tired and puzzled. He bent toward the baby politely and let him clutch an index finger.

The party was a small one, only five couples. Others had been kept away by the storm. People sat on floor cushions and canvas butterfly chairs, with spaces between them that seemed reserved for absent guests. There were spaces in the conversation, too. When Elizabeth had returned from a back room, stripped of her jacket and helmet, a silence had fallen. Timothy still stood in the doorway with Ian, carrying his coat draped over his arm. He ignored Elizabeth (let her manage for herself, if she was so independent) and she settled right away beside a boy with a mustache. "I rode down here with you last fall," she said. "You gave me a ride from Philadelphia, remember?"

The boy brightened; up till now he had been glumly snapping his watchband. "Oh, Mike's friend!" he said. "I didn't know you with your hair up. How is Mike?"

"Fine, I guess."

"Did you find a job all right?"

"The very first day," Elizabeth said. "I miss Philadelphia, though."

"Take it from me, there's nothing to miss about Philadelphia."

"I thought there was. I might never have left, if they hadn't fired me."

Timothy wanted to hear who had fired her, and for what, but now other people had pounced on the subject of Philadelphia. Conversation started darting around the room again, with Elizabeth at the center of it looking perfectly comfort-

able. She didn't need Timothy at all. He went off to find a drink.

The Schmidts were serving hot mulled wine. They were on a budget. Timothy sniffed gloomily at the kettle on the kitchen stove, and then he filled two mugs. He would have preferred something stronger. He had what he thought of as the medical-student syndrome—overworking and overdrinking, alternately, studying all one night on Dexedrine and drinking all the next to rid his mind of that heavy feeling. Hot mulled wine wasn't much good for getting drunk on. Standing by the stove he drank one of the mugs straight down, refilled it, and went back to the living room. The boy with the mustache had returned to the subject of Mike. Whoever Mike was. "If he would only put that Honda out to pasture," he was saying. "It's held together with paper clips. But you know Mike, he's too soft-hearted." Timothy handed Elizabeth a mug and passed on by.

He went to sit beside a blond girl whose turn it was to hold the baby. He was trying to think of her name; she had come to cook him dinner twice last spring. Now she had been passed on to another medical student, and probably at the next party she would come with still another. She turned the baby to face him and said, "Say hello, Chrissy, say hello."

"He did, he did," Timothy said. Jean, maybe. Or Betty. One of those plain names. She looked like half the girls he knew—feathered cap of hair, bright lipstick and blue eyeshadow, fine-boned figure that fit very tidily into a nurse's uniform. The other half of the girls he knew were from Roland Park, and their hair was smoother and hung gleaming to one side and they wore their clothes with a sloping, casual elegance. But they all had one thing in common: they treated Timothy like a teddy bear. They couldn't seem to take him

seriously. Was it because of his round face, or the curling-up corners of his mouth? "Show how you play patty-cake," the girl told Christopher. "Isn't he adorable?" Her tone was the same for Timothy as for the baby; it wasn't clear who she thought was adorable.

"I believe he's throwing up," Timothy said.

"That's not throwing up, he's just spitting a little milk. Tell him, Chrissy. Say, 'Don't you know anything about *babies*, fellow?' "

What he really wanted (and thought of whenever one of these girls showed off with a baby or a frying pan) was to get married and settle down, have two or three children. He had been planning on that all his life, even when he was in the girl-hating stage and when, much later, he had turned into a Hollywood-style bachelor with an apartment full of dim lights and soft music always waiting on the record player. Only he seemed to keep choosing the wrong girls. Even Elizabeth was wrong, and look at him: still tagging after her, still mulling her over all day and half the night until he grew weary at the thought of her. Elizabeth took him no more seriously than any of the others did. She could have, once, maybe at the beginning. He thought she had been swayed by public opinion. He imagined his family and a whole string of girls drawing her aside, one by one, to say, "You know that Timothy is a clown, of course. Always good for a laugh. Never really *feels* anything." Now she was as gay and careless with him as if he were a brother. When he took her home after a date she gave him a companionable good-night kiss and slid out of his hands like water. When he said something important to her she ignored it, or dodged it, or laughed it off. Why did he keep on seeing her, anyway? She would make someone a terrible wife. She was too lackadaisical. There was something frustrat-

ing about her. Any plan involving Elizabeth was bound to fall
to pieces in a stream of irrelevant side trips, senseless delays,
wild goose chases. "Why don't you get *organized?*" he had
asked her once. "What for?" she said.

What did she care?

He finished off his wine and let Lisa Schmidt ladle him
another mugful. She was passing around the room barefoot
with the steaming kettle. Jean or Betty, whoever she was,
untangled her beads from the baby's fingers and said, "How's
your cute little gerbil, Timothy?"

"I got rid of him," he said.

"Oh, why?"

"He was getting on my nerves."

"Well, I wish you'd've told me. I thought he was adorable. Who'd you give him to?"

"I flushed him down the toilet."

"Flushed—you didn't."

He nodded.

"You didn't really."

"Would I lie? Last I saw of him he was scrabbling with
his little paws, trying to climb back out. Then *whoosh!* down
he went."

"If that's really true," the girl said, "and not something
you just made up, I think you should be reported."

"Probably hell on the plumbing," said Timothy.

"You don't deserve another animal as long as you live.
I hope they blacklist you at all the pet shops."

"Now I have ants," he said.

"That's all you're worthy of."

"They come in a glass tray, you can watch them dig
tunnels. After a while it gets boring, though. And even ants
are a trouble. They're always asking for syrup, and every now

and then a drop of water. You have no idea how silly it makes you look with the neighbors. 'I'll be out of town a few days, could you water my ants?' "

"That cute little roly-poly gerbil," the girl said. "What's the matter with you? You must like to think you're funny. Well, you don't hear *me* laughing."

"Oh, don't take it to heart," Timothy said. "I gave him to one of the intern's wives."

She rested her chin on the baby's head and stared across the room, slit-eyed.

"Honest I did. He's much happier there. Got married and had a family."

"I don't know which to believe," she said, "but I'd hate to see the inside of that head of yours. How could you even make up a thing like that? Scrabbling with his little hands?"

"I have a cruel streak," Timothy said.

"Take another look. That's no streak, it's a yard wide."

Then she rose to pass the baby on, as if she didn't trust Timothy too close to him.

Elizabeth and three other people had progressed to the subject of jobs, all the odd summer jobs they had held down. Someone had worked in a funeral parlor. Someone had made hairbrushes. Elizabeth, whom he had imagined coming directly here from home, turned out to have wandered through various northern cities stuffing envelopes, proofreading textbooks, and substituting for mailmen. And been fired from every one. She had sent out a thousand empty envelopes by mistake, let horrendous errors slip by her in the textbooks, and on the mail route (her favorite job) given everybody the wrong letters, consistently. How was that possible, when he had seen her keep track of a dozen tiny wheels and screws while dismantling and reassembling the kitchen clock? He thought of her with her family, breaking more things than

she fixed. None of it fitted with what he saw of her here.

He stretched out on the floor with another mug of wine and imagined a federal law ordering everybody to switch parents at a certain age. Then butter-fingered Elizabeth, her family's cross, could come sustain his mother forever and mend all her possessions, and he could go south and live a happy thoughtless life assisting Reverend Abbott at Sunday vespers. There would be a gigantic migration of children across the country, all cutting the old tangled threads and picking up new ones when they found the right niche, free forever of other people's notions about them. He stared up at the ceiling with a blank smile while words buzzed over his head. His damp, stockinged feet were poked under a radiator. Elizabeth was next to him, and when the ceiling started whirling he turned to watch her hands clasped around her mug. His eyes became fixed on them. He sank into the grainy texture of her skin, he thought he could taste on his tongue the sharp, scraped knuckles. Who else would have hands in such terrible shape? There must be some special meaning to them. On her left wrist was a deep, slow-healing cut, running diagonally across the radial artery. She had done that in his presence. He had seen the knife flash too far along the grain of a carving, watched blood spurt instantly across the kitchen table. "Find the pressure point. Here," he had said, and wound a dishtowel around it and bundled her into his car. "Keep it tight. Push down harder." He had sped her to old Dr. Felson's office, frantically honking his horn. The dishtowel grew bright red. Elizabeth pressed beneath it with sawdust-covered fingers and watched the scenery through her side window. "What on earth?" she said once. She was looking at a man and woman struggling beside a bus stop, the man flailing his fists and the woman taking swipes at him with her pocketbook. Timothy slammed on his brakes, cursed, and speeded up again. He

hadn't known Elizabeth very well at the time. He had thought her unconcern was due to a misguided faith in medical students—people who could supposedly take charge of these things. Responsibility weighed on his head as if she had dumped it there. He was unable to tell her that for him, medicine was only so many words in a textbook; that humans were fragile, complicated networks encased in envelopes nearly as transparent as the diagrams made them out to be; that faced with blood, his stomach froze and his throat closed up and he wondered why his mother expected so much of him.

An image of his mother's house rose up, cupped in his own hands like the Allstate insurance ad.

Now Elizabeth was trying to convince some stranger that the length of a person's forearm was always exactly the length of his foot. "It's a scientific fact," she said (more earnestly than she had said anything else this evening, especially to him), and the boy said, "That's ridiculous." But he tried it, anyway—took off a shoe and knelt on the floor with his arm flat alongside his foot. All over the room, other people were trying it too. The place was turning into a contortionists' convention. Timothy felt like the lone human being in a jumble of machinery, intricate wheels and gears and sprockets, all churning busily. He closed his eyes and sank away, following green fluorescent threads that criss-crossed behind his lids.

Then Elizabeth was saying, "Timothy? Wake up, it's time to go." When he opened his eyes everyone was smiling down on him. He struggled to his feet, shaking his head, and let someone bundle him into his coat. The other guests were leaving too. The room had a ragged, broken look as they stood around in knots saying goodbye. Elizabeth led him over to Ian and Lisa, and then through the swamp of galoshes by the door. As she was pulling on her boots she said, "You want me to drive?"

"Why? Do you think I'm not able? I'm stone cold sober."

And he was, as soon as he hit fresh air. He stood on the sidewalk a moment, tilting his face into the falling snow while other people stepped around him and clapped him on the back and wished him good night. A headache started up and ran like a crack from one temple to the other, waking him fully. "I have never in my life let a girl drive me home," he said.

"Oh well, all right."

The car was buried. Timothy dragged handfuls of snow off the front windshield while Elizabeth, who seemed unable to do the simplest thing in a routine way, drew vertical and horizontal lines across the rear window until it looked like a stretch of plaid. Then, "Zzzip!" she said, and swooped off all the white squares in between and was settled in her seat by the time he had opened his door. "I had a very good time," she told him.

"Did you?"

He started the engine, and the wheels spun a moment before getting a grip. When he turned his head to back into the street he had a glimpse of Elizabeth peacefully chewing her chin-strap, unaware of the arrows of irritation he was sending her across the dark.

The snow was worse. Although the roads had been cleared, by now they were filling up again, and the soft flakes had grown smaller and faster. He inched along, screwing his face up with the effort of finding his way. When Elizabeth reached toward the radio button he said, "Do you *mind?*" She settled back in her seat. She jingled a boot-clasp with her fingernail and hummed a program of her own.

Once inside the city limits he thought he could relax, but in Roland Park the roads were deep with snow and rutted so that his car kept wavering. The engine made whining, straining noises like a sewing machine. "*Freen, freen,*" said

Elizabeth, imitating it. Ordinarily he would have answered with a sound effect of his own. That was one thing they had in common: an ability to fry like bacon, whine like mosquitos, jingle like his mother's bracelets, always fading into giggles while anyone around them looked baffled. It wasn't the kind of talent other people could appreciate. ("What's this?" Elizabeth had once asked, and then given a creak and said, "A tree growing. Ever put your ear to a treetrunk?" And the two of them had collapsed against each other, laughing not at the treetrunk but at Mrs. Emerson's bewildered face.) But now Timothy only scowled at a gust of white that slammed against the windshield. "Who was that character you were talking to so long?" he asked.

"Bart Manning, his name was."

"How come you know him?"

"He gave me a ride here. His mother'd just died; he worried all the way down because they put the wrong color eyes on her death certificate."

She sometimes offered him these sudden jewels, tacked to the end of dull facts. He nearly smiled, but then he rubbed the windshield with his coat sleeve and said, "Are you breaking that date with Matthew tomorrow?"

"No," she said.

Nothing tacked to the end of *that*.

"Well, in that case, Elizabeth—"

"Turn toward the skid," she told him.

But he couldn't. The car had started sliding in a slow, dreamy semicircle, and all he seemed able to do was hang on tight to the wheel. He had the sense of watching from far away, with only a passing interest, curious as to how this would all come out. When they stopped they were at right angles to the road. The nose of the car pointed into a bank. The head-

lights lit tall scrubby weeds growing from dimples in the snow.

"Looks like we get to walk off the wine," Elizabeth said.

Walk? In this weather? It was easily a mile or more. He thought of the other possibilities—sit here hoping for a police car to pass, go wake one of those sleeping houses and phone his family or an all-night service station. But he was too tired suddenly to bother framing the words out loud. And while he was looking at the houses—all of them huge and silent beneath a glowing sky, drinking in snow and giving back not so much as a gleam of lamplight—he began to feel unreal. It seemed possible he would die here. With somebody foreign, not even related to him. It seemed possible he was already dead.

"Elizabeth," he said, "did you ever get the feeling you had just died?"

"In a *skid?*"

"Did you ever think you might be making all this up— everyday life, the same as usual—and meanwhile your family had your body in a coffin and your funeral all arranged?"

Elizabeth seemed to need time to think that over. He watched her closely, as closely as his mother did when she was waiting for Elizabeth to solve all her problems. "*Did* you?" he asked.

"Oh, well, it must be the sign of a happy nature," Elizabeth said.

"What? A what?"

"Must be, if you think heaven is just everyday life."

"No, you don't—"

"And anyway, it's not such a bad idea," she said. "I never did think much of those streets of gold and pearly gates. Wouldn't you like to just go on like this forever? With something always about to happen and someone new always show-

ing up? Oh, wouldn't that make dying all *right?* I prefer reincarnation myself, more chance of surprise, but there's not
all that much difference."

Then she turned up her jacket collar and climbed out of
the car. After a moment Timothy followed. He was about to
poke fun at her—"Is *that* what you think? Is that how well
you understand? Are *you* the one my mother is leaning on to
patch her life together?" But something about the way she
walked ahead of him, with her shoulders hunched against the
cold and her shiny stockinged legs plowing awkwardly through
the drifts, made him keep still. He caught up with her and
trudged alongside, protecting her with his silence. The tight,
closed line of his mouth was a gift to her; his hand, guiding her
onto the curb, cradled her shoulder as gently as if she were
some sad little glass figurine that he could break in an instant.

But at the first streetlight she stopped, bent to take one
boot off, and handed it to him. "It's for you," she told him.
"Wear it and we'll be even." He put it on. When they set off
again their footsteps had a drunken, slaphappy rhythm—a
shoe squashing, a boot flopping, another shoe squashing. Their
shadows tilted from side to side, limping and draggled but
comical, so that when Elizabeth pointed them out Timothy
had to smile. Then he started laughing, and she joined in, and
they walked the rest of the way strung out across the sidewalk
holding hands stiff-armed, like tottering black paperdolls on
a field of white.

4

1961

"No fats, no butter," Mrs. Emerson said. "That I could stand for, I've always been a picky eater. I cut the fat off my meat as a matter of course. But no eggs, he said! Stop eating eggs! What will I do for breakfast?"

Elizabeth glanced in the rear-view mirror and watched Mrs. Emerson straighten her hat, which was circled with spring flowers. They were returning from a heart specialist that old Dr. Felson had recommended. Ordinarily Mrs. Emerson drove herself, but today she must have been nervous over the appointment. She had risen at five-thirty, and collected her gloves and hat two hours early. Then at the last moment she had looked at the cloudless April sky and said, "Will it rain, do you think? You'd better drive me, Elizabeth." So Elizabeth had put on the chauffeur's cap, once black but now gray with mildew, which she had found on a rafter in the garage the month before. "Oh, *must* you?" Mrs. Emerson always said when she saw it. Elizabeth thought it was a wonderful cap. Whenever she wore it she made Mrs. Emerson sit in back. If there had been a lap-robe she would have tucked it in;

if it hadn't looked silly with jeans she would have liked a gold-buttoned jacket and driving gloves. Only Mrs. Emerson would never have entered into the spirit of it. "Sometimes," she said now, "I feel you are making fun of me, Elizabeth. Did you have to stand at attention when I came back to the car? Did you have to click your heels when you shut my door?"

"I thought that was what I was *supposed* to do," Elizabeth said.

"All you're supposed to do is be a help, and it would have helped much more if you'd come in with me as I asked. Taken off that silly hat and come been a comfort in the waiting room."

"I tend to develop symptoms in waiting rooms," Elizabeth said. She drove lazily, one arm resting on the hot metal frame of the open window. Her hair whipped around her neck in the breeze, and sometimes she had to reach up and steady her cap. "Isn't it funny? If I go into a waiting room sick all my symptoms disappear. If I'm well it works the other way."

"Thank goodness there were no *real* chauffeurs around," said Mrs. Emerson. "I would have found you all playing poker, I'm sure. Discussing carburetors." But she watched the scenery as she spoke, as if her mind were only half on what she was saying. During these last eight months, her life and Elizabeth's had come to fit together as neatly as puzzle pieces. Even the tone of their voices was habit now—Mrs. Emerson's scolding, Elizabeth's flip and unperturbed. Outsiders wondered how they stood each other. But Mrs. Emerson, as she talked, kept dexterously erect in spite of Elizabeth's peculiar driving, and Elizabeth went on smiling into the sunlight even when Mrs. Emerson's voice grew creaky with complaints. "How will I manage *breakfast* now?" Mrs. Emerson asked.

"He say no eggs at all?"

"No more than two a week. A precautionary measure, he

said. He kept comparing me to clocks and machines and worn-out cars, and the worst of it was that it all made sense. You keep *hearing* about the body being a machine, but have you ever given it any real thought? Here I am, just at the stage where if I were a car I'd be traded in. Repairs growing more expensive than my value. Things all breaking down at once, first that bursitis last winter and now my chest grabbing, only it's worse than with a machine. All my parts are sealed in, air-tight. No replacements are possible."

"That's true," said Elizabeth.

She tried picturing Mrs. Emerson as a machine. Sprung springs and stray bolts would be rattling around inside her. Her heart was a coiled metal band, about to pop loose with a twang. Why not? Everything else in that house had come apart. From the day that Elizabeth first climbed those porch steps, a born fumbler and crasher and dropper of precious ob-jects, she had possessed miraculous repairing powers; and Mrs. Emerson (who had maybe never broken a thing in her life, for all Elizabeth knew) had obligingly presented her with a faster and faster stream of disasters in need of her attention. First shutters and faucets and doorknobs; now human beings. A wrist dangled suddenly over her shoulder. "See, how knobby?" Mrs. Emerson said. "Nobody ever *told* me to expect varicose *bones*."

Elizabeth touched the wrist and returned it, unchanged.

"Could it be all those pregnancies?" said Mrs. Emerson, sitting back. "Eight of them, Elizabeth. One born dead. Peo-ple are always asking if I'm Catholic, but the truth is I'm Episcopal and merely had a little trouble giving up the habit of a baby in the house. Could *that* harm my health?"

Elizabeth drove slowly, changing lanes in long arcs when the mood hit her. Buttery sunlight warmed her lap. The radio played something that reminded her of picnics.

"It doesn't seem just that I should be getting old," Mrs. Emerson said.

She removed her gloves and took a cigarette from a gold case—something she rarely did. Elizabeth, hearing the snap as she shut it, looked in the rear-view mirror. "Oh, don't *frown* at me," Mrs. Emerson said.

"I wasn't."

"I thought you were. The doctor told me not to smoke."

"It's all right with *me* if you smoke."

"I plan to stop, of course, but not till I get over this nervous feeling." She flicked a gold lighter which sputtered and sparked and finally rose up in a four-inch flame that blackened half the cigarette. She took a puff, not inhaling, and held it at an awkward angle with her elbow tight against her side. "What a beautiful day!" she said, just noticing. "It's nice to be driven places." And then, after a pause, she cleared her throat and said, "I don't know if I ever mentioned this, Elizabeth, but I appreciate having you here."

She had stepped far enough out of the pattern so that Elizabeth had to look at her again in the mirror. "That's all right," she said finally.

"No, I mean it. If I talked to my children this way they would get upset. Tell *them* I'm getting old, they'd feel forced to convince me I wasn't."

"Oh, well, getting old is one of the things I'm looking forward to," Elizabeth said. "I'd like the insomnia."

"The what?"

"The early-morning insomnia. I could have a lot more fun if I didn't sleep so much."

"Oh," said Mrs. Emerson. She took half a puff from her cigarette. "Now, a little worry wouldn't hurt the other children at all, but don't mention this new doctor to Andrew. He's subject to anxiety as it is. Sometimes he calls long dis-

tance asking if I'm sure I'm all right, wondering about things so specific you know they must have come to him in a dream, either waking or sleeping: have I had any falls recently? am I careful around blades? Well, nowadays we all know what *that* means, but even so, I don't want you giving him any grounds for concern."

"I don't even know Andrew," Elizabeth said.

"Yes, but this weekend he's coming for a visit."

"No problem, then. I won't be here."

"Oh, but you *have* to be here!" Mrs. Emerson said.

"I'm going home."

"What? Home?" Mrs. Emerson fumbled her cigarette, dropped it, and caught it in mid-air. "Not for *good*," she said.

"No, I just promised my mother I'd visit."

"Well, that's impossible," said Mrs. Emerson. "I mean it. Impossible. I won't let you go."

"I've put it off for months now. I can't do it again."

"You'll have to."

"I can't," said Elizabeth, and she crammed her cap down tight on her head and began driving with both hands.

"You never asked *me* about this. I never heard a word."

"My weekends are my own," Elizabeth said.

"Oh, listen to you. You're as set in your ways as an old maid," said Mrs. Emerson. She ground out her cigarette and then braced herself as they zoomed away from a traffic light. "I should have known better than to rely on you. You or *anyone*. I should have let Billy buy me a lingerie shop on Roland Avenue, sat there all day the way my friends are doing, drinking gin and writing up the losses for income tax. *Much* too busy to see my children. Then they'd come home every week; just watch. They only take flight if you show any signs of caring."

Elizabeth coasted past little Japanese trees that flowered

pink and white on the grassy divide. She kept time in her head to faint music from the radio.

"This is all taking place because I mentioned something about appreciating you," said Mrs. Emerson. "I am cursed with honesty. And where does it get me?"

"What would you want me for anyway?" Elizabeth asked. "I've kept even with all my work."

"No, you don't understand. I need a—Andrew and I manage better when there's a buffer, so to speak. Somebody neutral. His brothers are no help at all. Matthew is always in a daze anyway, and Timothy just flies off somewhere. These two weeks he's having a run of tests, isn't that typical? I be-lieve he arranged it that way, so that I'd be left alone with— oh, nothing that I say is what I mean. I *love* Andrew, some-times I think I might love him best of all. And he's so much better now. He's not nearly so—he doesn't have that—noth-ing's really *wrong* with him, you know."

Elizabeth peered into her side mirror.

"Why don't you say something?"

"Just trying to change lanes," Elizabeth said, and she leaned out the window. "How come this mirror is at such a funny angle?"

"I can't put the visit off," said Mrs. Emerson, "because he likes to come when things are in bloom. He's already missed most of it. I wonder why Timothy can't study at home? Talk to him, Elizabeth. Make him change his mind."

"I'm against things like that," Elizabeth said. "What if I changed his mind and he stayed home and got run over by a truck? What if the house burned down?"

"What?" Mrs. Emerson passed a hand across her fore-head. "I'm not in the mood for an outline of your philosophy, Elizabeth. I'm worried. Oh, wouldn't you think my children could be a little *happier*?" She waited, as if she really expected

an answer. Then she said, "I suppose you're going home with someone from a bulletin board."

"Well, no."

"You're taking the train?"

"I'm going with Matthew," Elizabeth said.

"Matthew?"

"That's right."

"Matthew *Emerson?*"

Elizabeth laughed.

"Well, *I* don't know all the Matthews you might know," Mrs. Emerson said. "I don't understand. What would Matthew be going to North Carolina for?"

"To take me home."

"You mean he's going especially for you?"

"I invited him."

"Oh. You're taking him to meet your family."

"Yes," said Elizabeth, and flicked her turn signal.

"Does that have any significance?"

"No."

"This is so confusing," Mrs. Emerson said.

Which made Elizabeth laugh again. The spring air gave her a light-headed feeling, and she was enjoying the drive and the thought of taking a trip with Matthew. She didn't care where the trip was to. But Mrs. Emerson, who misinterpreted the laugh, sat straighter in her seat.

"I *am* his mother," she said.

"Well, yes."

"I believe I have some right to know these things."

Elizabeth braked at a stop sign.

"That would explain Timothy's strange mood," Mrs. Emerson said.

"He doesn't know about it yet."

"Well, what are you doing? Are you playing off one

brother against another? Lately you've seen so much of Matthew, but you still go out with Timothy. Why is that?"

"Timothy invites me," Elizabeth said.

"If you tell me again that you accept all invitations, I'm going to scream."

"All right."

"I didn't want to mention this, Elizabeth, because it's certainly none of my business, but lately I've worried that people might think there's something *easy* about you. You can never be too careful of your reputation. Out at all hours, dressed any way, with any poor soul who happens along—and I can't help noticing how Timothy always seems to have his hand at the back of your neck whenever he's with you. That gives me such a *queasy* feeling. There's something so—and now Matthew! Taking Matthew home to your parents! Are you thinking of marrying him?"

"He never asked," Elizabeth said.

"Don't tell me you accept all invitations to marry, too."

"No," said Elizabeth. She wasn't laughing any more. She drove with her hands low on the wheel, white at the knuckles.

"Then why are you taking him home?"

Elizabeth turned sharply into the garage, flinging Mrs. Emerson sideways.

"Elizabeth?"

"I *said* it had no *significance*," Elizabeth said.

Then she cut the motor and slammed out of the car. She didn't open the door for Mrs. Emerson. She snatched her cap off her head and threw it in a high arc, landing it accidentally on the same rafter where she had found it. Was that how it got there in the first place? She stopped and stared up at the rafter, amused. Behind her Mrs. Emerson's door opened and closed again, hesitantly, not quite latching.

"Elizabeth?" Mrs. Emerson said.

Elizabeth turned and went out the side door, with Mrs. Emerson close behind.

"Elizabeth, in a way I think of you as another daughter."

"I'm already somebody's daughter," Elizabeth said. "Once is enough."

"Yes. I didn't mean—I meant that I feel the same *concern*, you see. I only want you to be happy. I hate to see you wasting yourself. I mentioned what I did for your own good, don't you know that?"

Elizabeth didn't answer. She was climbing the hill so fast that Mrs. Emerson had to run to keep up with her. *"Please* slow down," Mrs. Emerson said. "This isn't good for my chest. If you must play chauffeur, couldn't you have dropped me at the front door?"

"Oh, is that what they do?"

"It's just that you seem so—aimless. You don't make any distinctions in your life. How do I know that you won't go wandering off with someone tomorrow and leave me to cope on my own?"

"You don't," said Elizabeth. But she had slowed down by now, and when they reached the back door she held it open for Mrs. Emerson before she entered herself.

It was one of Alvareen's sick-days, and she had left the kitchen a clutter of dirty dishes and garbage bags that they had to pick their way through gingerly. Then when they reached the front hall they heard someone upstairs. Slow footsteps crossed a room above them. Mrs. Emerson clutched Elizabeth's arm and said, "Did you hear that?"

"Someone upstairs," Elizabeth said.

"Well, do you should we—could you find out who it *is?"*

Elizabeth tilted her head back. "Who is it?" she shouted.

"I could have done *that*," Mrs. Emerson said.

Then Timothy appeared in the upstairs hall, stuffing something into his suit pockct. "Hi there," he said.

"Timothy!" said his mother. "What are you doing here?"

"I was in my room."

"We thought you were à burglar. Well, it's fortunate you've come, I have a favor to ask you."

She climbed the stairs with both hands to her hat, removing it as levelly as if it were full of water. "Now, about this weekend—" she said.

"I thought we'd been through all that."

"Will you let me finish? Come with me while I put my things up."

Mrs. Emerson crossed the hall and entered her bedroom, but Timothy stayed where he was. When Elizabeth reached the top of the stairs he opened his mouth, as if he were about to tell her something. Then his mother said, "Timothy?" He gave one helpless flap of his arms and followed his mother.

Elizabeth went into her own room. She was fitting together a rocking horse that had arrived unassembled, a present for Mrs. Emerson's grandchild. He might be visiting in July. "Fix it up and put it in Mary's room," Mrs. Emerson had said. "I plan to be a grandmother well-stocked with toys, so that he looks forward to coming. In time maybe he can visit alone, they say it's quite simple by air. You tag the child like luggage and tip the stewardess." The rocking horse had been packed with the wrong number of everything—too many screws, too many springs, not enough nuts. Elizabeth had spread it on the floor of her room, and now she sat down on the rug to look at the diagram. Across the hall, behind a closed door, Mrs. Emerson murmured endlessly on. When the words were unintelligible she always sounded as if she were reading aloud.

It was the positive way in which she put things, without breaks or fumbles. From time to time Timothy's voice rode over hers, but it never slowed her down.

Elizabeth emptied out a mayonnaise jar full of stray nuts from the basement. She picked up one after another, trying to fit them to the extra screws. "Now, this for this one," she said under her breath. "This for this. No."

"I already *told* you—" Timothy said.

Mrs. Emerson went on murmuring.

"Don't you ever take no for an answer?"

Elizabeth shoved the nuts aside and went back to the diagram. She already knew it by heart, but there was something steady and comforting about printed instructions. "First assemble all parts, leaving screws loose. Do not tighten screws until entire toy has been assembled." The author's voice was absolutely definite. Timothy's was frazzled at the ends. What was she doing here, still in Baltimore? She should have left long ago. She awoke almost nightly to hear the tape-recorder voice—"Why don't you write? It's not that I care for my own sake, I just think you'd wonder if I were dead or alive"—and she lay in bed raging at Mrs. Emerson and her children too, all those imagined ears putting up with such a loss of dignity. She kept promising herself she would leave. But never see Matthew again? Never play chess with Timothy? Lose the one person who leaned on her and go back to being a bumbler? She set a deadline: at the first mistake, the first putty knife through a windowpane, she would move on. *That* shouldn't take long. But her magic continued to hold. What she couldn't solve the hardware man down on Wyndhurst could, and there was always *The Complete Home Repairman* in her bureau drawer. All she had to do was disappear for a moment and refer to it, like a doctor keeping his patient waiting while he thumbed through textbooks in some hidden room. At this

rate she would stay here forever. And always knowing, to the end of her days, that she should be out in the world again.

"You mistake the kind of twins we are," Timothy said. "Did you think we were Siamese?"

"Fit tab A into slot B, making sure that . . ."

"We're not even identical. Not even close to identical. We were an accident of *birth!*"

Elizabeth sighed and dropped the diagram. She rose to circle her room, twice, and then she padded out the door and down the stairs. In the kitchen, where she had meant to stop for milk, the clutter seemed like an extension of the argument above. She went through without slowing and continued on down to the basement. There everything was dim and silent, flickering like a pool of water in the sunlight that sifted through dusty windows. Dark, battered doors closed off the old servants' rooms, with transoms above them that reminded her of school corridors and church fellowship halls. In the central part were tangled metal cast-offs, bicycles, a workbench, hunks of monster household appliances. There was a cabinet door laid across the zinc laundry tubs, with two huge canning kettles on top of it. Elizabeth and Matthew were making wine together. They had split the cost of the ingredients and shared the work, but it was up to Elizabeth to stir up the dregs once a day. She took a long-handled spoon from a nail, rolled the cheesecloth off the first kettle and dipped the spoon deep inside. A yeasty, spicy smell rose up, with bubbles that churned and snapped in a film across the surface.

"Where will we get the grapes?" Matthew had asked, and Elizabeth said, "Oh, grape wine we can *buy*. Just look in this recipe book—tomato wine, dandelion wine. Let's make something different. Is there such a thing as mushroom wine?" And she had laughed at his expression. He was slow, thorough, too serious; she provided the lightness for him. What answer-

ing glimmers she found in him she nourished along, and then he would surprise her by laughing too and losing that dark, baffled look on his face. He was the only Emerson she knew of who was short of money. She seized on that as a base for all the flights she took him on—painting, wine-making, installing a shower in his cracked old bathtub. Once they mixed up a week's supply of something called sludge that they found in a cookbook for the poverty-stricken. With Timothy it would have ended in silliness; sludge might have been rolled into balls and flung all over the kitchen. Well, that was fun too, of course. But Matthew enjoyed it in his own way, following a plan systematically with that knotted gaze he turned on everything, giving his slow smile when it was done.

They had made a batch of orange wine and another of wheat. They had chopped oranges, lemons, and raisins endlessly, baked wheat on cookie sheets in the oven until a musty golden smell filled the kitchen, all while Mrs. Emerson was out at a meeting. (She might not take to having a brewery in her basement, and they had never bothered about a government permit. Matthew was all for sending off for one but Elizabeth was too impatient to begin.) They had lugged the kettles down the stairs and filled them with buckets of water and sacks of sugar. "It may turn out too sweet," Matthew said gravely. "It may," said Elizabeth. They never talked much. When he found out she was planning a visit home he said, "I'll miss you," and Elizabeth, instead of answering as she would to someone else (*"Miss* me, what for? I'm only going for the weekend"), said, "I'll miss you too. Want to come with me?" "That would be better," he said, "and you won't have to ride with strangers." He was forever protecting her, but not in that fretful way that wore on her nerves. He lent her his rain-hat, and scooped her hair out of the way when she shrugged herself into her jacket. On walks through the

woods to his house he would let her go single-file, unhampered by hand-holding or the troublesome etiquette of briars held back for her and roots pointed out; but once inside, in a living room splintery with cold, he might come up behind her to stand motionless and silent, his arms folded around her and his chin resting on her head, warming the length of her back.

"Any time the basement door is open there's the strangest smell coming up," Mrs. Emerson once said. "Have you noticed?" She thought it was a new kind of detergent Alvareen was putting in the washing machine. Elizabeth never told her anything different.

She twirled the spoon dreamily, resting her head against a shelf, listening to the fizz of the bubbles. Up in one corner a spider spun a web between two waterpipes, but the strands looked like another slant of sunlight. Leaves that had sifted through the grate rustled in the window-well, as dry and distant as all the past autumns that had dropped them there.

Footsteps crossed the kitchen. "Elizabeth?" Timothy called.

"Down here."

He came to the doorway above the basement steps; she saw the darkening of the patch of light on the floor. Then he snapped a switch on, paling the sunbeams. "Where?" he said.

"Here by the tubs."

While he descended the stairs she uncovered the second kettle and began stirring it. It had a burned, toasty smell. She was afraid they might have overbaked the wheat. She lowered her head and breathed deeply, inches from the wine. "Ah," said Timothy. "Eye of newt. Toe of frog." But the scene upstairs must still be hanging over him; his voice was as heavy as the hand he laid on her shoulder. "What *is* it, anyway?" he asked.

"Just wine."

"You handymen certainly have some odd chores." He moved toward the window, and peered up at the spider in its web. "I came to see if you wanted to take a drive. Have lunch at my place or something." He poked at the web and the spider scuttled higher, a fat brown ball with wheeling legs. "Are you scared of spiders?"

"Nope."

He turned away, hands back in his pockets. "I hear you're going home," he said.

"That's right."

"But just for the weekend."

"That's right."

Elizabeth straightened up. She hung the spoon on its nail, pulled the cheesecloth back over the kettles and knotted the strings that held it there. When she turned to go, she found Timothy just taking something from one pocket: a pistol, bluish-black and filmed with grease. "What on *earth*," she said. He shifted it in his hands, as carelessly as if it were a toy.

"Evil-looking, isn't it?" he said. "I found it in Andrew's room."

"Is it real?"

"Well, probably. How can you tell? I would break it open but I'm scared of the thing."

"Put it down, then," Elizabeth said. "Stop tossing it around like that, will you?"

"Me? Two-Gun Tim?" He set his feet apart like someone in a western, one thumb hooked in the pocket of his slacks, and tried to twirl the pistol by its loop but failed. When it dropped they both sprang away and stared at it, as if it might explode spontaneously. Nothing happened. Timothy bent to

pick it up, holding it this time by the barrel, firmly, the way his mother must have taught him to hold scissors. "Ah, well," he said.

"What would Andrew want with a gun?"

"He collects them."

"Well, that's a very silly hobby," said Elizabeth, and she led the way to the stairs, making sure to keep out of the pistol's aim.

"Oh, I don't mean *collects*. I don't mean as a hobby. I mean he collects them like a boat collects barnacles; they flock to him. What are you laughing at? I'm serious. When Andrew takes a walk he finds guns under bushes, when he goes to the attic he stumbles over them, when he answers the doorbell it's a mailman with the wrong package, and what's in the package? Guess. He's never bought a gun in his life, he wouldn't think of it. He's the gentlest soul you can imagine. He spends all his days in the New York Public Library doing research for professors, but when he comes out to go home what does he find in the litter basket? A gun among the orange peels, handle up. It's crazy."

"He wouldn't have to *accept* them," Elizabeth said.

"Why not? It's fate."

"Then what does he do with them?"

"Oh, stows them away."

They were in the kitchen now. Timothy had forgotten all his caution; he dropped the gun in his pocket, carelessly, and then gave the pocket a pat. "We don't mention this to Mother, you understand," he said. "I come pistol-hunting before every visit, just to be on the safe side. Not that he would *do* anything. I don't want you thinking—oh, there *was* a sort of accident once, someone got shot through the foot. But you're an outsider here. You don't know what Andrew's really like. He felt terrible about it. He was just—"

"Oh, stop, I'm not interested," Elizabeth said, although up till then she had been. She had the sudden feeling that troubles were being piled in front of her, huge untidy heaps laid at her feet, Emersons stepping back waiting for her to exclaim over the heaps and admire them. She headed out the back door, toward the toolshed. Timothy followed. When he came up beside her she saw that one of his pockets hung heavier than the other. She thought of an old Sunday comic strip: Dick Tracy's crimestopper's textbook, warning against men with lopsided overcoats. "You be careful you don't get yourself arrested," she told him. Then she reached inside the toolshed for a hoop of hose, closing the subject.

But Timothy said, "The worst is getting rid of the damn things. You'd never believe how hard it is. The last one I sent out with the garbage, under the coffee grounds. Elizabeth?"

"What," said Elizabeth. She backed across the lawn, feeding out coils of hose.

"I cheated on a test."

Another trouble, added to the heap. "Did you?" she said.

"This is serious, Elizabeth."

"Well, why tell *me* about it?" she said. "It's always something. Tomorrow it'll be something else. Go tell a professor, if it bothers you so much."

"I can't," Timothy said. "I've already been caught."

Elizabeth looked over at him.

"I was just walking past his desk, after it was over. He said, 'Emerson, I'd like to have a word with you,' and I knew, right then. I knew what he would say. It felt as if my stomach had dropped out."

"What will happen?" Elizabeth said.

"I'll be expelled."

"Well, maybe not."

"Of course I will. Those guys are tough as nails. And you

know something? I knew that answer I cheated on. I didn't have a shadow of a doubt about it. I wrote it down, and I turned to my left, and I read off the other guy's answer just as cool as you please. It was like I forgot where I was, suddenly. I forgot the customs of the country. I just wanted to see if Joe Barrett knew the answer too."

"Maybe if you told them that," Elizabeth said.

"Not a chance. It wouldn't help." He kicked at the hose. "Come on, will you? It's getting to be lunchtime."

"The grass is drying up. If I don't—"

"Look," said Timothy. "I've been walking around by myself ever since this happened. Can't you just drop everything and come with me?"

"Oh well. All right. Let me go and tell your mother."

"Call from my place. Don't go back in, she already knows something is wrong. Oh Lord, this is going to kill her."

"I doubt it," said Elizabeth.

But she didn't go back in, even so.

Timothy's apartment was downtown, in a dingy building with a wrought-iron elevator. All the way up to his floor, with the cables creaking and jerking above them, Timothy stood in the corner staring at his shoes. His face reflected the bluish light, giving him a pale, sweaty look. His silence was heavy and brooding. But once they entered his apartment, where tall windows let the sun in, he seemed to change. "*Well* now," he said. "What shall we eat?" And he went off to the little Pullman kitchen while Elizabeth settled herself on the couch. His apartment had a smothered look. It was curtained, carpeted, and upholstered until there were no sharp corners left, and in the evenings carefully arranged lamps threw soft, closed circles on the tabletops. Elizabeth felt out of place in it. She

shucked off her moccasins and curled her legs beneath her, but everything she looked at was so padded and textured that she couldn't keep her eyes on it long. Finally she closed them, and tipped her head back against the couch.

"Here," said Timothy. "Corned beef on rye. That all right? Cold beer."

"Well, thanks," said Elizabeth, sitting up. She took the plate and peered between the slices of bread. "Corned beef is what we had two weeks ago. Is this the selfsame can?"

"I don't know."

"Can you get food-poisoning from canned corned beef?"

But Timothy, in a chair opposite her with his sandwich halfway to his mouth, stared into space.

"Timothy."

"What."

"Look, it's not so bad. Find something else to do."

"Like what, for instance," he said.

"Well, *I* can't tell you that."

"Why not? Say *something*, can't you? Give me a treatise on reincarnation, convince me I'm full of lives and can afford to throw one away. Convince my mother too, while you're at it."

"Well, it is a point," Elizabeth said.

"Ha." He took a swig from his beer can. "Women have it easy," he said. "You can work or not, nobody minds. Men are expected to be responsible. There's no room for variation."

"Maybe you should make a *big* switch. Lumberjack? Fur-trapper? Deck-swabber?"

"I could answer one of those DRAW ME ads on the matchbooks," Timothy said. He laughed.

"You could be a state hog inspector."

But then he leaned forward, his elbows on his knees, his sandwich still untasted. "I can't seem to picture a future any

more," he told her. "There's nothing I hope for. No one I want to be. Yet I started out so promising, would you believe it? In grade school they thought I was a genius. No one but Andrew even knew what I was talking about. I invented weird gadgets, I played chess tournaments, I monitored Stravinsky on an oscilloscope that I rebuilt myself. Did you know that?"

"No," said Elizabeth. "I don't even know what an oscilloscope is."

"Why is everything you say so *inconsequential?* Can't you understand when something serious is going on?"

But it was hard to take him seriously when he looked so much like the child he had been talking about. There was one of him in every classroom Elizabeth had ever sat in—chubby and too clever, pale and scowling, wearing an old man's suit and cracking elderly jokes that made his classmates uneasy. She could picture him scuffing around the playground with his hands in his pockets while the others chose up softball teams; his name would come up by default, at the end, and he would play miserably and dodge the ball when it crossed the plate and then hit some pathetic, ticked-off foul and fling his bat in a panic and run toward first base anyway, hunched and desperate, until the hoots and curses called him back. "Oh, aren't you glad you're not still *there?*" she asked suddenly, for in spite of the traces of that child on his face he had at least grown into his suit, and his friends had grown into his jokes. He had passed the age for softball and learned when not to sling long words around. But Timothy, off on some track of his own, merely blinked.

"Elizabeth," he said. "Don't go home this weekend. Let's take a trip together."

"Oh, well, no."

"We could start off for anywhere! Drive without a plan.

Stop when we felt like it." He paused, having just then heard
her answer. "What's the matter with you? You love sudden
trips. Are you worried what people might think?"

"I just—"

"I never thought you would be, somehow." He looked
down at his sandwich, and began tearing pieces out of it and
dropping them on his plate. "We would have separate rooms,
of course," he said.

"No, you see—"

"If *that's* what's bothering you."

"No."

The sandwich had turned into a pile of shreds. "Maybe
you think—we wouldn't *have* to have separate rooms," he
said. "I just meant—I don't know what you expect of me.
What do you want, anyway? What am I supposed to be
doing? Just tell me, can't you? I don't know why I should be
making such a mess of saying this."

"Oh well, that's all right," Elizabeth said helplessly.
What she wanted to say was, "Of *course* I'll come." When
would she learn not to plan ahead, when always at the last
minute she felt tugged by something different? "I'm sorry,"
she said. "I really would like to."

"Or take me home with you."

"I don't think I can."

"Why not? If you want I could stay in a hotel, I wouldn't
be bothering your family then. Would that be better?"

"You see, Matthew is coming," Elizabeth said.

He stared at her.

"I invited him."

"But why *Matthew*? Why does he always keep popping
up like this?"

"I like him," she said. And she decided she'd better go

on with what she had planned to tell him earlier: "While we're on Matthew, Timothy, I thought I should say something about—"

"You are going to turn into a very objectionable old lady, Elizabeth. You know that. The opinionated kind. 'I like this, I don't like that,' every other sentence—it's fine now, but wait a while. See how it sits on people when you've lost your looks and you're *croaking* it out."

"That is something to think about," said Elizabeth, glad to change the subject.

"Call up Matthew. Tell him *I'm* the one that *needs* to go."

"Timothy, I've been up since six o'clock this morning and every single minute there's been some Emerson dumping crisises on me."

"Crises," Timothy said into his beer can.

"Picking and bickering and arguing. Raking up all these disasters and piling them in front of me. Well, I've had my quota. I don't want any more. I'm going to call your mother, and then I'm going off for an afternoon on my own and not coming back till supper."

"Wait, Elizabeth—"

But she left. She went into the bedroom, sat down on the edge of the bed, and lifted the telephone from the table. Then she couldn't remember Mrs. Emerson's number. All this chaos was disrupting her mind. There were tatters of old arguments in the air around her, and she had a restless, hanging-back feeling as if there were something she had not done well. She listened to the dial tone droning in her ear and watched Timothy pace back and forth in the living room with his eyes averted, his face pink and rumpled-looking. Then Mrs. Emerson's number flashed before her, and she leaned forward to dial.

The telephone rang four times. (Was Mrs. Emerson in some new frenzy, twirling through the house wringing her hands and far too upset to answer?) The fifth ring was cut off in the middle. "Hello!" Mrs. Emerson said.

"It's Elizabeth."

"Elizabeth, where are you? There's a man here delivering big sacks of something."

"Oh, that'll be the lime."

"What will I do with it? Where will I tell him to put it? I thought you were around the house somewhere."

"The lime goes in the toolshed," Elizabeth said. "I'm at lunch. I may be late getting back, I'm spending the afternoon downtown."

"Downtown? What—and I can't find Timothy. One minute he was here and the—now, don't take *all* afternoon, Elizabeth."

"Okay," Elizabeth said. "Bye."

She hung up. Timothy was leaning against the doorframe, watching her. "Now call Matthew," he said.

"I'm through with that subject."

"That's what *you* think."

He took a step back and slammed the door between them, with a noise that shook the room. She heard the key in the lock. *"Call* him!" he shouted from the other side.

"Oh, for—"

She stood up and went to try the door. It was firmly locked. Timothy was standing so close behind it that she heard his breath, which came in short puffs. *"Timothy,"* she said. He didn't answer. She gave the door a kick and then turned an oval knob at eye level that locked it from inside—a useless move, but the final-sounding click was a satisfaction. Then she flung herself on the bed again and lay back to stare at the ceiling.

When she had been there a few minutes she began to see some humor in the situation. She got off the bed and circled the room, stopping to look out the window. "I'm stripping your bed, Timothy," she called. "Now I'm tying the sheets together. Now I'm tying the blankets. I'm knotting them to the headboard, I'm hanging them out the window. Whee! Down I go."

Timothy said nothing. She imagined him waiting aimlessly, feeling sillier by the minute but unable to back down.

She went over to the bureau, found two military brushes, and brushed her hair with both at once. She picked up a textbook and went back to the bed with it and looked at a diagram of the circulatory system. There seemed no point in memorizing it. She went through her pockets, hoping to find something time-consuming—a scrap of sandpaper, maybe. Timothy's windowsill was scarred and peeling. But all she came up with was a rubber band, an unwrapped stick of chewing gum, six wooden matches and an envelope flap with a number on it. The rubber band she flipped into a light fixture on the ceiling, and the gum she dusted off and popped into her mouth. The matches she struck one by one on the windowsill and then held in her fingers, testing to see if telepathy could make a flame go out before it burned her. It couldn't. She was relieved to see the flickering knot of blue proceed steadily downward, unaffected by anything so insubstantial as her thought waves, which flickered also, veering from the match in her hand to the silent figure behind the door. When she had blown the last match out, and wiped the sting from her fingers, she dialed the number on the envelope flap. "Hardware," a man said. She dialed again, choosing the numbers at random. "I'm sorry, we are unable to complete your call as dialed," someone told her disapprovingly. "Please hang up and dial again, or ask your operator for assistance. This is

a—" Elizabeth slammed the receiver down. "Timothee," she said, in the tone she might use for the cat, "I'm ready to come *out* now."

"Did you call Matthew?"

She blew a strand of hair out of her face and tried another number. This time she hit on one that existed. A woman said, "Hello? Barker residence."

"Oh, Mrs. Barker," Elizabeth said, shifting her chewing gum to the back of one cheek. "This is Miss Pleasance calling, from Baltimore Gas and Electric? Your name has been referred to us for an in-depth study. Would you care to answer a question?"

"Why, surely," Mrs. Barker said.

"Could you tell me if—"

"But first, I want to say that I just love the little leaflets you send out. The ones with the bills? Your recipe-of-the-month is especially helpful and of course I'm always interested to see what new appliances are out. Why, every time the bill comes I just sit right down and read every word."

"You do?"

"Oh, my yes. And try the recipes. Living on a budget, you know, I especially appreciate those meals-in-a-skillet. Rice and what-not. Of course my husband prefers straight meat. 'I'm a meat-and-potatoes man,' he says, but I say, 'Joe, you supply the money and then I'll supply the meat. Until then,' I say, 'it's meals-in-a-skillet for *you*, my friend.' Well, he's very good-natured about it."

"Mrs. Barker," Elizabeth said, "is your—"

"One thing I might mention, though—"

"Is your *refrigerator* running, Mrs. Barker?"

"Oh, you're preparing for summer, aren't you. I read what the leaflet said about summer: don't leave your icebox door open and then come crying to *us* if the bill is high. Well,

you don't have to worry, Miss Pleasance. I know how you people are working to save us money and I do try to co-operate in every way I can. One thing I might mention, though, is the amount you depend on tomato sauce in your recipes. I wouldn't bring it up except you did ask, and I feel it might be helpful for you to know. My husband doesn't like tomato sauce. He says it's too acid. I don't know about other families, maybe they *love* tomato sauce, but it's something for you people to think over. Have you considered chicken broth? Look, I'm so glad you called. Any time, any questions at all, you just feel free to give me a ring. I'm home all day. I don't go out much. We just moved here and we don't find Baltimore very friendly, although I hope I'm not stepping on your toes when I say that. But I just know we'll settle in. And I take a great deal of pride in my home and feel sure I could tell you just anything you want to know about the typical housewife's opinions. Are you concerned about your meter-reading service?"

"Well, not just now," Elizabeth said.

"Any time you are, then—"

"Fine," said Elizabeth. "Thank you very much, Mrs. Barker."

"You're very welcome."

Elizabeth hung up. "Oh, my," she said, and pressed her index fingers to her eyelids. Then she rose and went over to the door. She knocked. "Timothy, I want to come out," she said.

"Did you call Matthew?"

"This is getting silly."

"Call Matthew."

She went back to the telephone. With the receiver to her ear she stared vacantly out the window a minute, popping her chewing gum, and then she smiled. She dialed the oper-

ator. "I'd like to make a long-distance call," she said, "to Ellington, North Carolina. Person-to-person. First class. Any *other* special charges you can think of." Then she settled back, still smiling, unraveling a thread from the ribbing of one sock.

It was her mother who answered. "Oh, Elizabeth, what now," she said.

"What?"

"Aren't you calling to put off your visit again?"

"Not that I know of," Elizabeth said.

"What is it, then?"

"I'm just saying hello."

"Oh. Hello," her mother said. "It's nice to hear your voice."

"Nice to hear *yours*."

"Do you have enough money to be spending it like this?"

"That's no problem," Elizabeth said. "How *is* everything? Everybody fine? Spring there yet? Trees in bloom?"

"Well, of course," said her mother. "Bloomed and finished. You're using up your three minutes, Elizabeth."

"How's that dog getting along? Pop used to her yet?"

"You know he doesn't like you calling him Pop."

"Sorry. Well. Is Dommie still hanging around?"

"Elizabeth, that's the saddest thing. I told you how often he's asked after you, well, then Sunday he came to church with a red-headed girl. I didn't think anything of it at the time, she could have been his cousin or something. But *now* what I hear: they're engaged. Planning a fall wedding. Well, I suppose you could care less, I know you're bringing home some Baltimore boy, but I always *hoped*, don't you know, just way in the back of my—"

Oh, Dommie was good for a full fifteen minutes. Elizabeth stretched out on the bedspread and listened, every now

104 : *The Clock Winder*

and then sliding in a question to keep the flow going. When that was exhausted they talked about her father. ("I feel I ought to warn you," her mother said, "that he looks upon this visit as a sign of some turning point in your faith. What are you laughing at? I won't have you hurt his feelings for the world. He expects you to have changed some, and if you haven't I don't want to hear about it.") Then Polly's new baby. ("Her hair is brown, and I believe it's going to curl. I'm so glad she *has* some, I never could warm to a bald-headed baby. Her eyes are a puzzle to me. They're blue but may be turning, there's that sort of opaque look beginning around the—") Once, in mid-sentence, the bedroom doorknob rattled. What would happen if she said, "Excuse me, Mother, but I just wanted to say that I've been taken prisoner"? The connecting of her two worlds by a single wire made her feel disoriented, but when her mother ran out of conversation Elizabeth said, "Wait, don't hang up. Isn't anyone else there who would like to talk?"

"Have you lost all common sense? How much is this going to cost you?"

"I don't know," Elizabeth said.

But she found out, as soon as the call was finished. She dialed the operator, who said, "Eight-sixty," and then "Ma'am?" when Elizabeth laughed. "Ho there, Timothy," she said. "Can you hear me? I just made an eight-sixty phone call."

Silence.

"Timothy? Now I'm going to call California station-to-station. I'm going to tell some store they delivered the wrong package, and get switched from department to department to—"

Something was thrown against the door. Then he kicked the door until it shook, and then he turned the key and

rattled the knob. It was still locked from inside, but Elizabeth didn't open it. "Damn it, let me in," he said.

"You're beginning to get on my nerves," she told him.

"Do I have to break the door down? I want to talk to you."

"Say please."

"I'm warning you, Elizabeth."

"Pretty please?"

There was a pause. Then he said, "I'm pointing a gun at you."

"Ho ho, I'm scared stiff."

"I'm pointing Andrew's gun. I'll shoot straight through the door."

"Oh, for goodness sake," Elizabeth said. The whole situation was getting out of hand. She slid off the bed and went over to open the door. "You're lucky I'm not the hysterical type," she said, brushing past him. "How do you know that's not loaded? Put it down. Send it out with the garbage."

She stopped off by the couch to slip into her moccasins, and then she headed out to the entrance hall. It was a pity she had no money; she would have to thumb her way home. Or take a taxi, and have Mrs. Emerson pay for it.

Behind her there was a click, a metallic, whanging sound. She wheeled around.

"Stop there," Timothy said.

But it wasn't at her the gun was pointing, it was at himself, at an upward angle near the center of his chest. His wrist was turned in a sharp, awkward twist. "Timothy Emerson," she said. "Did you just pull that trigger? What if there'd been bullets in it? Of all the—"

"No," Timothy said, "I think I took the safety catch off."

She started walking toward him, slowly and steadily.

Timothy kept his eyes fixed on her. His hand was shaking; she saw a glimmer trembling on the gun barrel. "Stop there," he said. But an edge of something was moving into his face, and she could tell that in a moment there would be a shift in the way he saw all this: he would laugh. Didn't he always laugh? So she kept chewing her gum all the way across the room, the eternal handyman, unafraid. "This family is going to drive me up a wall someday," she told him. "What did you do before *I* came along? What will you do when I'm gone?" Then she lunged.

Her hand closed on his. She felt the short blond hairs prickling her palm. There was an explosion that seemed to come from somewhere else, from inside or behind him, and Timothy looked straight at her with a face full of surprise and then slid sideways to the floor.

⬥ 5 ⬥

It was all up to Matthew. It was Matthew who made the funeral arrangements, brought his mother endless cups of tea that he had brewed himself, met his brother and sisters at the airport and carted them home, answering their questions as he drove. "But why—?" "How could he—?" "I really don't know," Matthew said. "I'll tell you what little I've pieced together, that's all I can do."

Peter came from college, looking young and scared with his hair slicked back too neatly. Mary flew out from Dayton with her little boy; Margaret came from Chicago and Melissa from New York. Andrew had not been told. He would arrive on Saturday, as he had planned before all this happened. Then they could sit him down and lay comforting hands on his shoulders and tell him gradually, face to face. The funeral would be over by then, but just barely, which made Matthew picture his family burying Timothy in haste. They didn't really, of course. There was the usual waiting period, with the usual tears and boredom and the sense that time was just creeping until they could get this business

finished. They wore out the subject of Timothy; they began to feel bruised and battered at the sound of his name. People kept paying formal calls, requiring them to make hushed and grateful conversation that did not sound real even though it was. No one ate regular meals. No one went to bed at regular hours. Any room Matthew went into, at any time of day, he might find several members of his family sitting in a silent knot with coffeecups on their knees. Sometimes a piece of laughter broke out, or an accidental burst of enthusiasm as they veered to other subjects. Then they caught themselves, checked the laughter, dwindled off in mid-sentence, returning to a silence that swelled with inappropriate thoughts.

It used to be Elizabeth who managed this family. Matthew had never realized that till now. She was the one they had leaned on—he and his mother and Timothy, and the house itself, whose rooms had taken on her clear sunny calmness and her smell of fresh wood chips. Only now, when she was needed most, Elizabeth had changed. With the others present she looked bewildered and out of place, like any ordinary stranger who had stumbled into the midst of a family in mourning. Mrs. Emerson called on her continually, but she answered with her mind on something else. Her caretaking had descended to the most literal kind: errand-running, lawn-sprinkling, lugging down more toys for Mary's Billy. At twelve o'clock one night Matthew found her on a stepladder in the pantry, changing lightbulbs. She wandered through crowded rooms winding clocks or carrying table-leaves, her face set and distant, and while Father Lewis was in the parlor offering his condolences she stayed on the sunporch, yanking weather-stripping from all the windows.

"Why are you working so hard?" Matthew asked her.

"This is my job," she said, and dumped tangles of

cracked stripping into a garbage can that she had brought in from outside.

"So that's Mother's famous handyman," said Mary. "Is she always so grim?"

"No, not ever," Matthew said.

Then he removed his glasses and rubbed the inner corners of his eyes. Mary looked at him a moment but said nothing more.

Late Friday afternoon, Elizabeth came into the kitchen while Matthew was making a sandwich. She was in her oldest jeans, carrying a curved pruning saw that she set on a counter. "I thought you would be the one to tell," she said. "After the funeral I'm going home for good."

Matthew spread jam over peanut butter and patted another slice of bread down on top of it. Then he said, "I don't know what I'd do if you left."

"I think I'd better."

"Is it because of the trouble with the police?"

"No."

"Mother's going to rely on you to keep her going, these next few months."

"I don't want to be relied on," Elizabeth said.

Matthew laid the sandwich carefully on a plate and offered it to her. She shook her head. He set the plate on the drainboard. "If you would just give it a little more thought," he said.

"I have."

"Or if you held off till things here were settled. Then I could come with you. I'm still planning on it."

"No," she said.

"Well, all right. Not now. But as soon as you want me to."

She said nothing. He laid a hand over hers, over cool

rough knuckles, and she kept still until he removed it. Then she picked up her saw and left.

"Where is Elizabeth?" Mrs. Emerson said. "Why don't I see her around any more?"

"She's out cutting that hanging branch, Mother."

"*That's* not what I need her for."

"Shall I call her?"

"No, no, never mind."

He set a tray on her nightstand, tea and a perfectly sectioned orange, and then straightened to watch his mother pace between the bed and the window. There was nothing broken about her, even now. She continued to wear her matched skirts and sweaters and her string of pearls, her high-heeled shoes, her bracelet with the names of all her children dangling on gold discs. She spoke when spoken to, in her thin, bright voice, and she kept in touch with the arrivals and the sympathy cards and the funeral arrangements. It was true that she spent more time alone in her room, and there were sometimes traces of tears when she came downstairs, but she was one of those women who look younger after crying. The tears puffed her eyes slightly, erasing lines and shadows. Her skin was flushed and shining. She moved with the proud, deliberate dignity she had had when her husband died. Once, months ago, Matthew had asked Elizabeth if she found his mother hard to put up with. "No, I like her," she said. "Think what a small life she has, but she still dresses up every day and holds her stomach in. Isn't that something?" Now that Elizabeth seemed so removed, Matthew tried to take over for her. He shielded his mother from visitors, and answered her telephone, and brought her food that she never ate. When she paced the room he watched with his hands slightly flexed, as if he were preparing to leap forward any minute

and catch her if she stumbled, or prevent her from ricocheting from wall to wall.

He was the one who broke the news to her. Elizabeth had called him from the police station and asked who should do it: he or she. "I should," he told her. "I couldn't decide," she said. "I thought, you're her son after all, she might prefer it. Then I thought no, it's something I should do"—as if she saw herself as a culprit, duty-bound to face in person someone whose dish she had broken or whose message she had forgotten to deliver. He couldn't understand that. Everyone knew she was not to blame. He had called for her at the police station, searching her out through long flaky corridors and finding her, finally, pale and stony-faced in a roomful of officials. "Wait in the hall," they told him, but instead he crossed to stand behind her chair, one hand on the back of it. He had waited through the endless questions, the short, stark answers, the final re-reading of her statement. The policeman who read it stumbled woodenly over her words, so that it sounded as if she herself had stumbled although she hadn't. His voice was bored and dismal; he was like someone reciting lists. Even her useless repetitions had been conscientiously recorded—"I don't know. I don't know," which she must have said before Matthew came in, and surely not in such a despairing drone. She would have been quick with it, flicking it off her tongue like a dismissal, the way she always did when she felt cornered. The thought made Matthew want to move his hand from the chair to her shoulder, but he kept still.

On the telephone he had not even asked her the cause of death, but when it came out at the police station he wasn't surprised. He had assumed it was suicide from the start. Now he wondered why. He had never known that he expected such a thing of Timothy. Why not a car accident? He was a short

tempered driver. Why not a hold-up man, a hit-and-run, one of those senseless pieces of violence that happened in this city every day? He couldn't answer. When he fixed an image of his brother in his mind, trying to understand, he found that Timothy had already grown flat and unreal. "He had a round face," he told himself. "He had short blond hair, sticking out in tufts." The round face and blond hair materialized, but without the spark that made them Timothy.

He had driven Elizabeth home and left her outside, sitting on the porch steps facing the street, while he went into the house. He found his mother writing letters in the bedroom. The little beige dictaphone was playing her voice back, as tinny and sharp as a talking doll's: "Mary. Is Billy old enough for tricycles? Not the pedal kind, I know, but—"

"I have bad news," Matthew said.

She spun around in her chair with her face already shocked. "It's Andrew," she said instantly.

"No, Timothy."

"Timothy? It's Timothy?" She had dropped the pen and was kneading her hands, which looked cold and white and shaky. "He's dead," she said.

"I'm afraid he is."

"I thought it would be Andrew."

Behind her the mechanical voice played on. "Does he have a wagon? A scooter? Ask Peter about his plans for the summer."

"How did it happen?" she asked.

"He, it was—"

"How did it *happen*?"

Timothy should have to be doing this; not Matthew. It was all Timothy's fault, wasn't it? Anger made him blunter than he had meant to be. "He shot himself," he said

—flatly, like a child tattling on some dreadful piece of mischief that he himself had had no part in.

"Oh, no, that's so *unfair!*" his mother said.

"Unfair?"

He paused. Nothing he had planned covered this turn in the conversation. Mrs. Emerson felt her face with her hands, sending off icy trembling sparkles from her rings. "Mother," Matthew said, "I wish there was something I—"

"Did he suffer any pain?"

"No."

"But how did it come about?" she said. "What was the cause? Where did he find a gun?"

"I'm not too sure. Elizabeth said—"

"*Elizabeth!*" Her face had the stunned, grainy quality of a movie close-up, although she was across the room from him. She felt behind her on the desk and brought forth an inkbottle. Without looking at it she heaved it, overhand, in a swift, vicious arc—the last thing he had expected. He winced, but stood his ground. The inkbottle thudded against the curtain on the door, splashing it blue-black and cracking one of the panes behind it. In the silence that followed, the dictaphone said, "Would Margaret like Mr. Hughes to print her up more of those address labels?"

"Oh, I'm so sorry," Mrs. Emerson said.

She flicked the dictaphone off, and then bent to pick up a sheet of stationery that had floated to the floor. "There was no excuse for that," she said.

"It's all right."

"What were you saying?"

"Well—" He hesitated to mention Elizabeth's name again, but his mother prompted him.

"Elizabeth said?"

"She said she went to eat lunch with him. She was just walking down the hall to his apartment when she heard the shot."

"Oh, I see," his mother said.

She never gave any explanation for throwing the inkbottle. She had Elizabeth replace the pane immediately, and Alvareen washed the stain from the curtain. And in restless moments, pacing the bedroom or waiting out some silence among her family, she still said, "Where is Elizabeth? Why isn't she here with us?" Matthew watched closely, less concerned for his mother than for Elizabeth herself, but if anything she seemed closer to Elizabeth now than before. He saw her waiting at the kitchen window for Elizabeth to come in from staking roses; he saw her reach once for Elizabeth's hand when they met in the hallway, and hold onto it tightly for a second before she gave a little laugh at herself and let it go. The inkbottle settled out of sight in the back of Matthew's mind, joining all the other unexplainable things that women seemed to do from time to time.

He didn't believe what Elizabeth had told the police. Too many parts of it failed to make sense. It came out very soon that she and Timothy must have driven downtown together, and then a neighbor of Timothy's said she had heard people quarreling, and the police discovered a long distance call that had been made to Elizabeth's family. "I was with him but left, and then came back," Elizabeth said. Well, that was possible. If they had had an argument she might have stormed out and then changed her mind later and returned. But what would they argue about, she and Timothy? And when had she been known to leave in a huff? And if she did leave, was she the type to come back?

One of the things he had long ago accepted about Elizabeth was that she didn't always tell the truth. She seemed to

view truth as a quality constantly shifting, continually reshaping itself the way a slant of light might during the course of a day. Her contradictions were tossed off gaily, as if she were laughing at her stories' habit of altering without help from her. With the police, now, she confined herself to a single version, remodeled only once when they discovered her earlier visit. Yet there were points at which she simply shut up and refused to answer. "You apparently don't realize that you could be in serious trouble over this," the policemen said. But that was where they were wrong. She must have realized, to have stopped so short rather than spin whatever haphazard tale came to mind.

"Where did he get the gun?" they asked.

"I don't know."

"It just came out of nowhere? What were you two arguing about?"

"Arguing?"

"Why were you shouting?"

"Shouting?"

"*Miss.*"

Elizabeth looked at them, her face expressionless.

"Why did you call home?"

"To say hello."

"Was that during the earlier visit?"

"Of course."

"Did the argument arise from that phone call in some way?"

"Argument?"

They gave up. There was no doubt it was a suicide—they had the powder burns, the fingerprints, the statement of his professor providing motivation. Elizabeth was only the last little untied thread, and although they would have liked her to finish wrapping things up they had never thought of her

as crucial. They layered death over with extraneous interviews and coroners' reports and legal processes until Timothy himself was all but forgotten. Then, almost as an afterthought, they declared the case closed. The deceased could be buried, they said. That was the end of it.

"Mother," Matthew said, "come drink this tea."

"In a minute."

She was standing by the window, moving a plant into a pool of sunlight.

"I've been talking with Elizabeth," Matthew told her.

"Oh?"

"She wants to leave her job."

Mrs. Emerson's hands dropped from the flowerpot. She straightened her back, so that her sharp shoulderblades suddenly flattened.

"She's going to wait till after the funeral, though," he said.

"But leaving! Why? What did she say about me?"

"Well, nothing about *you*."

"Did she say I was the cause?"

"Of course not."

"She must have given you a reason, though."

"No. Not really," Matthew said.

His mother turned. Her eyes, when she was disturbed, never could rest on one place; they darted back and forth, as if she were hoping to read her surroundings like a letter. "And why tell *you*?" she said. "I am her employer."

"I guess she thought it was a bad time to bother you."

"No, she blames me for something. But *now!* To leave now! Why, I've been thinking of her as one of the family. I took her right in."

"Maybe you could talk to her," Matthew said.

"Oh, no. I couldn't."

"If she knew how you felt about it—"

"If she wants to leave, let her go," said his mother. "I'm not going to beg her to stay."

Then she settled herself in a flowered armchair, arranging her skirt beneath her, and pushed her bracelet back on her wrist and leaned forward with perfect posture to pour herself a cup of tea.

Matthew went downstairs and into the kitchen, where he found Peter eating the sandwich that had been on the drainboard. "Oh, sorry," Peter said. "Was this yours?"

"I didn't want it."

"Just got to needing a little snack," Peter said. He gulped down one more bite and then set the rest of the sandwich aside, as if he felt embarrassed at being hungry. He was forever embarrassed by something, or maybe that was just his age— nineteen, still unformed-looking, clomping around in enormous loafers bumping into people and saying the wrong things. He had come at the tail end of the family, five years after Melissa. The others had no more than a year between them and some of them less; they were a bustling foreign tribe, disappearing and reappearing without explanation, while Peter sat on the floor beside his rubber blocks and watched with surprised, considering eyes. Then the oldest ones were given quarters on the third floor, into which they vanished for all of their last years at home. They read in bed undisturbed, visited back and forth in the dead of night, formed pacts against the grownups. Peter stayed in the nursery, next door to his parents. No one ever thought to change the pink-and-yellow wallpaper. He grew up while their backs were turned, completely on his own, long after the third floor was emptied and echoing. Now when he came home on visits he bumped into doors and failed to listen when he was spoken to, as if he had given up all attempts at belonging here.

"Mother's upset because Elizabeth is leaving," Matthew said, trying to draw him into the family.

"Gee, that's too bad. Who's Elizabeth?"

"*Elizabeth*. The handyman."

"Oh. I guess she must think we're a bunch of kooks after all that's happened."

"No, she—"

"Is that Elizabeth? I thought her name was Alvareen."

"No—what? *Whose* name? Oh, never mind."

Matthew left, bypassing the living room. He was tired of talk. He went out through the sunporch, a quiet place lit with diagonals of dusty orange light. Alvareen stood ironing a table cloth while tears rolled down her cheeks. (She had shown up two days in a row, on time, impressed by tragedy.) Margaret was curled on the windowseat reading a book and chewing on tight little cylinders that she had made from the page corners. Neither of them looked up as he passed.

"Elizabeth," he said, standing under the poplar tree.

"Here I am."

She sat on a branch above the one she had just cut off, leaning sideways against the trunk.

"Shall I help you down?"

"I like it here."

"I'm going home now. I'm not coming back until the funeral."

"Oh. All right."

"Could you come down? I'd like to talk some things over with you."

"No, I don't think so."

"Well, would you rather I stayed here? What do you want to do?"

"I want to sit in this poplar tree," Elizabeth said.

He nodded, and stood around for a while with his hands in his pockets. Then he left.

Matthew's house was out in the country, part of a rundown old farm that his father had somehow come into possession of. His family called it a shack, but it was more than that. It was a tiny two-story house, the front a peeling white, the other three sides unpainted and as gray as the rick-rack fence that separated it from the woods behind. To get there he had to leave the highway and drive down a rutted road that rattled the bones of his old car. At the end of the road he parked and walked through new, leafy woods up to the front yard, which was a floor of packed earth. A rotting tire hung from an apple tree. A Studebaker rusted on concrete blocks out back. His mother had come here only once and, "Oh, Matthew," she had said, looking at the porch with its buckling slat railings, "*I* can't go in there. It would make me too sad." But she had, of course. She had perched uneasily on a squat rocking chair and accepted Oreos and lemonade. Her hair and the glass lemonade pitcher had been two discs of gold beneath the high smoked ceilings. Then forever after that she begged him to find some place nicer. "I'll pay for it myself, don't think about the money," she said. "I'll fix it up for you. I'll shop for what it needs." When he refused she settled for buying what she called "touches"—an Indian rug, homespun curtains, cushions from Peru. She comforted herself by imagining that the house was meant to be Bohemian, one of those places with pottery on the windowsills and serapes draped over the chairs. Matthew didn't mind. He had chosen to live here because it was comfortable and made no demands on him, and all the cushions in Peru couldn't change that. His father had been

happy to give his permission. (He liked to see every last thing put to use.) Then at his death he had willed Matthew the house outright. The others got money; Matthew got the house, which was what he really wanted.

He walked through the front room, where each board creaked separately beneath his feet. He went into the kitchen and took a roll of liverwurst from the yellowed refrigerator. Leaning against the sink, paring off slices with a rusty knife, he ate liverwurst until he stopped feeling hungry and then put it away again. That was his supper. There was a table, of course, and two chairs, and a whole set of dishes in the cupboard (his mother's gift, brown earthenware), but he rarely used them. Most meals he ate standing at the stove, spooning large mouthfuls directly from the pot to save dishwashing. Once when Elizabeth came for supper he had started to do that—dipped a fork absentmindedly into the stew pot, before he caught himself—and all Elizabeth did was reach for the potato skillet and find herself another fork. Halfway through the meal they traded pans. If he narrowed his eyes he could see her still, slouched against a counter munching happily and cradling the skillet in a frayed old undershirt that he used for a pot-holder.

Then sometimes, when living alone depressed him, he set the table meticulously with knife, fork and spoon and a folded napkin, plate and salad plate, salt and pepper shakers. He served into serving dishes, and from them to his plate, as if he were two people performing two separate tasks. He settled himself in his chair and smoothed the napkin across his knees; then he sat motionless, forgetting the canned hash and olive-drab beans that steamed before him, stunned by the dismalness of this elaborate table set for one. What was he doing here, twenty-eight years old and all alone? Why was he living like an elderly widower in this house without children, set in

his ways, pottering from stove to table to sink? The carefully positioned salad plate and the salt and pepper shakers, side by side in their handwoven basket, looked strained and pathetic. He went back to eating at the stove, with salt from a Morton's box and pepper from an Ann Page pepper tin.

In the living room he picked up old *Newsweeks* and placed them in a wooden rack. He straightened a rug. He aligned the corners of the slipcover on the daybed. Then, since it was growing dark, he lit a table lamp and sat down with that morning's paper. Words jerked before his vision in scattered clusters. He felt like a man in a waiting room before a dreaded appointment, reading sentences that skipped along heartlessly in spite of the sick feeling in his stomach. He raised his eyes and looked at the walls instead—tongue-and-groove, shiny green, with an oval photograph of someone long dead leaning over the fireplace. The fireplace itself was black and cold, in spite of the chill in the air. A brown oil burner fed its pipe into one side of the chimney, and clanked periodically as if its metal were still contracting after all the winter months it had tried to heat this room.

"Aren't you *freezing?*" his mother had asked. And Elizabeth had said, "You want to go hunt firewood?" His father, rocking in that chair with a glass of warm bourbon, had said, "When *I* was a boy, rooms were always this cold. We were healthier, too." His father had come visiting often, mumbling something about business carrying him in this direction. He had supplied the bourbon himself, and occasionally fresh vegetables or a slab of bacon—country things, which he had purchased in the city to bring out here. He liked to have the fire lit. He liked to rock in silence for hours. "Now, this is the way to live," he said. "At heart, I'm a simple man," but there had been nothing simple about him. Every quality he had was struggling with another its exact opposite. If he rocked so

contentedly here, in the city he was a whirlwind. Always selling, pushing, buying, bargaining, sometimes bending the law.
"Remember this," he kept telling his children. "If you want to
rise in the world, smile with your eyes. Not just your mouth. It
gets them every time." His children cringed. Momentarily,
they hated him. (Yet every one of them, blond and dark both,
had his pure blue eyes that curled like cashew nuts whenever
they smiled.) He mourned for weeks when Mary refused to be
a debutante, and he joined the country club on his own and
played golf every Sunday although he hated it. "What do I
go there for?" he asked. "What do I want with those snobs?"
He was made up of layers you could peel off like onion skins,
each of them equally present and real. The innermost layer
(garage mechanic's son, dreaming of a purple Cadillac) could
pop up at any time: when he watched TV in his undershirt,
when he said "like I said" and "between you and I," when he
brought home an old tire to whitewash and plant with gera-
niums. "Oh, Billy," his wife said of the tire, "people just don't
—oh, how can I explain it?" He was hurt, which made him
brisker and more businesslike, and he stayed late at the office
for weeks at a time. Then he bought her a ruby ring too big
to wear under gloves. Then he took all his sons hunting although none of them could shoot. "I like the natural life," he
told them. "I'm a simple man, at heart."

Matthew's father was clearer in this room than Timothy;
his death seemed more recent, more easily mourned. He had
gone unwillingly, after all—taken unawares, in his sleep, probably looking forward to tomorrow's wheelings and dealings.
But how could you mourn a suicide? Complications arose
every time Matthew tried. On top of the oil burner was a sheaf
of photographs he had been puzzling over the night before:
Timothy in his mother's yard, last summer when Matthew was
trying out his new camera. He had not yet learned how to use

it. The focus was blurred, and in every print Timothy's laughing face had extra outlines around it, as if he had been moving, lunging toward the lens, as if laughter were some new form of attack. However Matthew tried to imagine him sober-faced, he couldn't. He pulled up images in his mind, one by one: Timothy laughing with that girl he had brought to dinner once, his arm around her shoulders; Timothy laughing with his mother, with Melissa, with his father at his college graduation. Then a new picture slid in, clicking up from the back of his head: Timothy quarreling with Elizabeth. Only what was it about? Had she broken a date? Refused one? Shown up late for something? All he remembered was that it had happened on the sunporch, over the noise of a TV western. "If you persist," Timothy said, "in seeing life as some kind of gimmicky guided tour where everyone signs up for a surprise destination—" and Elizabeth said, "What? Seeing what?" "Life," said Timothy, and Elizabeth said, "Oh, *life*," and smiled as fondly and happily as if he had mentioned her favorite acquaintance. Timothy stopped speaking, and his face took on a puzzled look. Wispy lines crossed his forehead. And Matthew, listening from across the room, had thought: It isn't Timothy she loves, then. He hadn't bothered wondering how he reached that conclusion. He sat before the television watching Marshall Dillon, holding his happiness close to his chest and forgetting, for once, all the qualities in Timothy that were hard to take (his carelessness with people, his sharp quick tongue, his succession of waifish girls hastily dressed and combing their hair when Matthew came visiting unannounced). He forgot them again now, and with them the picture of Timothy triumphantly cocking his pistol and laughing in his family's face. All he saw was that puckered, defeated forehead. He adjusted his glasses and cleared his throat. He felt burdened by new sorrows that he regretted having invited.

. . .

That night he dreamed that Elizabeth had gone away. She was *long* gone, she had been gone for years, she left behind her a dark blue, funnel-shaped hollow that caused his chest to ache. Then his mother died. She lay on a table with her head slightly propped and he stood beside her reading a newspaper. All the headlines contained numerals. "783 SUNK; 19 SUR-VIVORS; 45 BURIED IN MINE DISASTER," he read, but he understood that this was her will leaving everything to Elizabeth. It made sense; on the table his mother had changed into a frail, lavender-dressed old lady, the kind who would make eccentric wills in favor of pets and paid companions. He began searching for Elizabeth, combing through long grasses with his fingers and coming up with nothing. She never appeared. Her absence caused an echoing sound, like wind in the tops of very tall pines. "What shall I do about the money?" he asked the old lady on the table. "If you fail to find the beneficiary it must be buried with me," she said. "*You'll* never get it." He let the money float into the coffin. He was crying, but it wasn't because of what she had said; it was the wastefulness, the uselessness, the lost look of all that fragile green paper waiting forever for Elizabeth to come home.

At the funeral the immediate family filled one pew—Mrs. Emerson, her three daughters, two of her sons, and her sister Dorothy, who was barely on speaking terms but always showed up for disasters. In the pew behind sat Mrs. Emerson's two cousins, Mr. Emerson's strange brother, and Elizabeth. Matthew felt uncomfortable so close to the front. He had entered with his eyes lowered, guiding his mother by the elbow, and because it was his first time here since his father died he was

uncertain of anything that lay behind his own pew. He disliked sitting in places that he had not taken measure of first. Once he turned partway around, but his sister Mary jabbed him in the side. She was staring straight ahead, with her plump, pretty face set in stern lines. Little pockets of irritation shadowed the corners of her mouth.

Irritation was the mood of this whole funeral, for some reason. All down Matthew's pew, exasperated jerks traveled like ripples. Margaret tore triangles off the pages of her hymnbook, until Melissa slammed it shut. Aunt Dorothy tapped Peter for cracking his knuckles. Matthew shoved his glasses higher for the dozenth time and received another jab in the side. His mother, listening to the generalities of the service, twisted restlessly in her seat, as if she wanted to jump up and make additions or revisions. Even Father Lewis seemed annoyed about something. He was deprived of most of the phrases he liked to use—fruitful lives and tasks well done, happy deaths and God's design—and when he had finished the few vague sentences left to him he briskly aligned two sheets of paper on his pulpit, heaved a sharp sigh, and frowned at someone's cough. Before him lay the pearly gray casket, hovering, weighing down the silence, waiting for something more that never came.

By the time they returned from the cemetery it was nearly one o'clock. Three limousines left them at the door. People alighted in straggling lines, and unbuttoned their gloves and removed their hats and commented and argued and agreed all the way up the walk. "He never liked that hymn, he would have poked fun at us for singing it," Melissa said. Mrs. Emerson's two cousins climbed into their car, murmuring soft sounds that might not even have been words. It looked as if

only the immediate family and Aunt Dorothy were staying to dinner. "You'll stay, Uncle Henry," Mary told Mr. Emerson's strange brother, but Uncle Henry (who was strange because he never talked, not ever, but merely bobbed his Adam's apple when confronted with direct questions) waved one red, bony hand and went off stiff-legged to his pickup truck. "We'd better tell Alvareen," Mary said. "Eight for dinner, if she hasn't yet fed Billy."

"But how about Elizabeth?" Mrs. Emerson said.

"Elizabeth, oh. Does she eat with us?"

"I'll get something later," Elizabeth said. She was zig-zagging across the front lawn, gathering the debris left by last night's rainstorm. In church, in her beige linen dress, she had looked like anyone else, but there was nothing ordinary about her now when her arms were full of branches and rivulets of barky water were running down the wrinkles in her skirt.

"Is that girl all *right*?" Mary said. "You'd think she'd change clothes first."

Billy was waiting on the top porch step, guiding his mother back with his intense, unswerving stare. Alvareen stood behind him in a shiny black party dress. "Dinner's set," she called. "Come on in, you poor souls, I got everything you'd wish for right on the table." When Mrs. Emerson came near enough Alvareen patted her arm. "Now, now, it's finished now," she said. Mrs. Emerson said, "I'm quite all right, Emmeline."

"Shows you're not," said Alvareen. "I'm Alvareen, not Emmeline, but don't you mind. Come on in, folks."

Then she led the way into the house, shaking her head and moving her lips, no doubt preparing what she would say to her family when she got home: "Poor thing was so tore up she didn't know me. Didn't know who I was. Called me Emmeline. Didn't know me." Behind her, Melissa stumbled

against a step and laid one hand on Matthew's arm, but so lightly that the stumbling seemed artificial. Margaret followed, swinging a weed that she had yanked from the roadside. Mary bent to scoop up Billy, and at the end of the line came Aunt Dorothy, talking steadily to Peter although he didn't appear to be listening. "Now what I want to know is, who made the arrangements? Don't you people believe in the old-fashioned way of doing things? First no wake, no one at the funeral home, just the remains waiting all alone. Then that scrappy little service with hymns I surely never heard of, and the casket closed so that I couldn't pay my—why was the casket closed?"

"I asked it to be," Matthew said. "I thought it would be easier."

"Easier!" She paused in the doorway, her mouth open, a wrinkled, scrawny caricature of Mrs. Emerson. "Easier, you say! My dear Matthew, death is never going to be easy. We accept, we endure. We *used* to put them in the parlor. Now you're telling me—or was he, um, I hope the bullet didn't—"

Nobody rescued her. She closed her mouth and entered the house, leaving Peter horror-struck behind her. "Did it?" he whispered, and Matthew said, "No, of course not. Go on in." (And pictured, clearer than Peter there before him, Timothy's dead, toneless face, so solemn that it had to be a mockery—much worse than blood or signs of pain, although he never could have explained that to Peter.)

Alvareen stood scolding in the dining room. Nobody was coming straight to the table. They were milling in the hallway, or heading for bathrooms, or going off to put away hats and gloves. "You're breaking my heart," Alvareen said. "Here, little Billy, *you'll* pay me mind." She hoisted him into a chair with a dictionary on it and tied a napkin around his neck. He ducked his round yellow head to examine the tablecloth

fringe. There was always something he was checking up on—
as if he considered himself the advance scout for the grandchildren yet to be born. He peered at people suspiciously, drew
back to study Mrs. Emerson when she kissed him, cautiously
surveyed all offerings from his aunts and uncles. Sometimes
he repeated whole conversations between his relatives, word
for word, out of context, as exact as a spy's tape recording.
" 'Where you going, Melissa?' 'Out for a walk, can't stand it
here.' 'When'll you be back?' ' 'Spect me when you see me.' "
" 'Why don't I ever hear from you, Peter?' " he said now, and
then frowned at his silverware, as if turning the question over
for all possible implications.

When they were finally seated, their elbows touched. No
one would have guessed how many people were missing. Alvareen had chosen her own menu: ham and roast beef, three
kinds of vegetables, mashed potatoes and baked potatoes and
sweet potatoes. "Oh, my," Mrs. Emerson said, and she sighed
and refolded her napkin and sat back without taking a bite.
Only Margaret had any appetite. She ate silently and steadily
—a lanky-haired, pudgy, flat-faced girl. Beside her, Billy
whacked his fork rhythmically against the table edge. "In a
bottom drawer, under the tea-towels," he chanted. "In a
bottom—" "Cut that out, mister," Mary said. She buttered
a roll and laid it on his plate. "Eat up and hush."

"In a bottom—"

"It was nice of Father Lewis to do the services," Mrs.
Emerson said.

"*Nice?*" said Mary.

"Well, he could have refused. He had the right, in a case
of . . . case like this."

"I'd like to see him try," Mary said. She had changed
since the days when she lived at home. She looked calmer,
softer around the edges, especially now when she was expect-

ing another baby. Her face, with its lipsticked mouth and pale eyes, was settling along the jawline, and she wore her dark hair medium-length, average-styled, marked with crimp-lines from metal curlers. Yet while her looks had softened, her opinions had hardened. She passed judgment on everything, in her mother's sharp, definite voice. She was forever ready to turn belligerent. Motherhood had affected her in the way it did she-bears, but not only in matters relating to her child. "You know what I'd have said if he refused," she said. "I'd have marched straight up to him. Oh, he'd be sorry he ever mentioned it. Quit that, Billy. Give it to Mother. 'Father Lewis,' I'd say, I'd say straight to his face—"

"But he didn't," Margaret said.

"What?"

"What's the point?"

"Oh, Margaret, where are you, off in a daze some place? We were talking about—"

"I know what you were talking about. What's the point? He didn't refuse, he never said a word about it. He went right ahead and performed the services."

"Well, I was only—"

"Funerals are for the living," said Mrs. Emerson. "That's what all the morticians' ads say."

"Of course, Mother," Mary said. "No one denies it."

"Well, Father Lewis was very kind to me. Very thoughtful, very considerate. I don't want to disappoint you children in any way, but the fact is that I have never felt all that religious. I just didn't have the knack, I suppose. Now, Father Lewis knows that well but did it stop him? No. He came and spent time, he offered his sympathy, he never even mentioned the manner of Timothy's going. He was no help at all, of course, but you can't say he didn't try."

"No, of course not," Mary said.

"The trouble with ministers," said Mrs. Emerson, "is that they're not women. There he was talking about young life carried off in its prime. What do I care about the prime? I'm thinking about the morning sickness, labor pains, colic, mumps—all for nothing. All come to nothing. You have no idea what a trouble twins are to raise."

"Can't we get off this subject?" Melissa said.

"Well, it is on my mind, Melissa."

"I don't care, you're making me nervous. All this talk about Timothy, who has just played a terrible trick on us and left us holding the bag. Hymns. Sermons. Religion. Why do we bother?"

"*Melissa!*"

"What. There's nothing *wrong* with what he did, it was his own life to take. But we don't have to sit around discussing it forever, do we?"

"That's quite enough," said Mrs. Emerson, and then she set her glass down and turned to Alvareen, who was just coming in with more rolls. "Everything is delicious, Alvareen."

"How can you tell? You ain't eat a bite."

"Well, it *looks* delicious."

"It is," said Mary, taking over. "You must give me the recipe for the gravy, Alvareen. Is it onion? Is this something you get from your people?"

"All I done was—"

"Matthew," Mrs. Emerson said, "I have to know. Was death instantaneous?"

Everyone froze. Instantaneous death, which sounded like something that happened only around police lieutenants and ambulance drivers, seemed undesirable; and before Matthew had thought her question out he said, "No, of course not." Then when their eyes widened he realized his mistake. "Oh," he said. "No, it *was* instantaneous. I didn't—"

"Which is it? Are you keeping something from me?"

"Oh no, I just, you see—"

"Elizabeth? Where's Elizabeth?"

"Here we go again," Mary said.

"Here we go *where* again?"

"You'd think you could get along five minutes without Elizabeth."

"Mary, for heaven's sake," Margaret said.

"She *was* on the *scene*," said Mrs. Emerson.

"Ha," Mary said.

"Just what does that mean?"

There was a silence. Alvareen, who was propped against the wall with her arms folded as if she never planned to leave, suddenly spoke up. "All I done with the gravy," she said, "was throw in a pack of onion soup mix. Lady I used to work for taught me that. You might like to write it down."

"Oh, is that what it was," said Mary. "Thank you very much."

The silence continued. Forks clinked on plates. Billy's head slid slowly sideways and his eyes rolled, half-shuttered, fighting sleep.

"I do a lot of extries," said Alvareen. "Sometimes I cater for parties, I mention that in case you're interested. I spread cream cheese over Ritz crackers, I dye it however they want. Green, like, to match the carpet. Pink or blue, to go in with the decor. Little things is what makes them happy."

She went out through the swinging door, hands under her apron, probably telling herself she had done all that could be expected to liven this funeral party. Mary said, "I believe Alvareen is even stranger than Emmeline."

"There was nothing wrong with Emmeline," said Mrs. Emerson.

"What'd you fire her for, then?"

"What I mind about Elizabeth—" said Melissa.

Margaret said, "Oh, can't we get off Elizabeth?"

"She's creepy," Melissa said. "Never says anything. I distrust people who don't take care of their appearance."

"Wake up, Billy," said Mary. "Eat your beans. Well, I'll say this about her and then we'll drop it: I hate to see people taking advantage. It seems to me, Mother, that girl knows a good thing when she stumbles on it—settled down to live off a rich old lady forever, she thinks, and you should make it plain to her that you have children of your *own* to rely on. Plenty of your own without—"

"Well, I like her," Margaret said.

"What do you know about it?"

"I've had to share a room with her, haven't I? She talks to *me*."

Melissa said, "I don't hear Matthew speaking up."

"What about?" said Matthew, pretending not to know.

"Aren't you always hanging around Elizabeth?"

She smiled at him from across the table—a cat face, sharp and bony, with that thin, painful-looking skin that some blondes have. Who could have foretold that modeling agencies would consider her a beauty? Matthew decided suddenly that he disliked her, and the thought made him blink and duck his head. "Anyway, she's going," he said.

"Aren't you going to mope around, or follow after her or something?"

"Stop it," Mrs. Emerson said.

They looked up at her, all with the same stunned, pale eyes.

"Oh, what makes you act like this?" she said. "They say it's the parents to blame, but what did *we* do? I'm asking you, I really want to know. What did we do?"

No one answered. Billy slumped against Margaret, his

lids glued shut, exhausted from having so much to watch out for. Peter speared beans with all his concentration, and Aunt Dorothy began examining her charm bracelet.

"Just loved you and raised you, the best we knew how," Mrs. Emerson said. "Made mistakes, but none of them on purpose. What else did you want? I go over and over it all, in my mind. Was it something I did? Something I didn't do? Nights when you were in bed, clean from your baths, I felt such—oh, remorse. Regret. I thought back over every cross word. Now it's all like one long night, regret for anything I might have done but no fresh faces to start in new upon in the morning. Here I am alone, just aching for you, and still I don't know what it was I did. Was it me, really? Was it?"

"Mother, of course not," Mary said.

"Then sometimes I think you were all in a turmoil from birth, nothing I did could have helped. Can you deny it?"

"Mother—"

"What about Andrew? What about Timothy? I was such a *gentle* person. Where did they get that from?"

Her face was blurring, crumpling, dissolving. And all the movements made toward her were bluffs. Some cleared their throats and some leaned suddenly in her direction, but nobody did anything. In the end, it was Matthew who stood up and said, "I guess you'd like to rest now, Mother."

"*Rest!*" she said, with her mouth pressed to a napkin. But she allowed herself to be led away. The others scraped their chairs back and stood up. Alvareen, bearing a hot apple pie, stopped short in the doorway. "We won't be needing dessert," Mary told her. "Now, aren't you an optimist. Have you ever known this family to make it through to the end of a meal?"

"Your mama and Elisabeth always did," Alvareen said.

The others were filing out of the dining room. Mary bore

a sagging, boneless Billy toward a rocking chair by the fireplace. Mrs. Emerson, composed again, mounted the stairs
with Matthew close behind. "I'll just turn down the spread for
you," he told her. "You'll feel better when you're not so
tired."

"It's true I haven't slept much," said Mrs. Emerson.

But instead of going straight to bed, she stopped at the
doorway of Margaret's room. Elizabeth was wrapping pieces
of wood in tissue paper and stuffing them into a knapsack.
"Elizabeth," Mrs. Emerson said, "was death instantaneous?"

Elizabeth didn't even look up. "Oh, yes," she said, without surprise, and she folded down the flap of the knapsack and
buckled the canvas straps.

"Then he didn't have any, say any last—"

"No."

"Well, thank you. All I wanted was a clear-cut answer."

"You're welcome," said Elizabeth.

Matthew took his mother's arm, thinking she would go
now, but she didn't. "You're packing," she said. "I never
thought you would actually go through with this."

"Well, there's a lot I need to get done. I have to reapply
at the college."

"Can't you do that by mail?"

"I believe it'd be better just going down there," Elizabeth
said.

She still hadn't looked up. She had started folding shirts
into squares and laying them in a suitcase. For once, there was
nothing that could sidetrack or delay her. His mother must
have seen that too. "*Why*, Elizabeth?" she said. "Do you
blame me?"

"Blame you for what?"

"Oh, well—could you really just leave me like this? Are

you going to let me live through these next few months all alone? The *last* time you didn't."

"I'm sorry," Elizabeth said.

Mrs. Emerson raised a hand and let it fall, giving up. She allowed herself to be led across the hall to her bedroom. "I never did wholly trust that girl," she said.

Then she lay down, and shielded her eyes with her forearm. Matthew drew the curtains and left her there.

When he crossed the hall again, Elizabeth's door was closed. It was a message; it seemed meant for him alone. He stood there for a minute, slouched and empty-handed. When she didn't come out he went on downstairs.

Melissa and Peter were playing poker. "He's very successful," Melissa was saying. "He owns his own company. But he nags at me, we fight a lot. You know? Sometimes when he invites me out he makes me change what I'm wearing, just to suit him. He goes charging into my closet and pushes all my dresses down the rod, figuring what he'd like better. What can you do with a person like that?" Peter frowned at his cards. He wasn't even pretending to listen.

Margaret was talking about a man too, but in her own toneless way. She lay on a couch with her feet up, twining a limp lock of hair around her finger and telling Mary about someone named Brady. "I was planning to bring him home, before this happened," she said.

"Oh, don't," said Mary, rocking Billy serenely. "Everything goes wrong in this house."

"But he keeps asking me to marry him. Mother would have a fit if she didn't meet him first."

"Well, coming from someone who *eloped*—"

"Mother met *him* first."

"Only if you count when he brought in the groceries,"

Mary said. "She's not much for heart-to-heart talks with stray delivery boys."

"You don't have to be so snide about it."

"I'm not. Can't we have a normal conversation? I don't know why you want to get married anyway—you're not the type." She arranged Billy more comfortably, checking his sleep with her mouth tucked in and competent-looking. "Too disorganized. Any man would be climbing the walls. You must still think marriage is floating around in a white dress. Well, it isn't."

"*I* know that, *I* read the ladies' magazines."

"They expect *you* to take care of *them*, it's not the other way around. Always asking you to pick up, put away, find things for them. Look at Morris—every morning I tell him the butter's kept in the butter bin. He never listens. He opens the refrigerator and panics. 'The butter, where's the butter, we've run out of butter again.' 'It's in the butter bin, dear.' Oh, you'd never last through that. I often think of chucking it all myself."

The telephone rang. Matthew crossed to the armchair and lifted the receiver. "Hello," he said.

"Oh, Matthew," said Andrew.

"Hello, Andrew."

"What's wrong?"

"Nothing's wrong. Why?"

"You aren't glad to hear from me."

"Of course I am," said Matthew.

"I can tell from your voice."

"Don't be silly," Matthew said. "Were you calling about anything in particular?"

There was a chipping sound at the other end of the line—Andrew doing something nervous with the phone. His hands were always busy, twisting or fidgeting or kneading his thumbs, while the rest of him was limp and motionless. Like a rag doll,

he tended to remain where he was left—New York, in this case, after a try at college there. It took vast amounts of other people's energy to change his life in any way, and lately no one had felt up to it. What was the use? In New York he lived in a pattern as unvarying as the tracks of a toy train—from rooming house to library to rooming house, lunch every Wednesday with Melissa in the only restaurant he approved of (the only one he had *been* in; someone had once taken him there) and home three or four times a year, shattered and white over the change in his schedule. He distrusted planes (a family trait) and panicked at the swaying of trains, and had never learned to drive. All he had left were buses. Buses, Matthew thought, and started. "Holy Moses," he said. "You're in Baltimore."

"You forgot," said Andrew.

"Oh no, I just—"

"You forgot I was coming. Would you rather I just went back again?"

"No, Andrew."

"There are plenty of buses out of here."

"I knew you were coming. I just never heard what time," Matthew said. "I'll be right down."

"Oh, well—"

"Wait there."

"Well, if you're sure you're expecting me," said Andrew.

"We are. *Stay* there, now. Bye."

He hung up and started out of the room immediately. "I have to get Andrew," he said.

"Oh, Lord," said Melissa. "This is too much at once."

"I'll be back in a while."

"Tell him in the car, Matthew. Get it over with."

"Are you crazy?" Mary asked. "Why did we keep it from him, if we're just going to dump it on him now? Don't you say

a word, Matthew. Bring him on home. Maybe we'll wait till tomorrow."

"I think I'm going to throw up," Melissa said. "I have a nervous stomach."

Matthew left. In the hallway he met Elizabeth, who was just coming down the stairs with her suitcase and knapsack. Her burdens made her look lopsided. She still wore her church dress, with pieces of damp bark down the front. When she saw him, she stopped on the bottom step. He had an urge to trap her there, under glass, complete with her baggage and her peeling handbag and her falling-down hairdo, until life was sorted out again and he could collect what he wanted to say to her. "Can't you wait?" he asked. "Don't go yet. Won't you just wait till I get back from the bus station?"

"Oh, the bus station," Elizabeth said. "That's where I'm going."

"What for?"

"Well, I'm catching a bus. You could give me a lift."

"Oh, I thought—I had pictured you getting a ride."

"Not at such short notice," Elizabeth said.

She handed him the suitcase. Of all the sad things going on today, it seemed to him that the saddest was that single motion—Elizabeth flashing the luminous inner side of her wrist, with its bulky leather watchstrap, as she passed him her suitcase. Where were her bulletin board drivers, those laughable old cars full of Hopkins students that used to draw up at the door? Where were her blue jeans, and her moccasins with the chewed-looking tassels, and her impatient, brushing-away motion when he tried to help her with loads that looked too heavy?

"Are you waiting for something?" Elizabeth said.

"No."

"Let's go, then."

"But—so fast? You haven't said goodbye yet. Mother's still in her room."

"I'll write her a bread-and-butter letter."

"Well, if that's the way you want to do it," Matthew said.

They hurried down the sidewalk, with Elizabeth's turned-up pumps making clopping sounds and her knapsack swinging over one shoulder. "Hop in," Matthew said. "We have to get to Andrew before he takes the next bus out again."

"Oh, Andrew," said Elizabeth, but her voice was dull and tired. It sounded as if she had had enough of Emersons.

All the way downtown, Matthew kept choosing words and then discarding them, choosing more, trying to make some contact with Elizabeth's cold, still profile. He drove absentmindedly, and had to be honked into motion at several traffic lights. "You won't get to see how those new shrubs make out," he told her once. Then, later, "Will August be a good time for me to visit you?" She didn't answer. "I get my vacation then," he said. Elizabeth only drew a billfold from her handbag and started counting money. "Do you have enough?" he asked her.

"Sure."

"Did Mother ever pay you for this past week?"

"Pay me?"

When Elizabeth answered questions with questions, it was no use trying to talk to her.

They passed dark narrow buildings that had suddenly brightened in the spring sunlight, old ladies sitting on crumbling front stoops taking the air, children roller-skating. In the heart of the city, in a tangle of taverns and pawnshops and cut-rate jewelers, black-jacketed men stood on the sidewalks selling paper cones of daffodils. Matthew drew up in front of the bus station, where he parked illegally because he was afraid of losing both of them, Andrew and Elizabeth, if he

took more time. "Don't get away from me," he told Elizabeth. "Wait till I find Andrew. Don't leave."

"How could I? You're carrying my suitcase."

"Oh."

They went through the doors and toward the ticket counter. Only two people were waiting in line there, and the first was Andrew. "Andrew!" Matthew called. He ran, but he had sense enough to keep hold of Elizabeth's suitcase. Andrew turned, still offering a sheaf of bills to the man behind the counter. He was nearly as tall as Matthew, but blond and pale and fragile-looking. His suit hung from him in loose folds. His face was long and pinched. "I'm arranging to go back," he said.

"You can't do that."

"I can if I want to."

"This is all a misunderstanding," Matthew said. He took hold of Andrew's sleeve, and the ticket agent folded his arms on the counter and settled down to watch. "They're waiting for you at home," Matthew said. "They expect you any time now." Then, to the ticket agent, "He won't be going." He pulled Andrew out of the line, and the fat lady behind him moved up to the counter with a huffy twitch of her shoulders.

"Now you've lost my place," Andrew said.

"You know yourself you're acting like a fool."

"Oh, am I?" Andrew said. "Why didn't she think to tell you, then? Did she forget I was coming? Or did she remember and *you* forgot. Did you decide just not to bother?"

His eyes seemed deeper in their sockets than usual, and closer together. His arm, still in Matthew's grasp, was struggling away, and he was moving by fractions of inches back to the counter. Yet if he had really wanted to, he could have shaken Matthew off entirely. Returning to New York was

another of his passing impulses, already deserting him, leaving him to fumble on in his course out of sheer inability to back down. All he needed now was some dignified alternative. "Look," Matthew said, but Andrew's arm, which was bare and skinny beneath his coat sleeve, seemed to infect him with some of Andrew's shaky tension. He couldn't get his words out. "You could, could—"

And to make it worse, the fat lady at the counter moved away and the person behind her stepped up: Elizabeth. Composed and distant, she unsnapped the clasp of her billfold. "Ellington, North Carolina," she said.

"Elizabeth!"

But she wasn't so easily pulled from the line. She went on counting out bills, and the ticket agent gave Matthew a peculiar look from under his eyebrows.

"Elizabeth, too much is going on right now," Matthew said. "Will you wait? Will you come back with me, and take a later bus? There are things I want to get settled with you."

"May I have my ticket, please?" Elizabeth said. The agent shrugged his shoulders and moved off to the ticket rack. Elizabeth spread her money in a fan on the counter. "I'm in luck, there's a bus leaving right away," she said. "I want to get on it."

"I know you do. I don't blame you at all, but I can't let you go yet. I haven't *said* anything to you."

"There's nothing to say," Elizabeth said.

There was, but it was difficult with Andrew there. He was standing between them, teetering on his heels and looking curiously from one to the other. "I don't believe we've been introduced," he said.

"Elizabeth," Matthew said, "I love you. I think we should get married."

"*Married?*" said Andrew.

"I'm not interested," Elizabeth said.

"Why not?"

"I just want to get out of here. I'm sick of Emersons. Thank you," she told the agent, and stuffed the ticket into her bag.

Andrew said, "How do you know the Emersons aren't sick of you too, whoever you are?"

"Andrew, keep out of this," Matthew told him.

Andrew turned on his heel and went up to the counter.

"Andrew!" Matthew said. "Will you come back here?"

"See what I mean?" said Elizabeth.

"Look, you can't refuse to marry me just because I've got a crazy brother. Andrew! Elizabeth, listen to me."

"It isn't only Andrew that's crazy," Elizabeth said. "It's all of you. Oh, I knew I should have left before. How could I make so many mistakes? Give me my suitcase, please."

"No," said Matthew. He held onto it. "Elizabeth—"

She turned and left, walking fast and swinging her knapsack. She was heading out toward the buses, but he couldn't believe she would really go. He still had the suitcase, after all. He was holding it tightly. When Andrew reappeared, waving a ticket, Matthew said, "Here, take this suitcase. Don't let it go. I'll be back in a minute." Then he pushed through a crowd of ladies in hats, past a girl with a French horn case and a tiny old black woman with a caged parakeet. He thought he saw Elizabeth, but he was mistaken; the beige he had his eyes fixed on was a soldier's uniform. He pushed through the doors and outside, where rows of buses were revving their motors and men were rushing by with baggage carts. One bus, already backing out, had stopped to unfold its doors to Elizabeth. "Wait!" he called. "I have your *suitcase!*" If she heard, she didn't care. She scrambled up the bus steps, hoisting her knapsack higher on her shoulder. The last he

saw of her was one upturned shoe sole with a wad of pink bubble gum stuck to the toe. Then the doors folded shut again.

When he returned to the terminal, Andrew was waiting meekly beside the suitcase. He touched Matthew's shoulder. "Let's go home, Matthew," he said, and his voice was as gentle as a child's after a scolding. "I wouldn't let it bother me," he said. "She looked kind of strange, anyway. Nobody we would have much to do with."

◧ 6 ◧

Elizabeth had a nightmare which she couldn't remember. She awoke and sat up, her heart thudding, while vague, malevolent spirits swooped over her head. But the room was warm and sunlit, and a breeze was ruffling the dotted swiss curtains. She lay down and went to sleep again. She dreamed she was mending a quantity of buttons—the finish to every nightmare she had had this month, as boring and comforting as hot milk. She was riffling through a cascade of chipped and broken buttons in a cardboard box. Plastic, glass, leather, gold, mother-of-pearl. She fitted together two halves of a tiny white button that belonged on a shirt collar. She rewove an intricate leather knot from a blazer. She glued a silver shank to a coat button, and a pearl disc back into its round metal frame; she found the missing piece of a pink plastic heart from a baby's cardigan. Her hands moved surely and deftly, replacing the gagging horror of the nightmare with a quiet calm. More buttons appeared, in cigar boxes and coffee cans and Band-Aid tins. Sometimes she grew discouraged. Why mend things so fragile? Why couldn't they let her

throw them out and buy new ones? But there was some joy in doing her job so well. She worked on, plowing through a torrent of colored discs. She awoke feeling as exhausted as if she had been laboring all night long.

Her mother was out in the kitchen, running the Mixmaster. "I hope you know what time it is," she told Elizabeth.

"Eleven-fifteen," Elizabeth said. She got herself a glass of orange juice and sat down on a stool.

"You never *used* to get up so late. Do you feel all right?"

Mrs. Abbott was pouring evaporated milk into the beater bowl. Her face from a distance was young and thin and bright, but up close you could see a network of lines like the creases in crumpled, smoothed-out tissue paper. She wore a gingham dress and canvas slip-ons, and she moved with a quick, definite energy that made Elizabeth feel all the more lumpish. In two swift motions she had scraped down the sides of the beater bowl, slapping the scraper sharply against the bowl's rim. "Maybe you're coming down with something," she said.

"I feel all right."

"You look a mite yellowish."

"I'm fine."

But she wasn't. Her head ached, her throat was dry, her eyelids stung. Her joints seemed in need of oiling. She wondered if she were falling apart, like the machine Mrs. Emerson had talked about. Maybe, at twenty-three, she had passed her peak and started the long slope downhill. "Twenty-three," Timothy said out of nowhere, "is a woman's sexual prime, and you are going to be very very sorry you didn't take advantage of it." His voice brushed past her right ear. She flicked it away. Ghosts in the daytime were easily dealt with.

Her mother broke eggs into the beater bowl, and then

dumped in an unmeasured amount of salt. Two or three times a year she spent a morning in the kitchen brewing up this mixture—chicken and rice in a pale cream sauce, a dozen portions at once, laid away in the freezer until some church member should sicken or die. The pans were aluminum foil, disposable, to save the bereaved the effort of washing and returning them. How thoughtful can you get? And what would old Mr. Bailey say, or that sickly Daphne Knight, if they knew that even now their funeral baked meats were lying in wait for them in the freezer? She watched her mother disjoint a row of stewed chickens on the counter, tossing the slippery gray skin to the collie who fidgeted at her feet. "This is what you were doing the *last* time I was here," Elizabeth said. "They must have been dying off like flies."

"Oh, they have," said her mother. "I made another batch while you were gone." She sounded cheerful and matter-of-fact. On the surface she was the perfect minister's wife, tilting her head serenely beneath his pulpit on Sundays and offering the proper sympathy in the proper soft, hesitant voice; but underneath she was all bustle and practicality, and if she could have deep-frozen her sympathy ahead of time too she probably would have. She yanked a thighbone from a hen and tossed it toward the garbage bin, but Elizabeth reached out to catch it and offer it to the dog. "Oh no, Elizabeth," her mother said, and grabbed it back without altering the rhythm of her work. "No bones for *you*, Hilary," she told the dog. "They'll give you splinters."

"Oh, I doubt it," Elizabeth said.

"Do you want to pay the vet's bills?"

"Nope, she's not worth it."

Elizabeth scowled at Hilary, who was beautiful but stupid. She had a white mane and a long sharp nose. Because she was untrustworthy around henhouses she was kept in the

house like any city dog, and pent-up energy made her nervous and high-strung. She prowled restlessly around the linoleum with her toenails clicking. "I don't like you," Elizabeth told her. Hilary moaned and then zeroed in on a place to lie down.

"Your father's having trouble over tomorrow's sermon," her mother said. "He's working on it now, but when he's through he wants to have a talk with you."

"What about?"

"That's for him to say."

"Slothfulness," said Elizabeth. "Aimlessness. Slobbishness."

"Oh, Elizabeth."

"Well, that is it, isn't it?"

"If you know what it is," her mother said, "why don't you *do* something about it?"

Elizabeth stood up. "I believe I'll walk the dog," she said.

"Go ahead. The leash is on the doorknob."

She stalked through the house, with Hilary leaping and panting and whimpering behind her. There was nothing about this place that made her feel comfortable. Until a few years ago they had lived in an old Victorian frame parsonage, but then the church ladies (always in a flutter over how to make life easier for Reverend Abbott) had arranged to have a brick ranch-house built. It was nearer the church, which was no advantage because the church sat in the middle of a tobacco field out on R.F.D. 1. The outline of the house was bland and shallow. Even the sounds there were shallow—wallboard thudding flimsily, carpets purring, water hissing into a low-slung modern tub. Mr. Abbott, who was subject to drafts, loved it. Mrs. Abbott hated it, although only Elizabeth guessed that. Mrs. Abbott was very much like Elizabeth; she

liked wood and stone, she had enjoyed outwitting the bucking hot water heater and the back screen door that was forever sticking shut in the old house. Moving around her new stream-lined kitchen, she sometimes stopped to throw a baffled look at the stove that timed its own meals. Then Elizabeth would say, "We could always move back again."

"Move *back?* What would the congregation think? Besides, they're tearing it down."

Elizabeth clipped the leash to Hilary's collar and stepped out the front door. Blazing heat poured down on her. It was only the beginning of June, but in this treeless yard it felt like August. She crossed the flat spread of grass and descended the clay bank to the highway. Just to her right sat the church, raw brick that matched the house, topped by a white steeple. Gravestones and parking space lay in back of it. The Sunday school bus sat beneath a pecan tree at one side. FAITH BAPTIST CHURCH, its sign read. "THE DIFFERENCE IS WORTH THE DISTANCE." She never could get that phrase straight in her head. At night sometimes it came to her: The difference is worth the distance, the distance is worth the difference. Which was it? Either would do. She stopped to let the dog squat by the mailbox, and then moved on up the road.

Neat white farmhouses speckled the fields, as far as the eye could see. Each had its protective circling of henhouses and pigsties, barns and tobacco barns, toolsheds and white-washed fences. Occasionally a little dot of a man would come into view, driving a mule or carrying a feedsack. Nobody seemed to notice Elizabeth. She imagined that the neighbors thought of her as a black sheep—the minister's ne'er-do-well daughter who lay in bed till eleven and then had no better occupation than walking the dog.

There in that green field, where nothing useful grew, a circus tent rose up every August and a traveling revivalist

came. He stood behind a portable pulpit, sweating from all
his flailing and shouting beneath the bug-filmed extension
lamps. His message was death, and the hell to follow—all for
people who failed to give in to God in this only, only life.
Elizabeth's father sat to one side of him in a folding wooden
chair. "Wouldn't you be jealous?" Elizabeth had asked him
years ago. "Having someone else to come and save your own
people?" "That's a very peculiar notion you have there," her
father said. "As long as they arrive at the right destination,
does it matter what road they come by?" She hadn't taken
his words at face value; she never did. She had watched, in her
white puff-sleeved dress on a front row seat, and come to her
own conclusion: the revivalist picked sinners like plums, and
her father stood by with a bushel basket and smiled as they
fell in with a thud. His smile was tender and knowing. Ordinary Baptist housewives, stricken for the moment with tears
and fits of trembling, flocked to the front with their children
while the choir sang, "Stand Up, Stand Up for Jesus," and her
father smiled down at them, mentally entering their names
on a list that would last forever. What if they changed their
minds in the morning? Maybe some did; for next year they
were at the front once more as if they felt the need of being
saved all over again. A girlfriend of Elizabeth's had been
saved three times before she was fourteen. Each time she
cried, and vowed to love her mother more and stop telling
lies. She gave Elizabeth her bangle bracelets and her bubble-
bath, her movie magazines and her adjustable birthstone
rings from Dick Tracy candyboxes and all other vain possessions. "Oh, how could you just *sit* there?" she said. "With
that preacher's voice so thundery and your father so quiet
and shining? This has changed my whole life," she said. Although it never did, for long. But Elizabeth was always
stunned by those brief glimpses of Sue Ellen in her altered

state, with her face flushed and intense and the centers of her eyes darker. And then at breakfast the next morning there would be her father and the revivalist calmly buttering buckwheat muffins, never giving a thought to what they had caused.

Hilary was begging to run, yelping and shaking with excitement. "Oh, all right," Elizabeth told her. They took off across a field. Elizabeth's moccasins sank deep into plowed orange earth. The collie in motion rippled like water, her tail a billowing plume, her white forepaws landing daintily together. But Elizabeth only felt heavy and out of breath, and an ache between her shoulderblades was spreading down her spine. "Stop, now," she said. She drew the leash inward and Hilary slowed, still panting, and chose her way between clods of earth. From behind she was bulky-hipped and dignified. The long hair on her hindlegs looked like ruffled petticoats. That should have made Elizabeth smile; why did she want to cry? She studied the petticoats, and the stilt-like legs beneath them—old-lady legs. Mrs. Emerson's legs. She saw Mrs. Emerson gingerly descending the veranda steps, slightly sideways, with her skirt swirling around her thin, elegant shins. Sun lit her hair and the discs on her bracelet. She was looking down, concentrating on the precise placement of her pointy-toed alligator shoes. Was it worry that puckered the inner corners of her eyebrows?

Pieces of Emersons were lodged within Elizabeth like shrapnel. Faces kept poking to the surface—Timothy, Mrs. Emerson, Margaret cheerfully sharing her sawdusty room. And Matthew. Always Matthew, with his dim eyes behind his glasses asking why she had been so curt with him when she left. Why had she? She wanted to do it all over again, take more time explaining to him even if it meant catching a later bus. Take the time to tell Mrs. Emerson goodbye, and to

put away her tools properly. No one else would. But most of all, what she wanted was to change all those days with Timothy. "Whatever it was that happened," Matthew had told her, "you can't blame yourself for it." Well, why not? Who else could she blame? She had done everything wrong with him from the very beginning, laughed off all he said to her right up to the moment when the gun went off, misread every word; and what she hadn't misread she had pretended to. She thought of that snowy night when he worried that he had died, and she had acted as if she didn't understand. If she couldn't help him out, couldn't she at least have *admitted* she couldn't?

"Don't mull it over," Matthew had said. But he was under the impression that they were talking about a straightforward suicide. And he didn't have the picture of death from a bullet wound to struggle against every night of his life.

She tapped Hilary with a loop of leash. "Let's go," she said. Then she set off toward the ranch-house, with Hilary trotting beside her casting helpful, anxious glances. Red dust had worked into the stitches of Elizabeth's moccasins. A hot wind stiffened her face. Everywhere she looked seemed parched and bleak and glaring, but at least she was back where she was supposed to be.

When she got home Polly was in the kitchen with her baby, the smallest, fattest baby Elizabeth had ever known. Creases ringed her wrists like rubber bands; she not only had a double chin but double thighs, double knees, double ankles as well. Polly jostled her in her lap absentmindedly, speaking over her wispy head. "Look at you," she said. "I wish *I* could just go tearing off with the dog any time I wanted."

"Why don't you?" Elizabeth said. "Leave Julie with Mother."

"Oh, no," said Polly. She sighed. She was smaller than Elizabeth, with a heart-shaped face and a tousle of yellow curls like a frilled nightcap. "You're the one with the cute little sister," people used to tell Elizabeth. In high school Polly had been Queen of May Day. She had kept to the style of the fifties ever since—spitcurls framing her forehead, her lipstick a pure bright pink. Her flower-sprigged shirtdress was immaculate, except where the baby had just spit down the front. "Hand me a Kleenex, will you?" she asked Elizabeth. "What did I take all that Good Grooming for, if this was what I'd come to?"

"If you wore a bibbed *apron*—" her mother said. "That's what I always did." She was laying sheets of foil across the casseroles, which lined one counter from end to end. Without looking around she said, "Polly brought the mail in with her. What'd you do with that letter, Polly?"

"Here it is."

From the look Polly gave her as she handed her the envelope, Elizabeth guessed that they had been discussing it before she came in. She made a point of ripping it open in front of them, not even bothering to sit down. It was written in Matthew's looped, rounded hand. *Dear Elizabeth, Why don't you ever answer my letters? Did your suitcase arrive safely? Why do you—* She folded the sheets of paper and replaced them in the envelope. "What's for lunch?" she asked her mother.

"One of these casseroles."

"*Funeral* food?"

Polly settled her baby into a new position and studied Elizabeth's face. "You certainly have been getting a lot of mail these days," she said.

"Mmm."

"All from Baltimore. You used to be the world's worst

letter-writer. Have you changed? Or is someone an optimist."

"Oh, you know, these are just people I met," Elizabeth said vaguely.

"People? They look like mostly one handwriting."

"Now, Polly, leave her alone," her mother said. "Elizabeth, honey, I wish you'd take these down to the freezer for me."

She stacked foil pans into Elizabeth's outstretched arms. They were still warm, almost hot. Elizabeth rested her chin on the uppermost pan and started for the basement. Behind her, a deep meaningful silence linked her mother and Polly.

Most of the basement was a recreation room, which smelled of asphalt tile. A phonograph sat in one corner. When she was still in secretarial school Polly used to bring her friends here, and they had danced and drunk Cokes and eaten endless bags of Fritos. Then Carl had proposed to her on that vinyl loveseat in front of the TV. Elizabeth remembered the night it happened—Polly making the announcement, smiling up at Carl as she spoke. She was still the younger sister then; it wasn't until she was married that she somehow bypassed Elizabeth and began exchanging those knowing glances with her mother over Elizabeth's head. She had hugged Elizabeth tightly and suggested they have a double wedding. A what? Elizabeth thought she had lost her mind. By then Elizabeth was in her junior year of college, living at home, and she had brought no boys back with her except the laundromat burglar once and you couldn't count poor sweet Dommie. She had never used this recreation room. It affected her the way New Year's Eve parties did: you were supposed to have fun there, you were pressured into it, and the obligation weighed her spirits down.

She crossed to the dark cubicle behind the record player, partitioned off by cinderblocks, containing only a fur-

nace and a freezer. On the floor by the freezer a batch of orange wine was brewing up in a canning kettle. "What's that stuff you have down there?" her mother had asked the day before. "It's a new kind of preserves," Elizabeth said. "Preserves? What on earth kind of preserves . . ." Elizabeth had cut all the oranges and lemons herself, regretting it before she was halfway done; every whiff of lemon reminded her of when she and Matthew had done this job together. She had a mind like a tape recorder, an audial version of a photographic memory, and each chop of knife blade against breadboard brought her bits of things that Matthew had said. " 'Two cups raisins, minced'—*how*, when they stick together so?" "Did you ever make pomander balls?" "When the wine has aged we'll go on a picnic. I'll bring a chicken, you bring the wine in some nice, round jug with a cork plugged in . . . ." Now the wine was probably rotting away on the sink, and she would never know how it came out. That was why she was brewing more now—that and sheer devilment. She liked the idea of strong spirits bubbling in Reverend Abbott's basement. She had sent off this time for the special government permit, just so she would know that the parsonage was a licensed brewery even if no one else ever did.

When she had stashed the casseroles away she bent to lift the cheesecloth from the canning kettle. Warm spicy smells rose up. Bubbles stung her nose. Matthew lifted his head and gave her a long, slow, puzzled look from behind his glasses.

It was late afternoon before her father was finished with his sermon. He pushed away the papers on his desk when she came in. "Every week, the sermon gets harder," he told her. "Now I wonder why that should be. I always reach a

point where I think I'm beaten, I can't go on, I have finally found a sermon that can't be written." He smiled and rubbed his eyes with a long angular hand. His face was made of straight lines; his skin was stretched over fine, narrow bones and his fair hair conformed exactly to his skull. When he opened his eyes they were like blue glass globes, but tired veins were traced across the whites. "I need a vacation," he said. "I believe it's showing in my sermons."

"Take one."

"Well, but there's always someone needing me, you know."

"They'll manage," Elizabeth said.

"Have a seat, will you? Just clear those things off the chair."

She handed him what she collected—mimeographed pages and a stack of manila folders—and sat down in the captain's chair opposite his desk. He spent some time aligning the corners of the mimeographed pages. Then he cleared his throat and said, "Well now, Liz, it seems to me we were going to have a little talk."

"That's what Mom said."

"Your mother, yes. Now last week you said, if I'm right—" He slumped in his seat and stared at a letter opener. It always took him some time to get started. In these preliminary stages, before he grew sure of himself, Elizabeth kept feeling she had to help him out. "I said I would look for a job," she reminded him.

"Yes. A job."

"And that—"

"And that you were reapplying to Sandhill. I remember. My point is, do *you?*" He straightened his back suddenly, and stared at her so directly that his eyes seemed to grow square. "Are you planning to go on like this forever?" he asked. "The

last thing I want to do is pressure you, Liz, but I never *saw* anyone live the way you do. Week after week you rise late and lie around the house all day, your appearance is disorderly and your habits are slovenly, you go nowhere, you see no friends, you stay up till all hours watching television so you can rise late the *next* day—and your mother says you are no help at all."

"Did Mom say that?"

"She has enough to do as it is."

"How can she say that? I help out. I did the dishes the last four nights running. Why didn't she come to *me* about it?"

"It's not only the dishes," said her father. "It's your general presence. You're disrupting an entire household. Now I suggested, if you remember, that you find something to keep you busy until fall term. 'I'm sure you wouldn't want to remain idle all that time,' I told you. Well, it seems I was mistaken. You *do* want to. Your mother says you've taken no steps whatever toward finding a job. You haven't even left the house, except to walk Hilary. What kind of life do you call that?"

"I can't think of any job I'd be good at," Elizabeth said. She drew a pack of Camels from her shirt pocket, causing her father to wince. "It's not as if I could type, or take shorthand, or do anything specific," she said, tamping a cigarette on the edge of his desk.

"You know what smoke will do to my asthma," her father said. "Liz, honey. I know all about young people. It's part of my job. But you're twenty-three years *old*. We've been waiting twenty-three years for you to straighten out a little. Isn't it time you shaped up? Don't you think you're past the stage for teenage rebellion? It's just not becoming. Why, I

would expect you to be married and starting a family by now. Whatever happened to young Dommie?"

"He's engaged," Elizabeth said. She slid the cigarette back into its pack and studied a double photograph frame on the desk—Polly at eleven, dimpling and looking upward through long lashes; Elizabeth at twelve, an awkward age, with her face sullen and self-conscious and her organdy dress too tight under the arms. "I bet you were a tomboy," Timothy once said, but she never had been. She had dreamed of being rescued from fire or water by some young man; she had experimented with lipsticks from the five-and-dime until she realized she would never look anything but garish in make-up. She grimaced, and without thinking took the Camel out again and struck a kitchen match on the arm of her chair. Her father buried his face in his hands.

"I wouldn't worry," Elizabeth told him cheerfully. "I'll find something. And school begins in September."

"*September!*" her father said. "You'll have rotted away by then." He raised his head and stared at the photograph. Long deep lines pulled the corners of his mouth down. Was he thinking of when she had been twelve, when he still had some hope she might turn out differently? She suddenly felt sorry for him, and she leaned forward to pat his knee. "Look," she said. "Maybe I could ask if they need help at the news-paper office."

"I already did."

"Oh. You did?"

"I even asked my secretary if she needed an envelope-stuffer. She doesn't. There is something at the hospital, though—a sort of nurse's aide, working on the children's ward—"

"I wouldn't like it," Elizabeth said.

"How do you know that?"

"Oh, well, seeing all those children with leukemia and things—"

"There's nobody in Ellington with leukemia."

"And there's so many things you could *cause* there, I mean, giving out the wrong paper pill cup—"

"I'm sure you wouldn't do that."

"Someone did it to *me* once," Elizabeth said darkly. "When I was there having my wisdom teeth cut out."

"That was only a vitamin, Liz."

"If I did it, it would be cyanide."

"Dear heart," said her father, gathering himself together again, "I don't know where you get all these thoughts, but if you keep on with them you're going to render yourself immobile. Now, I gather something must have happened up there in Baltimore. All you say is there was a death in the family. Well, it must have been a mighty important death to make you come live here so suddenly, but if you don't want to discuss it I surely won't press you. You know, however, that my job has given me right much experience in—"

"No!" said Elizabeth, surprising both of them.

"Was the person who passed on very close to you?"

Passing on made her think of Matthew, not Timothy. She blinked at Matthew's face, which used to be so warm against her cheek and now made her feel merely cold and shut away.

"Well, we won't go into that if it bothers you," her father said after a pause. "But do you know what I would tell you if you were a member of my church? 'Young lady,' I'd say, 'you need to get *outside* yourself a little. Join a group. Do volunteer work. No man is an—' "

"Maybe I could be a garbage collector," Elizabeth said.

"Please try to be serious a moment. Now, there is one opportunity I haven't brought up yet. A sort of companion for old Mrs. Stimson's father. I mention this as a last resort because, frankly, I consider the man beyond need of companionship. His mind is failing. Taking care of him would be a waste of your talents, and I recommend—"

"Would I have to give him pills?"

"Pills? No, I don't—"

"I'll take it," Elizabeth said.

"Liz, honey—"

"Why not?" She rose and stubbed out her cigarette in a paper clip tray. "When do I start work?"

"Well, there *is* the matter of an interview," her father said. "We'll have to let you talk to Mrs. Stimson. But I wonder if you shouldn't think this through a little more."

"Didn't you tell me to get a job? I'm ready to go any time you are."

"All right," her father said. He pulled a leather address book toward him and leafed through the pages. "I'll just give her a ring. Meanwhile, could you change?"

"Change?" Elizabeth stared at him.

"Your clothes. Change your *clothes*, Liz. Put on a nice frilly dress."

"Oh," said Elizabeth. "Okay."

When she left, her father was just reaching for the phone with that broad, sweeping gesture that meant he was back to being a minister again.

She went to her room and changed into the wrinkled beige dress that she had worn home. She slipped her bare feet into ballerina flats and pulled her hair off her face with a rubber band. Then she went out to the living room, where her parents were waiting. They sat side by side on the couch, like

a wedding picture. Her mother looked unhappy. "Elizabeth," she said immediately, "I don't think this is the job for you at all."

"Well, that's what I'm going to find out," Elizabeth said.

"Honey, Mr. Cunningham needs a practical *nurse*. That's what you'd be doing. Why, they say they can't make sense out of half he says, you'd go out of your mind in a week."

"It's only till September."

"John?" Her mother looked at her father, waiting for him to help out—a rare thing for her to do. ("Don't tell your father," she had once said, "but it's a fact that from the day they're born till the day they die, men are being protected by women. Here at least. I don't know about other parts of the world. If you breathe a word of this," she said, "I'll deny it.") Her father only frowned and smoothed his forehead. "It's better than wasting away at home," he said.

"She'd be more wasted there. Here at least she could— oh, I don't know—"

"Walk the dog," Elizabeth suggested.

"Oh, Elizabeth."

Her mother went back to her mending, shaking her head. Elizabeth and her father left. Behind them, Hilary yelped anxiously and flung herself at a picture window.

The Stimsons lived in town, in a narrow frame house whose sides were windowless. Wooden curlicues ran under the eaves of the porch. It was Mrs. Stimson who answered the door for them. "Oh, Elizabeth, honey," she said, "isn't it nice to see you again. Jerome, *you* remember—"

"Yes indeed, yes indeed," said Mr. Stimson from behind her. "And how are you, Reverend?"

He stepped forward to shake hands. He and his wife could have been twins—both small and round, middle-aged. When he shook hands Elizabeth's father laid his other hand

on top of Mr. Stimson's—a habit he had when greeting church members. "Good seeing you, Mr. Stimson," he said. "How's that lumbago doing?"

"Oh, can't complain. Just a twinge now and then, don't you know, when the—"

"Well, let them in, Jerome. Won't you all come in?"

Mrs. Stimson led the way into a tiny living room, which had heavily veiled windows and plush furniture with carved legs. Everything wore a settled look, as if it had been there for centuries. Even the seashells and gilt-framed photographs seemed immovable. "Sit down, won't you?" Mrs. Stimson said. "Elizabeth, I declare, are you still *growing*? Why I remember when you were no bigger than a Coke bottle and *now* look. How tall are you, honey?"

"Five-nine," Elizabeth said glumly.

"Hear that?" Mr. Stimson asked her father. "Kind of takes you by surprise, don't it?"

"Oh, yes, yes it does. All you have to do is turn your back a minute and—"

"Now tell me about your boyfriends," Mrs. Stimson said. "I just know you must have dozens."

"What I really came for was to talk about the job," Elizabeth said.

She had thrown the conversation out of rhythm. Everyone paused; then her father said, "Yes, honey, but first I just have to ask, I can't believe my eyes. Mrs. Stimson, are those African *violets*? Why, you must have the greenest thumb in Ellington!"

Mrs. Stimson smiled into her lap and made tiny pleats in her print dress. "Oh, pshaw, that's not anything," she said. "Well, I do have this love of flowers, I guess you might call it—"

"Now, Ida, don't go being modest," Mr. Stimson said.

"She could make an old stick bloom, Reverend, she's got the damnedest—or, excuse me. But she does have a way with growing things."

"I can see that," Elizabeth's father said. "It's a shame that more people don't have your talent, Mrs. Stimson."

"Oh, nowadays, nowadays," said her husband. "Who takes the time any more? Why, I remember back in '48 or '49, over Fayette Road way. Old Phil Harrow, remember him? No kin to Molly Harrow that runs the beauty parlor. He grew melons that could break the table legs, had squash and corn and his own asparagus bed. How many years it been since you see asparagus growing? I believe they make it out of nylon now. And beans. Down to the right, you see—say this rug is Fayette Road—to the right would be the corn, and then *between* the rows, two or maybe three rows of—"

"Jerome, *he* don't want to hear about that."

"Well, *I* say he *does*, Ida."

"This is all very interesting," Elizabeth's father said. His voice had grown deeper and more southern. His face, when he turned toward Mrs. Stimson, had a kindly, faraway smile, as if he were making a mental note to relay to God everything she said. "There is something truly healing about raising little green things," he told her.

In the bookcase behind Mrs. Stimson's head was a line of pastel paperbacks. If she squinted, Elizabeth could just make out the titles. *Nurse Sue in the Operating Room*, she read. *Nurse Sue in Pediatrics. The Girl in the White Cap. Nancy Mullen, Stewardess. Nurse Sue in Training.* She veered to an enormous spiny conch shell, and was just deciphering what beach it commemorated when Mrs. Stimson leaned forward and said, in a whisper that stopped all conversation, "Elizabeth, I just know you want some Kool-Aid."

"No, thank you," Elizabeth said.

"*You* do, Reverend."

"Why, that would be very nice," said Elizabeth's father.

"I'll just have it ready in a jiffy, then. You want to come keep me company, honey? *You* don't want to hear about farmland and all."

Elizabeth rose and followed her out to the kitchen. Everything there was spotless, but orange cats had taken over all the windowsills and counters and the linoleum-topped table. "I'm just a fool about cats," Mrs. Stimson said. "I guess you can tell. Eleven, at last count, and Peaches here is expecting any minute." She opened the refrigerator door, dislodging the cat sitting on top of it. "We never had the fortune to be parents, don't you see. I guess the Lord just didn't will it that way. Jerome says I pour all my love out on the cats, he says I would have made just a wonderful mother if you can judge by how I treat animals."

She went from cupboard to sink and then back again, mixing up a packet of grape Kool-Aid. Her small cushiony body was packed into some tight undergarment that she kept pulling down secretly at the thighs. Her dress was a church dress, flowers on a shiny black background, and she wore tiny round patent leather pumps. She must have dressed up as soon as she heard the minister was calling. Her husband, who was in a collarless shirt and work pants, would have grumbled over all the fuss and refused to change. Now Mrs. Stimson kept stopping work to listen for his voice, as if she worried that he would say something inappropriate. "Talk?" she said. "That man could talk the ears off a donkey. Oh, your poor father. Honey, your father is a magnificent human being, don't you ever think otherwise. And when he called today about finding Daddy a companion I thought, Praise be, Reverend Abbott, if you aren't "

"Well, about that job," Elizabeth said.

"Oh, it don't pay much, I know, but the hours aren't long and the work is easy, just so you don't mind elderly men. He's well-nigh bedridden, you see. Has to be helped to his chair by the window—that's where he stays. Nice view of the street. I'm gone most of the day, I clerk at Patton's. Ladies' wear. I could get you a discount on your clothing. Jerome's gone too, and *now*, well, I don't feel comfortable leaving Daddy up there alone all day. He's getting on. I won't mince words, his mind is failing. Times he's clear as a bell, other times he thinks I'm Mama who's been gone these twenty years. Or what's worse, his *own* mama. He asks after these names I never hear of, never even knew were in the family. 'Daddy,' I say, 'it's me, it's Ida.' Then he'll get right quiet. Then, 'Ida,' he'll say, 'I know I'm slipping. I feel it,' he tells me. 'Feels like my mind is flickering, feels like I'm a lightbulb just about to burn out. Ida,' he says, 'tell me straight, am I going to die now?' Oh, it breaks my heart. I love him so. I've been looking into those eyes of his for sixty years, and now all of a sudden there's nobody behind them. You know? Like all he left with me was their color, and he went somewhere else. Then when he clears he gets so scared. 'Don't let them take me away,' he says, 'when I am off like that.' 'You know I won't,' I tell him. I never would, I'd sooner they take me. I love him more than ever now that he's so helpless."

She stirred the Kool-Aid endlessly, her little feet set apart on the floor and her face pouched with worry. In the other room her husband said, "We had what they call a railroad apartment, I'm sure you know. Say this coffee table was the hallway. To your left, now, just as you enter, was the living room. No, wait, the coat closet. *Then* the living room." Mrs. Stimson sighed and set her spoon down. "I expect you'd like to see him," she said.

"Well, yes."

"Come upstairs, then. I got him sitting by the window. I told him company might be coming."

They filed up narrow dark stairs, through a wallpapered hall and into what was plainly the best bedroom. Light poured in from a tall window, whitening everything—the tufted bedspread, the polished floor, the bony old man sitting in an armchair. A shock of silver hair slanted across his forehead. He was tilting his face upward, letting the sun shine on sunken, gleaming eyelids. For a moment Elizabeth thought he was blind. Then he turned and looked at her, and his hand fluttered up to make sure his pajama collar was buttoned.

"Daddy, honey," Mrs. Stimson said.

"They got me in pajamas," the old man told Elizabeth. "Used to be I never wore pajamas if there was company coming."

"How you feeling, Daddy?"

"Why, I'm all right." He squinted at his daughter—nothing failing about those eyes of his, which were chips of bright, sharp blue. "Later I might come down and see the people," he said.

"Well, I got someone I want you to meet. This is Elizabeth Abbott, the preacher's daughter. Remember? I know you must have seen her when she was just a youngster. This is my daddy, Mr. Cunningham."

"How do you do," Elizabeth said.

Mr. Cunningham nodded several times. A metallic flash moved back and forth across his shock of hair. "I was an usher when the old one was there," he said.

"The old—?"

"The *old* pastor, the one before Reverend Abbott."

"Oh, Mr. Blake," Elizabeth said.

"That's the one. What became of him?"

"He died."

Mrs. Stimson made a sudden clutch in the air with both hands, as if she wanted to grab Elizabeth's words and reel them back in, but Mr. Cunningham only went on nodding. "*That's* right," he said. "Died. Now I remember."

"Daddy, the nicest thing—"

"Aren't you the one got married?" Mr. Cunningham asked Elizabeth.

"That was her sister, Daddy. The other daughter."

"Well, anyone could make that mistake."

"Of course they could," said Mrs. Stimson. "I'll tell you why she's here, Daddy—"

"I would advise you against the marriage, young lady," Mr. Cunningham said. "Call it off. Get a divorce. *I* married." He turned and looked out the window again. "She aged so," he said finally.

"Daddy?"

But he went on staring at framed squares of blue, with his hands limp on the arms of the chair. His feet in their leather slippers hung side by side, not quite touching the floor, as neat and passive as a well-cared for child's.

When they had tiptoed out to the hall again Mrs. Stimson said, "Oh, my, I wish you had seen him more at his best." And then, on the stairs, "He can be so smart sometimes, you wouldn't believe it. Please don't judge him by this."

"No, I won't," Elizabeth said.

"You mean you'll take the job?"

"Sure."

"Oh, that's *wonderful!*" She beamed and squeezed Elizabeth's arm. Her skin seemed suddenly clearer, two shades lighter. "You don't know what this means to me," she said. "Could you start on Monday? Eight o'clock? I'm not due for work till nine, but I'll want to show you what he eats and all."

"Okay," Elizabeth said.

They carried the Kool-Aid in to the men. Mr. Stimson was still talking. He broke off to say, "I was just remarking on the bum, the atom bum. I blame it for the increase in rainfall. *Ida* can tell you. Used to be we could plan a Sunday drive with some hope of carrying it out. Not any more. Bum's changed the cloud formations."

"What does Reverend Abbott care about cloud formations?" Mrs. Stimson asked. She settled herself in her rocker with a tinkling glass. "Jerome, Elizabeth says she'll come look after Daddy for us."

"Is that a fact," said Mr. Stimson. "Well, you surely will be taking a load off my wife's mind there, young lady."

"And they hit it off just beautifully, Jerome."

"Is that a fact."

"Some people," Mrs. Stimson told Elizabeth, "seem to irritate him, like. I've noticed that. We had a colored girl cleaning up for me on Fridays, he didn't take to her at *all*. Then people with a lot of make-up on, he don't like that. Well, he's just old-fashioned is all. I notice *you* don't wear make-up. I expect that's from being a preacher's daughter."

"Ah well," said Elizabeth's father, "I'm glad things worked out. Any time these little problems come up, Mrs. Stimson, that's what I'm here for."

"I know that," Mrs. Stimson said. "I don't know what I'd do without you, Reverend. Why, I was about to have a collapse, worrying like I did all the time I was at work. I thought, if I could find *someone*—but I never dreamed your Elizabeth was back in town. I must've missed her in church."

"I don't go," Elizabeth told her.

"Oh?"

There was a silence.

"Elizabeth's one of these *modern* young people," her father said. He laughed lightly. "*She'll* get straightened out.

We don't see eye to eye on—what is it this week? Reincarnation."

"You don't say," said Mr. Stimson. "Why, I never knew it was in any question. Don't you believe in the reincarnation of Christ on the third day, young lady?"

"It's a thought," Elizabeth said.

"What?"

"*She'll* get straightened out," said her father.

"Why, of course she will. Of course she will," Mrs. Stimson said. She beamed at Elizabeth and rocked steadily, holding her Kool-Aid glass level on her knees. Elizabeth's father cleared his throat.

"*Well* now," he said, "I expect we better be moving on. Got a busy day tomorrow."

"Yes indeed," said Mr. Stimson. "We surely do look forward to those sermons of yours, Reverend."

"That one about pride!" his wife said. "Well, I can't tell you how much it meant to me. And we appreciate this so much, you helping out about Daddy and all."

"Glad to do it, glad to do it."

"Be nice to have a young person about," Mr. Stimson said. "Never had the fortune to have kids of our own."

"That's what I said earlier, Jerome."

"And it takes the burden off Ida some. Old people tend to get difficult sometimes, not that they—" He grinned and rubbed his chin. "Dangedest thing," he said. "The other day he took me for one of them quack medicine peddlers. Must have been forty years since they been through here last, wouldn't you say? Believe it was back in '21 or '22, I was just a —well, he gave me hell, or heck. Seems I had sold him some little bottle I swore would cure anything. 'Where's your conscience?' he asks me. 'Can you get up in the morning and look yourself in the eye, knowing how you let a man down?'

Well sir, there I stood, wondering who in Hades I was taking the rap for. Probably long dead, by now. Probably died a quarter century ago. Maybe more."

Nobody said anything. Elizabeth's father sat sharply forward, as if he were about to speak, but all he did was stare into the diamond formed by his knees and his laced hands. One wisp of hair had fallen over his eyes—a single flaw that made him look haggard and beaten. Elizabeth imagined that all his disappointments could be read in the grooves around his mouth: Why couldn't his family see him the way his congregation did? Why had his daughter stayed glued to her seat in the revival tent? What gave him the feeling sometimes that his wife viewed God indulgently, like an imaginary playmate, and that she prepared her chicken casseroles as she would tea-party fare for children on a Sunday afternoon? He shook his head. Elizabeth leaned over to lay a hand on his arm. "We should go home, Pop," she said gently.

He flinched, and she remembered too late that she should have called him Father.

When she went to bed, fragments of last night's dreams puffed up from her pillow like dust. She lay on her back, clamping her forehead with one hand. She saw a tea-tin spilling out buttons—self-buttons with their fabric frayed, wooden buttons with the painted flowers chipping off, little smoked pearls knocked loose from their metal loops. The self-buttons she cut new circles of material for. The wooden ones she retouched with a pointed paintbrush. She dipped the metal loops in glue and set them into the pearls, holding them there until they dried, pressing them so tightly between thumb and forefinger that she could feel, even in her sleep, the dents they made in her skin.

☒ 7 ☒

Dear Elizabeth,

I don't understand why you don't answer. I keep thinking up possible reasons, new ones every time. Are you angry? But when you are you generally say so, you don't just fade away like this. I'll keep on writing, anyway. I'll come down in August even if I don't hear from you. I would like to see you before then, maybe for a weekend, but for that I'll wait till you tell me how you feel about it.

Sometimes I imagine you just walking up my path, some sunny morning. It wouldn't bind you to anything. If you wanted I wouldn't even make a fuss about it—just say hello and peel you an orange to eat on the front steps for breakfast.

Mother is well. She totaled the car last week, which shook her up a little, but she escaped without a scratch. Now she has a Buick. Walked into the car lot and bought one, on sight— said a friend had told her they were all right. I was sorry to see the old Mercedes go. You wouldn't like the Buick at all, you always had such fun maneuvering the gear shift. Whatever

*happened to your chauffeur's cap? I looked for it in the old
car before they took it away. I'd hate to think of it in some
auto graveyard.*

*Andrew has been in a rest home in upstate New York.
They expect to release him any day now. I wonder if he
shouldn't come back here, but there would be so many diffi-
culties that I haven't suggested it. He claims he'd rather be
alone now, anyway; he was very insistent about it. I don't
think he has recovered from Timothy. He keeps writing
Mother and asking questions and more questions, two letters
a day sometimes—all about Timothy, irrelevant things like
what he was wearing that day and what he ate and who he
was talking to. Mother is very patient about answering him.
She says that now that Timothy's gone she doesn't worry so
much about Andrew. It's like some quota has been filled.*

*You said we were all crazy. Maybe you said it just for the
moment, not meaning it, but it's all I have to go on so I keep
trying to relate it to your not writing. I don't see how it fits in.
I do see how it could make you want to leave us. Do you think
craziness is catching? It could be, of course. It is, if you still
blame yourself for what happened. If that had anything to do
with you at all, it was only on the surface.*

*I just remembered one time when I was downtown with
Andrew, Christmas shopping, years ago. We were standing on
a corner waiting for a light to change. This car passed us, going
very fast, and just as it reached the corner all four doors popped
open. One of those fluky things, I just laughed. But Andrew
didn't. He got scared. He said, "I can't understand it. Why
do these things happen to me? Why on my corner? I can't
grasp the significance of it," he said. Well, I'm not saying
you're like Andrew. But things have been happening to us for
years, long before you came along. Before you were born, even.
Look at last summer, when we didn't know you existed. My
father died, my mother tangled with a hold-up man, Margaret*

got engaged to a middle-aged widower but broke it off and Melissa had a ten-day crying jag thinking she was pregnant. That's just what I remember offhand; there's more that got crowded out. We're event-prone. (But sane. I'm sure of that. Even Andrew is, underneath.) Probably most families are event-prone, it's just that we make more of it. Scenes and quarrels and excitement—but that part's manufactured, just artificial stitches knitting us all together. What would we say to each other if we had to sit around in peace? I may not make scenes myself but I allow them, I go along with them. I see that. It's my way of making connection with my family. Like Andrew's peculiarities. He chose them. Every trouble he causes is just another way of talking. If you look at it like that, doesn't it seem a waste to leave us?

I know I'm talking a lot of bull.

I love you. Why won't you marry me? I think you love me too.

Matthew

JUNE 27, 1961

Dear Elizabeth Abbott:
Having thought it over I am going to kill you.
Yours very truly,
Andrew Carter Emerson

Dear Mrs. Emerson,
How are you? I'm doing just fine.
I'm writing to see if you could send me my combination drill. It's down on the workbench in the basement. It has a metal box that you can pack it in. I'll be glad to pay the postage.
Thank you.

Sincerely,
Elizabeth

JULY 2, 1961

Dear Elizabeth,

Well here is half of that ten dollars you loaned me that I bet you thought you seen the last of, ha ha. I would send it all but my nephew's wife is in the hospital getting her nerves fixed and I just didn't have the heart to say "no." It seems like this summer we been ailing so. My husband has the arthritis so bad he can't leave the bed and my sister's getting the Change and myself I have the headache alot. Well I shouldn't complain, I can still get around thank the Lord and have a job for what its worth. Mrs. Emerson is changing ageing before my eyes and the symptom is parsimonousness. Turning into one of those old ladies that checks on every dime when there's a fortune in the bank. She saves moldy old leftovers and gripes do I take some of the ham for my lunch then goes out and buy herself a Buick. I have talk to her about getting some new handyman as washing outside of windows is not my job but she says "no" they all steal you blind. Well Elizabeth didn't I was quick to say and she says no, that's true, "I never had to lock up the valubles or the liquor around Elizabeth but she was such a magpie junky things was never safe around her, old doorknobs and screws and caster cups disappearing and coming back in the shape of paperweights and chest men and rubber stamps." I thought you would want to know how she is talking about you. She is ever criticizing how I do my work. On the phone she was telling about "my maid is going to drive me up the wall one of these days." Lady take care who you call yours I wanted to say but held my peace. She is all the time talking like she owns people, my florrist and my pharmacist and my meat man. Well Lord knows that woman has had her share of trouble though. I must close for now as it is hospital visiting hours. I will get that other five to you when my troubles eases up.

Sincerely,
Alvareen

JULY 3, 1961

Dear Elizabeth,

I tried to call you this morning but your mother said you were at work. I didn't even know you had a job. Then by evening I'd changed my mind. You are one of those people who deflect what is said to you and then hang up, bang. But I have seen you reading everything, instructions and Occupant ads and cereal boxes, and I can't imagine you throwing an envelope away without looking to see what's in it. Writing's better.

You must not know what it's like to wait for a letter. I leave for work late, just to catch the postman. I listen for his car on the highway. Cars that aren't his I hate, I despise the way they creep past my eyes taking up road space on trivial errands. Then I go to the back of the house and pretend I'm not interested. It's a superstition. When he comes he's always so cheerful. I reach the end of the driveway before he's finished loading my mailbox and he tells me it's just bills and grins from ear to ear. I pretend that's all I expected. It worries me the sloppy way he handles mail; anything could get lost, fall on the ground or under his car seat and he would never notice. In grade school they showed us a film about how letters travel —canceling machines and sorting machines and finally just the feet of a mailman down a sidewalk. Now that I think about it, there were so many ways those machines could lose a thing.

Mary's baby was born premature, a girl, and she telephoned all in tears at having to leave the baby in an incubator so mother's flown there to keep her company. Margaret has married again, nobody knows who to. I think Mother's going to check him out on the way back. It will do her good to travel a while. I go by the house often, just to make sure Alvareen's taking care of things okay. The place is going to hell—grass turning brown, leaky faucets. You know Mother never got

another handyman. She was distrustful of all the people the employment agency sent out to her.

Andrew is back at his old job and doing fine. I called him on his first night home to invite him here, but he says he'd like to be alone awhile.

Mr. Smodgett at the paper is drunker than ever and now the linotype operator has taken up drinking too, but come August I'm leaving no matter what. I have two weeks off and I'm spending them with you. Don't tell me not to. I would like to take you back with me. We could live at my house or someplace better, I don't care. If you still don't like children, that's all right. I won't expect you to change in any way. I love you.

Matthew

JULY 3, 1961

Dear Elizabeth,

I don't know if you remember me very well or would even be interested in hearing from me, after all the trouble you've been through with my family, but this morning when I was trying to think of someone I'd like to announce my marriage to yours was one of the few names that came to mind—

Not that you would be all that interested in my wedding, I guess, but it seemed like a good excuse to get in touch with you and tell you a lot of other things I've wanted to say—

When you left so suddenly I realized that those last few days must have been hell for you, only none of us thought of it at the time, and I wanted to apologize on behalf of my family and also to thank you for taking such good care of Mother— she used to write about you and she was always so pleased to have something offbeat, like a girl handyman, that could make her feel unconventional right in the safety of her own home—

I hope you aren't too disgusted with us. We are not as unhappy as we must seem. Sometimes when we are all together things start going wrong somehow, I don't know why,

and everybody ends up feeling they can't do anything right, and anything they try to do will make it worse. Everybody. Even Mother, maybe. But we love her very much, and we are a very close family, and Matthew is closest of all. I wish I could make you see that.

Well, so I am married—my husband's name is Brady Summers and he's in his last year of law school—next year we'll be moving to New York where he has a job with a corporation—

I'm going to like being so near Melissa and Andrew, who is the most interesting of all my brothers although of course Matthew is very interesting too—we will all have lunch together on Wednesdays at this little restaurant Andrew likes to go to, which will be fun—

I should say also that I'm not a frequent letter writer, so if it should happen that you'd like to keep in touch I won't be disappointed if you wait months to answer—then too you might not want to write at all, which I would understand. Thank you again—

> Sincerely,
> Margaret Emerson Summers

JULY 4, 1961

Dear Elizabeth Abbott:
I picked a revolver off a policeman at a parade today. It's for you.

> Yours very truly,
> Andrew Carter Emerson

Dear Matthew,
How are you? I'm doing just fine.
I have a job taking care of an old man who I like very much. I'm having a nice summer.
The reason I'm writing is to tell you not to come in

August. I'm not angry or anything, I just don't think there would be any point to it.

> Sincerely,
> Elizabeth

JULY 11, 1961

Dear Elizabeth,

What do you mean, point? When did you start caring whether things had a point?

I'm coming anyway. This is important. You are the first person outside my family I've ever loved and I'm worried you may be the last.

> Matthew

Dear Margaret,

Congratulations on your recent marriage which I was very happy to hear about. I'm not much for writing letters but will try to keep in touch.

I know that your family is very nice and I always did like your mother, only I had to start school again. Thank you for writing.

> Sincerely,
> Elizabeth

JULY 15, 1961

Dear Elizabeth,

I know that my last letter must have sounded rude. I've been thinking things over since then. I woke up last night and suddenly I saw this whole situation in a different light—not me being steadfast and patient but just pushing you, backing you against a wall, forcing a visit on you and talking on and on about love when you don't want to listen. Is that how you see it, too? You're younger than me. Maybe you're just not interested in settling down yet. Maybe I was always afraid of that underneath, or I would have called you on the phone or come down there one of these weekends.

You will have to discuss this with me somehow. I don't know what to think any more.

Mother is back from visiting Mary and Margaret. I don't know that traveling did her that much good after all. She looks tired. When I went to see her yesterday she was just putting the permanent license plates on the new car. She didn't have the faintest idea how to go about it. I suppose Dad or Richard always did it before, and then you last March. Anyway she was just circling the car with them, looking at the plates and then the car and then the plates again and holding a little screwdriver in her hand like a pen. I would have given a million dollars to see you coming across the grass with your toolbox. I even thought you would, for a minute. I kept looking for you. Then when I was putting the plates on for her Mother started crying. Without you we are falling apart. The basement has started seeping at the corners. Mother says she wouldn't even know what to look under in the yellow pages, for a job like that. Elizabeth should be here, she said. She knew the names of things.

I don't know how to think all this through any more, except to ask if you would mind writing and just telling me if you love me or not, no strings attached. If you don't want me to come in August, I won't.

Matthew

Dear Alvareen,

How are you? I'm doing just fine.

I'm writing because I asked Mrs. Emerson to send my drill, but so far she hasn't. Could you do it, please? The combination one, that sands and grinds and all. It's on the left-hand side of the workbench. There is a metal case you can put it all into compactly. If you mail it to me you can keep that other five dollars, I bet the postage will come to nearly that anyway. Thank you.

Sincerely,
Elizabeth

JULY 18, 1961

Dear Elizabeth Abbott:
   The bullet will enter your left temple. Although I prefer the heart, for reasons which I am sure you understand.
                              Yours very truly,
                              Andrew Carter Emerson

JULY 23, 1961

Dear Elizabeth,
   Well I have mailed the drill like you asked. It's no surprise about Mrs. E. not sending it as I believe she is mad at you, also out of town quite alot. Turning into one of those visiting mothers. She had a fight with Margaret's new husband who she didn't hit it off with and came back early. Now she's off seeing Peter in summer school. Melissa up there is going through some kind of breakup with her boyfriend and always calling on the phone "where is she, you think she'd be home the one time I wanted to talk to her." Honey I don't know I tell her. I only come in with my key and dust out these rooms that is seldom used anyway. If I had the strenth I would find me another job. My husband is so bad with the arthritis he just all the time moans and groans. Well the Lord knows what He is doing I suppose. I must close for now as I am not feeling too well myself these days.

                              Sincerely,
                              Alvareen

July 25, 1961

Dear Elizabeth Abbott:
   Now prepare to die.

                              Yours very truly,
                              Andrew Carter Emerson

Dear Andrew Carter Emerson:
   Lay off the letters, I'm getting tired of them. If I'm not left alone after this I'll see that you aren't either, ever again. I'll fill

out your address on all the magazine coupons I come across. I'll sign you up with the Avon lady and the Tupperware people. I'll get you listed with every charity and insurance agency and Mormon missionary between here and Canada, I'll put you down for catalog calls at Sears Roebuck and Montgomery Ward. When they phone you in the dead of night to tell you about their white sales, think of me, Andrew.

Sincerely,
Elizabeth Abbott

🔷 8 🔷

"This is a story about an outlaw," Elizabeth said. "I got it from the library."

"Let me see the cover," said Mr. Cunningham.

She held it up for him—a pulpy book too lightweight for its size, with a picture of a speeding horseman looking over his shoulder. Mr. Cunningham nodded and let his head fall back onto his pillow.

He was growing smaller day by day, Elizabeth thought. He reminded her of a fear she used to have: that once grown, free to do what she chose, she might dwindle back into childhood again. Life might be a triangle, with adulthood as its apex; or worse yet, a cycle of seasons, with childhood recurring over and over like that cold rainy period in February. Mr. Cunningham's hands were as small and curled as a four-year-old's. His formless smile, directed at the ceiling, had no more purpose than a baby's. He was in bed nearly all the time now. He lay propped on his back exactly as she had placed him, his arms resting passively at his sides. "I do like westerns," he said.

His S's whistled; his teeth were gnashed helplessly in a glass on his nightstand.

"Chapter one, then," Elizabeth said.

"Couldn't you just tell it to me?"

"It's better if we read it."

"I'm not up to that."

She flattened the book open and frowned at him, considering. They were doing battle together against old age, which he saw as a distinct individual out to get him. They read books or played checkers, pinning his thoughts to the present moment, hoping to dig a groove too deep for his mind to escape from. His attention span grew shorter every day, but Elizabeth pretended not to notice. "Isn't it depressing?" people asked when they heard of her job. They were thinking of physical details—the toothlessness, the constant, faltering trips to the bathroom. But all that depressed Elizabeth was that he knew what he was coming to. He could feel the skipped rhythms of his brain. He raged over memory lapses, even the small ones other people might take for granted. "The man who built this house was named Beacham," he would say. "Joe Beacham. Was it Joe? Was it John? Oh, a common name, I have it right here. Was it John? Don't help me. What's the matter with me? What's happening here?" When he awoke in a wet bed, he suffered silent, fierce embarrassment and turned his face to the wall while she changed his sheets. He viewed his body as an acquaintance who had gone over to the enemy. Why had she supposed that people's interiors aged with the rest of them? She had often wished, when things went wrong, that she were old and wise and settled, preferably in some nice nursing home. Well, not any longer. She sighed and creased the book's binding with her fingernail.

"We can read tomorrow," Mr. Cunningham said. "Today, just sum things up."

"If that's what you want," said Elizabeth.

She turned to the first page and scanned it. "It seems to be about someone named Bartlett. He starts out getting chased by a posse. He's riding through this gulch."

"What's he wanted for?" Mr. Cunningham asked.

"Well, let's see. They say, 'In the course of his career as a gunman . . . .' Probably one of those guys that hires out. Now he's coming to a shanty, there's a woman hanging out the wash. Her hair is the color of a sunset."

"Red, they mean," Mr. Cunningham said dreamily.

"Who knows? Maybe purple." Elizabeth snorted, and then caught herself. All these westerns were getting on her nerves. "He asks her for a dipper of water from the well. Then when the posse comes up she hides him away, she tells them she hasn't seen a soul. She brings him beef stew and a canteen, and he sits there eating and admiring her."

"This talk about water is making me thirsty," Mr. Cunningham said.

She laid the book on its face and poured him water from an earthenware pitcher. "Can you sit up?" she asked him.

"I just don't know."

She helped him, raising his head in the crook of her arm while he took small, noisy gulps. His head was strangely light, like a gourd that was drying out. When he had finished he slid down and wiped his mouth with the back of his hand. Even that much movement had been an effort for him. Resettling himself among the sheets, he gasped out the beginnings of defeated protests. "I can't get—" "It don't seem—" Elizabeth smoothed her denim skirt and sat back down. She was conscious of the easy way her joints bent and the straightness of her back fitting into the chair. Wouldn't he think of it as a mockery—even such a simple act as her sitting down in a Boston rocker? But it didn't seem to occur to him. He stared

at the ceiling, flicking his eyes rapidly across it like a man checking faces in a crowd. Sometimes it seemed to her there *was* a crowd, packing the room until she felt out of place— dead people, living people, long ago stages of living people, all gathered at once into a single moment. She waited for him to call out some name she had never heard of, but he was still with her. "Go on," he told her. "Get to the good part."

"Okay." She turned pages, several at a time. "He's boarding with this woman, taking care of her livestock and such. He goes into town for provisions. Now he's—" she skimmed the paragraphs. "He's in the saloon, getting challenged by a tough guy."

"What about?"

"They don't make it clear."

"People in those days were so *cranky*," Mr. Cunningham said.

"They have this fistfight."

"Where, out in the street?"

"Right in the saloon."

"Oh, good."

"Bottles smashing," said Elizabeth. "Mirrors breaking. Chairs going through the windows."

"*That's* right."

"Well, in the end he knocks the other guy out," Elizabeth said. "Then he has about a page and a half of bad mood, wondering why people will never allow him to go straight and lead a peaceful life. Let's see. But they don't know he's thinking that, they offer him a sheriff's badge."

"I don't want the responsibility," said Mr. Cunningham.

Elizabeth glanced over at him and turned another page. "He has to be argued into it, there's quite a stretch of arguing. Then—"

"I couldn't be expected to take on that kind of burden," Mr. Cunningham said.

"Well, it would be quite a job. But this is only a story. We're reading a story now."

"*Oh* yes. I knew that."

"Where was I? They want him to be sheriff."

"It's too much. It's too much. It's too much."

"I'll just lower the shades," said Elizabeth. She set the book down and went over to the window. Mr. Cunningham rolled his head from side to side. "It's time to sleep," Elizabeth told him.

"I'm too little."

Elizabeth stayed at the window, looking down into the front yard. Heat waves shimmered up from the pavement, and the grass had an ashy, flat, washed-out look. She was glad to be here in the dimness. She pulled the paper shade, darkening the room even more, and then looked back at Mr. Cunningham. His eyes were blinking shut. He kept his face set toward her. In the night, Mrs. Stimson said, he sometimes woke and called her name—"Elizabeth? Where'd you get to?"—turning her into another ghost, one more among the crowd whose old-fashioned faces and summer dresses filled this room. "He just dotes on you," Mrs. Stimson said, and Elizabeth had smiled, but underneath she was worried: Wasn't he sinking awfully *fast*? Just since she had come here? Maybe, having found her to lean on, he had stopped making an effort. Maybe she was the worst thing in the world for him. When she read aloud so patiently, and pulled his mind back to the checkers, and fought so hard against his invisible, grinning, white-haired enemy in the corner, it was all because of that worry. She was fighting for herself as well—for her picture of herself as someone who was being of use, and who would never cause an old man harm.

She watched him drop off like this a dozen times a day, maybe more. He swam in again and out again. Mrs. Stimson would say, "Oh, bless his heart, he's sound asleep," but there was nothing sound about that sleep. He seemed to have gone somewhere else, but always with a backward glance; returning, he glanced backward too, and mentioned recent experiences that he had never had.

His eyes were flinching beneath the lids. His mouth was open. Short breaths fluttered the hollows of his cheeks. The fingers of one hand clutched and loosened on a tuft in the bedspread.

Now was her time for just sitting. She had sat more this summer than in all the rest of her life put together, and when she bothered to think about it she wondered why she didn't mind. Day after day she rocked in her chair, staring into space, while the flattened old man on the bed stirred and muttered in his sleep. Sometimes her eyes seemed *hooked* in space; to focus them took real effort, so that she would be conscious of a pulling sensation when Mr. Cunningham woke again. Her mind was unfocused as well. She thought about nothing, nothing at all. She was not always conscious of the passage of time. It would have been possible to start a woodcarving, or to read some book of her own, but whenever she considered it she forgot to do anything about it. She would think of her whittling knives, which she had brought here on her first day of work along with two blocks of wood. She would picture the set of motions necessary to rise and fetch them, and then the wood itself: how the first slash along the grain would leave a gleaming white strip behind it. But from there her thoughts blurred and vanished, and when the old man awoke he would find her rocking steadily with her empty hands locked in her lap. It was as if she were asleep herself, or in that space on the

edge of sleep where people make plans for some action but only dream they have carried it out.

The doorbell rang. Elizabeth rocked on. The doorbell rang again, and she gathered her muscles together to rise from the chair. "Coming," she called. Then she glanced at Mr. Cunningham, but he only frowned slightly and stirred in his sleep.

The front door was open, so that as she came down the stairs she could see who stood behind the screen. But it took her several seconds, even so, to realize who it was. He was too much out of context. She had to assemble him piece by piece—first that stooped, hesitant posture, then the frayed jeans, finally the tangle of black hair and the smudged glasses. She stopped dead still in the hallway. "Matthew," she said.

"Hello, Elizabeth."

Then, when she didn't open the door, he said, "It's August. Here I am."

"I wasn't expecting you."

"Is it all right if I come in?"

"I guess so."

He opened the screen door, but she led him no farther inside the house. If he had tried to kiss her she would have dodged him, but when he didn't there was another awkwardness—how to stand, what to do with her hands, how to pretend that there was nothing new about the cold, blank space between them. "Did you have any trouble finding me?" she asked.

"Your mother gave me directions."

"How'd you find *her?*"

"Asked in town."

He shifted his weight and put his hands in his pockets. "None of it was easy," he said. "Not even locating Ellington.

I was wondering if you hoped I would just get lost and never make it."

"I wrote you not to come."

"Only the once. You didn't say why. I can't leave things up in the air like this, Elizabeth."

"Well," said Elizabeth. "How's your family?"

"Fine. How's yours."

"Oh, fine."

"Is there somewhere we could sit and talk?" Matthew asked.

She scratched her head. Then Mr. Cunningham rescued her. Her name creaked down the stairs: "Elizabeth? Elizabeth?"

"I have to go," she said. "He worries if I'm not there."

"Could I come with you?"

"Maybe you could just meet me somewhere after work."

"I'd rather stay," Matthew said. "I took a summer and seven hours getting here, I'm not going to lose track of you again."

"Well, for goodness sake. Do you think I would just run off?"

Apparently he did. He only waited, blank-faced, until she said, "Oh, all right," and turned to lead him up the stairs.

Mr. Cunningham lay motionless in his bed. He was nothing but shades of white—white hair and white pajamas, pale skin, white sheets—so pure and stark that Elizabeth felt happy to see him. "I'm sorry, Mr. Cunningham," she said.

"I called and called."

"Here I am. Come in, Matthew. This is Mr. Cunningham."

"How do, Mr. Cunningham," the old man said.

"No, this is Matthew Emerson. *You're* Mr. Cunningham."

"Well, I knew that." He raised his chin, sharply. "I thought you were pointing out *another* Cunningham. The name's not all that singular."

"You're right," Elizabeth said.

"I'm glad to meet you," Matthew said.

Mr. Cunningham frowned at him. "Are you any kin?"

"Kin? To whom? No."

"To *me*."

"No."

"Do I look like a man that would forget his own name?"

"No, you don't," said Matthew.

"I keep in pretty good touch, for my age. I'll be eighty-seven in November."

"That's amazing."

Mr. Cunningham turned his face away, irritably, as if something in Matthew's reply had disappointed him. "I'd like more water," he told Elizabeth.

"All right."

"Believe you salted that egg too much."

She poured the water and helped him raise his head to drink it. When he was finished she wiped a dribble off his chin. "I'll just raise the shade now," she told him.

"What's it down for?"

"You were asleep."

"You *thought* I was asleep."

She rolled the shade up. Sunlight poured into the room. When she turned back, Matthew had settled himself on the cane chair at the foot of the bed and was watching her. She had forgotten how open his face looked when he was staring at something steadily. Other people, returning from the past, could make her wonder what she had seen in them; with

Matthew, she *knew* what she had seen. It was still there, even if it didn't reach out to her any more. He studied her gently, from a distance, puzzling over something in his mind but not troubling her with questions. All he said was, "I never expected to see you in this kind of job."

"This here is a very good nurse," Mr. Cunningham said.

"Yes, but—"

"When I'm well we're going on a trip together. Get Abigail to arrange that, will you?" he said to Elizabeth. "Maybe Luray Caverns."

"All right," she said. There was no telling who Abigail was. She bent close to his ear, so that a wisp of his silvery hair feathered her lips. "Mr. Cunningham," she whispered, careful of his dignity. "Would you like to go to the—"

"Later, later," he said, with his eyes on Matthew. "I can hold out. I have a guest. Hand me my teeth."

She passed him the glass. He dabbled in the water a minute with shaky fingers, but he didn't take the teeth out. Maybe he thought he did; he rearranged his lips and gave her back the glass. "Now then," he said. "Just imagine, a relation I didn't even know about. How's your family, boy?"

"Mr. Cunningham," said Matthew, "I'm not—"

"Family all right?"

"Yes, fine," Matthew said.

"Parents okay?"

"Oh, yes."

Mr. Cunningham looked at him a minute, and then he gave a cross little laugh. "You ain't exactly *colorful*, are you?" he said. "Are you shy? What grade you in, anyhow?"

Matthew threw a quick glance at Elizabeth—asking for help, maybe, or wondering how soon he could get out of this.

"Matthew is a grownup, Mr. Cunningham," she said.

"Is that so. Why? How old are you?"

"Twenty-eight," said Matthew.

"*That* all you are? Call *that* grown up? The real growing up is between twenty and thirty. That's what I meant. I knew you weren't no *child*." He hugged himself suddenly, as if he were cold. "How's that pretty aunt of yours doing?" he asked.

"Uh, fine."

"She should take better care of herself," Mr. Cunningham said.

"I'll tell her that."

"Summer or no summer. Those skimpy little bathing suits are ruining the nation's health. You can get pneumonia in August, did you know that?"

"No, I didn't," Matthew said.

"Quick summer pneumonia, they call it. Now who did I—? Yes. Took my little brother when he was two. Not a thing they knew could save him. How old would he be today, I wonder? What was his name?"

He was about to start fretting over his memory again, Elizabeth thought. She leaned forward, but before she could change the subject he shook his head. "It don't matter anyway," he said. "He'd be an old man. What's the difference? I want a piece of whole-wheat toast, Elizabeth."

She had been hoping he would go on forever, wearing Matthew down till he left without saying what he had come for. So she tried not answering (he might forget) but Mr. Cunningham gave her a sharp look from beneath his pleated lids. "Toast," he said.

"Buttered?"

"Dry, just dry. I want things back to simple."

She nodded and left, and Matthew followed just as she had known he would. "You could stay here, if you like," she told him.

He didn't bothering answering that.

.　　.　　.

In the kitchen he said, "Where are your blue jeans?"

"Mr. Cunningham doesn't like women in pants," she told him. She heaved a cat off the breadbox.

"You look so different."

She concentrated on making toast, plugging the toaster in and emptying its crumb tray and carefully rolling the cellophane bag after she had taken out a slice of bread. Matthew sat down in a kitchen chair. "Would you like something to eat?" she asked him.

"Everything about you has changed. I don't understand it. There's something muffled about you."

"Oh well, I'm taking care of a very old man," she said.

"Elizabeth."

She jammed the toaster lever down.

"Look, this is such a *waste*," Matthew said. "What are you doing in this hot little house?"

"I like being here," Elizabeth said. "I like Mr. Cunningham. I'm going to miss him when I leave for school."

"For school. You're not coming back with me, then."

"No," said Elizabeth.

"Well, I knew that when I came, I guess. But I thought —and I never expected to see you like *this*."

"Like what?"

"You're so changed."

"You *said* that," Elizabeth told him.

He was quiet a moment, looking down at his hands. "Well, I didn't want to fight about it," he said finally.

"Who's fighting?"

"I came to get things straightened out. I didn't know what to think, way off in Baltimore. You weren't much help. You don't say what you feel, you *never* say what you feel."

He looked up, sending her one sudden spark of anger. "Why is it that sometimes the things I like most about you make me dislike you?"

"Oh, well, don't let it bother you," Elizabeth said. "Other people have told me that."

What she liked best about *him* was that slow, careful way of doing things—tracing the rim of a plate, now, stilling his hand when she laid the toast down. He had treated people just as carefully. He had never crowded her in any way. Watching her once in an argument with his mother, he had held back from protecting either one of them, although she had seen him lean forward slightly and start to speak before he caught himself. She could remember that moment clearly, along with the sudden ache of love that had made her stop in mid-sentence to turn to him, open-mouthed. Now the only feeling she had was tiredness. She sat down in the chair opposite him and set her hands on the table.

"I know I should have written again," she said.

"Then why didn't you?"

"It wasn't on purpose. I just seemed to be going through some laziness of mind."

"Try *now*, then," Matthew said. "Tell me why you left."

She didn't look at him. She waited till the words had formed themselves, and then she said, "That day with Timothy—" Then she raised her eyes, and she saw the fear that jumped into his face. What she had planned to tell him, relieving herself of a burden, was going to weigh him down. She changed directions, without seeming to. "That day after Timothy died," she said, "I stopped feeling comfortable there. I felt just bruised, as if I'd made a mess of things." She kept her eyes on his, to see if he understood. "Everything I'd been happy about before," she said, "seemed silly and pathetic."

"Do you mean me?"

"Well, yes."

"Did you stop loving me?"

"Yes."

"And you aren't the type who'd just say that. Just as some kind of sacrifice to make up for, for anything that might have happened."

"No, I'm not," Elizabeth said.

Matthew sat back.

"I should have said it in that letter, I know," she said. "Only I was trying to do it roundabout, and ended up making a bigger mess than ever."

"Don't you think you could change?" Matthew said.

"I know I won't," she said. "It's permanent. I'm sorry."

Then she was just anxious to have him go, to get the last little dangling threads tucked away. She watched him gather himself together too slowly, rise too slowly, scratch his head. There were things she wanted to ask him—Would he drive all the way back now? Was he angry? Was he all *right?* Even when she didn't love him, he could still cause a stab of worry and concern. But questions would prolong his going; she didn't want that. "I'll see you to the door," she said, and she walked very fast out to the hallway.

"I can find my way."

"No, I want to."

When they reached the screen door she went out first and held it wide open for him. He stopped on the braided mat to shake her hand. He held it formally, as if they were just meeting, but she couldn't see his expression because the light was reflected off his glasses. They shone like liquid, the plastic rims pinkish and dulled with fingerprints. "Well," he said, "I hope school goes all right."

"Thank you."

"Are you really *going* to school?"

"Well, of course."

"I can picture you not ever getting out of here," he said, and he gave her another long, stunned look so that she was suddenly conscious of her wrinkled denim skirt and the prison pallor of her skin. "Maybe I'll see you again sometime. Do you think so?"

"Maybe."

"And if you ever change your mind," he said, "or see things in a new light—"

"Okay."

"I won't have married anyone else."

She smiled, and nodded, and waved him down the walk, but she could picture him married to someone else as clearly as if it had already happened. She saw his life as a piece of strong twine, with his mother and his brothers and sisters knotting their tangled threads into every twist of it and his wife another thread, linked to him and to all his family by long, frayed ropes.

Elizabeth never did go back to school. By September Mr. Cunningham was much worse, and he cried when he heard she was leaving and clung to her hands. She stayed on. She failed him more every day in their battle against the enemy. Then a year and a half later he died, on a weekend so that she wasn't even with him. The last thing he asked, Mrs. Stimson said, was where Elizabeth was.

But she heard no more from Matthew. He never wrote her again.

🔯 9 🔯

1963

The trouble began on a Sunday morning in June. Margaret
woke early, before her husband. She lay in bed feeling
pleasantly hungry but too lazy to do anything about it, and
she spent some time making pictures out of a complicated
crack in the ceiling while she tried to remember a dream she
had had. None of it came back to her. Only vague sensations
—the smell of parsley in a brown paper bag, the feel of some
rough fabric against her cheek. Then the crack in the ceiling
dimmed, and she found herself looking directly into the face
of her first husband. He was laughing at something she had
just said. His black eyes were narrowed and sparkling; his
mouth was open, lengthening his pointed chin. He had the
carelessly put together look that is often found in very young
boys. While she watched he stopped laughing and grew
serious, but deliberately, exaggerating the effort, making a
mockery of it, as if the laughter were still bubbling within him.
He pretended to frown. All she saw in his eyes was love.

She buried her face in her pillow and started crying. Beside her, Brady stirred, and a minute later he had propped

himself on one elbow and was trying to turn her over. "Margaret? Margaret?" he said. She kept her face in the pillow. She cried on and on, while Brady first asked questions and then watched helplessly. When her tears seemed to be used up, she stopped. She sat against the headboard and brushed away the damp hair that was plastered to her face. "I'm sorry," she said. "I don't know why I'm doing this."

"You don't *know?* You've been crying for a quarter of an hour."

"It must have been a bad dream," Margaret said.

She watched him pacing the bedroom in his striped pajamas—a big, square, red-headed man with a kind face that screwed up into question marks when he was puzzled. In the sunlight, his hair turned orange and his eyelashes were white. He laid a hand on her forehead. "You sure you feel all right," he said.

"I'm fine."

"I think you have a fever."

"That's just from crying," Margaret said. Then she reached for a Kleenex and got up to fix Sunday breakfast.

He kept a close eye on her all that day, and every time she caught him looking at her she smiled. By evening he seemed satisfied that she was all right again. He might have forgotten all about it, if it weren't that from then on—every two or three days, just when neither of them were expecting it—the tears returned. She would be breaking an egg into a frying pan, and all of a sudden her face would crumple and she would sink into the nearest chair. "Margaret?" Brady said. "Honey? What's wrong?" She never told him. She didn't *know* what was wrong. Why should Jimmy Joe come back like this? (Even his *name* seemed unrelated to her.) Why just now, when she was finally settled and happy and in love with someone who loved her back? She kept picturing Jimmy Joe's ducktail hair-

cut, and the baggy, gray delivery coat he had worn the first time they met. Pieces of their apartment would suddenly appear before her—a dusty basement room in which they had lived out the five weeks of their marriage. Antimacassars on the sagging chairs, red checked oilcloth thumbtacked to the table. Turning the page of a book, she would see instead Jimmy Joe's bony, childish hands, with the nails bitten and the shiny new wedding ring much too loose once it got past the bulge of his knuckle. She ate breakfast staring blurrily at the sugarbowl, which had turned into the music box he brought her in a Kresge bag the night that they eloped. Subway wheels spun out the sound of his reedy voice, mocking lady customers, asking Little Moron riddles, telling her he loved her. "Honey? Honey?" Brady said. She looked at him from a distance, unable to remember for a moment what he had to do with her.

She gave him lists of reasons to explain away the tears. She had a headache. She had her period. She must be coming down with something. Brady didn't listen. He watched her constantly, wearing on her nerves until she snapped at him, which made her feel terrible and then she started crying all over again for a different reason. If she said what was in her mind, he would think she had stopped loving him. She kept it to herself. She began watching him as closely as he watched her. They were so careful of each other, so quick to protect each other, that even while she slept Margaret was conscious of a tense alertness arching between them in the dark. She would wake and reach toward his hand, or move to lay her head on his shoulder, and then stop herself. Let him sleep. One touch and he would spring awake, asking, "Are you all right? Are you happy?"

Over and over, Margaret's mother clicked through a long-ago shaft of sunlight in the basement room. She wore a cream wool dress. She lifted an antimacassar to stare at it

and then plunked it down again, lopsided. "Margaret darling," she said, "I'm sure you *think* you're in love. But you're only children! If it were really love would you be doing things this way—hidey-corner, fly-by-night?" And Margaret was crumbling, particle by particle, inch by inch, while she waited for Jimmy Joe to make a stand for her. He didn't. He never said a word. He sat on the arm of a chair with one sneaker propped on a radiator. His shoulders were hunched, his elbows were close to his sides, he chewed on a thumbnail and looked up at Mrs. Emerson beneath eyebrows that met in the middle. Other images—the music box, their dimestore goldfish, the pack of Marlboros by Jimmy Joe's side of the bed—came and went fleetingly, sometimes no more than once. The scene with her mother returned, and remained, and left only to return again. Mrs. Emerson's kid shoe prodded an issue of *House Beautiful.* Jimmy Joe chewed his thumbnail and did nothing, said nothing, allowed Margaret to be taken away from him and never saw her again.

"What you need is a trip somewhere," Brady said. She started to disagree. Travel? When even in her own apartment she was feeling torn out by the roots? But then she saw his face, which was strained and tired. "You're probably right," she told him. They dragged out road maps and travel brochures and puzzled over where to go. No place looked just right. Finally they flew to California to visit friends, and they spent a week lying on beaches and smiling at each other too often. Brady got sunburned. His back peeled, his nose was bright pink, but there were still smudges beneath his eyes. And Margaret sat on a towel in a black bathing suit, her skin eternally a pasty white, and imagined Jimmy Joe stalking toward her across the sand. She began to feel angry; the anger was so strong it caused ripples in everything she looked at. Why was Jimmy Joe doing this to her? If he was going to

hang around then why hadn't he stuck up for her all those years ago, when she needed him? She could feel the hurt and the shock all over again; she could see her mother repacking her clothes while Margaret herself stood numbly by. "This we can just leave behind, I believe," her mother said, and she lifted a black lace nightgown between thumb and forefinger and let it slip to the closet floor.

At the end of July, Brady's patience was beginning to show the strain. He suggested a minister, a doctor, a visit home. Margaret refused them all. "What *do* you want?" he said, and she said, "Nothing." What she wanted was a trip on her own, but at the same time she wanted to stay close to Brady. She shifted from one decision to the other, sometimes within minutes, without ever mentioning what was going through her mind. Then a chance for a trip rose all by itself: a wedding invitation. She met him at the door with it one evening when he came home from work. "Guess what," she said. "Elizabeth Abbott is getting married."

"Is that someone I'm supposed to know?"

"No, maybe not. She's just a friend of the family. I thought I might hop down," she said, speaking rapidly, slurring over what she was telling him. "It's just in North Carolina, I wouldn't be gone long."

"Are you saying you're going alone?"

"Well, I thought, *you* know—"

"Maybe you should," he said. "Do you good to get away a while."

She didn't know whether to feel relieved or worried, now that he had let her leave so easily.

The wedding was the second week in August. It was to be held in a Baptist church in Ellington. On the invitation, Elizabeth appeared as Elizabeth Priscilla—a middle name so unsuitable that Margaret had trouble making the connection.

The groom's name was Dominick Benjamin Whitehill. Margaret had never heard of him, but then there was no reason why she should have. Elizabeth's letters weren't that informative. She wrote only two or three times a year—always briefly, in direct answer to letters from Margaret. Mainly she just asked how Margaret was and said that she was fine. She gave no more details than a fifth-grader might. She was working in a shop, her last letter had said. But what kind of shop, what was she doing there? She was living in Raleigh. She was getting along okay. And then, out of the blue, this invitation, with one handwritten sentence scrawled on the bottom margin: "Come if you want to—E." As if she placed no real faith in all that copperplate engraving cordially inviting Margaret to attend.

Margaret couldn't locate Ellington on any Esso map. She called Elizabeth at her Raleigh address to find out how to get there, and Elizabeth said, "Oh, you're coming, are you?" Her voice was lower than Margaret had remembered it. And her face she could barely picture any more. After all, they didn't really know each other. Uncertainty made Margaret clench the receiver more tightly. "If you still *want* me—" she said.

"Well, sure."

"But I can't find Ellington."

"Just look for—no. Wait. This thing is taking place in the morning. If you're coming from New York, you'd better get to Raleigh the night before. I can put you up at my apartment."

"Won't I be in the way?"

"No, you'll solve the car problem. I can ride over with you in the morning."

"Well, if you're sure," Margaret said.

That was on Wednesday, her day for lunch with Andrew and Melissa. She avoided mentioning Elizabeth in front of

Andrew, but when she and Melissa were leaving together she said, "You'll never guess who's getting married."

"Everyone but me already *is* married," Melissa said.

"Elizabeth Abbott. Remember her?"

"No."

"*Elizabeth*. Mother's Elizabeth."

"Oh, her," Melissa said. She stopped in the middle of the block to peer into her compact. "Not to anyone in the family, I trust," she said.

"No, someone named Whitehill."

"Well, more power to her." She snapped her compact shut and continued walking.

"I thought I might go to the wedding," Margaret said. "It's down in North Carolina."

"Are you driving? You could give me a ride to Raleigh, if you're going near there."

"What for?"

"I need to see a woman in Raleigh who makes patchwork evening skirts. It's for the boutique."

"Oh, that," Margaret said. The boutique was a vague, half-hearted plan that Melissa had first mentioned last April, on her twenty-sixth birthday. She had short bursts of enthusiasm, where she spilled swatches and drawings from her purse and talked about leather and velvet and Marimekko, but then her modeling engagements picked up again and she would forget all about it. This must be one of her slack periods. It was always a bad sign when she looked in her compact too often. "This woman in Raleigh," she said, "sells her skirts for twenty dollars. We could get fifty, easily, if we could only pin her down. She hasn't got a phone and she doesn't answer letters. Just give me a lift there, will you?"

"I was thinking of going alone," Margaret said.

"Well, *go* alone, I'm not crashing the wedding. Just take

me as far as Raleigh." She hailed a taxi, which coasted to a stop at the curb. "When was it?" she asked.

"Saturday after next," said Margaret, giving up. "I'm going down that Friday."

"Well, give me a ring beforehand, then." And she slid into the cab, pulling her long, netted legs in last, and slammed the door. Margaret continued down the sidewalk with her handbag hugged to her chest. She was rearranging her vision of the trip to include Melissa. She pictured driving down hot southern highways with all the windows rolled up for the sake of Melissa's hairdo. Passing up Howard Johnson's (her favorite restaurant, with its peppermint ice cream) because Melissa would not be caught dead in such a place. Suffering through a hundred of those sharp, conclusive clicks Melissa's florentined compact made when she shut it. Then she thought, I'll just call her up and tell her I'm going alone, I don't want anyone with me. But she kept putting the call off from day to day, until it was too late.

Which was lucky, as it turned out. Because as soon as they had set off, on a bright Friday morning, with Brady still solitary and desolate in the rear-view mirror, Margaret started crying. She drove on until the car was out of his sight, and then she parked by the curb. "*You* drive," she told Melissa. "I can't."

"Margaret, what in the world?"

"*Drive*, will you?"

Melissa muttered something and got out of the car. When she was back in, behind the wheel, she said, "There's something you're not telling me. Have you had a fight with Brady? Is that why you're going off like this?"

"No, of course not," Margaret said. She blew her nose, but went on crying. Melissa, without a glance behind her, nosed the car into traffic again. Horns honked, brakes

squealed. She fluttered a hand out the window. "You're getting a divorce," she said.

"Oh, don't be silly."

"Well, *what*, then?"

But Margaret only buried her face in a Kleenex. She cried until they were well into New Jersey; she cried her way through half the Kleenex box, building a pile of soggy tissues on the seat beside her. She topped all the records she had set in the last two months. "Margaret, would you *mind?*" Melissa said. "Is this what you have planned for our whole *trip?*" Margaret turned further toward the window. She should have gone by train. This car was Brady's, and everything about it —the smudged radio dial, the leathery smell, the masculine-looking tangle of stray coins and matchbooks and tobacco flecks in the dashboard tray—made her wonder how she could have thought of leaving him. If she were alone, she would have turned the car around. (But then, when he opened the door and saw her, wouldn't that patient look cross his face again? He would shepherd her into the room, saying, "There, now," and making her wish she had just headed on south and never come back.)

In the middle of the New Jersey oilfields, she blew her nose a final time and blotted her eyes. "I'm sorry," she told Melissa. Melissa pushed the gas pedal and sailed past a Porsche. "Think nothing of it," she said.

"I just keep having these crying spells."

"Oh well," said Melissa, "so do we all."

Margaret, glancing sideways at her face, believed her. Melissa's mouth was a downward curve, dissatisfied-looking. Even behind her enormous sunglasses, fine lines showed at the corners of her eyes. "Everyone," Melissa said, "should have one day a month for nothing but crying. We'd all be a lot

better off. Crime would stop, wars would stop, generals would lay down their arms—"

"But not *unreasonable* crying," Margaret said.

Melissa only shrugged and passed another car.

In Pennsylvania they changed seats. Margaret drove, and Melissa filed her fingernails and polished her sunglasses and yawned at the huge, tidy farms that slid past them. "I could never live in the country," she said. "God, it's hot. I wish your car was air-conditioned."

"Roll down the windows," Margaret told her.

"Never. We're going to the *sticks*, there won't be a decent beauty parlor in the state."

Margaret didn't press her. She wasn't feeling the heat at all. She felt sealed in, immune. She was watching Jimmy Joe teach her how to drive, and he was laughing at her tense, forward-huddled posture behind the wheel until she lost her temper and they had their first and only argument. Jimmy Joe's left hand corrected her steering. A frayed gray Band-Aid looped his thumb.

They bypassed Baltimore. The countryside around it— more farms, pastureland, clumps of trees—reminded her of Matthew's place, and her mourning was extended to include him as well. He was the most loving of all her brothers. She might even have been able to tell him what was bothering her, except that it would just upset him. "Why can't we stop off at Matthew's?" she asked Melissa. "It isn't that far."

"He would be at work."

"Do you suppose he knows about Elizabeth?"

Melissa didn't answer.

"Do you?"

"Oh, I don't think they were all that serious anyway," Melissa said.

"Well, maybe not."

"Even so, I hope he hasn't heard. Weddings do funny things to people."

"I've hardly ever been to one," Margaret said.

"Well, I have. Dozens. Always a bridesmaid, never a—especially when the minister says to show cause why they shouldn't get married. *You* know. 'Speak now, or forever hold your peace' and sometimes the silence is so long, I start worrying I'll jump up and say something silly just to fill it."

In the back of her mind, Margaret's second wedding was moved into a church and it was Jimmy Joe's voice that broke the silence. "I can, I can show cause," he would say. "I still love her." "You should have thought of that twelve years ago," Margaret would tell him, and she would turn her back and take a closer hold on Brady's arm, shutting Jimmy Joe away forever.

In the afternoon they stopped at a restaurant Melissa approved of and ordered a late lunch. They sat across the table from each other, looking drained and frazzled, their ears humming in the sudden quiet. Melissa kept her sunglasses on. The tip of her nose poked out from beneath them, cool and white. "For someone you barely know," she said, "you're certainly going to a lot of trouble. A wedding? In this heat? Or was it just to get away a while."

"Both, I guess," Margaret said. "But I *would* like to see Elizabeth. I try to keep up a correspondence with her, not that she makes it all that easy."

"Andrew goes into a mental state if he even hears her name. He says it was her fault what happened with Timothy."

"That's ridiculous," Margaret said.

"I'm just saying what he told me."

"Well, don't."

"Why take it so personally? You only saw her the once."

"Whatever else she may have done," Margaret said, "she kept Mother company that whole awful year after Daddy died. Which was more than *we* did, any of us. I knew I should have, but I just couldn't. You should be thanking your stars she was around."

"Well, it's not as if there was nothing in it for *her*," Melissa said.

"Oh, stop," said Margaret.

After that, they ate in silence.

They entered North Carolina late in the afternoon. They seemed to have come during a dry spell; the red soil was baked, the pines were harsh and scrubby, the unpainted barns had a parched look. "KEEP NORTH CAROLINA GREEN," Melissa read off. "*Get* it green, first." She pulled out her compact and a zippered bag full of bottles and tubes. It took her half an hour to remove all her make-up and put on fresh—an intricate task which she performed without speaking. Margaret drove in a daze of exhaustion. She barely winced when Melissa snapped her compact shut.

In Raleigh, they found a hotel for Melissa and unloaded her suitcase. "Now, don't forget," said Melissa, standing on the curb. "The minute that wedding is over, I want to get *out* of here. Don't hang around all day. I plan on seeing this woman tonight; after that I'll just be twiddling my thumbs."

"All right."

"Don't go to any receptions or anything."

"All *right*," Margaret said, and she slammed the door shut and zoomed off.

Elizabeth lived in a green, wooded area that reminded Margaret of Roland Park, on the top floor of someone's garage. When Margaret climbed out of her car, twilight had just fallen and the lights in the garage windows were clicking on. She stood in the driveway, smoothing her rumpled dress,

and then she pulled her suitcase from the trunk and headed for the wooden staircase that ran up the outside of the building. She felt large and pale and awkward, top-heavy on the rickety steps. As she climbed she wiped her damp forehead and ran her fingers through her hair, and when she reached the top she paused a moment to catch her breath. Through the screen door she could see a bright, cluttered room, pine-paneled, sparsely furnished. Elizabeth was just crossing toward her. "Come on in," she said. "I heard you on the steps. Need a hand?"

She opened the door and reached out to take the suitcase. In two and a half years she had hardly changed at all. She wore jeans and a white shirt and moccasins; she might have been just about to go out and prune Mrs. Emerson's poplar tree. Only her hair was short—hacked off raggedly, at ear level, making her look like a bushier version of Christopher Robin. A little sprig of a cowlick stood up on the back of her head, as precise as the stem on a beret. "I'm making you some supper," she told Margaret.

"Oh, don't do that."

"Why not? I have to eat myself."

She slid the suitcase onto the daybed, which was already heaped with unironed clothes and a dozen blocks of wood. It must have been the wood that gave the place its workshop smell. Sawdust and shavings sprinkled the grass rug, and a stack of sandpaper sat on the table. In one corner was a large, mysterious object that turned out later to be a potter's wheel. "Sorry about the mess," Elizabeth said. "I have to pack tonight."

"*Tonight?* Don't you have to rehearse?"

"It's not going to be that complicated a wedding." Elizabeth picked up a head of lettuce and took it over to the sink. "At least, I hope it isn't," she said. "This whole thing is

getting out of my control. Well, *they* know how it goes, I'll let them handle it. Want a beer?"

"Yes, thank you," said Margaret.

Elizabeth got her one from the refrigerator and then hooked a chair with the toe of her moccasin and pulled it out from the table. "Sit and rest," she said. "I hope you like hamburgers."

"I do. It's nice of you to put me up like this. I know how busy you must be."

"Me?" she laughed. "No, I can use the lift to Ellington."

"Is that where you'll live? Ellington?"

"Mmhmm." She was cutting the lettuce into a wooden bowl. Margaret watched her and took sips from her beer, which instantly started to numb her. If she had any sense, she would stop drinking right now. Instead she kept on, dreamily fixing her eyes on Elizabeth's quick hands. Elizabeth poured dressing over the salad, slapped out some meat patties, dumped a can of beans into a saucepan. "I'm trying to use up most of the food," she said. "Then I'll give what's left to a guy I work with."

"Where *do* you work?" Margaret asked.

"In this handicrafts shop, over a tavern. I wait on customers and stuff. And they stock some of my carvings."

"Do many people buy them?"

"No," said Elizabeth. She looked toward the blocks on the daybed. "They keep coming in and picking them up, they say, 'Oh, I like this *type* of thing, do you have any more?' Then I show them more. They like that type, too, but they don't often buy them." She laughed. "I'm glad I'm quitting. I never did like waiting on customers."

"It's different from being a handyman," Margaret said.

"Yes."

"Did you like *that* job?"

"Oh, yes."

But she didn't say anything more about it. She hadn't even asked how Margaret's family was, and Margaret didn't want to bring them up on her own.

The whole of that evening, as it turned out, was centered on packing. Elizabeth packed the strangest things. Five cardboard boxes were filled with broken odds and ends—cabinet knobs, empty spools, lengths of wire, wooden finials. "What are they *for?*" Margaret asked, and Elizabeth said, "I may want to make something out of them." She dumped a handful of clock parts into a suitcase, and folded yards and yards of burlap down on top of them. Margaret watched in a beery haze. She was never able to remember much of her visit later— only in patches, out of chronological order. She remembered Elizabeth striding through a jumble of paint cans, munching on a hamburger. And her own trips from couch to refrigerator, and back to the couch with another beer. She sat in a slumped position, like something washed up on a beach and left to dry out and recover. Her shoes were abandoned on the rug; her dress became sprinkled with breadcrumbs and sawdust and bits of potato chips. "Oh, I feel so *relaxed,*" she said once, and Elizabeth stopped work to laugh at her. "You look it," she said.

"I'll never get up for the wedding tomorrow. Are there going to be many guests?"

"No. I don't know. Just whoever they invited."

"Why was *I* invited?" Margaret said—something she never would have asked sober. But Elizabeth didn't seem to mind. She straightened up from a pile of books, thought a while, and then said, "I don't know," and went back to work again. Margaret decided it was better than a lot of answers she could have been given.

Twice some people stopped by—a married couple with a gift, two boys with a bottle of champagne. The couple stayed only a minute and kissed Elizabeth when they left. The boys sat down for a beer. Margaret couldn't remember seeing them go.

And meanwhile Elizabeth worked steadily on, clearing the room. Her clothes were the last thing she packed. She threw them into a steamer trunk and slammed the lid. "Done," she said.

"How are you getting all this to Ellington?" Margaret asked.

"Dommie will move it in a truck, later on."

"Dommie? Oh. You haven't said anything about him," Margaret said. "What's he like? What's he do?"

"He's a pharmacist. He's taking over his father's drugstore."

"Well, that'll be nice."

"How's your family?" Elizabeth asked suddenly.

"They're fine."

"Everything going all right? Everyone the same as usual?"

"Oh, yes."

Margaret's mind was still on Dommie, trying to picture him. It wasn't until several minutes later that Elizabeth's questions sunk in. Had she wanted to hear about Matthew? There was no way of knowing. By then Elizabeth was making up the daybed, moving around with sheets and army blankets while Margaret watched dimly and sipped the last can of beer. "On the way down here," Margaret said finally, "we passed so close to Matthew's house I was tempted to stop in and see him."

Elizabeth folded the daybed cover, slowly and silently.

"He never married, you know," Margaret told her.

But all Elizabeth said was, "Didn't he?" Then she put a pillowcase on a pillow and laid it at the head of the daybed. "Well, here's where you sleep."

"How about you?" Margaret said.

"I have a sleeping bag."

She brought it out from the closet and unrolled it—a red one, so new that a label still dangled from the zipper-pull. "We're supposed to go camping on our honeymoon," she said.

"But you can't just sleep on the floor. Why don't we change places? You need to rest up for tomorrow."

"I don't mind the floor, it's the *ground* that's going to bother me," Elizabeth said. "Old roots and stobs and crackling leaves."

"Why are you going, then?"

"Dommie likes nature."

"Doesn't the bride have some say?"

"I did. I chose camping," Elizabeth said. "You don't know Dommie. He's so *sweet*. He makes you want to give him things."

"Well, still—"

"You want first go at the bathroom?"

"Oh. All right."

She had thought she would fall into a stupor the minute she was in bed, but she didn't. She lay on her back in the dark, watching the windowpane pattern that slanted across the ceiling. Music and faint voices drifted over from the main house. A screen door slammed; crickets chirped. On the floor Elizabeth breathed evenly, asleep or at least very relaxed, as if tomorrow were any ordinary day. Her white pajamas showed up blurred and gray—the same pajamas, probably, that she had worn back in Baltimore. There they had slept in Margaret's old twin beds, with fragments of Margaret's childhood

lining the bookshelves and stuffed in the closet. And she had lain awake, just as now. She had been going over and over Timothy's death—not yet wondering *why* he died, or picturing how, but just trying to realize that she would never again set eyes on him. Tonight he seemed faded and distant. The sadness that washed over her wasn't because she missed him but because she *didn't* miss him; he was so long ago, so forgotten, a tiny bright figure waving pathetically a long way off while his family moved on without him. They were caught up in things he had never imagined. He had never met Brady, or Mary's daughters, or Peter's strange girlfriend. And he wouldn't know what to make of it if he could see her here, in a garage in North Carolina the night before Elizabeth's wedding.

She flowed from Timothy to Jimmy Joe, to what would happen if *he* should see her here. Anywhere she went, after all, it was possible to run into him. Anywhere but Baltimore— he must surely have moved on. Maybe to New York, to materialize beside her at a counter in Bloomingdale's. Maybe to that beach in California. Maybe to Raleigh. He would come sauntering down the street with his windbreaker collar turned up, soundlessly whistling. His eyes would flick over her, veer away, and then return. "Oh," he would say, and she would stop beside him, poised to rush on to somewhere important as soon as she had said hello. "How are you?" she would ask him, smiling a social smile. "Oh, *how* could you just let me go, as if five weeks of me were all you wanted?"

She saw his mouth starting to frame an answer. His lips were slightly chapped, his shoulders were thin and high, and his hands were knotted in his windbreaker pockets. This time when the tears came she thought of them as a continuation, interrupted on some days by dry-eyed periods. She rolled to a sitting position, disguising her sniffs as long deep breaths, and

reached for her purse at the foot of the bed. Beneath the window, Elizabeth stirred.

"Are you in some kind of trouble?" she asked.

She must have been awake all along; her voice was firm and clear.

Margaret said, "No, I think it's an allergy."

She fumbled for a Kleenex. Then she said, "I seem to keep having these crying spells."

"Anything I can get you?"

"No, thank you."

"Well, if you should think of something."

"I'm really very happy," Margaret said. "I'm not just saying that. I *felt* so happy. Everything was going so well. Now all of a sudden I've started thinking about my first husband, someone I don't even love any more."

"Oh, well, he'll go away again," Elizabeth said.

Margaret stopped in the middle of refolding a Kleenex and looked over at her. All she saw was a dim gray blur.

"You don't know what it's like," she said. "Nobody does. I keep remembering things I'd forgotten. I keep thinking about the last time I saw him, when my mother walked in and just took me away and he never said a word."

"Took you *away*? How did she do that?"

"Just—oh, and he *allowed* it. I've never been so mistaken about anyone in my life. She packed me off to an aunt in Chicago. But do you think he even lifted a finger?"

"How did she find you?" Elizabeth asked.

"I'd written her a note once we got settled, telling her not to worry."

"But took you away! She's so little."

Through her tears, Margaret laughed. "No, not by force," she said. "She didn't drag me out by the hair or anything."

"How, then?"

"Oh, well—" Margaret stared past Elizabeth and out the window, where the sky was a deep, blotting-paper blue. Her tears had stopped. She zipped her purse and set it at the foot of the bed. "I feel much better now," she said. "I hope I didn't keep you from sleeping."

Elizabeth said nothing. Margaret lay down and watched the ceiling. It tilted a little from all the beer she had drunk. She was conscious of an alert, unsettled silence—Elizabeth still wakeful, still not saying, "That's all right," or, "This could happen to anyone," or some other soothing remark to round off the conversation. "You must think our family is pretty crazy," Margaret said after a while.

"More or less."

It wasn't the answer she had expected. "They aren't *really*," she said, too loudly. Then she sighed and said, "Oh well, I guess they *could* wear on your nerves quite a bit."

Elizabeth stayed quiet.

"Dragging you into all our troubles that way. It must—"

"Ha," said Elizabeth.

"What?"

"They didn't drag me *in*, they wanted me for an audience." She clipped off the ends of her words, as if she were angry. "I finally saw that," she said. "I was hired to watch. I couldn't have helped if I'd tried. I wasn't supposed to."

"Oh no, I think Mother just liked having you around," Margaret said.

"That's what I'm saying."

"But I don't *see* what you're saying."

"They were always asking me to do something," Elizabeth said. "Step in. Take some action, pour out some feeling. And when I didn't, they got mad. Then once, one time, I did do something. And what a mess. It was like I'd blundered onto the stage in the middle of a play. What a *mess* it made!"

"I think you must be talking about Timothy," Margaret said.

Elizabeth only rolled over and plumped her pillow up.

"But *you* didn't do anything," Margaret said. "Nobody thinks you're to blame."

"Talk to your mother about that."

"Why? Because she never kept in touch? Well, you have to see *that*—she just doesn't want to be reminded. If there's anyone she blames it's herself."

"Not that I ever heard," Elizabeth said.

"She blames herself for telling Timothy that you were taking Matthew home with you."

"Well, she—what?" Elizabeth sat up. "When did she tell him that?"

"Before he left the house, I guess," Margaret said. "That morning. She says she should have let *you* do it, however you were planning to."

"Before he left with *me*? Before we went to his place?"

"Sure, I guess so."

"He knew all along, then," Elizabeth said. "All the while he was asking to come with me. He *planned* it that way. He was trying to make me feel bad."

"Maybe so," said Margaret. "Anyway, I don't know how—"

"If I never see another Emerson in all my life," Elizabeth said, "I'll die happy."

Which should have hurt Margaret's feelings, but it didn't. She was feeling too sleepy. Sleep took her by surprise, dropping the bottom out of her mind, and suddenly she was blinking and floating, losing track of what they were talking about, spinning off into blurry unrelated thoughts. She was barely conscious of the sound of a match striking. She heard Eliza-

beth inhaling on a cigarette and crumpling cellophane—wakeful, daytime sounds, but they only made her sink further away. She slept deeply, feeling trustful and protected, as if Elizabeth sitting alert on the floor were a sentry who would keep watch for her through the night.

The wedding was held in a red brick church in the middle of nowhere. Elizabeth directed Margaret there, along glaring highways. She wore her jeans, and her hair was not combed; it blew out like a haystack in the wind. She was going to change at her parents' house, she said. In the back seat were her suitcase and her sleeping bag. A linen suit hung from a hook by the window. "Oh, you're not wearing a long dress," Margaret said. "No," said Elizabeth. All her answers this morning were brief and vague. Her mind must be on the wedding. She watched the road with narrow gray eyes that looked nearly white in the sunlight. Her face was calm and expressionless, and her hands, curled around her pocketbook, remained perfectly still.

"Here's where my family lives," she said finally, and Margaret pulled over to the side of the road. The driveway was choked with cars, each one crinkling the air with heat waves. A woman stood on the cement stoop of the ranch-house, and as soon as the car doors opened she called, "Happy wedding day, honey!" and started down the steps. Margaret hung back, although it was she who carried the white suit. She hated to be the only stranger in someone's family gathering. "I'll just go straight to the church," she told Elizabeth.

"Come in, if you want to."

"No, I'll just—"

She pushed the suit on top of Elizabeth's sleeping bag

and turned toward the church, barely taking time to wave at the woman. It must have been Elizabeth's mother. She was saying, "You haven't got much time, honey. Oh! Won't your friend stay? Mrs. Howard's already at the organ, you can hear her if you'll listen. Your flowers are in the icebox but don't you dare get them out till the very last thing, you know how they'll —where are your *shoes*, Elizabeth? Are you planning to get married in moccasins?" If Elizabeth said anything, Margaret didn't hear her.

She walked along the highway to the church, which had only one car in front of it and a Sunday school bus to the side. Although she felt awkward going in so early, it was too hot to stand out in the sun. She climbed the steps and entered through the arched door. Inside, she smelled lemon oil and hymn books. The light was so dim that she stood in the back of the nave for a moment, blinking and widening her eyes, listening to the organ music that wound its way down from the choir loft. The pews were empty, their backs long polished slashes. In front of the altar was a spray of white flowers. The windows were rose-colored and stippled with asterisks. Margaret crossed to the nearest one and opened the lower pane. Then she sat down in the pew beneath it, but still no breeze came to cool her. She picked up a cardboard fan stapled to a popsicle stick and stirred the warm air before her face.

At Elizabeth's house, now, they would all be gathered around and fussing over her, straightening her veil and brushing her suit. Margaret imagined her standing like a totem pole, dead center, allowing herself to be decorated. But she couldn't picture her coming down this aisle. She turned in her seat, looking toward the doorway, and saw the ushers just stepping inside with carnations in their buttonholes. They looked back at her, all out of the same perplexed brown eyes. Was she on the correct side of the church? Which was the bride's side?

She couldn't remember. She stayed where she was, to the right of the altar, and whisked her fan more rapidly.

People began filing in—old ladies, a few awkward men, women who took command of the church the moment they stepped inside. They clutched the ushers' arms and beamed at them, whispering as they walked ("How's your mama? How's that pretty little sister?"), while the ushers stayed remote and self-conscious, and the women's husbands, a few steps behind, carried their hats like breakable objects. The organ grew more sure of itself. A fat lady slid into Margaret's pew, trailing long wisps of Arpege. "I finally did make the Greyhound," she said.

"Oh, good," said Margaret.

The fat lady frilled out the ruffles at her elbows, touched both earlobes, and pivoted each foot to peer down at her stocking seams. Margaret turned and looked out the window. If she ducked her head, she got a horizontal slice of grass, ranch-house, and the lower halves of several pastel dresses and two black suits heading toward the church. In the center was Elizabeth's white skirt, drawing nearer—a sight that startled and scared her, as if she herself were involved in this wedding and nervous about its going well.

The fat lady had started talking, apparently to Margaret. "You knew Hannah couldn't make it," she said. "She's having such a lot of trouble with Everett. But *Nellie* will be here. 'Oh,' she told me, 'I wouldn't miss it for the world. Been waiting a long time to see that boy get married.' Well, *you* know. It came as quite a surprise. *I* had always thought he would marry Alice Gail Pruitt. I expected to see Liz Abbott die an old maid, to tell you the truth."

"Why is that?" Margaret asked.

"Well, she's been mighty difficult. Wouldn't you say?" She kept looking around the church while she spoke, as if she

had lost something. "Didn't they do a nice job with the flowers, now. A few more wouldn't hurt, but—*we* had thought she'd lost Dommie forever, but then he broke off with Alice Gail and came right back here where his heart had been all along. Talk about patient! That boy has the patience of a saint. I just hope Liz knows how lucky she is. And her parents! They've been angels to her. I said to Harry, I said, speaking for myself I just don't know how John and Julia do it. 'If it were me, Julia,' I told her once—"

As if on cue, Mrs. Abbott started up the aisle on the arm of an usher. She was an older, heavier Elizabeth, but her speech was a continuation of the fat lady's. Margaret could hear her clearly as she passed. "That child's *hair!*" she told the usher. "Oh, I begged her to leave it long. 'Just till after the wedding,' I told her, 'that's all I ask.' But wouldn't you know . . ." She passed on by, a whispering blue shadow wearing white roses and absently patting the usher's hand. He kept his eyes on his shoes.

Then the organ paused, and a door at the front creaked open and the minister came out. If she hadn't known ahead of time, Margaret would never have guessed that he was Elizabeth's father. He was tall and handsome and frightening, dressed in black with a small black book between his clasped hands. He was followed by two young men. When they had arranged themselves at the front, so that Margaret could tell which was the groom, she sat forward to take a closer look. She had noticed how Elizabeth described him. "Sweet," she had said—not a word that Margaret would have expected from her. But now she saw that nothing else would have been accurate. Dommie Whitehill's face was the kind that would stay young and trusting till the day he died; his eyes were wide and dark, his chin was round, his face was pale and scrubbed and hopeful. His short brown hair was neatly flattened with water.

If he had any last-minute doubts, none showed in the clear, shining gaze he directed toward the back of the church.

The organ started up, louder this time. What it played was not the traditional march, but then it couldn't be what Margaret thought it was either—the wedding music from *Lieutenant Kije*. She looked around her; no one else seemed to find anything funny. She looked toward the aisle and saw a frilly blonde in pink—Elizabeth's sister, it must be, but softer and prettier—keeping pace with some more dignified music in her head and carrying a nosegay. Behind her came Elizabeth, on the arm of a young man whom Margaret assumed to be the brother-in-law. Elizabeth's white suit was crisp and trim, but without her dungarees she seemed to lose all her style. She walked as if her shoes were too big for her. A short veil stuck out around her face like a peasant's kerchief. Her escort scowled at the carpet, but Elizabeth's face was serene and the music had brought out one of her private half-smiles. They passed Margaret and continued forward, beyond a multitude of flowered hats and whisking fans.

When everyone was in place, Margaret sat back and wiped her damp palms on her skirt. "Things are going to be all right, I believe," the fat lady whispered. Margaret watched Elizabeth's father open his black book and carefully lay aside a ribbon marker. "Dearly beloved . . ." he said. He was one of those ministers who develop a whole new tone of voice in front of a congregation. His words rolled over each other, hollow and doomed. Margaret forgot to listen and watched Elizabeth's straight white back.

But Elizabeth wasn't listening either. The moment her father started reading she turned toward Dommie, as if the ceremony were some commercial she already knew by heart. She spoke, not whispering but in a low, clear voice. Margaret was too far away to hear what she said. Dommie turned toward

Elizabeth and parted his lips; Elizabeth waited, but when he said nothing she went on speaking. Her father's voice crashed above their heads, unnoticed.

Now *no* one was listening. Everyone watched Elizabeth. Whispers traveled down the pews. "You would think just this *once*—" the fat lady said. Even Elizabeth's father seemed to have stopped hearing what he was saying. He spoke with his eyes on Elizabeth, his finger traveling lower on the page, line by line, without his following it. He was going faster and faster, as if he were running some sort of race. "Do you, Dominick Benjamin . . ." Dommie's face turned reluctantly from Elizabeth. "I do," he said, after a pause. He had the strained, preoccupied look of someone interrupted in the middle of more important things. "Do you, Elizabeth Priscilla . . ."

Elizabeth's pause was even longer. A fly spiraled toward the ceiling; someone coughed. Elizabeth drew herself up until she was straight and thin, with her elbows pressed to her sides and her feet close together.

"I don't," she said.

No one breathed. Elizabeth's father snapped his book shut.

"I'm sorry, I just don't," she said.

Then she turned around, and the organ gave a start and wheezed into *Lieutenant Kije* again. Elizabeth came down the aisle slowly and steadily with her nosegay held exactly right and her head perfectly level. Oh, why didn't she just turn and run out that little door at the front? How could she bear to travel all that long way by herself? Margaret thought of leaping up and shouting something, anything, just to pull people's eyes from Elizabeth. But she didn't. She stayed silent. After one glance at Dommie, frozen before the pulpit, she stared down the aisle as hard as anyone.

It took several minutes for people to realize what had

happened. They just sat there—even the fat lady. Then the
organ dwindled out in the middle of a note, and whispers and
rustles started up. Mrs. Abbott rose and marched firmly toward her husband. She looped one arm through his and the
other through Dommie's, and led them back out the little
door.

"Did you ever?" all the women were asking, rising and
clustering together. "Did you ever *hear* of such a thing?" the
fat lady said. "I always did want to see somebody do that," a
man told Margaret. She smiled and sidled out of the pew. In
the doorway, Elizabeth's sister stood circled by more flowered
hats. She looked dazed. "I don't understand, I just don't understand," she kept saying. A woman with feather earrings
said, "Now tell me this, Polly. Had they had a little quarrel
or something?"

"*Dommie* wouldn't quarrel," an old lady said.

"Did they—"

"She *told* us she'd changed her mind," Polly said. "Told
us just as we left the house. Father said no. He said, 'Liz, now
all the guests are here,' he said, 'and you owe them a wedding,'
and she said, 'Well, all right, if a wedding's what you want.'
But we never thought, I mean, we thought she meant—and
Father said she was sure to feel differently, once she was standing at the altar."

"Well, of course. Of course she would," someone said.
"*All* brides get cold feet."

"That's what he told her," Polly said. " 'And they forget
about it an hour later,' he told her, but Liz said, 'How do *you*
know? Maybe they're just saying that, and they regret it all
their lives. It's a conspiracy,' she said—oh, but still I never
thought—Mother asked if there were anyone else. I mean,
anyone, you know, but she said no, and you could tell she
meant it, she looked so surprised—"

"Excuse me," Margaret said. She slid sideways through the crowd until she reached the front steps. Then she shaded her eyes and looked all around her. The sun had bleached everything—the grass, the walk, the highway—but in all that whiteness there was no sign of Elizabeth's wedding suit. She had vanished. All she had left behind were two high-heeled shoes placed neatly side by side on the bottom step.

Margaret walked to her car very slowly. She wanted to give Elizabeth a chance to catch her, in case she needed a ride. But no one called her name. By the time she reached the highway she was feeling a letdown. Now I suppose I'll never hear from her again, she thought, I'll never know how this turned out. Then she opened her car door, and there was Elizabeth on the front seat.

She was slouched so far down that she couldn't be seen from outside, but she didn't have a fugitive look. She seemed flattened, exhausted, as if her sitting so low were merely poor posture. "Hi there," she said.

"Elizabeth!"

"You think you could get me out of here?"

Margaret slid in and slammed the door and started the car, all in one motion. When she pulled onto the highway she left streaks of rubber. Anyone watching would have known it was a get-away car. "Elizabeth," she said, "are you all right?"

"More or less," said Elizabeth.

But from the stoniness of her face, Margaret guessed that she wanted to be left in peace.

They flew down the highway, across mirages of water that streaked its surface. Margaret wanted to make sure where they were going, but she was afraid to break the silence. Then they entered Ellington, and Elizabeth sat up straighter and looked out the window. "There's where I went voting," she said.

"Boating?" Margaret asked. There was no water any-where, but she couldn't believe that Elizabeth would mention voting at a time like this.

"Voting. Voting," said Elizabeth. "Polly's husband said I ought to." She sighed and trailed a hand out the window. "There were all these people lined up. Shopkeepers and house-wives and people, just waiting and waiting. So *responsible*. I bet you anything they wait like that every voting day, and put in their single votes that hardly matter and go back to their jobs and do the same chores over and over. Just on and on. Just plodding along. Just getting through till they die. You have to admire that. Don't you? Before then I never thought of it."

"I admire *you*," Margaret said.

"What for?" said Elizabeth, absently. "But when I was waiting to vote I thought, Wouldn't you think *I* could do that much? Make some decisions? Get my life in order? Let my parents breathe easy for once? Well, I tried, and you see what happened. Just before the finish line I think no, what if I'm making a mistake? Sometimes I worry that everyone but me knows something I don't know: they set out their lives with-out *wondering*, as if they had a few extras stashed away some-where. Well, I've tried to believe it, but I can't. Things are so permanent. There's damage you can't repair."

"But it took a lot of courage, doing what you did today," Margaret said.

"*Flashes* of courage are easy," said Elizabeth, with her mind on something else. Then suddenly she spun around and said, "What's the matter with you? What are you admiring so much? If I was so brave, how'd I get into that wedding in the *first* place? Oh, think about Dommie, he's always so sweet and patient. And my family doing all that arranging, and people coming all that way for the wedding. But *Dommie*. He's never

said a mean thing in his life, or done anything but hope to be loved. What am I going to tell him now?"

From far back in Margaret's mind, where she hadn't even known it existed, came the picture of Dommie's face as he watched Elizabeth leaving him. His eyes were blank and stricken; his mouth was closed, unprotesting. He hadn't yet realized what was happening to him. He unfolded before her eyes as complete and as finely detailed as if the glance she had given him had taken whole minutes, as if she had known him for years and had memorized that picture of him line by line and dreamed of it every night. She blinked and widened her eyes, tightening her hands on the wheel as she drove.

"Well, shoot, Margaret," said Elizabeth. "It's weddings you cry at, not the escapes from them."

"So," said Melissa, settling herself in the car. "How'd the wedding go?"

"It didn't."

"It didn't? What happened?"

"She got to the altar and said, 'I don't,' " said Margaret. She laughed, surprising herself. "Well, it really wasn't funny, of course."

"Sounds funny to *me*," Melissa said. She frowned, briefly interested. Then she said, "Well, anyway, this patchwork skirt woman. She's a *nut*. I'm sorry I ever came down. Do you know what she said to me? I said, 'Look, you're getting twenty dollars for these things. I'll give you twenty-five apiece,' I said, 'if you'll supply me with a dozen now and all you can make from now on.' 'Twenty-five?' she said. 'Well, I don't know, there's something fishy about that.' You'd think I was trying to sell *her* something. 'Look,' I told her . . ."

Margaret gazed through a traffic light. She was thinking

of Jimmy Joe, who might be sauntering down the sidewalk just a block from here. His collar would be turned up, he would be whistling beneath his breath. When he saw her, he would stop and wait. She reached out and touched his wrist, which was frail and bony. "Jimmy Joe," she said, "I'm sorry I left you the way I did." He smiled down at her and nodded, and then he walked on. If he ever came back it would be dimly, for only a second, in the company of others whose parts in her life were finished.

" 'How do I know I'll *feel* like making all those skirts?' she asked me. *Feel* like it! What next? 'Oh, I believe I'll just go my own little way,' she said. Teeny old scrawny woman living all alone, you'd think she'd be jumping at the chance. In her front yard she'd set a bathtub on end and turned it into an icon."

Margaret laughed.

"Why do you keep laughing?" Melissa said. "I think you've spent too much time with Elizabeth."

"Elizabeth? No. She wasn't laughing at all."

"Oh, that doesn't matter," Melissa said. "She's all in the mind anyway. Margaret, what am I going to do? I was counting on patchwork skirts. What can I do instead?"

Margaret didn't answer. She was out on the highway now, concentrating on driving, trying to get home before nightfall.

◙ 10 ◙

1965

Mary's letter said, "Good news, Morris and I are going off for a week in July. Just the two of us, no children. Finally we'll be able to finish a conversation, I told him . . . ."

Mrs. Emerson read it several times, trying to figure out what was expected of her. Was this a hint? Was Mary hoping her mother would babysit? No, probably not. The last time she visited Mary she had overstayed her welcome. Only four and a half days, and she had overstayed. She had replaced a scummy plastic juice pitcher with a nice glass one—nothing special, just something she picked up in downtown Dayton— and Mary had thrown a fit. "What is my juice pitcher doing in the garbage?" she had said. "What is this new thing doing here? Who *asked* you? What right did you have?" Mrs. Emerson had packed and left, and held off writing for three weeks. Then just a bread-and-butter note, brief, formal, apologizing for waiting so long but life had been so cram-*packed* lately, she said. And now what?

She wandered through the house carrying the letter, pressing her fingers to her lips while she thought things over.

If she didn't offer to babysit she would be missing a chance to see her grandchildren. If she did offer, she might be turned down. The insult pricked her already; imagine how much worst if it actually happened! But if she didn't offer . . .

She climbed the stairs to her bedroom. Lately her legs had grown stiff. She moved like an old lady, which she had promised herself she would never do, and although her shoes were still frail and spiky she had lately been eying the thick, black walking shoes in store windows. If she wore sheer stockings with them, after all, if she bought the kind of shoe with a fringed flap so that people thought she had merely changed into a tweedy type . . . . Her hand rested heavily on the banister, and when she reached the top she had to pause to catch her breath before she went into her bedroom.

Dear Mary, she wrote on cream notepaper. *How nice to hear about the vacation. It will do you a world of good. You don't mention a babysitter, and maybe you've already found one, but I did want to let you know that just in case you haven't—*

She stopped to read over what she had written. Although she had chosen her words carefully, her handwriting was deliberately a little more slapdash than usual. Let it look casual, spur-of-the-moment. But when she took up her pen again, she paused and read the letter a second time. She was thinking of her grandchildren. Four of them, three girls and a boy, and she would like to know where people got the idea that girls were quieter. Oh, they ran her ragged. Climbing too high, jumping too far, running too fast. Talking in their high-pitched voices with excited gulps for air. Always hiding her things and giving shrieks of laughter when she missed them. Was she even sure she *wanted* to do this?

Grandchildren were not all they were cracked up to be. She held onto that thought a minute, enjoying it, before she

flicked it away again. Grandchildren were wonderful. What *else* did she have to live for? Her committee work was fading out; her friends were turning into droning old ladies or even, some of them, dying. Mornings, when she came downstairs in a fresh crisp dress and looked all around her at the high ceilings dripping cobwebs, she sometimes wondered why she had bothered to get up. The house seemed thinner-walled, like an old and brittle shell, and she was a little dried-up scrap of seaweed rattling around in its vastness. But then she would remember her children, who descended and spread out from her like a fan, and *their* children spreading out further; and she felt grand and deep and bountiful, a creamy feeling that she held to tightly all through her empty mornings. She felt it now. She rose and made her way to the hall again, for no other purpose than to fill all the other rooms with her richness while it lasted.

Down the stairs, which was harder on her legs than coming up but not so bad for her chest. Through the lower hall, touching pieces of furniture meaninglessly as she passed them. And into the kitchen, where she put a piece of bread in the toaster because it was possible that she had skipped lunch. While she waited for the toast she gathered dirty dishes and set them into the sink. Alvareen had not been by for a week. It looked as if she had finally quit, and all over a little spat that had no importance whatsoever. She had claimed she ought to be paid for her sick-days. "Seeing as you always save up what work I missed, every rag and tag," she said, "and I got to do it then when I get back, you ought to at least pay me for it." "That's rubbish, that's ridiculous," said Mrs. Emerson. "I don't have to stand for any smart talk, Alvareen, I can always find some clean hard-working girl to bring in from the country." "Suit yourself," said Alvareen. What Mrs. Emerson couldn't bring herself to tell her was that it wasn't just *work*

she paid Alvareen for, it was her presence in the house, something to drive the echoes away. But try letting her know that:
she would puff up immediately, maybe ask for a raise. Mrs.
Emerson would not even give her the satisfaction of a telephone call. If she quit, she quit. There *were* no more clean
hard-working girls in the country (where had they got to, anyway?) but good riddance, even so. She'd make do without.

The toaster clicked. Mrs. Emerson took the last clean
plate from a cabinet and went over to the table, but then she
saw that the toast had not come up. It was caught down inside
by one bent corner. Mrs. Emerson poked it with a finger, and
nothing happened. She circled the table thoughtfully. "Never
put a fork in a toaster," people were always saying. It might
have been the only advice she had ever been given; it came in
a chorus, from somewhere above her head. Lately she had been
noticing how many opportunities there were for painful
deaths. Anything was possible: gas heaters exploding, teenaged
drivers running her down, flying roof slates beheading her in a
windstorm, and cancer—oh, cancer most of all. Several nights
she had awakened with the certain, heart-stopping knowledge
that when she died it would be in some horrible way. She had
pushed it off, but the knowledge sank in and became accepted.
In the daytime she often found herself surveying her actions
from some distant point in the future. This was me, before It
happened, she would say, going about my business blissfully
unaware, never dreaming how it would end. The thought gave
a new tone to everything she did. Measuring out tea leaves or
folding back her bedspread was tinged with a lurking horror,
like the sunlit village scenes in vampire movies. And where
there was actually some danger—getting this toast out, for
instance—she became nearly helpless. She spent minutes just
staring at the toaster, plotting courses of action. A wooden
spoon, maybe—something non-conductive. But how did she

know it was non-conductive? She had only the scientists' word for it. Finally a channel seemed to break through in her brain, and she clicked her tongue at herself and bent to unplug the toaster. Even then, she didn't put her fingers in. She turned the toaster upside down and shook it, scattering crumbs all across the kitchen table.

When she had buttered the toast, she took it with her into the hallway. There she picked up the telephone and dialed Mary's number. Lines whirred and snapped into action halfway across the continent. The phone rang several times at the other end, and then Mary said, "Hello?"

"Oh, Mary," said Mrs. Emerson, as if she had forgotten whom she was calling. "How are you, dear?"

"Oh, fine," said Mary, and waited.

"How wonderful about the vacation," said her mother.

"Yes, isn't it?"

"And no children along."

"No."

"You'll be leaving them behind."

"Well, I don't see what's so wrong about *that*," Mary said. "You and *Daddy* went off sometimes. It's not as if—"

"No, no, it's a fine idea," said Mrs. Emerson. "I think it's just fine."

"Well, then."

"Now that you mention it though," Mrs. Emerson said, "do you have someone to stay with the children?"

"Oh, yes, that's all taken care of."

"No problem there, then."

"Oh, no."

"I see. Of course, if it's *settled*," Mrs. Emerson said. "But you know I'm willing to help out with them if I'm needed."

"Thank you, Mother. I think we can manage."

"Oh. All right."

"We'll leave them with Morris's mother, and that way there'll be less—"

"*Morris's* mother!" Mrs. Emerson said. She put her other hand to the receiver. "But *she* gets to see them all the time!"

"All the more reason," said Mary. "They're more used to her. We have to think of the children's side of this."

"But I am," Mrs. Emerson said. She picked up a ballpoint pen and bent over the telephone pad, although there was nothing she wanted to write down. Her voice was soft and feathery. No one hearing it would have guessed how tightly she held the pen. "It's for the children that I want to come, after all," she said.

"Yes, but with Pammie in this nightmare-stage, one more trauma is all she—"

Mrs. Emerson drew a straight slash across the pad and straightened up. "You have just said a word which I utterly despise," she said.

"Now, Mother—"

"I loathe it. I detest it. *Traumas.* How much harm can it do them to see their grandmother once in a while? How long has it *been*, after all? I so seldom—"

"It's been seven weeks," said Mary. "In the past year you've paid us four visits, and all but one lasted nearly a month."

"There, now. See?" said Mrs. Emerson. "You don't make sense. First you say the children aren't used to me and then you say I'm around all the time."

She smiled brightly at her wavery yellowed reflection in the antique mirror. Her hair clung to her forehead, which was damp. Although she wasn't hot, a flush of some sort was rising from her collarbones. She undid the top button of her blouse.

"It's not *my* fault I'm not making sense," Mary said. Her voice was younger and higher; she sounded as if she were back

at that terrible time in her teens, when all she seemed to do was cry and throw tantrums and pick out her mother's niggling faults. "Mother, can't you stand on your own *feet* any more? You're out here all the time, and every visit you make I have the feeling you might not go home again. You get so *settled*. You seem so *permanent*. You act as if you're taking over my household."

"Why, Mary," Mrs. Emerson said. She laid her fingers to her throat, which was tightening and cutting off her breathing. "Where could you get such a thought? Don't you see how careful I am to be a good guest? I help out with the chores, I give you and Morris a little time alone when he comes home in the evenings—"

"You circle around whatever room we're in, clearing your throat. You throw out all our food and buy new stuff from the health store. You make a point of learning the mailman's name and the milkman's schedule and the garbage days, as if you were moving in. You send my clothes to the laundry to save me ironing when ironing is something I enjoy, you buy curtains I can't live with and hang them in the dining room, you string Geritol bottles and constipation remedies all across my kitchen table—"

"Well, if I'd only—"

"*Then* you go off to Margaret's and spoil little Susan rotten. She told me so."

"Oh, this is unfair!" said Mrs. Emerson. "How was I to know, if no one tells me?"

"Why should we *have* to tell you?"

"Well, now that I've heard," said Mrs. Emerson, getting a tighter grip on her voice, "you'll have no further cause for complaint. I certainly won't be troubling you again."

"I might have known you'd take it that way," said Mary.

"Well, what am I supposed to say? Anything I do is wrong. I shouldn't visit, I shouldn't *not* visit. What, then, Mary? Why are my children so un—un—?"

Her tongue stopped working. It jerked and died. Her throat made an involuntary clicking sound that horrified her. She dropped the receiver, letting it swing over the edge of the table. "Mother?" Mary's voice said, tinnily. Long cold fingers of fear were closing around Mrs. Emerson's chest. She buckled her shaking knees and slid to the floor. Then, like a very poor actor performing an artificial death, she felt her way to a prone position and lay staring up at the underside of the table. "Mother, what *is* it?" Mary said. The swinging receiver was nauseating to watch. Mrs. Emerson closed her eyes and felt herself draining away.

When she looked up at the table again it seemed darker, clustered with spinning black specks. Was she going blind? She tried to work her arms, but only one responded. It moved to touch the other, which felt dead and cold and disgusting. She was dying in pieces, then. How fortunate that she had got the children grown before this happened. They *were* grown, weren't they? Weren't they? There seemed to be one baby left over. But when she tried to picture him she realized that she had never seen him; he was that poor little soul born dead, between Melissa and Peter. Well, but it was logical that she should have thought of him; she was going to heaven to meet him, after all. So some people said. Only he had managed alone so long, and the ones left here needed her so much more. How could she bear to look down and see her poor, unsatisfied children struggling on without her? And don't tell her she *wouldn't* see them. If heaven was where people stopped being

concerned with such things then no woman would be happy there.

The undersurface of the table was rough and unfinished, a cheat. From above, it had always been so beautifully polished. In one corner a carpenter's pencil had scrawled the number 83, and she spent a long time considering its significance. Her mind kept floating away from the problem, like a white balloon. She kept reaching out and grabbing it back by the string. Then she saw a small gray brain, a convoluted bulb growing on the inner side of one table leg. Shock caused new chills to grip her chest, before she realized that she was looking at a chewed piece of gum. Chewing gum. She saw cheerful rows of green and pink and yellow packets strung across the candy counter at the Tuxedo Pharmacy. She saw her children snapping gum as they came in for supper, a nasty habit. Chewing open-mouthed, on only one side, their faces peaceful and dreamy. Laying little gray wads on the rims of their plates before they unfolded their napkins. How often had she told them not to do that? The wads cooled and hardened; Margaret, her sloppiest child, would pry hers off the plate and pop it back in her mouth when she had finished eating. Was it Margaret who had stuck chewing gum to her mother's walnut table?

The children swam up from the darkness at the edges of the hallway. Not I, not I, they all said. They were happy and glowing, as if they had just come in from outdoors. Matthew and Timothy and Andrew, their voices newly changed, their hands newly squared and hardened so that she kept having an impulse to reach out and touch them. Teenaged boys are so difficult to live with, a friend whispered. Yes, difficult, Mrs. Emerson said politely, and she smiled and nodded, rubbing the back of her head against the floor, but inwardly she dis-

agreed. She was layered around with teenaged boys, all huge and gangling, making her feel small and frivolous and well-protected. In the middle of their circle she spun, laughing. She was going to stay at this moment in time forever.

It was some trouble with Mary that caused her to be lying here. She remembered now.

She was arguing with her husband, something about the baby. Matthew. This is the wrong one, she said. In the hospital he was fairer. How could I have such a dark-headed baby? She had made him drive her back to the hospital, she had carried the baby in naked, the way he had arrived, rolled in a blue receiving blanket. Would she ever forget how the nurses had laughed? They had called in doctors, orderlies, cleaning ladies, to share the joke with them. In their center she stood looking at the unwrapped baby and saw that he was hers after all— those level, considering eyes, wondering how much to expect from her. She had started crying. "Why honey," her husband said. "This isn't like you." And it wasn't. She had never been like herself again. All the rush of life in this house, that had carried her along protesting and making pushing-off gestures with both hands. All the mountains out of molehills, the mole-hills out of mountains. "The trifles I've seen swelled and magnified!" she said, possibly out loud. "The horrors I've seen taken for granted!"

She opened her eyes, although she had thought they were open already. There was something she had to do. Feed some-one? Take care of someone? Was one of the children sick? No, only herself. She had to call for help. She framed the word "Mama" and discarded it—too strange a mouthful, it must be inappropriate. Her husband? She worried over his name, which was almost certainly Billy. But would she have married a Billy? Oh, after all the hesitation and excitement, the plans,

the doubts, the final earth-shaking decision of whom to marry —and now look. She couldn't remember which man she had ended up with. It was all the same in the end.

She circled Billy, looked at him and then away again, finally made up her mind to speak. "But!" she said aloud. Her tongue was playing tricks on her. She tried again, making such an effort that her forehead tightened. "But!" she called, and saw Billy dead in his bed, his profile barely denting the pillow. Without taking time to mourn she went on to Richard. Would he help? But Richard was tinkling in the rosebushes. Men! His broad, sloping back reminded her of some sorrow. There was no one left. When she awoke in the night, the bed beside hers glowed white and leaped to her eyes at first glance as if it had something to tell her. So there! it said. She rocked her head from side to side.

Now, that clicking sound. Was it her throat again? Her heart? Her brain? No, only the telephone company, reminding her to hang up. She nearly laughed. Then she grew serious and gathered her thoughts together. It was necessary to call a doctor. She was quite clear about it now. She tensed her neck muscles and raised her head. Far away her feet pointed upward, side by side, ludicrous-looking, the feet of the wicked witch in *The Wizard of Oz*. Her good arm moved to support her. She was just fine; she could do anything. She sank back again and stared up at the table. Beneath it, wooden braces ran diagonally at each corner. They were held in place by screws, which were sunk in round holes so that the heads were flush with the wood. Wasn't it wonderful how the holes were so round? How the slant of the braces fit so well to the table angles? There was a word for that; she had heard it once.

"Mitering," Elizabeth said.

Elizabeth, she said silently but briskly, I'm going to want a new backing for that picture at the head of the stairs. Mend

the glass in the bookcase. Coil the hose, please. I can't go getting sued if it trips someone. Do you know how to restring a venetian blind?

Elizabeth's voice came in on a muffled jumble of sound, like a loudspeaker in a railroad station. She spoke in fragments. "The what?" she said. "What would he do *that* for?" "Oh, well—" She laughed. "If I have time, maybe," she said.

We are falling to pieces around here, Mrs. Emerson told her.

Elizabeth laughed. "So are most people," she said.

Elizabeth, we are—

"All right, all right."

Mrs. Emerson prepared to sleep, with everything taken care of. Then some irritating thought began drilling her left temple. She had forgotten: she'd stopped liking that girl a long time ago. Shiftless. Untrustworthy. The world was made up of people forever happy, wastefully happy, laughing at something too far away for Mrs. Emerson to see even when she stood on tiptoe. She craned her neck. She clutched at Andrew's elbow for support. What do you want from me? she asked him.

"Let us in," he said.

He left. She was all alone. She was back before the children, before her husband, back to the single, narrow-boned girl that had been looking out of her aging body all these years.

"Let us in," a man said. He rattled the front doorknob. "Mrs. Emerson? Are you there? Can you hear us? Let us in!"

She meant to answer, but forgot. Voices brushed against each other on her front porch. They were wonderful men, just wonderful. They were here for her. Love and trust washed over her in a flood, and she closed her eyes and smiled.

They broke the window of the front door. Now, why would they do such a thing? Large pieces of glass clanged on

the floor while she screwed up her face, trying to figure it out. Then she found the answer. She was pleased with the rapid way her mind was working. She turned her head to watch a blue-sleeved arm reach in and unsnap the lock. The door opened and two policemen entered, dressed in full uniform just for her. "Mrs. Emerson?" one said.

"Ham," she said, and then she went to sleep, finally in the care of someone competent.

◈ 11 ◈

Matthew sat by the hospital bed, looking at a *Saturday Evening Post* while his mother slept. He ran his eyes down a couple of lines, broke off in the middle, and turned the page. He glanced at a few more lines, turned another page. None of what he read was coming through to him. His mind was on his mother, who lay on her back with her hands by her sides. Her face seemed young and unlined. Her eyes moved beneath the veined lids, following dreams. When Matthew was small, coming in to wake her on a Sunday morning, he had watched her in just this way—jealous, back then, of her dreams, which might not be concerned with him at all. Now he hoped that he was farthest from her mind. "Don't give her anything to worry about," the doctor had said. "Let her sleep as much as she wants, keep her calm and quiet." Which made Matthew consider, and reconsider, before he even opened his mouth. The most trivial small talk might lead to something disturbing. When she slept, he was relieved. He willed her into dreams of a long ago time when she was young and untroubled. He sent her thought-waves of her youth, which for some

reason he pictured against a sunlit, windy meadow sprinkled with daisies. "Before you were born . . ." she used to tell him, and that meadow would rise in front of him, with his mother running through it dressed in white and laughing, free of quarrels and tears and insufficiencies of love.

He glanced across the bed at Mary, who was knitting a child's sweater. Every time she came to the end of a row she reeled more yarn off the ball with a long, sweeping motion and frowned into space a moment, as if she were trying to remember something. Once she sighed. "You must be tired," Matthew said. "Why don't you go on home?"

"Oh, no."

And then she returned to her knitting. She had spent more time here than Matthew, even—two full days, planted in that armchair. And at night, when he took her home, her mind was still back with her mother. "If only I hadn't *quarreled* with her," she kept saying. "I mean, stated my case, but quietly. Put her off a little instead of coming right out with things. Do you think she blames me?"

"No, of course not."

But there was no real way of telling. Their mother's speech was difficult; she could talk, but only after false starts and hesitations. To save effort she kept to the bare essentials. "Water," she said, and it could have been a polite request or a surly order, no one knew. Yet the doctor said she would be back to normal in no time. Already the paralysis was lifting. Her face merely had a numb look, as if she were under Novocain. Her hand was beginning to respond to massage, and she was anxious to try walking. "Your mother's a remarkable woman," the doctor said. Mary frowned, as if he had told her something she didn't want to hear.

Margaret had come, but she had had to bring the baby. She only visited the hospital when Mary was home to babysit.

And Andrew had arrived on the bus the day before, still pale and shocked over the news. "She's fine, she's going to be fine," they told him. But he barely heard. In the hospital room he prowled nervously, stopping every now and then to lay a hand on his mother's forehead, and finally they had sent him home in a cab. "But I want to be *with* her," he kept saying. "Hush, now," Mary told him, "you'll only make her worse, going on like this."

"Can I come back this evening?"

"She'll be *home* day after tomorrow, Andrew."

"Who will stay with her later on? Are you all going to leave her alone again?"

"No, no."

"*I'll* stay. I'll come here to live, I've been meaning to for years."

"No, Andrew."

But who *would* stay with her? It was on all their minds. The girls had to go home soon. Matthew was planning to spend his nights there for a while, but his mother needed someone in the daytime. "Where is Alvareen?" Mary asked. No one had thought to wonder before. They looked at the house, which seemed stale and dusty. Not even Alvareen would have let it get that way. Had she quit? They asked Mrs. Emerson, who merely closed her eyes. "What's her last name?" Mary said. "Do you have her phone number? We want her to come look after you."

"No," said Mrs. Emerson.

"No, what? You don't have her number? Or you don't want her to come."

"I don't want—"

"You don't need a nurse, exactly," Mary said.

"No."

"Is there someone *you* can think of?"

Mrs. Emerson raised her good hand to her lips and frowned. She sighed, apparently about to give up, and then just as she was turning her head away she said, "Gillespie."

Mary looked at Matthew, puzzled. "Gillespie?"

"Gil—" Mrs. Emerson struggled to a half-sitting position. She looked irritated. "*Gillespie*," she said.

"Elizabeth," Matthew said suddenly.

"Elizabeth? The handyman?"

Mrs. Emerson sank down again. Mary raised her eyebrows at Matthew.

"She'd be good if she'd do it," Matthew said. "I saw her taking care of a sick old man once."

"But you don't think she'd do it," Mary said.

"I don't know."

"You know better than anyone else."

"What makes you say that?" Matthew asked. "Do you think I keep in touch with her or something?"

"Well, excuse *me*," said Mary.

"Sorry," Matthew said. "Well, give it a try, if you want. *I* don't know what she'll say."

Mary tracked down Elizabeth's parents right then, from the phone in the hospital room. She had the operator place the call person-to-person to Elizabeth. While she waited Matthew stood at the window with his back to the room, pretending to be looking at the view. He wound a venetian blind cord around his fist. "Lots of visitors today," he told his mother. Mrs. Emerson made some small, impatient gesture that rustled the sheets. Then Mary tensed, listening. "I see," she said. "Well, place the call there, then. Thank you." She cupped the receiver and turned to Matthew. "They say she lives in Virginia now. They gave us the number to call her at work— some kind of children's school."

"School? *Elizabeth?*"

"They said—" She uncupped the receiver. "Yes? All right, I'll hang on. They're trying to reach her now," she told Matthew.

But Matthew didn't stay to hear. He had a sudden urge to get away, as far as he could from Elizabeth and even from the phone that connected her. "Think I'll buy a cup of coffee," he said, and he bolted from the room while Mary stared at him. Once he was outside he took several deep breaths. He pressed the elevator button, and then when it didn't arrive immediately he pushed out the swinging door beside it and started down the stairs.

Elizabeth would never come. He didn't even want her to. He had stopped thinking about her long ago. The hole she left, after the last time he saw her, had made him realize that he wasn't happy living alone; and he had conscientiously taken out several other girls in that first empty year. One he had grown serious about. He had considered asking her to marry him. Then Elizabeth had unfolded herself from a dim corner in the back of his mind, shaken the dust off her jeans and stretched her legs. Her face was bright, threaded across with wisps of blond hair blowing in the wind. She was laughing with a careless kind of joy that took itself for granted. But once he had made his decision—broken off with the other girl, although he sometimes regretted it—he was no longer troubled by Elizabeth. His life had solidified. He was a man in his thirties who lived by himself, encased in a comfortable set of habits and a plodding, easy-going job. He liked things the way they were. Change of any kind he carefully avoided.

He bought a cup of coffee from a vending machine and drank it very slowly. Then he returned to his mother's floor, using the stairs again, and when he got back Mary was peacefully knitting in her armchair. "Sssh," she told him. "Mother's asleep."

He went over to the window. "Sun's out," he said.

"Is it?"

"The forecast was rain."

"I talked to Elizabeth," Mary told him.

He stayed quiet. Mary untwined another length from her ball of yarn.

"I asked if she could come, but she said no. She's not interested."

"Oh. Well, then," Matthew said.

"Then I thought of Emmeline. Remember her? Do you happen to know what her last name might have been?"

"Why are you asking *me* all these things?" Matthew said. "Ask Mother, she's the one who keeps using people up and throwing them out. Wouldn't you think she could just once *keep* someone?"

"There, now," Mary said. "Keep your voice down, Matthew." And she went on serenely knitting that endless sweater.

Mrs. Emerson came home in an ambulance, pale and mysterious on a wheeled stretcher. Mary rode with her; the others stayed at the house to meet her. As soon as the ambulance drew up to the curb Mary leaped out, all energy and efficiency. "Coming through! Coming through!" she called, and chased Matthew from the front door so that she could open it wider. "Is the room ready? Are the sheets turned down?" The men bore the stretcher up the steps. Mrs. Emerson stared straight into the sunlight with the corners of her mouth slightly curled. "Where is the *doorstop?*" Mary asked. Beside her, the others seemed drab and subdued. Margaret stood next to Matthew, with little Susan over her shoulder. Andrew waited just inside. His face loomed out of the dimness like a sliver of moon on

a cloudy night. "Out of the *way*, Andrew," Mary told him, but he paid no attention. "Should you be so loud?" he asked. "Mother? Are they going too fast?" The men navigated the stretcher through the house, calling out warnings and cursing newel posts and doorframes. Mrs. Emerson's smile seemed to be apologizing for her sudden awkwardness. She had been so small, all her life. Now she had grown to the size of a bed, with four square corners to catch on furniture.

She was taken to the sunporch, which Mary had converted to a sickroom. Her twin bed filled one wall, with a table beside it already bearing a tumbler and a water pitcher, flowers in a vase, a pile of slick new magazines. At the other end were all the chairs that had once been scattered through the room. They were placed in a double row, as if Mary had planned on the family's sitting there as rigid and watchful as an audience. Beneath one window was the television, its face newly Windexed, waiting to be depended upon.

"Easy, easy now," one of the men said, and they lifted Mrs. Emerson from the stretcher. She held her neck stiff and clutched at her bathrobe. Matthew, watching her face, could tell when she tried to move her paralyzed hand and failed. There was a shift in her expression, a momentary distance in her eyes, as if she were surprised all over again at the failure and was just recollecting how it had come about. Then she was settled. Her lips moved, and firmed themselves, but instead of speaking she merely nodded to the men. They backed out of the room with the stretcher between them.

For the first hour, there was a concentrated flurry centered in the sunporch. A servant's bell was brought in, and a reading lamp. Andrew put ice in the water. Susan was set on the bed but she cried and had to be taken away again. And everyone, without intending to, kept speaking for Mrs. Emerson. "How nice to be *home!*" Mary said. Then she caught herself, and

laughed. Mrs. Emerson raised her head. "It fools—" she said.

"Feels? Feels too hot?" said Matthew.

"Too cold," said Mary.

"Strange," said Andrew.

Mrs. Emerson brushed them all away. "Summery," she said. Then she closed her eyes, as if she were disappointed at such a pointless remark after all that effort. Everyone rushed to make a fuss over it. "It *does*," Mary said, and Andrew said, "It's June now, you know. Good time to be on the sunporch." They fell silent and looked at the slant of yellow light. "Tomorrow," said Mary, "I'll get the window washers in."

Mrs. Emerson didn't open her eyes.

Pianists, Matthew thought, are the ones that get arthritis, and artists go blind and composers go deaf. And his mother, who pulled all the family strings by words alone, was reduced to stammering and to letting others finish her sentences. All morning they supplied her words for her—never exactly the right ones, never in the proper tone. Tears of frustration kept slipping out of the corners of her eyes and forming gray discs on the pillow. Her chin trembled and her mouth turned downward. She gave her children the feeling that it was they who had failed.

They found her a memo pad, and closed her fingers around a ballpoint pen. But what good was that? Even writing letters to her children, she had preferred using a dictaphone first to try out the words on her tongue. She threw the pen away, with such a jerky movement that it landed in the bedclothes. Then she shook her head, over and over again. "Sorry," she told them.

"It's all *right*," said Mary. "Nobody blames you at all. Do we? We know how hard it must be."

Lunch was eaten in the sunporch, with Mary beside the bed helping her mother and the others in the lined-up chairs.

Susan was put on the windowseat, where she popped all her peas with one finger and babbled to herself. Everyone was grateful to have her there. During breaks in the conversation they watched her intently, implying that there was much more they could be saying if only she hadn't distracted them.

Supper was easier; their mother was asleep. But by then they were all exhausted. They ate sandwiches by a dim light in the dining room, on a table cluttered with bills and playing cards which no one had the energy to move. "How do *nurses* do it?" Margaret asked. "There are four of us. Wouldn't you think we could manage better than this?"

Mary raised her chin from her hand and said, "Margaret, do you know Emmeline's last name?"

"Emmeline. Emmeline—it will come to me. Why?"

"We figured she might take care of Mother after we leave."

"Well, that's a thought," Margaret said.

"*Mother* knows her name, I'm sure of it, but she pretends she doesn't. She's latched onto the idea of Elizabeth."

Andrew lowered his sandwich carefully to his plate, and Margaret shot a glance at him. "Then why *not* Elizabeth?" she asked.

"Margaret?" Andrew said.

"She won't come," said Mary, ignoring him.

"Did you try her?" Margaret asked.

"We called her this morning."

"Really? Where's she at?"

"Virginia," said Mary. "I thought you kept in touch with her."

"Oh, no. Not since, not for years. I wrote but she never answered. What'd you say to her?"

"This conversation is pointless," Andrew said. "I would never allow her to come back here."

"Well, she isn't, so don't go into a stew over it," Mary said.

"Stew? Who's stewing? I merely feel—"

"She isn't *coming*, Andrew."

"Can you guarantee that?" Andrew said. "She's packing her bags right now, I can feel it. Wild horses couldn't keep her away. Well, if necessary I'll bar all the doors and lock the windows. I won't allow it. *Mother* wouldn't allow it."

"Mother's the one who asked for her," Matthew said.

"There are other people she likes in this world."

"But not that she asked for."

"I'm surprised at her. I don't understand her, she used to not even want to hear her name. Are you sure she said *Elizabeth*? Does she *remember*?"

"*Mary*," said Margaret, "what did you *say* to her?"

"Just asked if she could help out with Mother a while. She said no."

"Did you say it would only be for a short time? Did you tell her we'd just need her till Mother's herself again?"

"She didn't give me a—"

"Did you say all we wanted was a nurse, pure and simple? No other problems dumped on her? Did you tell her we'd let her go back afterward to her old life?"

"Well, of *course* we'd let her go back," said Mary. "Why should I bother telling her *that*?"

"You did it all wrong, then," Margaret told her.

"I did the best I knew how."

"We should call her again and give her a limit. Six weeks, say. Tell her six weeks is all she'd—"

"Margaret," said Andrew, very quietly, "I'd like to state a preference, please."

"*You* get sick and you can state your preferences," Mar-

garet told him. "This time it's Mother that's sick. Shall I call Elizabeth now? Matthew?"

"Babcock," said Matthew.

They stared at him.

"I just remembered Emmeline's last name. Babcock."

"You're right," Mary said.

But Margaret said, "*Emmeline's* not the one Mother asked for."

"She's much superior, though," Andrew said.

"Emmeline wouldn't even *come!* I'm sure of it! She never forgave Mother for firing her like that. Can't I call Elizabeth?"

It was Matthew who settled it. "No," he said. "I'm too tired. I don't feel like any more complications."

They finished their supper in silence. Even Andrew wore a defeated look.

At night they watched television. Mrs. Emerson had awakened but refused to eat. She stared at the ceiling while her children watched westerns they had no interest in, and when the picture grew poor no one had the strength to do anything about it. The frames rolled vertically; their eyes rolled too, following the bar that sliced the screen. "I'm sorry," Mary said finally. "I seem to be sleepy. I don't know why." She kissed her mother good night. "Well, Susan will be up so early in the morning—" Margaret said, and she left too. Matthew followed shortly afterward. Andrew stayed behind, gazing at them reproachfully, but before Matthew was even in his pajamas he heard Andrew's feet on the stairs.

Matthew slept in his old room on the second floor. He associated the room only with his early childhood; in his teens he had moved to the third floor with the others. The finger-

prints on the walls here reached no higher than his waist, and the scars were from years and years ago—crayon marks, dart punctures, red slashes of modeling clay rubbed into the screens. Even the bed, which was full size, seemed hollowed to fit a much smaller body. He sank down on it and stretched out, without bothering to turn down the blankets.

There was some disappointment far in the back of his mind, a dull ache. Elizabeth. Had he really wanted her to come, then? But even thinking of her name deepened his tiredness. He pictured all the strains she would have brought—his own love and anger, knotted together, and Andrew's bitterness. "I hate her," Andrew had once told him. "She killed my twin brother." "That's ridiculous," Matthew had said, but he had had no proof of it. He had spent years wondering exactly how Timothy's death had happened; yet the one time Elizabeth seemed likely to tell him, down in Mr. Cunningham's kitchen, he had been afraid to hear. Now he felt grateful to her for keeping it to herself. The worst strain, if she came, he thought, would be Elizabeth's own. At least she had been spared that. Then he relaxed and slept.

When he woke it was still dark, but he heard noises downstairs. He switched on a lamp and checked his watch. One-thirty. Someone was running water. After a moment of struggling against sleep he rose, felt for his glasses, and made his way down the stairs. It was Mary in the kitchen, heating something in a saucepan. She looked blowsy and plump in a terry-cloth bathrobe, with metal curlers bobbing on her head. "What are you doing here?" he asked her.

"Mother wants hot milk."

"Have you been up long?"

"All night, off and on," Mary said. "Didn't you hear the bell? She wanted water, and then a bedpan, and then another blanket—"

"Why didn't you wake me?"

"Oh, we're *all* tired," said Mary. "You too. And each time I thought it would be the last. It's not even two o'clock yet. Do you think this will go on all night?"

"Maybe she's uncomfortable," Matthew said.

"She's nervous. She wants someone to talk to. That water she didn't even drink, and I bet it will be the same with the milk. Oh, *I* don't know." She slumped over the stove, stirring the milk steadily with a silver spoon. "I ended up getting cross with her, and now I feel bad about it," she said. "There's too much on my mind. I worry how the children are doing. And Morris, he can barely tie his own *shoelaces*, and his mother will be feeding him all that starchy food—"

"Go to bed," said Matthew. "Let me take over."

"Oh, no, I—"

But she gave up, before she had even finished her sentence, and handed him the spoon and turned to leave. Her terrycloth slippers scuffed across the linoleum, and the grayed end of her bathrobe sash followed her like a tail.

He filled a mug with hot milk and brought it in to his mother, who lay rigid in the circle of light from the reading lamp. "Oh," she said when she saw him. Since the stroke, she had not spoken his name. She must be afraid that it wouldn't come out right. She hadn't said Margaret's or Andrew's names, either, and although he could see why—they were all such a mouthful—still he wished she would try. The only one she mentioned was Mary. Was there some significance in that? Was it because Mary was the only one who hadn't eloped or had a breakdown or refused to give her mother grandchildren?

He propped up a pillow for her and handed her the milk, but after one sip she gave it back to him. "I hear you're having trouble sleeping," he said. "Would you like me to read to you?"

She shook her head. "When—" she said, and then struggled with her lips. "When you were—"

"When we were children," Matthew said, knowing how often she began things that way.

She nodded and frowned. "I, I read to—"

"To us," said Matthew.

She nodded again.

"I remember you did."

"I never—"

"You never?"

"I never—"

"You never refused?" said Matthew. "You never got tired? You never—"

"No."

He waited, while she took a deep breath. "I never asked, asked *you* to—"

"You never asked *us* to read to *you*," said Matthew. But that made so little sense that he was surprised when she seemed satisfied. He turned the sentence over in his mind. "Well, no," he said finally, "you didn't."

"Money, *Mary*, Mary nooting, knitting—"

"Mary knitting," said Matthew. "Beside your bed? In the hospital?"

"Gave my life," his mother said.

"Oh. Saved your life. By calling the police."

"*Gave.*"

"*Gave* your life?"

"Like a mud, a mother," his mother said.

Matthew puzzled over that for a long time. Finally he said, "Are you worried that it's us taking care of *you* now?"

She nodded.

"Oh, well, we don't mind," he said.

His mother didn't speak again, but she might as well have. The words locked in her head crossed the night air, crisp and perfectly formed: *I do. I mind.* But all she did was turn on her side, away from him. Matthew switched off the lamp, unfolded an afghan, and settled himself in an easy chair at the other end of the room. Shortly afterward he heard her deep, even breaths as she fell asleep.

In this sunporch, where the family had always gathered, Mrs. Emerson's long-ago voice rang and echoed. "Children? I mean it now. *Children!* Where is your father? When will you be back? I have a right to know your whereabouts, every mother does. Have you finished what I told you? Do you see what you've done?" On Timothy's old oscilloscope, she would have made peaks and valleys while her children were mere ripples, always trying to match up to her, never succeeding. Melissa was a stretch of rick-rack; Andrew's giggles were tiny sparks that flew across the screen. Margaret only turned the pages of her book and tore the corners off them. She was a low curved line, but Matthew was even lower—the EKG of a dying patient. He pulled the afghan up closer around him. His mother slept on, her moonlit profile sharp and strained, her mouth pulled downward with the effort of accepting when she had always been the one to pour things out.

He slept, and she woke him three times—once for water, once for the sound of his voice, once for a bedpan. For the bedpan she insisted that he call one of the girls. He climbed the stairs in the dark, hesitated at Mary's door, and then woke Margaret. While she helped her mother he stayed in the living room and kept himself awake by watching a pattern of leaves moving over the Persian rug. Then Margaret came back out and tapped him on the shoulder. "Do you want me to take over?" she asked. "You look dead on your feet."

"No, I'm all right."

"I called Emmeline. She won't come," Margaret said.

"We'll find someone."

"Matthew, you *know* that I could change Elizabeth's mind. Mary didn't put it to her right."

"No," Matthew said.

"I could have her here in an hour, if she took a plane."

"There are agencies all over Baltimore that can help us out with Mother," Matthew said.

He went back to the easy chair. Its rough fabric had started prickling through his pajamas, and he kept shifting and turning and rearranging the afghan while his mother lay tense and wakeful at the other end of the room. "I want—" she said. But in her pause, while he was waiting for her to finish, Matthew fell asleep.

He awoke at dawn. Every muscle in his body ached. "Oh, Matthew," someone said, and for a moment he thought it was his mother, finally getting around to saying his name; but it was Margaret. She stood over him, fully dressed, holding Susan. Susan wore a romper suit and straddled her mother's hip with small round legs still curved like parentheses. She looked down at him solemnly. "Hi there," he told her. "Matthew, you look terrible," Margaret said.

"I'm okay."

He looked over at his mother. She was watching them out of eyes the same as Susan's—round and pale blue and worried. "How you doing?" Matthew asked her.

"I fool—"

"You feel?"

"I fool I'm—"

She flattened the back of her hand across her mouth. Tears rolled down her stony face, while she stared straight ahead of her. "Mother?" Matthew said. He struggled up out

of his chair, but then there was nowhere to go, nothing to say. He and Margaret stood there in silence, already defeated by the day that lay ahead of them.

Everyone agreed that Matthew should go to bed now—even Matthew himself. But first Mary brought him a breakfast tray in the sunporch, and while he was buttering a roll his head grew so heavy that he laid his knife down and leaned back and closed his eyes. He felt the tray being lifted from his knees—a falling sensation, that made him jerk and clutch at air. "You should go upstairs, Matthew," Mary said. But he only slid lower in his seat and lost track of her voice.

He dreamed that he was in a forest which was very hot and smelled of pine sap. He was walking soundlessly on a floor of brown needles. He came upon someone chopping wood, and he stood watching the arc of the axe and the flying white chips, but he didn't say anything. Then he felt himself rising out of sleep. He knew where he was: on his mother's sunporch, swimming in the bright, dusty heat of mid-afternoon. But he still smelled the pine forest. And when he opened his eyes, the first thing he saw was Elizabeth in a straight-backed chair beside his mother's bed, whittling on a block of wood and scattering chips like fragments of sunlight across her jeans and onto the floor.

◈ 12 ◈

The first thing Elizabeth did with Mrs. Emerson was teach her how to play chess. It wasn't Mrs. Emerson's game at all—too slow, too inward-turned—but it would give her an excuse to sit silent for long periods of time without feeling self-conscious about it. "This is the knight, he moves in an L-shape," Elizabeth said, and she flicked the knight into all possible squares although she knew that Mrs. Emerson watched in a trance, her mind on something else, the kind of woman who would forever call a knight a horse and try to move it diagonally.

She set up game after game and won them all, even giving Mrs. Emerson every advantage, but at least they passed the time. Mrs. Emerson cultivated the chess expert's frown, with her chin in her hands. "Hmmm," she said—perhaps copying some memory of Timothy—but she said it while watching her hands or the clock, just tossing Elizabeth a bone in order to give herself more empty minutes. Elizabeth never hurried her. Mary, passing through the room once, said, "Hit a tough spot?" And then, after a glance at the game, "Why, the board's

wide open! All that's out is one little pawn." "She doesn't like standard first moves," Elizabeth explained. Although eventually, when Mrs. Emerson had collected herself, all she did was set her own king pawn out.

Every time Elizabeth looked up, Mary was somewhere in the background watching her. Margaret was standing in the doorway hitching her baby higher on her hip. Well, Margaret she had always liked, but still, she kept having the feeling that she was being checked out. Were they afraid she would make some new mistake? Under their gaze she felt inept and self-conscious. She plumped Mrs. Emerson's pillow too heartily, spoke to her too loudly and cheerfully. All of Thursday passed, long and slow and tedious. No one mentioned going home.

For them—for Margaret, who had sounded desperate and offered double pay and a six-week limit and a promise of no strings attached—she had taken a leave of absence from her job with only ten minutes' notice and flown to Baltimore when she had never planned on seeing it again. She had minded leaving her job. She was a crafts teacher in a girls' reform school, which was work that she loved and did well. The only mistake she had made there was this one: that she had left so suddenly, and lied about the reason. Told them her mother was sick. Oh, even the briefest contact with the Emersons, even a long distance phone call, was enough to make things start going wrong. She should have kept on saying no. She should be back in Virginia, doing what felt right to her. Instead here she was pretending to play chess, and all because she liked to picture herself coming to people's rescue.

She moved out pawns, lazily, making designs with them, sustaining over several turns the image of some fanciful pattern that she wanted them to form. No need to watch out for attacks. Mrs. Emerson would never attack; all she did was buckle, at the end, when she found her king accidentally

surrounded by half a dozen men for whom Elizabeth had forgotten to say, "Check."

"Could I bring you two some tea?" Mary asked, hovering. "Does anyone want the television on?" Margaret said, "If you'd like a breath of air, Elizabeth, I can stay with Mother. Feel free to go to the library, or draw up lesson plans." They thought she was a teacher in a regular school. Elizabeth hadn't set them straight. She kept meaning to, but something felt wrong about it—as if maybe the Emersons would imagine her students' crimes clinging to her like lint, once they knew. She wondered if the school smell—damp concrete and Pine-Sol disinfectant—was still permeating her clothes. While Mrs. Emerson struggled for a word Elizabeth's mind was on the paper towel roll on the nightstand: two more towels and the roll would be empty, and she could hoard it in her suitcase for an art project she had planned for her students. "I want—" Mrs. Emerson said, and Elizabeth's thoughts returned to her, but only partially. Piecemeal. Neither here nor there. She felt suddenly four years younger, confused and disorganized and uncertain about what she could expect of herself.

Mrs. Emerson said, "Gillespie. Gillespie." Elizabeth jumped and said, "Oh," She wasn't used to this new name yet. She wondered how it felt to have Mrs. Emerson's trouble. Did the words start out correctly in her head, and then emerge jumbled? Did she hear her mistakes? She didn't seem to; she appeared content with "Gillespie." "I'm—" she said. "I'm—" Her tongue made precise T sounds far forward in her mouth. Elizabeth waited. "Tired," Mrs. Emerson said.

"I'll put the board away."

"I want—"

"I'll lay your pillow flat and leave you alone a while."

"No!" said Mrs. Emerson.

Elizabeth thought a minute. "Do you want to sleep?" she asked.

Mrs. Emerson nodded.

"But you'd rather I stayed here."

"Yes."

Elizabeth put the chess pieces in their box, tipped her chair back, and looked out the window. She kept her hands still in her lap. From her months with Mr. Cunningham she had learned to lull people to sleep by being motionless and faceless, like one of those cardboard silhouettes set up to scare burglars away. Even when Mrs. Emerson tossed among the sheets, Elizabeth didn't look at her. If she did, more words would struggle out. She imagined that coming back would have been much harder if Mrs. Emerson could speak the way she used to. Think of what she might have felt compelled to say: rehashing Timothy, explaining those years of silence, asking personal questions. She shot Mrs. Emerson a sideways glance, trying to read in her eyes what bottled-up words might be waiting there. But all she saw were the white, papery lids. Mrs. Emerson slept, nothing but a small, worn-out old lady trying to gather up her lost strength. Her hair was growing out gray at the roots. The front of her bathrobe was spotted with tea-stains—a sight so sad and surprising that for a moment Elizabeth forgot all about those students that she was missing. She rocked forward in her chair and stood up, but she watched Mrs. Emerson a moment longer before she left the room.

Matthew was in the kitchen, eating what was probably his breakfast. He had shaved and dressed. He no longer had that uncared-for look that he had worn asleep in the armchair, but his face was older than she remembered and a piece of adhesive tape was wrapped around one earpiece of his glasses. "Can I pour you some coffee?" he asked her.

"No, thank you."

"How's Mother?"

"She's asleep."

"How does she seem to you?" he asked her.

"Oh, I don't know. Older." She wandered around the kitchen with her arms folded, avoiding his eyes. She didn't feel comfortable with him anymore. She had thought it would be easy—just act cheerful, matter-of-fact—but she hadn't counted on his watching her so steadily. "Why are you staring?" she asked him.

"I'm not staring, you are."

"Oh," Elizabeth said. She stopped pacing. "Well, the *house* seems *terrible* to me," she said. "Much worse off than your mother. How did it get so rundown? Look. Look at that." She waved to a strip of wallpaper that was curling and buckling over the stove. "And the porch rail. And the lawn. And the roof gutters have whole *branches* in them, I'm going to have to see to those."

"You're not the handyman here anymore," Matthew said.

She thought for a moment that he had meant to hurt her feelings, but then she looked up and found him smiling. "You have your hands full as it is," he told her.

"When she's napping, though. Or has visitors."

"I've been trying to do things during the weekends. I mow the grass, rake leaves. But it's a full-time job, I never quite catch up." He looked down at his plate, where an egg lay nearly untouched. "Before she got sick I'd just finished cleaning out the basement," he said "*Shoveling* it out. All that junk. Remember our wine?"

"Yes."

"I found it in the basement six months after you left. White scum on the top and the worst smell you can imagine."

"I wondered what you'd done with it," Elizabeth said.

A younger, shinier Matthew flashed through her mind. "When the wine has aged we'll go on a picnic," he had said. "I'll bring a chicken, you bring a . . ." As if that picnic had actually come about, she seemed to remember the sunlight on a riverbank and the flattened grass they sat on and the feel of Matthew's shirt, rough and warm behind her as she leaned back to drink from a stoneware jug.

"What would it have tasted like, I wonder," Matthew said.

She knew she should never have come back here.

The first time she realized that Andrew was home was at supper. They ate in the dining room—Elizabeth, the two sisters, Matthew, and Susan. Elizabeth kept hearing clinking sounds coming from the kitchen, separated by long intervals of silence. "What's that?" she asked, and Mary said, "Oh, Andrew."

"Andrew? I didn't even know he was here."

"He's going back on Sunday."

Nobody pretended to find it odd that he should be eating in the kitchen.

That night, from the army cot that had been set up for her on the sunporch, she heard Andrew cruising the house in the dark. He slammed the refrigerator door, creaked across floorboards, scraped back a dining room chair. He carried some kind of radio with him that poured out music from the fifties —late-night, slow-dance, crooning songs swelling and fading as he passed through rooms, like a bell on a cat's collar. In the morning when she went upstairs his door was tightly shut, sealed-looking. When she returned from the library with a stack of historical romances for Mrs. Emerson she found flo-

rists' roses by the bed—nothing any of the others would have thought of buying—and the smell of an unfamiliar aftershave in the air. He ate his lunch in the kitchen. That weighty, surreptitious clinking cast a gloom over the dining room, but no one mentioned it. "We seem to be missing the butter," Elizabeth said, and Mary rose at once, letting a fork clatter to her plate, as if she feared that Elizabeth would go out to the kitchen herself. "Sit still, I'll get it," she said. But Elizabeth hadn't even thought of going. She avoided Andrew as much as he did her. Otherwise, even in a house so large, they would have had to bump into each other *sometime*. She kept an ear tuned for the sound of his approach, and circled rooms where he might be. Why should she bother him, she asked herself, if he didn't want her around? But she knew there was more to it than that: she didn't want *him* around, either. He had passed judgment on her. Once or twice, during the afternoon, she caught glimpses of him as he crossed the living room—a flash of his faded blue shirt, a color she associated with institutions —and she averted her face and hunched lower in her chair beside Mrs. Emerson. She should have gone right out to him, of course. "Look here," she should have said. "Here I am. Elizabeth. You *know* I'm in the house with you. I feel so silly pretending I'm not. Why are you doing this? Or why not just go back to New York, if you can't bear to see me?" But she already knew why. He had summed her up. He was afraid to leave his family in her hands. He alone, of all the Emersons, knew that she was the kind of person who went through life causing clatter and spills and permanent damage.

A man from an orthopedic supply house delivered an aluminum walker. It sat by Mrs. Emerson's bed most of Friday afternoon, but she made no move to use it. "Try, just try it," Mary said. Mrs. Emerson only sent it slit-eyed glances full of

distrust. She felt strongly enough about it to frame a very complicated sentence about walkers reminding her of fat old ladies in side-laced shoes, which made Elizabeth laugh. "You're right, come to think of it," she said. Mary frowned at her. When they were alone she said, "Elizabeth, I hope you'll *encourage* Mother a little. The doctor says she'll be back to normal in no time if she'll just take things step by step." "Oh, she'll be all right," Elizabeth said. And she was. With no one watching, with Elizabeth's back deliberately turned, Mrs. Emerson looked at the walker more closely and finally reached out to test its weight with one hand. Within a few hours, she had allowed herself to be lifted to a standing position. She clomped around the sunporch, leaning heavily on the walker and puffing. Elizabeth read a magazine. "I think—" Mrs. Emerson said.

"You should probably get some rest," Elizabeth said. She had figured out by now how to carry on their conversations. As soon as she got the gist of a sentence she interrupted, which sounded rude but spared Mrs. Emerson the humiliation of long delays or having words supplied for her. It seemed to work. Mrs. Emerson released the walker, and Elizabeth closed her magazine, helped Mrs. Emerson back to bed, and took her slippers off. "Before supper we'll try it again," she said.

"But I—"

"Yes, but the more you practice the sooner you'll be free of the walker."

Mrs. Emerson closed her mouth and nodded.

Matthew and his mother and Elizabeth went over Mrs. Emerson's checkbook together. Mrs. Emerson wanted Elizabeth to pay bills and keep her records; she had had Elizabeth's signature cleared at the bank. "But why?" Elizabeth asked her. "*You* can write *that* much. Why me?" She felt herself sinking

into some kind of trap, the trap she had been afraid of when she first said no to coming back. "I'll only be here six weeks, remember," she said.

"Oh well," said Matthew, "I suppose it's tiring for her, dealing with all this."

But Elizabeth was still watching Mrs. Emerson. "Six weeks is all the leave I have," she said. "That's understood. Margaret told me so."

Mrs. Emerson merely aligned a stack of envelopes. She moved her lips, forming no words, pretending it was the stroke that kept her from speaking.

Matthew smoothed open the pages of the budget book and explained how it was kept—a page for every month, an entry for every expense, however small. Matches, stamps, cleaning fluid. Her children thought of the book as a joke. Matthew showed Elizabeth the first page, started two years ago: "This book, 69¢; envelope for this book, 2¢." He pointed it out silently, smiling. Elizabeth barely glanced at it. "Why couldn't *you* do this?" she asked him. "You're here all the time."

"But I won't be after Sunday."

"Why? Where are you going?"

"Well, I have to get back to work. I can only stop by in the evenings."

She looked up and found him watching her. His glasses had slipped down his nose again. His shoulder just brushed hers. He smelled like bread baking, and always had, but until now she had forgotten that. Caught off guard, she smiled back at him. Then Mrs. Emerson cleared her throat, and Elizabeth moved over to sit on the foot of the bed.

All Friday evening she worked on the bills, staying close by Mrs. Emerson in case questions arose. "Who is this Mr.

Robbins? Why the two dollars? Where is this bill they say you've overlooked?" She decided that budget books were more revealing than diaries. Mrs. Emerson, who had been born rich, worried more about money than Elizabeth ever had. Her business correspondence was full of suspicion and penny-counting, quibbling over labor hours, threatening to take her business elsewhere, reminding everyone of contracts and estimates and guarantees. Her bills were from discount stores and cut-rate drug companies, some of them clear across the country, and to their trifling amounts interest rates and penalties had been tacked on month after month while Mrs. Emerson hesitated over paying them. Her checks were from an inconvenient bank at the other end of town—lower service charges, Matthew said. Yet Elizabeth found a seventy-dollar receipt from a health food store, and a sixty-dollar bill for a bathrobe. She whistled. Mrs. Emerson said, "What, what—"

"Your spending is all cock-eyed," Elizabeth told her.

"I worry—"

"I would, too. What kind of bathrobe costs sixty dollars? *Health* food! You can live in perfect health on forty-nine cents a day, did you know that? For breakfast you have an envelope of plain gelatin in a glass of Tang, that's protein and vitamin C, only you have to drink it fast before the gelatin sets. For lunch—"

"But stone-ground—"

"Fiddle," said Elizabeth. "And forty-watt lightbulbs, so you'll ruin your eyes and need to buy new glasses. I'll have to change all the bulbs in this house, now. And five cents postage to save four cents on aspirin."

"I worry—"

"But what *for*? You never used to."

"I don't know," Mrs. Emerson said clearly. Then she

slumped against the pillow and started plucking at her sheet. Worry radiated from her in zig-zags that Elizabeth could almost see. Crotchety lines were digging in across her forehead— just what Mr. Emerson had set up all these trust funds to keep her from, never dreaming that they would be no comfort. "Oh, well," said Elizabeth, sighing. She tapped Mrs. Emerson's hand lightly and then went back to the bills. She wrote out neat columns of numbers, as if by her careful printing alone she could salvage all Mrs. Emerson's hours of fretting and hand-twisting and helplessness.

By Saturday morning, Mrs. Emerson had grown more adept with the walker. She had turned it into an extension of herself, like her little gold pen or her tortoise-shell reading glasses—lifting it delicately, with her fingertips, setting it down almost soundlessly. "Now we can go out," Elizabeth told her. She flung open the double doors off the sunporch and then went ahead, without looking back at Mrs. Emerson. "I think—" Mrs. Emerson said.

"Aren't you planting any annuals this year?"

Mrs. Emerson moved out into the yard. Elizabeth heard the barely perceptible clink of screws against aluminum, but still she didn't look around. She walked on ahead, sauntering in an aimless way so that it wouldn't seem she was deliberately slowing down. "We *could* pick up some marigolds," she called back.

"I fool so—so—"

Unseen, Mrs. Emerson's struggle for words seemed more difficult. Elizabeth winced and held herself rigid, staring at a flowerbed.

"Gillespie. I fool so—"

"Take your time," Elizabeth told her. "I'm not in any hurry."

"I fool so *clumsy,*" Mrs. Emerson said.

"Oh, well. That'll pass."

She ambled toward a trellis, poking stray weeds with the toe of her moccasin. "Plantain is taking your yard over," she said. "Something's wrong with your grass. Don't you ever feed it anymore?"

She turned and found Mrs. Emerson smiling at her, with the pale yellow sunlight softening her face.

While Mrs. Emerson napped, Elizabeth wound all the clocks. She nailed up a kitchen spice rack that was dangling crazily by one corner. She dragged the aluminum ladder out from under the veranda and stood on it to clean the gutters, until Matthew found her there. "I thought I told you not to do that," he said. He held onto the ladder, steadying it, while she took swipes at damp black leaves that had rotted into solid clumps. "This isn't your job any more," he said. "And it isn't safe. Will you let me take over, now?" The force he put into his words traveled through his hands and shook the rungs, so that she felt she was standing on something alive. When she descended with an armload of twigs it was he who moved the ladder to a new position and climbed it, and Elizabeth who held it steady. "You were supposed to be mowing the grass," she called up to him.

"Never mind, I'll get to it later."

They were at the back of the house, above the steepest part of the lawn, and when she looked down the hill and then up at Matthew he seemed dizzyingly high. How old was this ladder, anyway? Did it have to shake so? What was that flimsy twanging sound? She leaned forward until she was braced full length along its slant, with her arms woven through

the rungs and her head hanging down to study her feet. When Matthew shifted his weight, a tremor ran through the metal like a pulse.

For supper that night, Mrs. Emerson came into the dining room. They lit candles to celebrate. She sat in her old chair at the head of the table, her back beautifully straight, her right hand folded in her lap while she managed her fork with her left. If she was surprised to see Andrew's place empty, she didn't show it. When Matthew offered her more meat she said, "No. Ask—ask—" and waved her hand toward the kitchen. Mary went out and there were low murmurs; then she came back in. "No, thank you," she told Matthew. She threw a quick, embarrassed look at Elizabeth, who hardly noticed. Now that she had spent the afternoon repairing things, Elizabeth was thinking like a handyman again. She was making a mental note of the knobs on the corner cupboard, both of which had come off. They were sure to be in the silver candy bowl on the top shelf. How many times had she fished them out of that bowl and fitted them back on? She knew exactly how they would feel in her hand, the chipped, rounded edges pressing into her thumb and the way the left one always went on crooked unless she was very careful. She seemed to have memorized this house without knowing it. Between the main course and dessert she slipped out of her chair and stood on tiptoe to feel in the candy bowl, and sure enough, there they were. A little dirtier, a little more chipped. She squatted by the lower door and screwed the first one on. "Elizabeth?" Mary said. "Would you care for coffee?" Elizabeth turned and said, "Oh. No, thanks." Mary's face was puzzled and courteous. "If you have things to do," she said, "maybe you want to be excused." But Matthew was smiling at Eliza-

beth as if she'd done exactly what he'd always known she would.

In the night Mrs. Emerson kept calling for things. She wanted food brought in, or errands run, or the sound of someone's voice in the dark. "Gillespie. Gillespie," she said. Elizabeth, on her cot, slept on, incorporating Mrs. Emerson's voice into her dreams. "Gillespie." Then she opened her eyes, and struggled up among a tangle of sheets.

"What," she said.

"Water."

She lifted the pitcher on the nightstand, found it empty, and padded off to the kitchen. While she was waiting for the water to run cold she nearly went to sleep on her feet. The name Gillespie rang in her ears—the new person Mrs. Emerson was changing her into, someone effective and managerial who was summoned by her last name, like a WAC. Now Mary had started calling her Gillespie too. It was contagious. She jerked awake, filled the pitcher, and brought it to the sunporch. "Here," she said, and dropped into bed again.

"Gillespie."

"What."

"A blanket."

The third call was for pills. "Pills?" Elizabeth said blurrily. "Sleeping pills? You've had them."

"I can't—"

"The doctor said no more than two. Remember?"

"But I can't—"

Elizabeth sighed and climbed out of her cot. "How about warm milk," she said.

"No."

"Would you like a glass of wine?"

"No."

"*What*, then."

"Talk," said Mrs. Emerson.

Elizabeth sat down on the foot of the bed, and for a minute she only frowned at the moonlit squares on the floor. Soft night air, as warm as bath water, drifted in the open windows. Her pajamas smelled of Ivory soap and clean sheets, a dreamy, comforting smell. But Mrs. Emerson said, "Talk," and sat straighter, waiting.

"When you called, I was asleep," Elizabeth said.

"Sorry," said Mrs. Emerson.

"I dreamed that your voice was a little gold wire. I was chasing a butterfly with my fourth-grade science class. My fingers would just brush the butterfly; then the wire pulled it away again. There was gold in the butterfly, too. Threads of it, across the wings."

She pulled her feet off the cold slate floor and tucked them under her. "You may be scared of the dark," she said.

"No."

"Why not? What would be so strange about that? Look at all the dark corners there are, and the moonlight makes them look darker. I used to think that skinny ladies in bathrobes were waiting in corners to get me. *I* don't know why. My father had a lady like that in his church—sick for years, about to die, always wore a pink chenille bathrobe. Whenever my mother said 'they'—meaning other people, just anyone— that's who I pictured. 'They've put a stop sign on Burdette Road,' she'd say, and I would picture a whole flock of ladies in pink bathrobes, all ghostly and sure of themselves, hammering down a stop sign in the dead of night. Funny thing to be scared of. They weren't only in corners, they were in the backs of closets, and under beds, and in the slanty space below the stairs. Now I'm grown up and don't think of them so much, but if something is worrying me, dark corners can still make me wonder what's in them. Possibilities, maybe. All the

bad things that can happen to people. Or if I'm worried *enough*, ladies in pink bathrobes all over again."

"Yes," said Mrs. Emerson. But she didn't seem to be dropping off to sleep yet.

"When you're independent again it won't be so bad," Elizabeth told her. "It's feeling helpless that scares you."

"But I won't—"

Elizabeth waited.

"I won't *be*—"

"Of course you will. Wait and see. By the time I leave you'll be running this house again."

"Gillespie."

Elizabeth stiffened.

"Can't you—"

"No," said Elizabeth. "I have a job now. One I like."

"You never *used to*—"

"Now I do, though," Elizabeth said. "I stay with things more. I don't go flitting off wherever I'm asked nowadays."

But she hadn't guessed the words correctly. "Never used to like, like *children*," Mrs. Emerson said.

"Oh. Well, not as a group, no. I still don't. But these I like."

She passed a hand across her eyes, which felt dry and hot. She was going to be exhausted by morning. "Are you sleepy?" she asked.

"Talk," said Mrs. Emerson.

"I *have* talked. What more is there to say?" She wound a loose thread around her index finger. "Well," she said finally, "I'll tell you how I happened to start working at the school. I was leaning out the window of this crafts shop where I used to sell things, watching a parade go by. There were people crammed on both sidewalks, mothers with babies and little children, fathers with children on their shoulders. And

suddenly I was so *surprised* by them. Isn't it amazing how hard people work to raise their children? Human beings are born so helpless, and stay helpless so long. For every grownup you see, you know there must have been at least one person who had the patience to lug them around, and feed them, and walk them nights and keep them out of danger for years and years, without a break. Teaching them how to fit into civilization and how to talk back and forth with other people, taking them to zoos and parades and educational events, telling them all those nursery rhymes and word-of-mouth fairy tales. Isn't that surprising? People you wouldn't trust your purse with five minutes, maybe, but still they put in years and years of time tending their children along and they don't even make a fuss about it. Even if it's a criminal they turn out, or some other kind of failure—still, he managed to get grown, didn't he? Isn't that something?"

Mrs. Emerson didn't answer.

"Well, there I was hanging out the window," Elizabeth said, "thinking all this over. Then I thought, 'What am I doing up here, anyway? Up in this shop where I'm bored stiff? And never moving on into something else, for fear of some harm I might cause? You'd think I was some kind of special case,' I thought, 'but I'm not! I'm like all the people I'm sitting here gawking at, and I might just as well stumble on out and join them!' So right that day I quit my job, and started casting about for new work. And found it—teaching crafts in a reform school. Well, *you* might not think the girls there would be all that great, but I like them. Wasn't that something? Just from one little old parade?"

"Yes," said Mrs. Emerson. Then she was silent.

"Mrs. Emerson?"

But all Elizabeth heard was her soft, steady breathing. She slid off the bed and found her way back to the cot. She

stretched out and pulled the cool sheets over her, but then she couldn't sleep. She stayed wide awake and thoughtful. She was awake when Andrew's shadow crossed a moonbeam, heading all alone to the gazebo. When she propped herself on an elbow to look at him, he had stopped close beside the sunporch. A thin silvery line traced the top of his head and slid down the slope of his shoulders, stopping at the white shirt whose collar was pressed open in a flat, old-fashioned style. Although he was looking toward the windows, he couldn't see her. His face was a blank oval, pale and accusing. After a moment he turned and wandered off behind the tangled rosebushes.

"Look," Matthew said. "From here you would think the house was on fire."

Elizabeth followed the line of his arm. They were in the gazebo, balanced precariously on a rotten railing, and from where they sat they could look up and see the house reflecting the sunset from every window. Not as if it were on fire, Elizabeth thought, so much as *empty*. The windows were glaring orange rectangles, giving no sign of the life behind them. The scene had a flat, painted look. "I wonder why she keeps the place," Matthew said.

"Maybe for her children to come home to."

"We never come all at once anymore."

He picked up her hand and turned it over. Elizabeth wasn't surprised. At this time of day, in this stillness, it seemed as if she had never been away; his hardened palm was as familiar as if she had last held it minutes ago. She rested lightly against his side, which felt warm on her bare arm. Matthew was in a suit. He was dressed to take Andrew to the bus station and the girls to the airport. Elizabeth wore only jeans and a

short-sleeved shirt. When she shivered he said, "Do you want my jacket?"

"No, thanks. It's time for you to be going."

But Matthew didn't move. "My father bought this house when they were married," he said. "Before they even had children. They moved in with nothing more than Grandmother Carter's parlor furniture, in all this space. He said they were going to live here till they died. He expected to have a long life, I guess. They were going to celebrate their golden anniversary here, all white-haired and settled with the third floor closed off except when children and grandchildren came to spend their summer vacations."

"Vacations in *Baltimore?*"

"If you were to marry me," Matthew said, "we could stay in this house, if you liked."

Which surprised her no more than his hand had. Why should it? Life seemed to be a constant collision and recollision of bodies on the move in the universe; everything recurred. She would keep running into Emersons until the day she died; and she and Matthew would keep falling in love and out again. If it snowed, wouldn't Timothy be waiting for her to shovel him a path? Wouldn't he emerge from those bushes if she took it in her head to walk another turkey?

"When I picture *our* golden anniversary," Matthew said, "I think of us in a supermarket. One of those cozy old couples you see telling each other what food they like. 'Here's some nice plums, Mother,' I'd say, and you'd say, 'Now, Pa, you know what plums do to your digestion. Remember back in '82,' you'd say, 'I fixed stewed plums for supper and you never got a wink of sleep. Remember?'" He made his voice old and crotchety, but Elizabeth didn't laugh.

"It's funny," she said. "I picture us with your family tangled up in everything you do, and me brought in to watch.

Your mother living with us, and long distance phone calls from sisters divorcing and brothers having breakdowns, and quarrels among the lot of you every evening over the supper table. And me on the outside, wondering what next. Putting on the Band-Aids. Someone to impress."

"Is *that* how you see yourself?" Matthew asked. "On the outside?"

"Of course I do."

"Then what are you doing here now?"

"Putting on the Band-Aids," Elizabeth said.

"But who *asked* you to do it? Mother. She didn't want anyone else. She thinks of you as family. They all do."

"Mighty strange family," Elizabeth said. "She didn't write for four years, I never once got one of those little letters of hers all rehearsed on the dictaphone. What do you say to that? I used to think of *them* as family too, I always did want a little more sinful family than the one I've got. But then I caused all that trouble with Timothy, and your mother didn't write and we all went our separate ways. Now I'm back for six weeks. Period."

"You and I don't see things the same," Matthew said. "Do you think you're just standing off aloof from us?"

"Well, I'm surely not collecting guns," Elizabeth said, "or eloping, or having spells of insanity or shouting quarrels."

"We're having a shouting quarrel right now," said Matthew.

"Matthew, will you *go*? Your sisters are going to miss their planes."

"There's plenty of time." But even as he spoke, the back door slammed and Mary called, "Matthew? Are you coming?"

"Go on, Matthew," Elizabeth said.

"In a minute. We haven't—"

"*Matthew!*" Mary called.

"Oh, all right," he said. He slid off the rail and stood there a minute, scratching his head. "Tomorrow I go back to work," he told Elizabeth.

"All right."

"I can only come here in the evenings. Will you be here?"

"Where else?" Elizabeth said.

She watched his loose-boned figure shambling up the hill toward Mary, with his awkward suit that looked too short and his hair shaggy and ruffled. Then Margaret came out of the house, carrying Susan, and Mary started speaking. Whatever it was she said—scolding Matthew, or asking where Andrew was, or worrying about plane schedules—Elizabeth couldn't catch, but she heard her thin, sharp voice and Susan's irritable fussing. The scraps of their quarrel and the fluttering of Mary's skirt in the breeze made them seem remote, like little figures under glass. They stood with their backs to Elizabeth. In a minute Andrew would come out and they would leave, confident that Elizabeth would keep things going somehow while they were away. Elizabeth slid off the railing and wandered through the grass, feeling cold and tired. She ought to say goodbye. Instead she moved in a wide slow circle around the gazebo, picking up twigs and fallen branches out of habit although she had nowhere to put them.

One long branch refused to be lifted, and when she tugged at it, it broke off in her hands. It was weighted at the other end by a pair of shoes, slim and elegant but scuffed across the toes; above them, a gray suit, and a faded blue shirt pressed open at the collar.

She straightened, holding the branches close to her chest, and looked squarely into Andrew's long, sad face. "Well," she said.

Andrew said nothing. He held a little steel pistol whose eye was pointed at her heart.

Now, why should that make her want to laugh? The blue of the steel was lethal-looking, and she was holding the branches so tightly that her muscles were trembling. And above all, she had been through this before; she knew now that it was something to take seriously. Laughter tended to set explosions off. "Why is everything you say so *inconsequential?*" Timothy had asked, but now the most inconsequential remark of all came into her head, and she said it in spite of herself.

"Where did you get *that* gun, I wonder," she said.

Andrew winced, as if he knew what a mistake she had made.

"Plucked it off a tree? Found it in your mother's sewing box?"

"It was left with me by a friend," said Andrew. "He went to Europe."

"Funny friend," Elizabeth said.

"Things always come to you somehow, if you want them badly enough."

She had never heard his voice before, except above the noise of the bus station. It was light and frail, breakable-sounding. There was a pulse ticking in his forehead. The hand that held the pistol was shaking, which gave her some hope that his aim might be poor. "Andrew," she said, "give me the gun now."

"I can't. I didn't *want* to do this. I warned you and warned you, I wrote you letters. Nothing stops you. *I* know what you were up to in the gazebo."

"Really? What was I up to?" Elizabeth asked.

"You'd better take this seriously. I mean it."

"I am. I know you do," said Elizabeth. And she did. It was beginning to seem possible that this was the way she would die—in a numb, unreal situation in the orange half-

light of a Sunday evening. How could she have guessed, when she woke up this morning and brushed her teeth and chose what shirt to wear? She didn't even know what date it was. "What's today's date?" she asked.

"June seventh," said Andrew.

She thought it over. June seventh had never had any significance before. She pushed her mind back to Timothy, who had died one day in April because of mistakes that she had made and had rehashed again and again since then, but she had never been sure what she should have done instead. Started crying? Run away? Said she would take him south with her after all?

She made up her mind. She said, "Well, I can see how you feel. Shall I leave Baltimore and not come back?"

Then she spun away from him to start toward the house. She had completed the turn already (she saw Matthew with a suitcase, his back to her, his sisters straggling behind him) and she was just wondering what to do with these dead branches when the gun went off.

The sound had nothing to do with her. It was as distant as the diminished figure of Matthew, who pivoted in mid-step without a pause and dropped the suitcase and started running toward her. The others were a motionless, horror-struck audience; then they came running too. But the first to reach her was Andrew himself. He knocked away the branches she held and picked up her arm. Blood was soaking through the cuff of her sleeve. She felt a hot stab like a bee-sting, exactly where her smallpox vaccination would be.

"Oh, Elizabeth," Andrew said. "Did I hurt you?"

When Matthew reached her she was laughing. He thought she was having hysterics.

·   ·   ·

They took her to old Dr. Felson, who wouldn't make trouble.
He had a dusty, cluttered office opening off his wife's kitchen.
It smelled of leather and rubbing alcohol. And Dr. Felson, as
he hunted for gauze, talked like someone out of a western. "A
graze," he said. "A flesh wound. Would you happen to be
sitting on my scissors? I've seen you here before, I believe."

"You sewed up a cut for me," Elizabeth said. "A knife
wound on my wrist."

"Came with young Timothy, didn't you?" He straightened up from a desk drawer and scowled at Matthew, who
was holding tight to Elizabeth's bleeding arm. "Don't go
getting germs on that," he said. "Well, Lord. Who was it cut
your wrist now? I forget."

"I cut my wrist," Elizabeth said.

"You Emersons could support me single-handed."

"I'm not an—"

"Mind if your blouse is torn?"

"No."

He slit her sleeve and put something on her arm that
burned. Elizabeth hardly noticed. She felt silly and light-
headed, and the pain in her arm was getting mixed up with
the stab of light that cut through her brain: Now we are even,
no Emersons will look at me ever again as if I owe them
something; now I know nothing I can do will change a bullet
in its course. "This'll throb a little tonight," the doctor said,
but Elizabeth only smiled at him. Anyone would have thought
Matthew was the one in pain. He held her wrist too tightly,
and his face was white. "Don't worry," Elizabeth told him.
"It looks a lot worse than it feels."

"Of course it does," said Dr. Felson. He was wrapping
her arm in gauze, which felt warm and tight. "But how
about next time? You may not be so lucky."

"*Next* time!" Elizabeth said.

"What does Andrew have to say about this? I've looked the other way quite a few times in my life, but that boy's beginning to bother me."

"Oh, well, he's apologized," Elizabeth said.

Dr. Felson snorted and stood up. "If it gets to hurting, take aspirin," he told her.

"Okay."

She let Matthew lead her out again, across the wooden porch and into the street. He guided her steps as if she were an old lady. "I'm all *right*. Really I am," she said, but he only tightened his arm around her shoulders. His car was waiting beside the curb, packed with people who had missed their travel connections all on account of her. Mary in the front seat, Margaret and Susan and Andrew in the back—peering out of the dusk, their faces pale and anxious, waiting to hear the outcome. "What's he say?" said Andrew. "Is she all right? Will you be all right?" He loomed out through the window to take a better look, and at the sight of him bubbles of laughter started rising up again in her chest. "Of course I will," she said, and laughed out loud, and opened the door to pile in among a tangle of other Emersons.

⬧ 13 ⬧

1970

While Peter drove P.J. slept, curled in the front seat with her head in his lap. Long skeins of tow hair strung across his knees, twined around the steering wheel and got caught between his fingers. He kept shaking his hands loose, as if he had dipped them in syrup. Then the hot wind blew up new strands. "P.J.?" he said. "Look, P.J., can't you stretch out in the back?" P.J. slept on, smiling faintly, while blocks of sunlight crossed her face like dreams.

They were driving back to New Jersey after a week with P.J.'s parents—an old tobacco farmer and his wife who lived on a rutted clay road in Georgia. The visit had not been a success. The gulf between Peter and the Grindstaffs had widened and deepened until P.J., the go-between, could cause a panic if she so much as left the room for a glass of water. She had ricocheted from one side to the other all week, determinedly cheerful and oblivious. Now her head was a weight on his right knee every time he braked; she was limp and exhausted, refilling her supplies of love and gaiety while she slept.

Just past Washington, he pulled into a service station and woke her up. "Would you like a Coke?" he asked her. P.J. lived on Cokes. And she was a great believer in breaking up trips—for sandwiches, restrooms, Stuckey's pecan logs, white elephant sales, caged bears and boa constrictors—but now she only looked at him dimly. "A what?" she said.

"A Coke."

"Oh. Well, I guess so."

She yawned and reached for the door handle. While the attendant scraped bugs off the windshield Peter watched her cross the concrete apron—a thin, tanned, rubber-boned girl with red plastic rings like chicken-bands dangling from her ears. She swung her purse by its strap and tugged at her shorts, which were brief enough to show where her tan left off. The attendant stopped work for a moment to watch her go.

From the glove compartment Peter took stacks of maps— Georgia, New England, even eastern Canada, and finally Baltimore. He had promised P.J. they would stop over to see his family. It was three years since he had last been there. When he opened the map to check the best route the half-forgotten names of streets—St. Paul and North Charles, criss-crossed now with grimy folds that were beginning to tear—gave him the sudden, depressing feeling that he was a teenager again. He remembered hitchhiking on North Charles, sweating in the damp heavy heat, fully aware that his mother would go to pieces if she ever saw him doing this. He pictured Baltimore in an eternal summer, its trademark the white china cats, looking fearfully over their shoulders, which poor people riveted to their shutters and porch roofs. And then his mother's house—closed, dim rooms. Gleaming tabletops. What was the point of going back?

P.J. came in sight, picking her way across the cement on

narrow bare feet. When she caught the attendant watching she grinned and raised her Coke bottle in a toast. Then she leaned in the window and said, "Come on, Petey, get out and stretch your legs."

"I'm comfortable here."

"Out back they have garden statues, and birdbaths and flowerpots. Want to take a look?"

"I'd rather get going," Peter said.

She climbed into the car, wincing when the backs of her thighs hit the hot vinyl. Down her cheek were the stripes of Peter's corduroy slacks. Her eyes were still sleepy and rumpled-looking. "They have the cutest little plaster gnomes," she said. "On spikes. You just stick them into the grass. I bet Mama would love one of those."

"I bet she would," said Peter.

She looked at him sideways, and then took a sip of her Coke. "Shall I get her one?" she asked.

"Why not?"

"As a sort of making-up present?"

Peter handed a credit card to the attendant. "*You* don't have to make up," he said.

"I was thinking of sending it in your name."

"Well, don't."

She drank off the last of the Coke, wiped the rim of the bottle, and set off toward the case of empties beside the vending machine. The minute she was gone Peter felt sorry. "P.J.!" he called.

She turned, still cheerful. He slid out of his seat and ran to catch up with her. "Of course we can buy one," he said. "Put my name all over it, if you like."

"Oh, good," P.J. said. "I'll do the wrapping and mailing and all, you won't have to lift a finger, Petey."

She led him around the back of the filling station.

toward a field of plaster flamingos and sundials and birdbaths. The gnomes stood in a huddle, their paint already flaking, grinning at a cluster of little black boys who held out hitching-rings. The saleslady wore a straw hat and a huge flowered smock that blazed in the sunlight. "Aren't they darling?" P.J. said. "Or would she rather have an eentsy wheelbarrow to plant her flowers in. Which do you think?"

"You know her best," Peter said.

"Or then these deer. *They're* nice." She wandered through the field, unable to make up her mind, patting the heads of little painted animals and returning the smile of any statue that smiled at her. Her bare feet stepped delicately between the grass blades, as if she had no weight at all. "How much do you reckon it would cost to mail a sundial?" she asked. The saleslady said, "Oh, no, honey, you don't want to *mail* them, it'd take a fortune." Peter hated people who called their customers "honey." But P.J. only shifted her smile to the saleslady's face, and the two of them stood beaming at each other like very dear friends. Oh, it would take a lot to make P.J. start frowning. He thought of all this last week, all the times her parents must have whispered, "Paula Jean, what's the *matter* with that boy?" all the children who, coming upon him unexpectedly, lost their bounce and seemed to sag under the weight of his gloom. Yet P.J. had continued smiling. She had led him by the hand through the barnyard, hoping that he would make friends with the animals. She had introduced a hundred topics of conversation that Peter and her family might seize on. "Petey's just got out of the Army, Daddy, you and him ought to compare experiences. Petey, don't you want to see Mama's herb garden?" Peter had tried, but nothing came to his mind to say. He floated in a weariness that made him want to escape to some hotel and sleep for days. "Petey, darling," P.J. said, "don't you *like* them?" I

do," he said truthfully, "but I just can't—" "Talk about the crops. Daddy likes that. Talk about baseball, or what's on the television." So then, back among the others, Peter said, "How're the crops, Mr. Grindstaff?" "Just fine," said Mr. Grindstaff, and Peter said, "Oh, good," and subsided, unable to think of what came next.

"He's just back from Vietnam," P.J. would tell people. Everyone murmured, as if that explained things. But Peter had been gloomy long before the Army. War only added a touch of fear and the sense of being out of place, neither of which seemed to leave him when he came back. He was still afraid. He still felt out of place. He had a job now, teaching chemistry in a second-rate girls' school, where the pupils whispered and giggled and knit argyle socks while he lectured. "All of you," he would tell them, "missed the second equation on the last hour quiz. Now I would like to go over that with you." The girls looked up at him, still moving their lips to count stitches, and Peter fell silent. *Why* would he like to go over it? What difference did it make? How had he come to be here?

P.J. settled on a gnome with a pointed red cap, cradled it in her arms all the way to the car and rolled it in a picnic blanket in the trunk. "I just know she's going to love it," she said. And then, when they had pulled out into traffic again, "I know things will work out all right. Won't they? Everything will be just fine now."

"Of course," said Peter, but he had no idea what she was talking about. This trip? The two of them? He and her family? If he found out he might have to disagree. He kept quiet, and smiled steadily at the stream of oncoming cars while P.J. slid down and set both feet against the dashboard. Her hair blew out behind her, knotting itself and slipping out of the knots. She seemed to glint and shimmer. When Peter

first met her, in the school cafeteria, she had stood out among the pasty dull students like a flash of silver. She had worn a white uniform and collected dirty dishes off the tables with pointed, darting hands. He took her for a student with a part-time job. When she turned out to be a real waitress he was relieved, since it was against school rules to date students. Then later, after they had begun to grow serious, he had some doubts. A *waitress?* What would his family say? He pushed the thought away, ashamed that it had come up. He started seeing her daily; he fit himself into her motionless, shadowless life: lying oiled and passive on a beach towel for hours at a stretch, watching television straight through till sign-off, sitting all afternoon in dusky taverns dreamily peeling the labels off beer bottles. She gave him the feeling that she could never be used up. Whenever he looked her way she smiled at him.

The rush hour was beginning. Traffic was bumper-to-bumper, and the flashes of sunlight off chrome stung his eyes. "Where are we now?" P.J. asked.

"Close to—just past Washington."

"Close to Baltimore."

"Well, yes."

"How much longer to your mother's?"

"Well, I've been thinking," Peter said.

"Oh, Petey, don't say we can't go. After all this time that I've been counting on it?"

"If we drove straight through, we could be home by bedtime," Peter said. "Besides, she might not even be there."

"Didn't you tell her we were coming?"

"I meant to drop a postcard, but then I forgot."

"You're ashamed to show me to her."

"No, Lord," he said. "I've kept away long before *you* were around."

"That's just not natural, Petey. Not and you living so close."

"But I wasn't always close, I was in the Army."

"When Barney Winters went overseas, down home," P.J. said, "they let him have some time with his folks after basic training. Then when he came back he spent a month there, just filling up on that good home cooking he said. Fat? In that one month he must have gained thirty pounds. You never would've known him."

"I went to New York after basic training," Peter said.

"Gunther Jones, too, *he* visited home before he left. And would have after, I reckon, if he hadn't gone and got killed."

"Well, we all do our own thing," Peter said. "I went and saw a lot of art galleries."

"Before, you mean. I don't know how much you enjoyed it but afterward I *know*, you told me yourself. Up until the new semester opened you didn't do a thing but lay around a old rented room reading the beginnings of books. Call that a rest? Call that a recuperation? When you could have been home all that time eating your mother's good home cooking?"

"*I* can cook better than my mother does," Peter said.

"Petey, do you have some *reason* not to want to go there?"

"None at all," said Peter. Which was true, but he should have made something up—some feud or family quarrel that would have satisfied her. As it was, she thought he was putting her off. She considered the subject still open for discussion. "Barney *Winters'* mother met him when he landed," she said. "Bringing a whole chess pie that he ate right there by the plane."

"Oh, Lord," said Peter.

"Myself, I'm a family-type person. Just made that way,

I don't know why. We always were close-knit. Now I want to meet *your* family too, but if you think I wouldn't match up to them—"

"No, P.J. We'll go, if you're so set on it. But just for one night, is that understood? No hanging around. No getting caught up in anything."

"Whatever you like, Petey," P.J. said.

By the time they reached Baltimore, Peter had a long ache of tiredness running down his spine. He drove irritably, one hand always ready at the horn. Row houses slipped past him in endless chains, with clusters of women slumped on all the stoops, fans turning lazily behind lace curtains, parlor windows full of madonnas and globe lamps and plastic flowers alternating with windows boarded up and CONDEMNED signs on the doors. Children were drinking grape Nehis. Men scuttled out from package stores with brown paper bags clutched to their chests. "Are you still sure you want to stop in Baltimore?" Peter asked.

P.J. didn't bother answering. She was neatening the edges of her lipstick with the tip of a little finger. "Should I put my hair up?" she said.

"You look okay."

"My wig is right handy."

"No, P.J."

P.J. dumped her pocketbook on the seat and riffled through ticket stubs and loose change and wadded-up hair ribbons until she found the little plastic case containing her eyelashes. They were cut in a style called "Innocence"— spiky black lashes widely spaced, so that when she had put them on she looked as if she had just finished crying over some brief, childish tragedy. She blinked and turned to him. "How's that?" she asked.

"Very nice."

"Is it far to go?"

"Another fifteen minutes or so."

"Well, is there something I should *know* first. I mean, subjects not to bring up? People not to mention? You never tell me things, Petey. I want to do this right, now."

"Oh, just be yourself," Peter said. Which were her exact words on the way to Georgia, but she missed that. If he were to list forbidden subjects it would take him all night.

Once out of the downtown areas they drove faster, through streets that grew steadily greener and cooler. Then they entered Roland Park, and Peter suddenly felt eager to be home. He forgot all the misgivings he had had. There was the old locked water tower, which he had once tried to break into. There was the Women's Club where his mother went for luncheons, always in a hat and gloves. And now the wooded road that led to the house, dark and cool and dappled with sunshine. He hid his eagerness from P.J. as carefully as if she might mock him for it, although he knew she wouldn't. "We're almost there," he told her, keeping his face blank. P.J. nodded and sat up straighter and wet her lips.

In this neighborhood, people stayed out of sight more. All he saw was one lone maid with a shopping bag, heading toward the bus stop. And his mother's house, when he drew up in front of it, was closed and silent. The curtains hung still, the veranda chairs were empty. A water sprinkler spun dreamily in the right side yard.

"Well," said Peter. He let his hands drop from the wheel. P.J. said nothing. She was looking at the house, taking in the rows of gleaming windows and the wide expanse of grass, the multitude of chimneys rising from the slate roof.

"You never told me it was a *big* house," she said finally.

"Shall we go in?"

P.J. began gathering up her possessions. She had a purse,

sandals, a scarf, a sack of licorice shoestrings which had already lined her lips with black although Peter didn't tell her so. When she had climbed out of the car she tugged at her shorts and slid into her sandals—leather soles with yards of straps which would have twined all the way to her knees if she had tied them. She shuffled up the front walk, curling her toes to keep the sandals on. She looked like a seal on dry land. Peter stayed where he was, watching her. He didn't even open his door until she turned to look for him. "Aren't you coming?" she asked.

"Sure."

He had expected his mother to burst out of the house the moment he cut the engine, ending a three-year vigil at the front window.

It wasn't until he was halfway up the walk that he became aware of the noise. A clattering sound, like millions of enormous metal zippers stickily opening and shutting. It rose from every bush. It was so steady and monotonous that it could pass unnoticed, like a clock's ticking. "What *is* it?" he asked, and P.J. only looked at him blankly. "That noise," he said.

"Crickets? Locusts?"

A buzzing black lump zoomed into his face, and then veered and swooped away. He ducked, seconds after it had gone.

"Seventeen-year locusts," he said.

"Never heard of them," said P.J.

"Cicadas, in point of actual fact."

The words were Timothy's, dredged up from a long-ago summer, and so was the tone—dry and scientific, so unlike Peter that even P.J. noticed and looked surprised. The last time the locusts had been here, Peter was twelve. He remembered the fact of their presence, and Timothy's lecture on

them, but not what they were really *like*—not these viciously buzzing objects which, he saw now, swung through the air on invisible strings and hung like glittering fruit from all the bushes. P.J. had one on her shoulder; it rattled menacingly when he brushed it away. When he stepped on the sidewalk, he crunched countless pupa shells which lay curled and hollow, small beige shrimps with all their legs folded tightly inward.

They crossed the shiny gray floorboards of the veranda. P.J. knocked at the door. "Knock, knock!" she called out gaily. She always did that, but today Peter found it irritating. "There *is* a doorbell," he said, and reached around her to press it. P.J. looked up at him, her eyes like round, rayed suns in her Innocence eyelashes.

It was a child who opened the door for them. A squat little blond boy with a solemn face, wearing miniature Levis. "Hi," he said.

"Hi there," said Peter, too heartily. "I'm your Uncle Peter. Remember me?"

"No."

"So there, Peter Emerson," P.J. said. She laughed and bent down to the little boy's level. "I'm P.J.. What's your name?"

He studied her. Peter cleared his throat. "This is George, I believe," he said. "Matthew's boy. Is your grandma home, George?"

"Yup."

"Could we see her?"

"She's in the kitchen," George said.

He turned back in the direction he had come from. The cuffs of his Levis dragged on the floor. "Well," said Peter "Shall we go in?"

They followed George across the hallway—Peter leading

P.J. as if she were another child, clutching her by the arm while she looked all around her. They went through the butler's pantry, windowless and stale, and then into the sudden brightness of the kitchen.

His mother was standing just as he had imagined her—wearing soft colors, her hair a clear gold, surrounded by her family. The only thing wrong was that she and all the others had their backs turned. They were facing squarely away from him, watching something out the rear door. "It's the screens, they will have to be mended in the morning," his mother said. "Look at those holes! *Anything* could get through them."

"Hello, Mother."

She turned, but even when she looked directly at him she seemed distracted. "What?" she said. "What—*Peter!*"

Everyone turned. Their faces were momentarily surprised and unguarded.

"Peter, what are you *doing* here?"

"Oh, just passing through. Mother, this is P.J. P.J., this is my brother Andrew, my brother Matthew's wife Gillespie —where's Matthew?"

"He's still at work," his mother said. "Are you staying long? Why didn't you tell us? Have you eaten supper?"

"We were heading back from Georgia—" Peter said. His mother stood on tiptoe to kiss him. Her cheek felt withered and too soft, but she still wore the same light, powdery perfume, and she held her back as beautifully straight as ever. Her speech was slower now than her children's—as slow as Gillespie's southern drawl, and hesitating over consonants. "Georgia?" she said. "What would you go to *Georgia* for?"

"You look older," said Andrew. He looked older himself, but happy. His hair was thinning, and below his concave

chest a paunch had started. Someone's apron was tied around his middle. "If I'd known you were coming—" he said, and then P.J. stuck her hand out to him. He looked at it a moment before accepting it.

"I'm very glad to meet you all," said P.J.

Andrew frowned. He was nervous with strangers—something Peter had forgotten to warn her about. But before the silence grew noticeable, his sister-in-law stepped in. "We're glad to meet *you*," she said. "Good to see you again," she told Peter, and she shifted the diapered baby who rode her hip and held out her hand. Peter took it with relief; her cool, hard palm seemed to steady him.

"We were just on this trip, you see," he told her. "Passing through Baltimore. Thought we'd stop in. I wasn't sure you'd —are we interrupting something?"

"Oh, of *course* not!" his mother said gaily.

"But with everyone at the back door there, I didn't know—"

"It was a locust. Gillespie was shooing it out of the house for us. Oh, these locusts, Peter, you can't imagine. We keep the house just *sealed*, and still they get in. Will this screen be seen to, now?"

"I'll mend it in the morning," Gillespie said.

"Mother is scared of locusts," Andrew said.

"You're none too fond of them yourself, Andrew dear," his mother told him.

"Well, no."

And meanwhile P.J. stood smiling hopefully, with her belongings still clutched to her chest, looking from one face to another and settling finally on the baby, who was playing with a long strand of hair that had straggled from Gillespie's bun. "Oh, isn't it *darling*," she said. "What's its name?"

"She isn't an it, she's a she," Andrew said stiffly.

"Well, how could anyone tell?" Gillespie asked him. "All she's got on is a diaper."

"Her *face* is a girl's face. No one should mistake it."

"Oh, hush, Andrew, I never heard of such a thing."

Peter waited for Andrew to get insulted, to collapse in a kitchen chair or turn on his heel and leave, but he didn't. He had changed—a fact that Peter forgot all over again each time he left home. He was the only person in this house who had changed. His mother remained a gilded pink and white and Gillespie continued shuffling around in dungarees, her face a little broader and more settled-looking but her fingers still nicked by whittling knives and her manner with babies still as offhand as if she were carrying a load of firewood. But Andrew had mellowed; he had calmed and softened. ("Andrew is in such a state," Mrs. Emerson had written last winter. "You know how he gets when Gillespie's expecting, I believe he'd go through the labor pains *for* her if only he could." Only Peter seemed to remember the day after Timothy's funeral, when Andrew had paced the living room saying, "Where is that girl? Where? I'll get her for this.") Now instead of taking offense Andrew smiled, first at Gillespie and then at the baby, whose cheek he lightly touched. "Her name is Jenny," he told P.J.

"Oh," said P.J. She looked bewildered, but after a moment she smiled too.

"Now then," Mrs. Emerson said. "Shall we go into the living room where it's cool?"

She led the way, calming her skirt with her hands as if it were a long and stately gown. If the kitchen had become Gillespie's, with its wood chips across the table and its scatter of tools beside the breadbox, the living room was still Mrs. Emerson's. The same vases marched across the mantel; the same

dusty gray smell rose from the upholstery. The red tin loco-
motive under the coffee-table could have been Peter's own,
back in the days when he was a child here anxiously studying
the grownups' faces.

His mother settled in her wing chair, across from Andrew,
and Gillespie sat in the high-backed rocker with both children
nestled against her. Peter chose the couch, beside P.J. He felt
she needed some support. She was nervously twisting her purse
strap, and the licorice bag rustled on her knees like something
alive. "I just love old houses," she said.

"How long can you stay?" his mother asked Peter. "And
don't say you're just passing through. I want you to plan on a
nice long visit this time."

"I have a lot of work to get back to," Peter said.

"In the summer? What kind of work would you do in the
summer?"

But then, remembering her social duties, her face became
all upward lines and she turned to P.J. "I hope you're not tired
from the trip, J.C.," she said.

"P.J.," said P.J. "No ma'am, I'm not a bit tired. I'm just
so happy to finally *meet* you all. I feel like I know you already,
Petey's told me so much about you."

A lie. Peter had told her next to nothing. And he hadn't
even mentioned her to his family, but Mrs. Emerson continued wearing her bright hostess look and leaning forward
in that hovering posture she always assumed to show an open
mind. "Where are you from, dear?" she asked.

"Well, New Jersey *now*. Before it was Georgia."

"Isn't that nice?"

P.J. shifted in her seat, deftly smoothing the backs of her
thighs as if she wore a dress. "You look just like I thought you
would," she said—oh, always trying to get down to the personal, but she was no match for Mrs. Emerson.

"I suppose this heat is no trouble to you at all then," Mrs. Emerson said.

"Ma'am?"

"Coming from Georgia."

"Oh. No ma'am."

"Peter darling," Mrs. Emerson said, "I want you to tell me *everything*. What have you been up to, now?"

"Well, I—"

"Where are my cigarettes?" She slid her fingers between the arm of the chair and the cushion. Peter, who hadn't been going to tell her anything anyway, felt irritated at being cut off. He kept a pointed silence, with his arms folded tightly across his chest. He thought his mother was like a hunter who set traps and coaxed and baited until the animal was safely caught, and then she forgot she had wanted him and went off to some new project. "Nothing is where it should be in this house," she said. "Gillespie, I think we could do with some iced tea to drink."

"Oh. Okay."

Gillespie handed the baby to Andrew and went to the kitchen, with George tailing her. P.J. sat back and smiled around the room. The only sound to be heard was the clatter of locusts. Finally P.J. said, "Mrs. Emerson, have you got a family album?"

"Album?"

"I'd like to see pictures of Peter when he was a baby."

"Oh, there are hundreds," Mrs. Emerson said. She had filled more albums than any coffee-table could hold—rows upon rows of snapshots precisely dated—but she didn't offer to bring them out. "*Somewhere* around," she said vaguely, and she turned to stare out a window. What connection did this girl have with Emersons?

What connection did *Peter* have? He sat plucking the

knees of his slacks, as empty of things to say as he had been in
Georgia, as hopeful of acceptance as P.J. From the kitchen
came the smells of supper cooking, roast beef and baked potatoes. There was nothing like cooking smells to make you
feel out of place in someone else's house. While he was on the
open highway life here had been going on in a pattern he could
only guess at—meat basted, knife sharpened, bustling hunts
for misplaced spoons, systems and rituals and habits they never
had to think about. Mrs. Emerson lit her cigarette and reached
without looking for an ashtray, which was exactly where she
had known it would be. A silvery strand of baby-spit spun
down onto Andrew's hand, and out of nowhere Andrew produced a folded diaper and neatly wiped Jenny's chin. P.J. was
telling Mrs. Emerson how she just loved this section of Baltimore. (She just loved *everything*. What was the matter with
her?) At her first pause, Andrew turned to Peter. "How's the
job going?" he asked. Mrs. Emerson said, "Do you like New
Jersey?" To counterbalance P.J., he was blunter than he
should have been. "I hate it," he said.

"Oh, Peter."

"If there was another job open *anywhere,* I'd take it in
a flash."

"Why don't you, then?"

He peered at his mother. She was perfectly serious. Jobs
nowadays were scarce and money scarcer, and no one was
interested in chemists any more, but what did she know about
that? It was possible that she wasn't even aware there was a
war on. Since he first left home there had been upheavals of
every kind—assassinations, riots, not once referred to in letters
from his mother. Oh well, once: "Mrs. Bittern was just here
collecting food for riot victims. I gave her a can of pitted black
olives. . . ." "I had hoped you might teach in some university,"
she told him now. "Well, times are hard," was all he said. She

frowned at him, distantly, secure in her sealed weightless bubble floating through time. While he was in Vietnam, she had kept writing to ask if he had visited any tourist sights. And could he bring home some sort of native craft to solve her Christmas problems?

"Petey's school is just a *real* nice place," P.J. said. "He couldn't hope for a better job."

"That's all *you* know," Andrew said.

"What?"

"Peter made straight A's all through school. Are you qualified to say he should stay in some mediocrity in New Jersey?"

"Oh! Well!"

She looked at Peter to defend her, but he didn't. He was irritated by the soft, hurt look on her face. It was his mother who stepped in. "Now, Andrew," she said. "You mustn't mind Andrew, J.C. He's hard on outsiders. The second time he met *Gillespie*, he shot her." She laughed, and so did Andrew—a contented, easy sound. Peter heard her without surprise, although he had never been told about any shooting, but P.J. gave a little gasp and drew closer to him. "With a *gun?*" she said.

"Oh, Mother, now—" said Andrew.

But he was saved by a noise from the fireplace—a rattle as steady and senseless as some wind-up toy. Mrs. Emerson screamed. Her cigarette flew out of her hand and landed on the rug, and when Peter leaped up to stamp it out he collided with P.J., who reached the spot before he did but then tripped over one of her long twisted sandal straps. "Gillespie!" Mrs. Emerson screamed. "Gillespie, a locust!"

Then out came Gillespie, skating along levelly with a brim-full pitcher. She poured a dollop of tea on the cigarette

and set the pitcher down on the coffee-table. "Where?" she said.

"In the fireplace!" said Mrs. Emerson, already scuttling toward the dining room. "Oh, I *told* you you should stuff that chimney up! Anything, I said, could get down inside it and the flue handle came off in Matthew's hands two years ago—" Andrew followed her out of the room, shielding the baby, and Peter rose but had nowhere to go. He didn't feel up to helping out. He could imagine how cold and heavy a locust must be, slithering down the back of his neck, and he was relieved to see that Gillespie seemed to have the situation in control. She crouched before the fireplace with a rolled-up magazine. George stood by with the poker, scratching the front of his grimy T-shirt and looking bored. "Here, buddy," Gillespie told the locust. She poked at the ashes. "Come on, *come* on." The whirring grew louder. The magazine rattled as if a fan blade had hit it and then up swooped the locust, evading Gillespie, zooming toward the ceiling with an angry buzz. Mrs. Emerson screamed again. She ducked behind Andrew, clutching him by the sides. "Will I survive this summer?" she asked.

Andrew said, "There, Jenny, there, Jenny," although Jenny was happily gnawing his shirt collar without a care in the world.

"I will *never* get used to these creatures, never," said Mrs. Emerson. "I haven't stepped out of the house since they arrived. Gillespie? Why are you just standing there?"

"I'm waiting for him to come down," Gillespie said.

"Down? Where *is* he? Oh, on my damask curtains, I'm sure of it." She stepped back and sank into one of the dining room chairs. From the table behind her she took a bottle of vitamin C, uncapped it and gulped two pills, like a man down-

ing a glass of whiskey. Her hands were shaking. "They're everywhere," she said. "Chattering all day, bombing into people, and at night it's no better. They're silent then but it's a *planning* silence, they hang from all the leaves plotting how to get me in the morning."

"It's the oak trees," Gillespie said. "They favor oaks."

Her voice was calm and unemphatic, reducing monsters to mere scientific fact. But then the locust whirred up from the curtains and lit on the lampshade, and when George swung at it with the poker all he did was knock the lamp over. "Damn," said Gillespie.

"We're like in jail," Andrew said. "Matthew and Gillespie and George are the trusties, they get to go out for mail and food. Mother and I stay inside."

"I spend a summer in the house every seventeen years," said Mrs. Emerson. She thought that over a minute. Then she said, "The next time they come, I'll be dead."

"Oh, Mrs. *Emerson!*" P.J. said.

But Mrs. Emerson only looked at her as if she wondered where P.J. had come from. She said, "Peter, do you remember when they were here before? You were, oh, twelve, I suppose. You were *hopeless*. You made a necklace out of the shells and wore it everywhere. You had bottles in your closet packed full of locusts. *Black* with them."

"I did?" Peter said.

"You kept one on a string and took it for walks down Cold Spring Lane."

He still couldn't picture it. Like most youngest children, he had trouble remembering his own past. The older ones did it so well for him, why should he bother? They had built him a second-hand memory that included the years before he existed, even. He had a distinct recollection of Melissa's running away from home with a peanut butter sandwich and a pome-

granate, two years before he was born; but he himself, with his locust on a leash, had vanished.

There was another whir. George leaped straight up in the air, as if he were catching a fly ball, and came to earth with his hands cupped tightly around a rattling black shape. "Ha!" he said.

"Now, when I open the door," Gillespie told him, "throw him outside. *Far* out, Georgie. Don't let him fly back in or Grandma will have a fit."

They all went to the hallway—even Mrs. Emerson, hanging back a little. Gillespie opened the door and stood ready with the magazine. When George tossed the locust up it seemed to hang in mid-air a minute, and then Gillespie reached out and batted it on its way so violently that she lost her balance. It was Matthew who caught her. He was just crossing the porch with a folded newspaper.

"Not *another* one," he said, setting her on her feet.

"She says we'll have to stop up the chimney. Look who's come for a visit."

Matthew looked over Gillespie's head and said, "Peter! I wondered whose car that was."

"I was just driving through," Peter said.

"He brought a girlfriend, and we're going to get him to stay a good long time."

Peter said, "Oh, well, I don't—"

"Come on, we've got plenty of room," Matthew said. "Well! Looks like the Army's changed you a little."

But Matthew hadn't changed. He was still black-haired and stooped and skinny, still continually readjusting his glasses on the bridge of his long narrow nose. Gillespie, sheltered under his arm, smiled up at him and said, "You look tired."

"I am. Old Smodgett was drunk again."

He kissed his mother, who had come to the doorway but

not an inch beyond it. He clapped Andrew on the shoulder and ran a finger down the curve of the baby's cheek. P.J. stood waiting, next in line. "Oh," said Gillespie, "this is P.J. P.J.— what's your last name, anyway?"

"What?" said P.J. "Emerson."

"Oh, isn't that funny."

"What's funny about it?"

Peter cleared his throat.

"It's *customary* to have your husband's last name," P.J. said.

"Husband?" said Mrs. Emerson.

P.J. spun around and stared at Peter.

"Guess I forgot to mention it," Peter said.

"Mention what?" asked Mrs. Emerson. "What's going on here?"

"Well, P.J. and I got married last month."

He had startled everyone, but P.J. most of all. "Oh, Peter," she said. "Didn't you *tell* them?"

Then his mother's voice rose over hers to say, "I can't believe it. I just can't. Could this be happening to me *again*?"

"I thought they knew," P.J. said.

"Peter, I assumed she was a *friend*. Someone you had picked up along the way somehow. Is it just a joke? Are you making this up just to tease me?"

"Well, why? What would be funny about it?" P.J. said. She looked ready to run, but there was nowhere she knew of to run to. Mrs. Emerson ignored her.

"Is she pregnant?" she asked.

"Well!" said P.J.

"Now, Mother," Matthew said, "I believe the best thing might be to sit down and—"

But it was Gillespie who rescued P.J. "Well, that's one problem solved," she said cheerfully. "I didn't have two extra

beds made up anyway. Do you want to see your room, P.J.?"

"Yes, please," said P.J. Her voice was thin and muffled. She followed Gillespie up the stairs without a backward glance at Peter.

"I never expected this of you, Peter," his mother said.

"Now, let's sit down," Matthew told her. "What's that on the coffee-table? Iced tea? We can all have a—"

"I have five married children now. Five. And six weddings between them. Do you know how many I was invited to? One, just one. Mary's. Not Melissa's, not Matthew's, not Margaret's two. Just secrets! Scandals! Elopements! I can't understand it. Don't girls dream of big church weddings any more?"

"Sit down, Mother," Matthew said. "Do you want lemon?"

They grouped themselves around her on the edges of chairs, all uneasily aware of the footsteps over their heads. Matthew poured tea and passed out the glasses. Each time he crossed the rug he had to step over his mother's soggy cigarette, afloat in a puddle of tea, but he didn't seem to find it odd. "Well, now," he said, and he settled himself on the couch and began chafing his bony wrists. "What have you been up to, Peter?"

"We were just discussing that," said his mother.

"I meant—"

"I believe I'm going to be sick," Andrew said.

"Oh, Andrew. Pass me the baby."

But he only clutched her tighter, and Jenny squirmed in his arms and screwed her face up. She started crying, beginning with a little protesting sound and working toward a wail. Gillespie entered the room, scooped her up, and passed on through. "Supper will be ready in a minute," she called back.

"None for me," Andrew said.

She didn't answer him.

Peter rose and went upstairs, with the feeling that everyone's eyes were on his back. He found P.J. in Melissa's old room. She was in front of a skirted vanity table. Tears were running down her cheeks in straight, fine lines.

"P.J., I was *going* to tell them," he said.

"I don't believe you."

"You know how seldom I write them. I just hadn't got around to—"

"You wouldn't have told them. You'd have let them give us separate rooms, never said a word. Or asked to *share* a room, that's more like you. Let them think we were living in sin. That's your idea of a joke. And me just going on not realizing, thinking you had told them. Oh, I feel like such a *fool!* Here I was trying so hard, asking for baby pictures—they must have thought I was the pushiest girlfriend you ever had. I wondered why they kept mixing my name up. Did you even tell them I existed?"

"I might have. I forget," Peter said.

"You didn't, did you?"

He put his hands in his pockets and circled the room. It had the musty, dead feeling of a guest room—furniture bare and polished but thinly filmed with dust, bedspread perfectly smooth, all traces of Melissa gone except for perfume stains on the vanity table. When he reached the window he pulled it open and leaned out into the twilight. "Hot in here," he said.

"You never even told them you were dating me," P.J. said. "You kept us so separate you never even told *me* about *them*, not hardly enough to count. Not even their names, just sets of words—the Nervous Case, the Sister that Elopes, the Handyman's Husband. Like you'd met them only once or twice, and had to think up labels to keep them straight. And if you'll pardon me for saying so I get the feeling they do you

the same way. Which will you be, now? The Georgia Cracker's Husband? And not a word about we wish you a happy life together, or we hope you'll be like one of us—"

Peter watched her lips, which were puffy from crying. The paint was flaking off her ear-bangles. All he seemed able to think of was her grammatical mistakes, which chalked themselves up in his mind like a grocery list.

"Why, there I was with a wedding ring on!" P.J. said. "Did they think to notice? No. They were too busy chasing bugs around. That crazy old lady locking herself away from the bugs."

"Well, wait, P.J.," Peter said. "This is my *family* you're talking about."

"What do I care?"

"This afternoon you were going to be their long-lost sister."

"Me? Not now, boy. Not for a million dollars. That little closed-up family of yours is closed around *nothing,* thin air, all huddled up together scared to go out. Depending on someone that is like the old-maid failure poor relation you find some places, mending their screens and cooking their supper and fixing their chimneys and making peace—oh, she ended up worse off than *them.* I wouldn't move into this family for anything you paid me. You can just go on down to them and leave me be."

"P.J.—"

"Will you *go?*"

He made a grab for her—a mistake. He felt a cool smoothness slipping through his fingers and then she was gone, flashing white through the doorway and clattering down the stairs with her sandals flapping. The front door slammed. "Peter?" his mother called. "Is that you? Was that him?" The door spring twanged and hummed, and then fell silent.

Peter didn't go after her. He had been through this too many times—not the quarrels, she had never quarreled before, but the running away whenever his moods grew too much for her. She would stay gone for two or three hours before she wandered in, cheerful again. "What do you do when you're gone?" he had once asked her, and she had laughed and looked down at her hands. "Oh, walk around," she said. "Sit on park benches. Check the time every now and then to see if I've been away long enough to worry you." She should never have told him. Now he could afford to stay home and wait for her. Before, he had run after her in a panic at the thought of being left with no company but his own forever more.

He descended the stairs slowly, and found his family still sitting in the living room. There was no sign of supper yet, not even any silver on the dining room table, but they didn't seem concerned. In the kitchen, Gillespie whistled a tune; they waited, confident that food would arrive somehow, sometime.

"Where's P.J.?" Matthew asked him.

"She's taking a walk."

"I didn't warm to her," said Andrew.

"You don't warm to anyone."

"When I was married," Mrs. Emerson said, "my family disapproved very strongly. They said, 'Oh, certainly he's nice enough, and we have no doubt he can support you. But don't you want more than that? Pamela, he's not your *type*,' they said. 'He doesn't have, he has a different—' Well, I didn't listen. I will say this, though: I told them to their faces. I never snuck around. We had a perfectly beautiful church wedding with all my family in attendance, acting very civilized. Then later I thought, Well, now I know what they meant. I know what my parents meant. They had my best interests at heart, after all. But I only thought that later."

Andrew looked up from the asterisk he was drawing in a tea-ring. "What are you saying?" he asked. "Are you telling us that you and Dad didn't get along?"

"Oh, we got *along*," said his mother. "But there was so much—we were so far apart. Never understood each other. And I thought you children would take after my side. Even Billy wanted that. Why, it was he who named you—Matthew Carter Emerson, Peter Carter Emerson, every last one of you had my maiden name in the middle. 'It gives them something to be proud of,' Billy said. 'The whole world knows who the Carters are.' Oh, I had such *expectations* of you all! How did things turn out so differently? You're pure Emerson. You're all like Billy's brothers, separate and silent and with failure just built into you, and now looking back I can't even pinpoint the time when you shifted sides. Why did it work out this way?"

As if she were discussing some abstract problem, something that had nothing to do with them, her three sons sat looking detached and interested. Then Matthew said, "Oh, I don't know. I kind of liked Dad's brothers."

"You would," said his mother. "You most of all."

"They *were* sort of rednecks, Matthew," Andrew said.

"Well, wait a minute—"

Before it became an argument, Peter escaped. He went out to the kitchen, where he found George playing with a locust on the floor and Gillespie nursing the baby, sitting peacefully with her blouse unbuttoned like a broad golden madonna. The roast was cooling on the counter, but she didn't seem in any hurry. "Where's P.J.?" she asked.

"Gone out."

"Well, I wish you'd go get her. Supper will be on as soon as I'm through here."

"Maybe we could start without her," Peter said. A picture

of never finding P.J. at all flashed through his head. He might
jump in his car now and leave alone, light-hearted and full of
a pure, free joy. Then hours later P.J. would come straggling
in, with grass stains on the back of her shorts. "Where's
Petey?" "He's gone." "Well," she would say, trying to remain
dignified, acting as if this were all according to plan—"I believe I'll be getting along too now. I just loved meeting you
all." He imagined her out on the street thumbing rides, with
her purse hitched over her shoulder and her bare legs flashing
like knife blades in the darkness. Yet how could he be sure
that, halfway to New Jersey, he wouldn't start feeling lonely
and remorseful? Then too, he could stay here. This house
could expand like an accordion, with its children safe and
happy inside and Gillespie to take care of them. Why not?

Gillespie hoisted the baby on her shoulder and went to
the refrigerator for a carton of milk. She poured a saucer full
and set it out on the back porch. "Kitty kitty?" she called.
Then she returned and checked the biscuits in the oven, and
after that she placed the baby on the other breast. Jenny
screwed her face sideways, searching for the nipple. Gillespie
hummed beneath her breath—a juggler of supplies, obtaining
and distributing all her family needed. But when she caught
Peter watching her, she said, "I'd wish you'd go find P.J.,
Peter."

"I'd rather not," he said.

"*Emersons*," said Gillespie, but without much force. She
brushed back a wisp of Jenny's hair. In this position, with her
eyes lowered, with her mouth curved for the baby, she looked
younger than he had expected. He had pictured her as some
kind of family retainer, ageless, faceless, present for as long as
he could remember, although in fact she hadn't arrived till he
was in college and she was only a few years older than he was.
Now she stuck out a moccasin to stop the locust's progress

across the floor, and when she grinned at George she looked like another child. "You better not let that in where Grandma is," she told him.

"I'm going to teach him how to fly," George said.

"Don't you think he already knows?"

But George was wandering out of the kitchen now, toward the front door. Peter frowned after him.

"They think I've made a mistake," he told Gillespie.

Gillespie stayed quiet. The baby, intent on nursing, rolled her eyes up to study him.

"Maybe they're right," he said. "You shouldn't hope for anything from someone that much different from your family."

"You should if your family doesn't *have* it," said Gillespie.

Then she rose, with the baby clinging like a barnacle, and went to check the oven again.

Peter stood still a moment, watching her, but she seemed to have nothing more to say to him. Finally he went out of the kitchen, down the hallway, avoiding the rest of the family. He passed so close that he could hear his mother in the living room. "Why are my children àlways leaving?" she asked. Peter stopped, afraid for an instant that it was him she was speaking to. "Why are they always coming *back*?" Andrew asked her. "Scratching their heads and saying, 'What was it you wanted me to do?'" Mrs. Emerson murmured something Peter couldn't understand. Then a newspaper crackled, drowning out their voices, and under the cover of its noise he went out the front door and eased it shut behind him.

The dry, bitter smell of locusts hung in the dark, but they were silent now. The only locust to be seen was the one on the porch which George flung out, caught, and flung once again, never causing more than a buzzing sound and a dazed whirring

of wings. "Bye, fellow," Peter said. He rumpled George's hair.

"Bye," said George, without surprise. He caught the locust again and looked at Peter absently, as if, every day of his life, he saw people arriving and leaving and getting sidetracked from their travels.

Peter went out to his car, looked up and down the dark street, and then got in and started the engine. He rolled slowly and almost soundlessly, peering at everything his headlights touched. After a few hundred feet he stopped and leaned over to open the door. "Want a ride?" he asked.

"Might as well," said P.J.

She climbed in. When she slid over next to him her skin felt cooler than the night air, but the hand she laid on his knee was warm and she warmed the length of his side. By the time they had reached the main road again, she was asleep with her head in his lap.

A Note About the Author

Anne Tyler was born in Minneapolis, Minnesota, in 1941 but grew up in Raleigh, North Carolina, and considers herself a Southerner. She was graduated at nineteen from Duke University, where she twice won the Anne Flexner Award for creative writing, and became a member of Phi Beta Kappa. She has done graduate work in Russian studies at Columbia University and worked for a year as the Russian bibliographer at the Duke University Library. Miss Tyler has published two other novels, and her stories have appeared frequently in such magazines as *The New Yorker, The Saturday Evening Post, McCall's, Harper's,* and *The Southern Review.* She is married to a psychiatrist, Taghi Mohammad Modarressi, and she and her husband now live in Baltimore, Maryland, with their two young children.

A Note on the Type

The text of this book is set in Electra, a typeface designed by W. A. Dwiggins for the Mergenthaler Linotype Company and first made available in 1935. Electra cannot be classified as either "modern" or "old style." It is not based on any historical model, and hence does not echo any particular period or style of type design. It avoids the extreme contrast between "thick" and "thin" elements that marks most modern faces, and is without eccentricities which catch the eye and interfere with reading. In general, Electra is a simple, readable typeface which attempts to give a feeling of fluidity, power, and speed.

Composed, printed, and bound by The Book Press Incorporated, Brattleboro, Vermont. Typography and binding design by Christine Aulicino.

3